On Your Knees

A *Tradition Bound* Story

By Brynn Paulin

Resplendence Publishing

R·>♦<·P
www.resplendencepublishing.com
Gems of Romantic Fiction

On Your Knees
Copyright © 2016, Brynn Paulin
Edited by Liza Green and Tiffany Mason
Cover Art by Those Girls Designs/Chel Hickerty

Published by Resplendence Publishing, LLC
1093 A1A Beach Blvd, #146
St. Augustine, FL 32080

Print format ISBN: 978-1-62344-082-4

Print Release: June 2016

Books by Brynn Paulin

Taboo Wishes Series

Punished
Kidnap and Kink
Yuletide Greetings
Mr. Smith's Whip
Dick Does Jane
Sybil Disobedience

Tradition Bound Series

On Your Knees

Daly Way Series

Belonging to Them
Plays Well With Others
Fill Her Up
Briar's Cowboys
One for the Team
Roped by the Team

Daly Connection Series

His Old Kentucky Home

North Springs Series

Stocking Full of Cole
Love Notes

Books by Brynn Paulin

Dragon Clans Series

Dragon's Blood
Blood Bought
Blood of the Wolf

Erotic Gems

Orgasmatron
All In
Special Force
Winter Abandon

Standalone Books

Taken by Storm
Forbidden Obsession
Swapped
Feeling His Steel
Two Plus One
Heart of Ice
Harvest's Pride
Shifting Snows
Romero and Julian
Bound for the Holidays
In the Dark
Stealing the Bride
Strangers in the Night
Tribute for the Goddess
Wedding Jitters
Tuesday Afternoons

On Your Knees by Brynn Paulin

"Oops."

Being a control freak in a male-dominated profession is hard
enough without the complications of a workplace crush, yet
Jessica Rush finds herself struggling with all three. How can
she continue to work for a man who commands the leading role
in all her submissive fantasies? Thankfully, the solution to her
sudden lack of control comes in the form of a party invitation
to Pleasure Palace. Perfect. A kinky good time—on her own
terms—is all Jessica needs to boot her sexy boss right out of
her dreams. However, she never anticipated being chained up
in some Dom's dungeon. "Oops," indeed.

"You're mine, kitten."

Finally, Jessica is exactly where he wants her. Ryan Cress has
hidden his kinky lifestyle and his attraction to his subordinate
for years, but when Jessica Rush shows up at Pleasure Palace,
Ryan—*aka,* Master R—vows to claim her as his own and
introduce her to carnal pleasures untold. As far as he's
concerned, before the evening ends, she will be on her knees
for him. That's the plan, anyway. But what will happen when
the mask is removed? Can they move from Boss and employee
to Dominant and submissive so easily?

Jessica is not so sure. Offering her submission to Ryan means
giving up the only thing that has kept her anchored in life: her
control. But Ryan is about to teach Jessica three new words that
will shatter everything *she thinks* she knows about control and
show her a world of sensual delights found only at his loving
command...

"On. Your. Knees."

Dear Readers,

Thank you for your purchase of On Your Knees by Brynn Paulin. We hope you enjoyed the story, and will consider leaving a review at the eBook retailer website where you made your purchase.

Resplendence Publishing is proud to bring you high-quality romance and erotic romance titles each week. Please visit ResplendencePublishing.com every Wednesday for the latest from your favorite authors.

Don't forget to "like" our Resplendence Publishing, LLC page on Facebook to keep up with new releases, author news, special discount codes and sale announcements.

Happy reading!

To all the women who have to be in control,
but don't want to be.

To Jana and Veronica,
my gracious beta readers.
Thank you!

Author's Note

On Your Knees portrays some aspects of
Domination/submission and the BDSM
lifestyle, but is not intended as a true-to-life
account of this community or their practices. If
you are interested in further exploring these
ideas, please research the concepts fully and
always be Safe, Sane and Consensual.

Chapter One

"*Do you want me, slave?*"

She cast her eyes downward. "*Yes, Sir. I want to please you.*"

He stood over her while she knelt submissively with her mouth open, waiting for him to push his long, thick cock into her mouth. His hard, dove-gray eyes raked over her naked body, one side of his mouth tilting up in a dark smile as his black crop stroked down her arm. Right then, she knew he planned to make her wait for him, though she ached for his taste.

Determined to please him and earn the right to orally satisfy him, she remained still, her only movement that of her fingers curling and uncurling behind her as she tried to keep her need in check. She longed to touch him, to worship his body, to show him that his pleasure alone aroused her, but some sort of tape bound her wrists at the small of her back. She couldn't move. It wasn't allowed. Not until her Master removed the bindings then commanded her.

Still, he seemed determined to make her tremble then

writhe.

    Excitement burned through her as the crop's flat leather dragged between her breasts before he turned it and scraped the edge up the underside of one mound. She quivered as it circled her puckered areola. The slightly rough edge pulled on the crinkled skin, creating a pleasure/pain that ripped a moan from her. Turning the crop once more, he flicked the flat surface against her nipple just hard enough for her jerk.

    "Please," she begged as her pussy flooded with her need to be fucked by him.

    "Did you say something?" her Dom asked. She realized in an instant it wasn't him who'd spoken...

    Jessica Rush struggled to surface from beneath the memories of the erotic dream that had overwhelmed her last night and haunted her all morning. Again. How many times would this happen? She'd always found her boss mouthwatering, though she did her best to hide it. He might be perfect for what plagued her, but dear God...he was her *boss*!

    Standing before his desk, she met his gaze as he waited for her reply, and she desperately hoped he couldn't see the lust on her face as she fought the heat still burning through her. *Be cool,* she reminded herself as she stared into the gray eyes that matched those of her dream-Dom. In that same dream last night, Ryan Cress, second son of the Cress Construction family and the VP of Operations, her staid, unflappable *boss*, had fucked her until she'd woken on a loud cry, gasping for breath, an orgasm pulsing within her and her pussy flooded.

    "No," she breathed, summoning the cool professionalism that had earned her one of the company's coveted Project Management positions. She needed to get a grip; she prided herself on her control. Why the hell was he invading her fantasies? Now, after two years of working with him? Didn't she see enough of him here? He wouldn't be pleased if he knew the direction of her nightly thoughts. Nightly? She almost snorted. Lately, her days had been plagued, as well. Especially when she was near him.

"You're sure?"

I'm sure I could just die right now.

"Yes. Maybe you heard my stomach growl. Sorry," she offered, lying. Her stomach hadn't made a sound. "I skipped my morning bagel."

"Mmm," he replied noncommittally then returned his gaze to the sheet before him. Her hands laced behind her as she watched him, waiting and wishing she could just run back to her office and hide until the illicit images of him in leather, crop in hand, faded from her mind. So, yeah, that would be never. She'd be hiding until the end of time because she was pretty sure that dream would never leave her. And tonight, a new version of it would overtake her.

She shifted her weight from one foot to the other, keeping the move slow and controlled so she didn't appear impatient. She was glad she wore her favorite pencil skirt rather than pants. It hid her action as she pressed her thighs together, trying to alleviate some of the renewed moisture gathering in her pussy as her vivid thoughts continued assailing her. They were never far from the forefront of her recollection. *It's a wonder I get anything done lately with as oversexed as I am.*

She took a quiet, shaky breath through slightly parted lips as she studied the dark curls on the top of his head while he examined the paperwork she'd delivered. Hot prickles burned across her back as she tried to push back her embarrassment.

God! I'm a mess. Shit! Is that...? Panic clutched at her

as a trickle of moisture rolled onto her thigh. She pressed her legs even closer together to prevent further movement. It only seemed to make the situation worse. Would her predicament be better or worse if she could manage to slim down her curves and obtain the coveted thigh gap? Worse, she decided, giving herself a thumbs up.

What the hell would he think of her if he knew she'd been having crazy fantasies featuring *him* as a BDSM Master? Or that in those same dreams, she was his submissive? Him a Dom and her a sub? Right. As if that would ever happen. Ryan was far too laid back for that and she… Well, geez, the kinky books she read turned her on, but that didn't mean she was in to that stuff. It was too unlike her. She valued control above all things.

Trying to redirect her thoughts yet again, she glared at the crown of his head then flicked her gaze to the pen moving back and forth over her numbers as he read. The silence was unnerving. Was he doing it on purpose?

Was this some sort of power play? He'd claimed this schedule review would only take a minute—fifteen minutes ago. She'd been standing here in her black Manolos watching him for what seemed an eternity. Should she just sit? He hadn't invited her to. Maybe, he just didn't realize how long it had been or that she was still standing here in on four-inch heels. Ryan tended to get caught up in what he was doing.

"Do you have any questions on that?" she asked.

He didn't look up this time. "Not yet. You're very detailed."

"I try," she replied dryly. "Um…do you want me to just come back after you're finished looking over the numbers and my projections? I could answer any questions then."

His pen tapped on the printout then held there when

he looked up as if he were using the tip to hold his spot. "That won't be necessary." He lowered his chin slightly, his stare drilling into her. "Just be patient a moment longer."

That look. That fucking look right there. *That* was why he got her wet twenty-four-seven. That confident, sexy-as-fuck, master-of-your-universe, true-gift-from-God *and* I'll-prove-it look. A half-smile brought out a naughty dimple and she just wanted to lick it.

She bit the inside of her bottom lip and slid her gaze away from his to study the carpet at the base of his desk.

"Yes, Sir," she murmured, the words escaping a moment before her thoughts caught up with her mouth. Jesus! Why were her hands clasped together behind her? She quickly brought them to her sides. Were her cheeks blazing with color?

Ryan's nostril's flared, and his head tilted slightly, before he shook it, smiling. He looked back at the numbers, and she was sure she heard a quiet chuckle.

Is he laughing at me? Her fingers clenched, then realizing the action, she slowly opened them again and forced herself to be complacent yet detached.

She took a deep intake of breath then forced it out through her nose.

Her job situation wouldn't work much longer. Her recurrent dreams of her dark-haired, wide-shouldered, muscular boss just weren't going away as normal dreams did. It made work decidedly uncomfortable. Maybe, she should quit.

"Jessica?"

"Yes?"

"Are you okay this morning? You seem…not quite there. I just asked if you've heard back from Peterson Electrical on their timeline for the signage."

You know I'm not okay, Sir—asshole! The knowing

look in his eyes told her clearly that he *did* suspect something, and he was amused...and jealous? No, that couldn't be. He was just irritated that she wasn't paying attention. The VP was a busy guy.

"Oh, I—"

He cut her off with a slice of his hand through the air. "Email me about it later. I'd rather know what's going on with you. You're one of my best managers and your work remains top notch, but every time we've met the past few weeks, you seem like you're off in la-la land."

There was that gray stare, burning through her again. Crap...she wouldn't have to quit. She'd end up fired.

"Something going on at home? Some family issues?" he asked. "Something medical I should be aware of?"

"No. No, everything's fine. I mean...I haven't been sleeping the greatest." *That's for damn sure. Stop keeping me up at night, Master Ryan.* "But that's my issue. I'm sorry. I didn't realize it was impeding my work."

"It's not. I'm just worried about you. Lately, you seem...off." He stood and circled his desk, and she forced herself to breathe slowly, even as her heart raced and blood thrummed behind her ears.

Had there ever been a man more perfectly built? He wore a charcoal-gray suit today, but he'd shed the coat. Without it, his crisp dress shirt emphasized the width of his powerful shoulders and the way his torso tapered into slim hips and a flat stomach. His white shirtsleeves were rolled up, revealing his powerful forearms and reminding her he'd spent plenty of time out in the field before taking on an executive role in the office. He obviously kept up a rigorous fitness routine to maintain that rock-hard physique.

He leaned his perfect ass against the edge of his desk, crossing his arms over his chest. Suddenly, she felt very much like a quarrelsome student called before the principal.

I've been very bad. Spank me, Sir.

Fuck! Holy Jesus, what was wrong with her?

"I've seen you around other people, and you're fine. Did I...do something to upset you?"

Only in my dreams.

"No. No, you haven't. I apologize if I've made you feel that way. Really, I'm fine," she replied. "I'll get more rest this weekend and try to be more focused in the future."

He nodded, seeming appeased for the moment. "When's your next trip out to the site? I'd like to go with you, and you can take me through the progress."

"Um, Mon...Monday," she stuttered. *No. No. No!* Panic gripped her as she realized what he was telling her. The site was a few hours from here. Visits usually entailed a car ride, several more hours inspecting construction progress and talking to the construction manager and crew supervisors then an overnight stay at a hotel followed by a second site visit and travel home on the next day. How would she manage three hours confined to a car with him? Or all the hours basically attached to his hip as he shadowed her?

"Perfect. What time are we leaving?" he prompted. He smiled, the glint in his eye telling her he knew she wasn't pleased by this news.

"I usually leave by six-thirty. If that's too early—"

"Nope. Six-thirty is fine. I'll bring you a Starbucks. Still a caramel macchiato made with soy milk and extra shots?"

He remembers that?

"Um, yeah. Thanks." She looked down then realized she'd had her hands clasped behind her—*rather submissively*—again. She dropped them to her sides then, feeling odd that way, propped them on her waist. "Is there anything else? I have a ton to finish today since I'll be gone from the office Monday and most of Tuesday."

He shook his head and straightened from the edge of the desk. "No, that's all." Dismissing her, he turned to resume his seat. Jessica allowed herself a split-second to stare at his perfect ass then snapped around and practically ran for the door.

How much longer could she do this? Christ, she probably needed therapy or something. She groaned. She knew what that *something* was. She needed fucking. An honest to God, no-holds-barred, fast and hard fucking. Maybe, *that* would snap her out of this miasma of torrid need.

* * * *

Ryan watched Jessica practically sprint to the door, moving as fast as those sexy, tall heels could carry her. He'd always admired her, but lately, she perplexed him. She was so fucking beautiful that sometimes he made up reasons to meet with her, just so he could have her in his office.

It was crazy and perverse and probably a little stalker-y, but he seriously didn't care. Jessica consumed him. Lately, though, truth be told, she'd been kind of pissing him off. Without fail, whenever their paths crossed, even if they'd only bumped into one another in the corridor, she seemed to zone out, her dark-green eyes glazing over as if she were imagining herself anywhere but near him.

If she were his, he'd spank her for the behavior, but she wasn't his and never would be unless he were granted a small miracle.

This morning, she'd gotten spacey again, this time during the Project Management staff meeting, and he'd had it. Feeling peckish, he'd called her to his office.

Admittedly, he'd been playing a game with her. Indulging in his own agenda, he'd made her wait there before his desk while he pretended to review the paperwork he'd requested. Covertly, he'd watched her.

It wasn't hard to imagine her under him, her dark-red hair tousled around her head as he kissed the smattering of freckles across her nose. Her perfect porcelain skin would be gorgeous, naked for him from head to toe, her pretty nipples pouting for his mouth—

Fuck! His cock stirred. He'd only *just* gotten it back under control. As soon as her nipples had knotted beneath her blouse while she'd waited, blood had rushed to his dick. He'd almost groaned as she'd bowed her head slightly and locked her hands behind her back. He did groan now and allowed his hand to ease down over his rock-hard erection. He needed to stare into her moss-green eyes and sink balls-deep into her. Soon!

Never happening.

"Fuck," he growled. He surged to his feet. How long had it been since he'd screwed a woman? Too long apparently when his employee—*she was his employee for God's sake*—had become an obsession.

He paced the length of his office, occasionally glancing out the window at the expanse of Lake Michigan. With this location and view, the Cress offices were prime real estate. They were damn lucky his grandfather had purchased this parcel for the company sixty years ago.

A quick tap on the office door announced Ryan's brother, Theo, a moment before he barged in, looking as if he owned the place. Pretty much he did—or would anyway, when their father, Declan, retired. Theo's three younger brothers, Ryan included, would all get smaller shares of the company, but Theo was the one who'd been groomed since childhood as the grand successor.

"What?" Ryan asked. "I'm busy."

"Oh, I can see that," Theo scoffed. He sank into one of the comfortable chairs opposite Ryan's desk, chairs Ryan hadn't offered to Jessica when she'd been in here. Theo looked around while Ryan ignored him. "Why do you have a better office than I do?"

"You're office is exactly the same as mine," Ryan replied, nearly by rote since they had this conversation repeatedly over the years.

"Troubles?"

"What do you think?" Ryan turned and faced the man who looked so much like him, there was no denying they were brothers. Theo's hair was a few shades lighter— dark brown instead of black. In a subtle act of defiance for the role he'd had little choice in assuming, he wore the wavy strands to his shoulders, but he ruthlessly tied it back while at work. His skin was tanned from all his time outside, but their eyes were identical. All the Cress children had the same eyes as their father, Declan—pale- gray with blue undertones.

"I think you should just fucking take her out and show her how you feel." Theo was as much Ryan's best friend as he was his brother and boss. He knew about Ryan's stalker-y ways when it came to Jessica. Months ago, Ryan had stopped fucking other women because every time he did, he saw her face. The disappointment and guilt had been too much after a while. Not a good mix for a Dom. Abstaining until he rid himself of his obsession— an obsession he couldn't indulge in—had seemed the smart thing to do.

"Okay. So I take her out. Maybe, we'll even get along fine. Then what?" Ryan blew out a disgusted breath. "As if it even matters. She can barely stand to be in the same room with me anymore. I really am a masochist. I keep forcing it. By the way, along that line, I'm heading out to the mall site with her on Monday. See... I'm a fucking masochist." He shook his head. "What is wrong with me, Theo?"

"Besides turning into a whiny bitch?"

"Asshole," Ryan growled.

"That's better. Nothing's wrong with you, bro. Nothing that a little pussy won't solve. You just need to get your head back on straight. You want me to hook you up?"

"Does mom know you talk like that?" Another common joke.

Theo ignored him. "So is that a yes or no?"

"No," Ryan replied firmly. "I can get my own, thanks a lot."

"Not so I've noticed."

"Did you come in here for a reason? Or are you just here to interfere with my love life."

"You don't have a love life," Theo pointed out. "You don't even have a sex life, despite a long line of subs throwing themselves at your feet." He held up a hand. "I know, I know. That's not the sort of submissive you want."

Ryan's gaze shifted in the direction Jessica had gone minutes ago.

Theo cleared his throat then rolled his eyes in a clear message to his brother once Ryan refocused his attention. "That... *That* is a whole lot of work. She's had zero training, she's stubborn, driven, headstrong—"

"Perfect," Ryan interrupted.

"Is that really what you want?"

Did he want Jessica kneeling before him, waiting for his pleasure? Did he want her lips around his cock while he fucked her mouth? Did he want to tie her down and lose himself inside her while defiant fire burned in her eyes—a fierce strength and determination to please him above all others, to exert her will with everyone but him, because she was his. She'd be magnificent as his sub.

"Yes, that's exactly what I want."

Theo shook his head. "You *are* a masochist," he laughed.

Reaching into his pocket, Theo pulled out his iPhone. His thumb tapped then slid across the screen as he scrolled to something. "I had that gym chain, Fit-Life, contact me. They want us to do at least four new facilities for them as they break into this region. I asked them to send me specs. It looks good, but I need to know if we have the resources available to dive into this. These four are just the start, since they're talking about doing up to ten facilities in the next two years. If we don't screw things up, we'll get all of them."

Without Theo saying so, Ryan realized this was a multi-million dollar deal that could push Cress Construction to a higher level. They were already respected, but this kind of contract would attract like-minded companies and projects—as long as they proved themselves worthy of it.

He moved back to his desk and the oversized monitor placed to the far left side of it. "Send me the specs, and let's have a look."

Chapter Two

Please Cum…

Jessica raised an eyebrow. "That's crass, don't you think?"

She wrinkled her nose as she tossed the invitation onto the corner of her desk. A sex toy demonstration at an exclusive BDSM club? As if she needed *that* on top of her morning meeting with Ryan.

"No. Just…*no*," she told her friend, Keera Thornton. Keera rolled her hazel eyes. When they'd taken a break together this morning, she'd mentioned an invite for a party and promised to bring it by. This wasn't what Jess had expected.

"Mya is having this thing," Keera had said while stirring an excessive amount of sugar into her coffee. Jess had no idea how the woman didn't go into sugar coma by the end of the cup. Surely, no one needed that much sweetener.

"Are you having some coffee with that?" Jess asked.

Keera rolled her eyes and nudged the day planner Jess had placed on the table when they'd sat, adjusting the position off-kilter from Jess' precise angle to her body. Jess straightened it. "Whatever. But about the party… Since my guy can't get away tonight, I'm thinking of going to Mya's party instead. I can bring a guest. You should come along."

"Still seeing him? How long is it now? Three months?"

"Almost five," Keera replied absently, playing with the salt and pepper shakers. She set them on opposite side of the table.

"Cut it out," Jess laughed, moving them back beside the sugar packets that Keera had methodically rearranged, mixing the colors, earlier.

"You're so easy to mess with, Miss OCD," Keera laughed.

"And you're trying to distract me. So…are you going to tell who he is?" For some reason, Jess' friend insisted on keeping her guy on the DL. She insisted it would jinx things if she told Jess who he was.

Keera's dark-brown hair swung as she shook her head, making it clear her lips were sealed on that point. They'd repeated this same discussion many times over the past months. Jess had never seen her friend so happy and hoped the guy lasted.

"So…I probably know him."

"Not saying."

"I'll take that as a yes. If I know him then…maybe, he works here?"

Keera's eyes flashed. "Not. Saying."

Jess laughed. "Jason from the mailroom?"

"No!"

"Donny from HR?"

"No. I'm not telling you."

"Our illustrious Senior VP, Theo. I know you think he's the hottest thing around here."

"That doesn't mean I could date him," Keera retorted. "He's way out of my league. Speaking of out of one's league… Still having those dreams? Judging from those circles, last night's must have been out of this world. That Dom really put you through the ringer, huh?"

"Shut up!" Jess hissed, casting a glance around to see if anyone had heard Keera. Everyone else seemed oblivious. Thank God! A couple months ago, Keera had asked why Jess looked so exhausted, and in a weak moment, Jess had told the truth, telling her best friend about the x-rated dreams.

"Turnabout's not so much fun, is it, friend?"

"Fine." Jess ripped a piece off her bagel. "I'll stop asking about the boyfriend." *For today, anyway.* "Big plans for the weekend—other than the party tonight?"

"Don't know yet. He thinks he might be able to get away tomorrow. If so, we'll do something."

"Oh God, he's not married, is he?"

"No. Definitely not. I wouldn't touch that with a hundred foot pole. It wouldn't matter how spectacular the sex is."

Jess couldn't help herself. "So…good sex, then?"

"You are tenacious. And apparently, have sex on your mind. You really need to come to this party with me."

Right then, a page for Jess through the overhead system had effectively ended her break.

"I'll bring the invite to your office this afternoon," Keera had called as Jessica left the breakroom. "Think about it, okay?"

A couple of hours later, Keera leaned against the edge of Jessica's desk, her sleek espresso-brown tresses shifting around her in a glossy wave before settling into place in a smooth curtain that fell to the middle of her slim back. Jessica could only fantasize about having hair like her friend's. Her hair tended to be a wild cascade of auburn curls she couldn't dream of containing, even with hours of flat ironing. She wore it long, almost to her waist, just so the heavy weight would pull out some of the kinks and leave her with thick waves.

Self-consciously, she pushed an escaped strand behind her ear and quickly ran her hands over her twist to ensure pieces weren't sticking out in odd directions.

"Please," Keera pleaded, her hazel-green eyes imploring Jessica to give in. "It'll be fun. The whole place is set up for parties like this. I went to one last month. Very sexy. You'd love it."

Sexy. Right. Who needed a "sexy" party? She had dreams of "Dom" Ryan to arouse her. She had to stop thinking of her boss that way!

Deflecting her friend's oncoming wheedling, Jess pulled the latest construction schedule toward her. Since break this morning, her day had turned into a complete clusterfuck. *She'd* find it very sexy and arousing if her crew could bring in the mall project on time. Until then, she didn't have time for anything else, not even a distraction like the party Keera wanted her to attend. It didn't matter that a wistful part of her would like nothing more than to spend the night laughing with friends, talking orgasms and giggling over neon-pink vibrators or whatever other devices were trotted out. Maybe, she'd find something so mind-blowing that she'd be too exhausted to have dreams of being on her knees for her boss. And what the hell was with the kneeling fantasy anyway? That had never been her thing.

Keera picked up the invitation and dropped it in the middle of Jessica's paperwork. "You promised you'd think about it."

She had *not*.

"Come on. You need to think about something besides work."

That was easy for Keera to say. Her job overseeing the administrative personnel wasn't, by her own admission, as stressful as Jess' position as Project Manager for Cress Construction. Though Jess had a good record in the department, plenty of people thought she shouldn't have been promoted to a "man's" job, couldn't hack the work and ultimately shouldn't have been given the mall assignment—a major coup that could make or break the company. She was out to prove every one of the naysayers wrong. And that meant no time for play.

She glanced down at the square of light-blue cardboard in the middle of her work. Reluctantly, she flipped it over and read the formal, cursive font aloud. *"Pleasure Palace: Giving Single Women What They Want Most.* Hmph. Pleasure Palace..." she scoffed, rolling her eyes at Keera.

Jess had heard of that place—and stayed far from it. Pleasure Palace was a sex resort. The club catered to humanity's darker, deeply sensual tastes at a steep price that made it rather exclusive. However, a small portion of their business, the bit that never mixed with upper echelon of their clientele, was dedicated to these parties that gave a taste of kink but were fairly vanilla. From what Jess had heard anyway. She'd never attended one, but she'd heard about them. Pleasure Palace parties never disappointed and couldn't touch the similar home demonstrations from other companies.

"It's coed," Keera gushed. "Some of the guys coming are hot and available. I'm not interested, but you could hook-up. Blow off some steam." She nudged Jess' shoulder. "Fulfill some secret, pent-up desires."

"Right. Yeah, that would be great! You know what I really desire?" she whispered, her eyes wide. "Someone to clean my house."

"I love you, but when did you get so boring?" Keera

sighed, flipping her hair behind her shoulder where it rejoined the rest in its perfect *perfection*. Jess decided the woman must have a pact with some hair god.

"I've always been this way, babe."

She'd only known Keera a few years, but they'd been nearly inseparable friends since their first meeting. Their personalities might appear completely different to someone from the outside looking in, but where it mattered, they shared identical views. Still, no one was as in touch with their wild side as Keera was—well, no, it was more than that. No one was as capable of unleashing yet controlling their wild side as Keera was. The woman knew how to have fun, but never go off the rails. Jess wasn't sure she trusted herself that much. She'd grown up with parents who'd *always* been off-the-rails. Being a minor caught in the adult's runaway train had been, at times, terrifying.

"Look, let's just go to dinner then I can be home in time to finish my budget updates then get to bed early so I can come into the office early tomorrow—"

"Tomorrow's Saturday! Jess, come on!"

"And I still have a project to manage. If I screw up, it's more than my neck on the block. It will impact the whole company and plenty of jobs."

"No one expects you to work every weekend," Keera replied, waving away Jess' melodrama. "I know for a fact the construction crews won't be onsite again until Monday. There's no reason for you to be here managing paperwork and crunching numbers. The project will not fall apart because you take a weekend away from it."

"Keera, you know how hard it is to be a woman in this field—"

"And you have to prove yourself, blah blah blah. The only thing you're proving is that you're handily capable of killing yourself with stress and overwork. Stop being such a fucking perfectionist, give yourself a break and take the night off—take the whole fucking weekend off!"

Jessica sighed. Her friend was right. She was so damned tired. Maybe, she could leave here on time tonight, go to this thing Keera wanted her to attend and perhaps, come in during the early afternoon tomorrow instead of at eight a.m. "I'm still recovering from the last party you dragged me to," she hedged.

"What one? Oh! You mean the psychic bridal shower? It was fun, wasn't it?"

"What part? Watching the drunk bride-to-be model her TMI, wedding night lingerie? Dodging the skeevy stripper? Or getting tarot readings from that total fraud? I know more about tarot than she did." Jessica remembered the woman's mystic-tinged voice as she'd "revealed" Jessica's future. The woman had promised a fulfilling alliance, exploration and a happily ever after. Supposedly, Jessica's past hurts would be healed, she'd learn to trust and her dreams would come to pass.

Right.

So far, Jessica hadn't seen a single sign of any of that happening, and the likelihood of forgetting what screwups her parents had been was nil. Being forced to be the only grownup in the family had a way of shaping one's life and future.

And her dreams?

Out-of-control BDSM fantasies aside—and she wanted to eliminate those, not live them—Jessica couldn't say she *dreamed* of anything. Maybe, she *was* boring. All she wanted was order and control in her life. She needed to know everything that should be done *would* be done. Letting things fall through the cracks or wait until a different day only caused drama and fear.

She shook her head. At best, that woman at the party had been a charlatan. But Keera had a point, and Jess felt herself caving. She did need to relax.

"You're right. I need to get out and do something, but I don't want to go to a sex-toy party. Let's just go to a movie or something. We could go to that club near my place and crack open a bottle of wine to share. I'll even pay."

Keera rolled her eyes and snatched away the oh-so-tempting invitation. Truly, Jessica's pussy clenched at the idea of what she might find there, the things she might see or do—

Of course, from what she'd heard, Pleasure Palace shielded its members from the casual partygoers and vice versa. She'd never see the more sordid inner workings of the place.

Still, the hook-up her friend flippantly mentioned sounded far better than it ever should have. She really *did* crave something more than the small, vibrating bullet-of-wonder she used when her sexual needs grew too overwhelming. It easily brought her to orgasm during the two minutes she spared for pleasure before falling to sleep.

"Nope. I'm going to this," Keera declared, waving the card. "Seriously, I think it's a much better way to spend Friday night than the bore-fest you're suggesting." She swept her dainty, pink-tipped fingers hand toward Jess' desk and the papers strewn over it. "You've got ten minutes to change your mind then I'm on my way. The party starts at six."

"What party?"

Jessica's gaze shot to the entrance of her office, her wide-eyed stare colliding with her boss' sensual gray perusal. His full lips quirked, revealing he knew he'd intruded on a conversation Jess would rather he hadn't heard.

"Hi, Ryan. Bye, Ryan," Keera chirped as she headed

out the door. She waved the invitation over her shoulder as she left. "You'd better text me and tell me you're coming, Jess!"

Jess almost groaned as Ryan strolled into her office. Lately, every time she saw him, her thoughts seemed to get foggy. Her heart sped up, and her breathing grew rapid and shallow as he moved closer.

Heat flooded up her back as she once again remembered last night's erotic dream. On her knees before him. Her panties flooded. Damn it.

Business. Think about business. Construction schedules. Broken glass that was delivered today. The incident with the drunken plumber—crap! I still need to write a report on that.

Okay, that was better. She forced a smile for Ryan. At least once a day, he stopped by to check her progress— well, actually, the progress on the mall. Still it *felt* like he was checking on her, especially since they had update meetings throughout the week, as well. She'd like it better if he were checking *her* out. She supposed it was his right to be on top of things. Though…she wanted him on top of her—

Jesus! What was wrong with her. She'd never been as oversexed as she'd been lately. Maybe, Keera was right. She needed a random hookup to get this out of her system.

She needed to stop these thoughts. Ryan was her boss! This was his family's company. If he wanted to micro-manage her, it was his right. No…that wasn't fair. Ryan didn't micro-manage. That was just her skewed perception of things, brought on by her need to constantly prove herself.

Still, she didn't doubt he was here to check up on her. Mentally, she readied herself to give a quick update of the project while he folded his long frame into the chair across from her. A lock of his wavy, black hair drooped over his forehead while he studied her.

She stifled an appreciative sigh. She'd never seen another man wear business clothes as well as or as comfortably as Ryan wore his dark razor-creased slacks and starched white shirt. They hugged his body as if they'd been specifically made for his lean figure and they probably had been. He was perfection walking. All of the men in his family were, even his younger brother, the hell raiser, Josh.

"What party?" he repeated, dragging her from her scattered thoughts.

She shrugged dismissively. "A thing Keera's going to. She wants me to go with her."

"You're not going?"

She shook her head. "I've got things to do."

His gray eyes narrowed on her, growing troubled. "Work?"

"Well—"

"Jessica," he interrupted, his voice low and chiding.

A shiver snaked down her spine at his tone. No one except Ryan called her Jessica. To everyone else, she was plain old Jess, one of the guys.

Ryan took a deep breath then exhaled sharply. He leaned forward, resting his forearms across his knees. "You're working yourself to death. As far as our client is concerned, you're ahead of schedule. As far as I know, any problems are well in hand. Yet you insist on acting as if you're behind—"

"I am."

"You're not," he corrected, his calm insistence and deep voice brooking now argument. "You don't have to prove yourself."

Gah! He knew her too well, and that bugged her. Yet…didn't. She wanted him to know her. And yet, again, didn't. Lord, she was confused. She didn't know what she wanted anymore.

"Anyone who doubted you has long ago been convinced you're the right person for this job."

She bit back a protest. "Thank you."

"Do yourself a favor," he suggested. "Go do something fun tonight."

"I have too much to do," she replied weakly.

Shaking his head, he stood then leaned on her desk and bent toward her. His warm, minty breath brushed her skin. "Take the night off. If you don't, I'll reassign you. I will not have you killing yourself."

"You wouldn't!" She glared at him.

"Try me."

"You can't. I haven't done anything wrong."

He simply watched her, letting her come to her own conclusions. The authority in his gaze set her back in her chair. Captured by his demeanor, she fought an image of being reassigned to a position beneath his thrusting body.

"Fine. Whatever," she muttered and gathered up the schedule. She folded the sheets then shoved them into her briefcase. Her phone and iPad were snatched up then followed the papers. She stood, angry with him and angrier at herself.

"Don't forget to text Keera. Where is she going tonight, anyway?"

"Some party at Pleasure Palace."

Ryan tried to breathe as he realized where he'd ordered Jessica to go. Besides being the Senior VP here, his older brother, Theo, owned Pleasure Palace. He and Ryan had spent plenty of time there with their submissives. It wasn't a place he'd expect to find Jessica, as much as he wanted to. He hadn't been there in a longtime though.

As he watched Jessica turn from him to grab her purse from the bottom desk drawer, he imagined her on her knees, shoulders to the ground, presenting her ass to him. His cock sprang to attention, and he swore under his breath. What the hell was wrong with him? Learning to control his reactions was one of the first things he'd learned as a Dom. Still, every time he was in the same room with her, he got hard.

Watching her, knowing where she was going this evening, he suddenly knew. If Jessica didn't submit to him soon, he might go nuts. Tonight, this obsession would end. Tonight, he'd have her. Tonight, she'd start to learn how to let go.

She was so driven. Her need to control everything and to prove herself colored everything she did from her prim power suits and upswept deep auburn hair to her hard-as-nails attitude. Daily he watched her drive herself into the ground until the wee-hours of the night. Her security card swipe, in and out of the building revealed she left after everyone else. He knew she took home a briefcase full of paperwork which he'd witnessed her lugging back into work the next morning. Dark crescents lived beneath her tired green eyes. She never cut herself a break.

No matter how many times he warned her not to work so hard, she continued. He wanted to see her pale skin free of fatigue almost as much as he wanted to fuck her until her sweetly curved body collapsed beneath him and they both struggled to breathe again. Actually, he wanted it more.

Last month, she'd stopped smiling. He wanted her happiness back.

As she sat up, she pushed a strand of her long reddish-brown hair back into her twist. Her blouse pulled tight against her arm, showing how slim she'd become. It was past time to put a stop to this.

"Did you eat lunch today?" he asked, startling her with his sudden inquiry.

Still gathering papers from her desk, she shook her head without looking at him and missed his pissed off expression. Good thing. He might have scared her to death.

"I was in back-to-back meetings all day, which is why I'm behind this afternoon. I grabbed a Coke an hour ago."

It sat unopened on her desk.

"It tastes better if you open it," he grated, and her head snapped up.

"I'll grab something on the way home."

Ignoring the annoyance in her eyes, he forged ahead, his knuckles against the top of the desk as he leaned forward. "I'm giving you two minutes to get your butt out of that chair and get out the door. I swear if you take one scrap of paper with you—one bit of work—I will fire you before you hit the parking lot. Get moving. Your time started thirty seconds ago."

"You can't do that!"

"Try me. Get in gear and get out of here. I want a report on Monday."

Heat flooded her cheeks turning them bright pink. It was the most life he'd seen in her in weeks. If this is what it took to get a reaction, he'd sure as hell keep on. He had a plan and another reason to hurry her out the door. And he'd bet Theo would be interested in knowing where Keera planned to spend her evening. Nearly as interested as Ryan was at the prospect of finding Jessica there.

He looked at his watch. "Less than a minute. How much do you value your job?"

As he watched, she transferred her iPad and phone to her purse then shoved the briefcase beneath her desk. She swiped her ID badge from beside her blotter, grabbed the can of Coke then marched toward the door. He fell in step beside her.

"It should go without saying that I'm going to have Josh check your security punches and remote accessing for the weekend. I better find none." His brother, Josh, headed IT and would get him the information in minutes, not that Ryan supposed he'd need it. He planned to keep Jessica busy the next two days. By the time she fell into bed, Sunday night, she'd be too exhausted to consider working.

"Fine," she said again. The stiff set of her shoulders said anything but.

"I'll walk you to your car," he went on.

"For God's sake!" she exploded. "I'm going, okay? I won't slink back to my office to sneak paperwork from the building."

"I know you won't, but I'm walking you anyway."

He heard her irritated breath, but she didn't argue. Instead, she made a beeline for the elevators, probably hoping she could leave him here and get to the parking level on her own if he saw she was hightailing it that way.

"Did you need something?" she asked out of the blue.

"Excuse me?"

"You came to my office for some reason, but you never said. Did you need something?"

Ryan mentally rolled his eyes at himself. He'd been so distracted by her then the prospect of the night ahead that he'd forgotten why he'd come into her office in the first place. "I'm updating a report for HR and needed to ask you about the site manager on your mall project."

She made a face, and he knew Clive Honeycutt was being a pain in the ass. "What about him?" she asked.

"Nothing that can't wait until our drive on Monday. Just forget about it until then and enjoy your evening," he said as she stabbed the call button for the lift. "So…have you ever been to Pleasure Palace?"

"Jesus," she muttered under her breath, shooting a horrified glance around them to see if anyone had heard him. Not likely. It was Friday evening and most people were out of here nearly an hour ago. "No," she answered through clenched teeth.

The signal dinged then the doors slide open. Ryan stepped in on her heels, standing so close that he startled her as she turned to the control panel. Her eyebrows drew together and she stepped to the side.

"Have you?" she asked suddenly as the conveyance started to move downward.

"Been to Pleasure Palace? Sure, a few times." Hell, he had his own private rooms, a perk of being brother to the owner and owning a small stake in the place—not that he'd considered himself an owner, too. He just reaped a financial dividend every quarter. Ryan, Josh and Max, who were his other two brothers, had helped Theo out when he'd wanted to start the place. A fifth stake had gone to his sister's ex-fiancé, but Ryan was pretty sure Theo had bought him out after the breakup.

"Really?" she asked.

"Why so surprised?"

"I guess...I just hadn't pictured you there."

Oh, you should picture me, baby. Me and you...handcuffs. "I'm sure most of the men in the area have been at least once, if only for a bachelor party."

"I guess so." She pressed her lips together and he could nearly see the wheels turning in her head. She was intrigued, wasn't she?

The stepped from the elevator and headed for her car, parked halfway across the level. A silver Prius—last year's model. Of course. So sensible, of her. He'd love to see her in a little red sports car, the top down and her unrestrained auburn hair whipping around unfettered.

Someday, he'd make that happen.

"What's it like?" she asked suddenly.

"The club? Something you really need to experience for yourself to appreciate. It's décor is high class, you know? Expensive, classy, lush… the owners spared no expense since they wanted it to cater to an exclusive set. It can get wild, depending on the clientele for the night—that's on the member side though. The side that caters to special gatherings like the one Keera invited you to attend or for bachelor parties… It's still fancy but the décor is easier to replace. When people get drunk, things get broken."

She pulled her keys from her purse then opened her back door and dumped the bag on the seat. Closing the door, she turned and leaned on the side of the car. Her arms crossed and a speculative gleam lit her green eyes. "You've seen the member side."

"Sure. You can get a tour if you're curious. Once upon a time, I was." Of course, that was a long time ago before Theo had ever dreamed of opening the place. Though Ryan had grown up in a household that practiced the D/s lifestyle and his family belonged to a sect dating back hundreds of years, he'd never actually witnessed it firsthand. His father wasn't exactly putting their mother on display—thank God! That just wasn't their way. Like any kid was curious about sex, he'd been curious about BDSM. When he was eight, his father gave him the birds and the bees talk. When he'd turned thirteen, he'd been let in on the family secret and started his training, though there was nothing hands-on until he'd been sixteen.

And none of this he could tell Jessica right now.

"It's nothing to be scared of," he added.

"Well, if you're into that."

"Most everyone is…on some level anyway."

"Not me."

He had to admit it surprised him that she shared that—
and he also didn't believe her. He had no doubt Jessica
had a *very* submissive nature she'd buried deep inside,
and he intended to find it.

"So," he drawled, "since you haven't been there and
you don't have an actual invitation, you need to know
that you should go to the North doors, not the South."
The North entrance wouldn't get her where she expected,
but they would take her *exactly* where *he* wanted her to
go.

Chapter Three

Jessica drove slowly down the curved drive in front of Pleasure Palace and surveyed the sprawling structure before turning into a surprisingly small lot, occupied by less than twenty other cars.

Though, she'd never been here, she'd always pictured the place a bit like a renaissance fortress. There would be towering turrets, a drawbridge and a moat. A dungeon. The very name "Pleasure Palace" spoke of castles, and knowing what sort of activities happened here... Well, castles had dungeons, right? Her skin warmed, despite the bite in the fall air and she imagined herself chained to a wall, naked and waiting for the master of the keep. He looked strangely like her boss. Damn, she was back to that again?

"Jessica, you're a pervert and you've read one too many steamy books." Looking at the club, she pushed the thought of dungeons and inappropriate erotic fantasies from her mind. Instead of a castle, before her stood an old-world mansion with double doors and three-story pillars. Definitely no moats and probably no stone-walled dungeons here. For some reason, a thread of disappointment wound through her. And she couldn't figure out why. She was headed to a toy party, not a BDSM demonstration using her as a willing subject. What was wrong with her, anyway? Why was she getting all hot and bothered over the thought of being tied up? Giving up her control like that wasn't her thing. Damn, next thing she knew she'd be getting off on the thought of being spanked. Her pelvic muscles tightened, sending a tingle through her cleft.

And there it was. Her panties were wet at the ideas assaulting her pervy mind.

Yeah, she was a lost cause. She didn't understand it. Submitting to some man was the last thing in the world she wanted, yet she'd gotten aroused just considering the scenario. She should just turn around and go home before she managed to get herself into trouble. They'd probably be demonstrating bondage tools at the party. Sure, she was interested in that lifestyle—in theory *only*—but she certainly didn't want anyone else knowing her secret fantasies.

Nervously, she rounded a sculpted hedge and headed up the marbled path to the front doors. These parties were by invitation only and she was late. She and Keera had texted and because Jess wanted to run home and freshen up before getting her, her friend had gone ahead of her. Since Jess hadn't arrived with Keera, she wasn't even sure she would be admitted.

Smoothing her hands down her black slacks, she fought back her nerves. This was only a demonstration. Likely, there would be a bunch of giddy women giggling over huge purple dildos or the like. She'd kick back, look at the toys—maybe buy one—and be home in time to work on her project budget. Since it was saved to her Dropbox, Ryan wouldn't even know she'd accessed it.

But she'd have a good time while she was here. She wasn't a complete stick in the mud. Before she'd been assigned her new project and had to prove herself, she'd managed to party with the best of them.

This would be fun!

Or it could be as excruciating as a migraine.

But in the end, she'd at least have the bragging rights to say: I've been to Pleasure Palace and lived to tell about it. Maybe, they sold T-shirts here that said that. No...probably not.

Powered by her squirrely thoughts, she pressed the button on the intercom beside the red, double doors.

"Name?" came a disembodied female voice.

"I'm not sure I'm on the list—"

"Name?"

The woman sounded irritated. So...they weren't exactly cordial here.

"Jessica Rush," she answered. *Please, please, please don't let me be on the list,* she prayed as her nerves kicked back into high gear. The attitude behind her greeting didn't calm her agitation.

The attendant didn't speak again. Then the lock on the door clicked, disengaging to admit her. She dove for the knob before the lock re-engaged.

The entry hall was lit by a massive crystal chandelier, and just inside stood a woman in medieval wench garb. Actually, to be more accurate, it was the gothest, *briefest* wench outfit Jessica had ever seen and rounded out with jagged-cut black hair with electric-blue tips, heavy eyeliner and black lipstick. Jessica tried her best not to stare at the woman's excessive cleavage, amplified by her tightly laced corset. It was black with electric-blue dragons embroidered up both sides, the creature arms looking to reach for the girl's breasts. When she turned, Jessica saw a thick, black satin ribbon held the contraction closed. The attendant's short black skirt flared around her legs as she moved and Jess caught a glimpse of the lacy tops of the woman's stockings. She imagined herself in such and outfit. Would she feel sensual or embarrassed?

"This way," the goth wench said. She sighed and shook her head, visibly unimpressed with her duties.

Oh, I see. Miss Personality here was the one who answered the buzzer.

So far, Jessica wasn't exactly thrilled by the service. But maybe, the woman was irritated because of a latecomer. Jessica thought about turning around and leaving, but remembered Ryan's order. He intended to ask her about this on Monday and she'd better have answers. Since he'd been here, he'd know if she made up details.

Determined to take it all in, she let her gaze flit about the entry with an eye for the construction and decoration. It seemed pretty standard old-money decor. Several doors, all closed. Expensive wall treatments. Highly polished marble floors. The interior had been recently remodeled or exceptionally well-maintained.

She caught her breath when she stepped through the door leading to the inner portion of the house. The modern façade fell away, and she could have been deep inside a medieval castle complete with wall torches— thankfully, an electric simulation, she noted—and rough stone walls. Just like a dungeon.

Oh shut up! she told her inner voice. *There is no dungeon.*

She jumped as several screams erupted around her, echoing down the hallway. *Pleasure? Pain? Holy crap! Where the hell was the exit?*

Her guide turned and rolled her eyes. "Exhibitionists," she muttered in disgust. "Most of the rooms are soundproofed, but not these. Would you like to check in on what they're doing? They won't mind."

"Um, no."

"Okay. This way." She turned a corner, and Jessica froze. She considered turning around and running for the door. She had a feeling she'd just entered the Hotel California. She could check out, but never leave. A shiver ran down her spine. Trouble was…she wasn't so sure it was fear.

The woman huffed and grabbed her elbow. "You're going to get lost. I'll be in big trouble if you wander in to the wrong room." She hustled Jessica down another winding passageway then ushered her into a dimly lit room.

Jessica pulled her arm free and looked around the empty space. There was no one else here, just an exam-type table and a second, smaller table, much like a desk, near the wall. "I think there's been some mistake. I'm supposed to be—"

"You are Jessica Rush, right?"

"Yes."

"No mistake. This is the package your, uh, *friend* requested for you. Wait here, and the, uh, servants will be in to prepare you for your evening." She frowned at a paper held by a small silver clamp protruding from the rough-hewn brick beside the door. She sighed and shoved it into her pocket then turned to Jessica with a fake smile and wide eyes. "Happy fucking."

Jessica stared at her aghast. "You don't like your job, do you?"

Another long-suffering sigh burst from between the woman's black-painted lips. "No. I've got a busload of transvestites arriving in fifteen minutes, and I'm stuck fitting people into the schedule."

"I could leave."

"Oh hell no. That *would* get me fired." She pointed at Jess. "Stay." Then she stomped from the room and slammed the door.

Okay. Now what? Jessica, turned around in a circle, completely perplexed by the situation. They had her name right, but this was definitely not where she was supposed to be.

* * * *

Ryan looked up from the magazine he was flipping through as his baby sister, Francesca, stomped through the door and plopped herself into the chair beside the security intercom.

"She's here," she said sullenly, glaring from him to where Theo paced.

"Good," Ryan replied.

"Is Keera ready yet?" Theo snapped.

Someone was a little impatient, though Ryan couldn't much blame him. After Ryan had let him know about this "party" the girls were supposed to attend, Theo had hijacked Keera, just as Ryan had Jessica. Evidently, his brother felt the same edginess had sent Ryan flipping through three magazines and a romance novel already. The sooner he was alone with Jessica the better.

After a scowl at Theo, Francesca checked the schedule tracking system on her computer. "She's waiting for you in your suite. By the way, boss man, I want a raise. Facilitating my older brothers' sex lives is not in my job description."

Ignoring her, Theo darted from the room while she made a gagging sound.

Twerp, Ryan thought.

She turned on him, arms crossed. When had the little girl who'd planned Barbie weddings turned so militant?

He knew when. With their parents' consent, their sect had arranged a match for her to unite their family with another. She'd fallen in love and actually gotten engaged, despite learning her fiancé's family had stricter beliefs than the Cress family. When he'd broken it off, she'd going into a downward spiral of rebellion. The woman before him now was an improvement over the bitter, angry shell she'd been when she'd come home from across state.

"You know, this is really gross," she said, turning her complaints to Ryan. "I do not need to know about my brothers' hookups. Any of them. I might need therapy."

"You're already in therapy."

"Oh. Yeah. Right. You know, you look like a dork in that outfit."

He looked down at his black leather pants and boots and smirked. Women who'd seen him in this had drooled, especially if they were the focus of his attentions.

"Only to you."

"Can't you put on a shirt?"

"No."

"What are you supposed to be anyway? Who are you, masked man? The Lone BDSM Ranger?" She chortled in the way that only obnoxious little sisters could—and live. Barely. "Watch out, ladies! The Ranger rides again."

If he was lucky he'd ride.

"No hat. I might have a lasso," he offered, baiting her. "Or a riding crop."

"Ew!"

He shook his head and stood. Sometimes, his sister forgot she wasn't twelve anymore. "I'm going downstairs to my dungeon suite to get my tools ready." Like each of his brothers, he had two rooms designated for his use only.

"Oh man! I *so* didn't need to know that! Couldn't you

just say, 'I'm going downstairs?'"

"Shut up, 'Cesca."

She laughed, reaching up his discarded magazine. "Don't rush. I'm sure Finn and Bobby will take their time with her."

A wave of possessiveness stabbed through him along with the urge to kill his baby sister. "You sent Finn and Bobby to prep her?"

"Everyone else is busy. It's a full schedule tonight. I had to fit in you boneheads."

He tapped his fingers impatiently on his thigh. He'd go nuts if he waited downstairs for Jessica. And his sister sure as hell knew, judging from her shitty grin. She glanced at her watch. "You could go join the Masturbation Awareness Group in room 3D. You know, since you have time to kill."

He scowled at her as he left the room. His little sister was in dire need of a spanking. 3D was his private—and empty—room. Masturbation indeed. Why would he bring himself off when he'd soon be inside Jessica's tight little pussy? She'd be right where he wanted her. Hot, ready and panting for his cock.

Hell, he'd been watching Jessica since she'd started working for him, sizing her up. Assessing her. She worked her beautiful ass off, bringing in all her projects under budget and on time, keeping all the contractors in line, never missing a step. She was a formidable force to reckon with and she hated every minute of it, not that she'd ever admit it. He could *see* it. A submissive in wolf's clothing. He hated watching what it was doing to her. Every day, she fought for power and to prove herself. Fought to be in control of everything. Every day it burdened her more.

She didn't even realize it wasn't control she needed.

* * * *

This was the weirdest sex toy party ever. So where was the party? Jess was alone in an empty room, not a toy in sight, and someone was coming to "prepare" her. Prepare her? For what? More and more, she was sure there was some mistake.

She made her third circuit of the room, rounding the exam table in the middle. Why didn't this room have any chairs? This was so dumb. She had work to do at home. Gathering her purse from where she'd dropped it on the table beside the room's entrance, she yanked on the door.

It didn't budge.

"Oh, come on! You got to be kidding me." A torrent of prickles leapt down her back. She tried to push aside her fear. This was a public facility with a good reputation. Surely, it was a mistake that she'd been locked in. Miss Personality seemed to be more intent on things other than being sure she didn't accidentally confine a patron.

A few feet away, another door opened. She jumped, unaware it was there until she heard the scrape of it moving. This place was full of all the bells and whistles, wasn't it? Sulky attendants, doors made to blend into the wall, hulking men dressed in medieval gear...

Wait? No!

Terrified, she backed away from the two guys who entered. They had to be twice her size. Dressed in hose and tunics, they still looked like pro wrestlers gone bad.

"The door's locked," she blurted, although as an afterthought she wondered if she shouldn't have. "I want to leave."

The darker complected man plucked her purse from her fingers and lifted her onto the table, while his blond counterpart set a canvas bag on the table beside the door.

"There's been a mistake," she protested, immediately trying to scoot off the other side of the table, but she was snared and held in place by the man who'd originally placed her there.

"Miss Rush, just relax," the blond said. "We won't hurt you. It's merely time to prepare you for your evening's adventures. I'm Bobby, and this is Finn." He exchanged a glance with Finn, touching his arm as they shared a smile. "He's my *partner*."

Neither guy looked gay to her. But really, what did a gay man look like? It wasn't as if people wore signs announcing their sexuality. While she stared at Bobby, trying to comprehend his statement, Finn managed to remove her blouse.

"Stop!" she shrieked when he reached for the clasp of her bra.

He sighed as he studied her, obviously searching for a way to persuade her to cooperate. "Your evening will be more enjoyable if you let us ready you. You can rest, *relax*, and we'll rub you with creams and lotions." He paused, pulling out what he probably considered to be the international persuasion card when it came to women. "We have clothing."

She narrowed her eyes, but let the clothes remark slide by. "So what? We're talking like…a massage?"

"Just like."

"I need to be naked for this?"

"It would be helpful."

She considered it for a moment. "And you're not into women?"

"You're lovely, but no, not a bit."

Jess stared at the two men. So much of this seemed…wrong, like they had the wrong person. She couldn't imagine Keera, the only friend who knew she was here, ordering up this treatment. But…Pleasure Palace was a reputable business. High end. Not a whisper of complaints or shady behavior. What did she know about how the other end lived?

"You're sure this *massage* is for me?"

Bobby pulled out a card. "Full treatment for Jessica Rush, ordered and paid for. I assure you that you're quite safe. If you truly want to leave…"

He left the option open to her, the implication clear—leaving would be a bad decision that would cause her to miss out on a great time. She bit her lip. Now that she could go, now that she knew they'd let her walk out of here, she didn't want to. She was probably crazy, but… What the hell. She'd live a bit.

She'd never disrobed in front of a stranger—or two. If this was what was needed in order to get on with things and meet up with Keera, she'd do what was necessary. Besides, this was one of those forbidden fantasy moments, right? And this *was* the Pleasure Palace.

Adventure and exploration. That's what tonight would be about. And damn…a free massage? That would be good to release some tension.

Still, Jessica's fingers trembled as she removed her bra. Slipping from the table, she kicked off her shoes and slid off her pants. Neither man seemed affected by her nakedness. Relief filled her, followed by an irrational spurt of irritation. What kind of a place was this that a naked woman didn't warrant some sort of reaction?

Finn helped her back onto the table. When she attempted to roll onto her stomach for the massage, he propelled her onto her back while Bobby opened a hidden cupboard in the wall. Returning to them, he set several jars next to her legs and laid a warm, damp cloth over her mound. Mesmerized, she watched as he coated his hands with lotion. Slowly, he worked the emollient into her foot, working his way up to her calf.

Jessica sighed and laid her head on the rolled towel Finn placed beneath her neck. Bobby had enchanting fingers. Her muscles seemed to melt as he kneaded them. Lulled by his touch, she jumped when Finn began massaging lotion into her breasts. He worked more quickly than Bobby. His hands rubbed to her belly, down her arms, over her shoulders.

"Can I take you home?" she whispered, letting her mind drift as they worked her weary flesh.

"Sorry, not allowed," Bobby answered.

Too soon, the soothing touch receded, and the cloth over her sex was taken away. She shivered as the air cooled her warm flesh. Her lethargy persisted as she remained still for the men's ministrations.

"This won't do. It will need to be removed," he said. "Ideally, you should be waxed, but that will be too irritating for the night ahead."

She opened her eyes as Bobby brushed his fingers over the trimmed thatch of curling hair hiding her folds. She'd always wondered about what it would be like to have a bare pussy, but she'd never been bold enough to have it done by a professional.

"Okay," she answered, though she figured her opinion wouldn't matter. It hadn't so far.

While Finn retrieved supplies from the canvas bag, Bobby bent her knees and spread her thighs wide, planting her feet close to her ass but on opposite edges of the table. For the first time, she felt real trepidation. She shifted to pull her legs back together, but he held her still. "Relax."

Taking a bottle of cream from his partner, he lathered it over her sex. Jessica lay back determined to enjoy the decadent slide across her already slick folds. When she'd left home this morning, she'd never expected anything like this.

Thank you, Keera!

Finn resumed massaging her scalp and torso while

Bobby worked the shaving cream into her curls. She tried desperately to stay still as he began to slowly scrape the hair from her pussy. Meanwhile, Finn brushed then braided her long hair, binding it into a long plait.

Two strange men. Touching her. Delicious spirals of heat seeped through her.

Decadent. She imagined herself at a pricy spa then her mind emptied. There were no projects, no to-do lists, no responsibilities. There was only the sensation of these delightful hands working over her body.

She sucked in a breath and fought to remain relaxed as Bobby parted her folds to complete his task. The blade scraped over her delicate flesh to remove the last of the curls.

Sweet heaven, it was making her hot. Her cheeks heated. Could he see how excited he made her while he prepared her? Could he see the way her cleft flexed?

Maybe not. He didn't comment—perhaps he was paid not to—and a warm cloth replaced his fingers and cleaned her smooth skin. Then he massaged on soothing balm.

Together, the men shifted her to her belly. Finn's hands became more aggressive, kneading her thighs and buttocks. With her head turned, she watched Bobby unscrew the cap from a jar. He coated his fingers. Finn lifted her slightly then his partner slathered the emollient over her folds and rubbed it into her clit.

Jessica whimpered as hot tingles enveloped her vagina. They grew stronger by the moment, radiating out to her thighs and up into her belly. She gasped for breath as the strong sensations coiled through her. She tried to twist away from the fingers on her pussy.

Finn held her down. "Relax," he murmured. "Bobby won't hurt you. He's just getting you prepared."

She couldn't relax. The waves of prickling arousal

continued assaulting her pussy. Bobby applied another coat of his devil-cream, stroking his fingers deep inside her sheath. Finn bent over her. His iron grip on her back held her prone for his partner's work.

Just when she thought it couldn't get worse, Bobby smoothed more of the same along the tender skin between her pussy and anus. His fingers continued between her ass cheeks.

"Please stop," she whispered, trying again in vain to get away from Finn. No one listened to her.

Bobby's well-lubricated finger, prodded her ass, slowly slipping inside bit by bit. Her teeth sank into her lip to stop her scream. She couldn't help her hips' movement as she worked against his hand, her body demanding more. She grew dizzy from it, her mind fuzzy. She surrendered to the haze of overwhelming sensation. The two men flipped her over again. Bobby wiped his fingers on a cloth then continued his ministrations on her folds.

"Please," she begged. She tried to control her need and push aside the overwhelming desire, but she couldn't. Whatever gel he'd used seeped into her, warming a clawing path into her womb. Even with her most skilled lover—who hadn't been all that skilled, to tell the truth— she'd never become such a wallowing heap of arousal.

Her sheath clamped and released as it searched for something to fill it. What were the chances those men had a dildo in that nifty bag of theirs? Anything. She needed relief.

Finn roughly rubbed her breasts, applying some of the same emollient to her nipples. Ruthlessly, he pulled them to erect points.

She needed sex, and she needed it now.

She barely registered being dressed in the most transparent pink baby doll top she'd ever seen. Three tiny ties held the front closed between her breasts. The flimsy fabric still managed to drive her to madness as it caressed over her rigid nipples.

The garment left her belly totally bare. Coupled with a minuscule thong that tied on the sides, she was hardly clothed. The fabric chafed her clit, and she tried to push it away.

Finn pulled her hands away and lifted her from the table. He guided her toward the secret door. "Come with me," he instructed.

"No. I can't. I need—"

"Your needs will soon be fulfilled," he assured her.

Leaving Bobby in the room, he took her down a flight of stone steps that led to a long dimly lit hallway. They passed several iron-studded doors before Finn stopped in front of one near the end of the hallway. Moans punctuated the cool air around them.

Lucky people.

She had to join a party. No sex for her. Could she just peek in, say hi and dash home to her vibrator? She frowned, knowing she should be more concerned about joining the party dressed in a transparent scrap of lace and drenched panties, but the cream Bobby had rubbed into her breasts and pussy left little room for thinking of more than hot, pounding sex as fast as she could possibly obtain it.

Finn opened the door, revealing a deserted torch-lit chamber. She turned frantically as he shoved her inside. *Now* her freaking senses decided to return? Chains, cuffs and various whips lined the upper half of one wall, along with several other items she was hesitant to identify. The lower half was a bank of drawers. Hastily sizing up her situation, she scanned the rest of the room. An odd bench stood to one side of the room near another iron-studded door. A set of manacles dangled on a thick chain from the center of the ceiling.

Her knees buckled.

A dungeon! Every bit of her fantasies fell away, revealing terror in the face of reality.

"Wait! There's been a mistake!" she protested. "I'm supposed to be going to a toy demonstration. A party with friends."

"It's no mistake, miss." He pulled her toward the chain. She was no match for his strength as he fastened each cuff around her slim wrists. She yanked on them trying to get free. She couldn't. The increased movement only amplified the ache throbbing in her cleft and breasts.

"Let me go!"

"You can voice your complaints to the dungeon master."

The *who?*

"What! Let me go!" she demanded again.

Finn shook his head, wishing her a good night, then strolled from the room. The heavy door closed behind him with an echoing thud.

What had she walked right into? She closed her eyes as horrible, scary as hell images filled her head. Somehow, Jessica couldn't imagine anything happy beginning in a dungeon.

How did this happen? They'd said her friend had set this up. Her friend? She'd kill Keera for this. The woman knew Jessica's fantasies—on a vague level, anyway—but would she do this? Why? Why would she set up Jess like this?

Jess closed her eyes. And why was she dumb enough to just go along with it until it was too late? Now, that... That was the million dollars of therapy question.

Chapter Four

Ryan almost lost himself—*again*—when he entered
the dungeon. Damn, he was getting soft. Not a good
quality in a Dom. Surveying his woman, his body was
anything but soft. His cock throbbed against his thick,
leather pants.

Jessica, unattainable Jessica, whom he'd wanted for
months, stood in the middle of the room, her hands bound
above her head. His prisoner. Her thighs flexed as she
pressed and released them, fighting her arousal, low
moans escaping her lips as her head hung back.

He frowned, narrowing his eyes. He'd seen this
before. Damn it! Finn and Bobby weren't supposed to use
the XT gel on her. That was the only thing that would
have her practically writhing like this. This scene would
be difficult enough for her to accept without adding the
shame and confusion of mindless need. He'd wanted her
clear-headed. He'd wanted her sound decision to submit
to him…without the gray area of a stimulant.

Once XT gel was applied, only an orgasm would
relieve the sensations clawing over the submissive's

body. No amount of fighting, ignoring or waiting it out would help. It couldn't be simply washed off. The effect of the gel just got worse and worse, until the unattended need collapsed upon itself, succumbing to a release of dangerous proportions. There were reports of test subjects climaxing for nearly a half hour with no relief.

He wouldn't let Jessica's condition deteriorate that far.

Her head shot upright, and she turned when she heard the door shut behind him. Her sparkling green eyes narrowed with anger. "You must be the *dungeon master*," she spat out derisively.

Yes, this would be difficult.

"Let me go, you prick! I swear if you don't release me, I'm suing all your asses off. This place will be toast. I'll press charges!"

"Oh, I highly doubt that," he replied, coolly, taking care to add a rasp to his voice, disguising it from her. If things went further south, he could be in a metric shit ton of trouble, but his determination promised she'd leave here fulfilled, not pissed. He'd put her in this situation, but rape was not his thing.

"Fuck you," she screeched.

"Later, kitten. You won't regret a moment here."

"Try me."

"I intend to." He smiled at the phrase she'd picked up from him. As her boss, he'd used it many times in her presence.

Her anger sent strength through him. Training her, *disciplining* her, would be a pleasure. He crossed his arms over his chest, knowing the muscle beneath the tribal tattoo banding his right biceps would bulge, making it more prominent. Even so, she wouldn't know that mark was a symbol of his power—power granted over submissives, specifically *his* submissive.

She yanked on the cuffs, impotent anger making her shake. That and her arousal.

"Let. Me. *Go!*" she screamed.

He simply watched her without speaking, knowing it would unnerve her quicker than anything he could say. A good Master always communicated with his sub, but sometimes, silence spoke loudest. Sometimes, it was the clearest communication.

She was trying to be so strong. Nevertheless, he still heard the tremor in her voice. A flush pinkened her chest, a background to the dark, beaded nipples visible through the sheer lingerie he'd chosen for her.

His body tightened at the sight of her deep in the throes of desire. Each shallow breath lifted her full breasts, presenting those hard peaks to her Master...to him, the man who'd soon control her body and her pleasure. The muscles in her stomach trembled and flexed as arousal wound in her core. He'd bet everything he owned that, if he touched her cleft, she'd be soaked from her need.

"I'll go away," she begged, trying a new tack. "I won't say anything. Just please...let me leave, and you'll never hear from me again."

Like hell. He wanted to hear from her as often as possible.

He stepped closer, smoothing his hand over her firm ass. "I don't intend to harm you. And I won't rape you."

"Like I could stop you right now, you bastard. Like I could with that crap they put on me."

His jaw clenched. Later, he'd punish her for the name calling. "When I take you, you won't be under the control of the gel Bobby and Finn put on you. You'll be fully cognizant of the fact you want me deep in your pussy, fucking you until you scream for mercy."

He saw excitement flare in her eyes, before she shifted

her gaze away from him and shielding her desires from him. As soon as she was fully his, he'd teach her not to hide from him—even her emotions. He wanted to be inside that pretty head, her thoughts open to him, her body entirely his with just a few soft commands.

She shook her head. "Never."

"We'll see, kitten. First, you need to come or we'll never get to that."

He reached for her, and she shied from his hands. She tried to swing away, but the cuffs limited her progress. To his amusement, her attempt at escape ended with her slamming back into him, the complete opposite of her intent. Fruitlessly, she yanked at her restraints.

He cupped her chin and turned her to look at him. "I *will* touch you. *Whenever* I want to touch you. You can't control that. I own your body. You're mine, Jessica."

She sucked in a harsh breath. Though she didn't speak, rebellion blazed in her stare. Still holding her so she was forced to watch him, he reached his other hand between them to demonstrate his point. He cupped her pussy, nearly groaning at the first intimate touch. A drenched inferno met him. His fingers pressed in, barely hampered by the thin strip of fabric.

"Do you want me to ease this? The only relief is from orgasm."

He felt her jaw tighten beneath his grasp. Her eyes closed.

"Look at me," he barked in his most commanding Dom voice.

Her eyes snapped open, but she wasn't cowed enough by his sharp tone to keep from glaring at him.

His fingers stroked her heated flesh, circling her clit then sliding back to trace her opening. He knew she fought her reaction, yet her hips bucked into his caress. "Do you want me to help this?" he asked, his tone firm yet velvet soft. "Answer me."

"You said you wouldn't."

He chuckled, the sound a thin rattle against the dungeon walls. He'd never been so aroused. Neither had he held himself by such a taut, ever-fraying thread. He'd been a Dom for too long to have so little control. In all that time though, he'd always had subs who'd been broken in and well into the scene. Quite frankly, they'd been more into the scene than he was. Some in the general D/s community and the sect to which he'd sworn his oath looked down on him for that. Still, his women had never complained.

"There are ways to bring you to release without using my cock," he explained, his mouth nearly touching hers. He wouldn't kiss her. His kiss would betray everything he felt for her.

Her breath fluttered across his lips. "How?"

"Trust me."

She tried to shake her head, but he still held her chin. He knew she wanted to look away. She always looked away to hide what she was thinking.

"I trusted the people upstairs and look where it got me."

"Yes. Right where you should be. Right where you need to be. You should be thankful."

She made a disgusted sound. "*Right.*"

Jessica stared at the man who looked like the fucking Dread Pirate Roberts from the *Princess Bride*, only the dungeon master was far hotter than the Dread Pirate could dream to be. But what was up with the mask and head covering? She should be terrified. Instead, she was pissed. That didn't stop her from noticing his wide shoulders and slim hips. Nor did she miss the black swirling tattoos over his belly button and around one of his heavily muscled upper arms. And oh, sweet heaven, the way his ass and thighs filled out those leather pants… If she wasn't chained up in such an intolerable situation, she might not be able to keep her hands off him, nor would she be able to keep her mouth off his taut stomach and the sharp curve of muscle that sloped into his pants at either side of his pelvis. *Man, I could take a bite out of that.*

Obviously, that gel was fucking with more than her body. Her head was screwed up too. She was a freaking lunatic. She should be screaming herself hoarse, but no, she'd been sucked in by his deep commanding voice and those mesmerizing eyes. In the dim light, she couldn't tell their color. They were beautiful nonetheless, especially when he stared at her as if he had complete power over the universe. Her universe.

She swallowed hard.

Damn it! He *and* this situation were turning her on. She was a damned freak. Her traitorous body grew hotter with every word he spoke. Her cleft fairly vibrated with need while it flooded, the cream now seeping past her thong. It was on her thighs and filling his big hand.

He had to love that.

She squirmed at the thought of pleasing him. Why would she even care if he was happy? She'd been practically kidnapped, yet she wanted this man with every fiber of her being. Well, not *every* fiber. A tiny, ragged scrap of her still screamed that this was just that horrible, horrible, *wonderful* gel. She didn't really want him to bend her over that bench over there and fuck her like crazy. Did she?

Well, yeah, she did. It embarrassed and confused her. It railed against every female sensibility. She shouldn't want this, but she did. A part of herself she kept locked in a dark corner of her mind was inching out of the shadows, powerful and ready to take her over. Her desire wasn't just from the stuff those goons had put on her. Being chained up like this, helpless, in front of a stranger with his hand on her crotch made her hotter than she'd ever imagined she could be.

As insane as it was, she needed more. She didn't get it. She *wanted* him to take what he wanted. Yes, it was crazy. Insane. So unlike her. But she didn't care. The craving inside her grew painful as her muscles bunched and released searching for the cock she so desperately needed. If he laid her on the cement she'd probably spread her legs and beg to be fucked.

She whimpered as he pulled his hand from her. A moment later, she heard several clanks and the chain holding her arms loosened.

"Widen your stance," he commanded. "When you are standing before me, your feet will always be at least shoulder-width apart."

He made this sound as if he planned for more than just this one time. Was this more than Keera setting up a fantasy fulfillment? Had she been kidnapped? Fear tightened her throat, but she forced her arousal-hazed brain into gear. People knew where she'd gone. She'd be all right. Wouldn't she? She'd just cooperate, let him help her counteract this gel then figure out a way to get the hell out of here.

"Move your feet," he growled when she hesitated too long. When he spoke to her in the rumbling timbre, when he commanded her, his voice never raised much louder than a low, ultra-controlled intonation, not even as loud as a normal speaking volume. Yet, it demanded her full attention and obedience. She trembled inside at the fine edge of menace that lingered in the air around him. If she didn't obey him, what would he do?

"Why?" she asked, knowing she flirted with danger.

He glowered at her, and she distantly wondered what he looked like behind the half-mask hiding the upper portion of his face. His broad chest was impressive and the tattoos made her drool, but she wanted to see his eyes, his cheekbones, his hair… All of him really. She wanted to know if she'd met this fine specimen outside this dungeon. Did she know him? Would he even notice her if he saw her in clothes and without these chains?

It didn't matter. He was one of Pleasure Palace's dungeon masters. This was all an act. Something he was paid to do. He was saying these things for her pleasure. None of this was for real. The sex-slave fantasy was part of his routine. Did that make him like a prostitute? As quickly as the thought came, she pushed it aside.

Nothing mattered but this moment. She might as well go for it then leave. "Why?" she repeated.

"My flogger is going to love your ass," he growled.

"You wouldn't!"

"I will. This is your last chance. Move your feet, or I'll move them for you."

Flogger? What the fuck! She'd rarely been spanked as a child, and she wasn't letting someone start spanking her now. *A flogger is something completely different from a hand. It wouldn't be like a spanking.*

Well, she wasn't letting this go that far. She moved her feet.

Nodding his approval but still scowling, he went to the wall and pulled down a metal bar, easily a foot and a half wide, with short leather pieces hanging from either end. Her brow furrowed. That was *not* what she thought it was!

He knelt behind her and shoved it between her ankles, quite quickly confirming her suspicion. A spreader bar. There was nothing she could do to stop him from fastening the straps around each ankle. She would have toppled if not for the support of the chain holding her arms.

"I wouldn't have to do this if you weren't so rebellious," he told her.

She moaned, unable to halt the sound. She'd never find relief! At least before, she could squeeze her legs together. That had helped. Now, she was spread wide open, her cream flooding her panties unchecked.

Her fingers clenched. Why did she have to be so excited? Curiosity and lust had edged aside her healthy dose of fear and panic. This man delivered all her fantasies in one power-punch.

She was freaking crazy.

The demands of her body grew stronger. Spiraling tremors marched over her, demanding she surrender to him. Relentless, unquenchable need had turned into pain.

"Please," she choked.

"Will you let me relieve this?" he asked.

They were back to that? She thought her consent had been a foregone conclusion when he'd dragged down this bar. Or maybe, that had been to help her make up her mind and send her in the direction he wanted. Whatever.

"Yes. Yes," she replied, another spasm twisting her.

He smoothed his hands over her abdomen. "Shh. Take deep breaths. I'll take care of you."

She doubted it. No one ever took care of her.

His mouth flattened against her navel, tongue flicking in and out. Her keening wail echoed off the stone walls and probably into the hallway. Anyone could hear. She didn't care. No one save for the dungeon master could help her. She didn't want anyone else. He promised to ease this pain.

Going to the wall, he pulled out what was arguably the loveliest flesh-colored dildo she'd ever seen. Of course, at that moment, any dildo headed for her pussy would look good. He tugged the ties on the side of her panties. The garment fell into his waiting hand, and he lifted it to his nose.

"You smell good, Jessica. I can't wait to finally taste you."

She couldn't help mirroring his breath as he inhaled again. Dropping the lace beside him, he slipped his arm around her waist. His toy prodded at her slit. It slipped through her juices and slowly penetrated her tight sheath. She gasped at the girth of it parting her sensitive tissues. Arching her hips, she tried to take more. He kept pushing, shoving inch by remarkable inch inside her.

"More," she begged.

He leaned into her, his chest pressed to her hard nipples, his heat seeping into her. His lips brushed her ear.

"I lied," he whispered. His midnight, velvet voice raked down her skin. "This *is* my body taking you. This dildo was made from a mold of my cock. Take me , Jessica. Feel me. Feel me using your sweet passage. Feel me fucking you." With that revelation he proceeded to claim her with the replica of himself. Slicing the toy in and out of her in rapid strokes, his thumb pressing firmly over her clit each time it bottomed out.

The pleasure of it undid her and she screamed as her walls convulsed around the shaft, only heightening the rapture clamping over her.

"Do you like it?" he asked, though surely her cries told him she did. "Do you like me fucking you?"

"Yes," she sobbed, mindlessly working against it the best she could in her position. The cock surged deep, fully demanding her response. Tears streamed down her face at the intensity of it, at the wild tremors exploding through her body. She screamed again; she knew she did. Still, it barely registered as all her awareness focused inside her, centered on her core, captivated by the deep digs of that toy.

Shimmering heat flooded to every part of her. It pulsed over her rigid body driving her into the jerking rhythm of a shaken marionette. Even so, he drove on, drawing release after release from her until they piled one atop the other and she begged him to stop as her tortured sheath gushed around the silicone cock.

Time ceased to exist, until finally, weakly, she hung from the chain, each shallow pant tugging at her body.

The dungeon master pulled the toy from her.

"That was quite possibly the most beautiful thing I've ever seen," he murmured as he helped her to straighten. "A few more moments and your arms will be free."

Crossing the room, he opened a drawer in the wide cabinet beneath the rack that had held the spreader bar and pulled out a cloth. A basin she hadn't noticed sat on a nearby table, almost hidden from view in an alcove. He dampened the fabric then returned to her.

Slowly, he dragged it over her swollen folds wiping away any residue of gel that had tormented her, as well as her excessive arousal. She trembled as he pushed the cloth inside the crease of her ass to cleanse away the emollient Bobby had spread there, too.

"Better?" he asked.

She nodded, realizing she *was* better. Arousal still tingled through her body, but now, it was a pleasant buzz not the sting of swarming bees. It was still urgent though not as dire. And when she found the opportunity, she knew she'd be able to make it home without fucking some hapless pedestrian.

Now that she could think again, it was only a matter of time before she escaped to her real life.

Chapter Five

Since Jess had orgasmed, he removed the bar from
between her ankles. Apparently, he'd only wanted to
keep her from pressing her legs together to lessen her
need. Left with thighs parted, she'd begged to come,
begged for him to soothe the itch. Ire wove through her.
Tricky bastard. No doubt every move he made tonight
would be carefully planned and calculated to bring her to
her knees.

A vision of her bowed before Ryan shot through her
mind. What the hell! Hastily, she pushed aside the
picture. Despite her rampant fantasies, Ryan had nothing
to do with this. And she didn't want to think about
subjugating herself before anyone. It wouldn't happen. A,
she wasn't doing it. And B, Ryan didn't fit into this
scenario. Her boss and this Dom were far too different
from one another.

She glanced at the man who'd commanded her body
moments ago. Though he'd freed her ankles, she
remembered what he'd said and kept her feet about
shoulder-width apart.

"I'd like you to let me go now," she announced.

His dark gaze studied her, and he tilted his head. "Would you?"

Why did he sound so amused? She yanked on the chains, her anger growing now that the ache from her arousal had greatly diminished. "Yes."

"It's not your decision."

"Look, that was fun—"

"This is all a game for you, isn't it?" He circled her, his glower growing again. "You don't think any of this is real?"

"There's been a mistake…"

"There's no mistake. I know exactly who you are. I know exactly why you're at Pleasure Palace." He stepped close to her, and she smelled his deep masculine scent. "And I know *exactly* why you're here. You think you're in charge of this? You're not. You like this, don't you? You wanted this. You wanted to be powerless. You still want it."

"No." She shook her head. She never wanted to be powerless…helpless. Still, his words both frightened and aroused her. His complete control, the self-assurance, his dominance all nudged up her boiling desire. God, she loved assertive, confident men like him. Unfortunately, in real life, she'd never found one who wasn't a complete asshole just trying to be tough. She'd only read about Doms—that's what he was. A Dom, right?

"Then how did you get here? Like this?" he asked.

"I thought it was something else."

"You thought it was something else?" His mask shifted, and she knew he was lifting his eyebrows in disbelief. "So you let them touch you? Shave you? Dress you? Chain you here? You were fooled?"

"Yes," she answered in a small voice.

"No, you weren't." He drew his finger down her inner

arm, leaving goose bumps in the wake. "You let them."
His finger slid beneath the strap of the baby doll top.
"You let them." Over her belly. "You let them."

He cupped her smooth mound before pushing his
fingertip inside her still-dripping pussy. "You *let* them."
He lifted his hand, coated with her arousal, between
them. She smelled her scent as he sucked the juice from
his fingers. Even more collected between her legs,
seeping onto her thighs again.

"Please, don't…"

"You *let* me."

She could only shake her head as the deep need
started again, a need that had nothing to do with any
stimulant. A need he'd predicted, and she couldn't
prevent. Every word he said was true. She'd let this
happen because it was her deepest desire. It was a fantasy
that had long lurked in her darkness, coming out to play
every time she found pleasure in the quiet of her lonely
bedroom.

Suddenly, he stepped back, breaking the disquieting
intimacy building between them.

"Let, let, let… It's all about power for you. Isn't it?
It's all about you being in control."

She didn't want to hear any more about herself. He
couldn't delve into her psyche and pull out her secrets,
putting them on lurid display.

"Let me go!"

"Let?" he mocked. "Doesn't it get tiresome for you?
Always being in control of everything?"

Her lips pressed together as she fought her emotions
and the tears suddenly pricking her eyes. She sucked in a
breath through her nose. "There's nothing wrong with
being in control."

Her voice trembled, and even to herself, she didn't
sound as if she believed the words.

"There is if you hate it. You hate it, don't you?" He stepped back into the intimacy. With him close, a warm, protected feeling enveloped her, totally incongruous to her situation. "You resent it. I can see the unrest seething inside you."

"No one else is going to take care of things. No one else ever has."

"I would," he replied, his deep, velvet voice wrapping around her. He released the ties on the front of her top, and it gaped open. Within the security of this moment, she didn't think to protest.

He tapped the center of her chest. "What about in here? Don't you want someone else to be in charge?"

"Sometimes," she admitted, half-heartedly. Sometimes, she hated her structured existence. She resented always being the responsible one. Sadly, there was no one in her life she trusted to take some of the weight from her shoulders.

"You don't like power."

"Yes, I do," she lied, unwilling to give over everything.

"No. You embrace it because you feel like you have to. You try to control everything even though you don't like it." He lightly drew his thumb over the shadows she knew lurked beneath her eyes. "These circles testify to how much you don't."

How did a stranger know her so deeply? "I do what has to be done."

"Do you? You don't trust people. You think they'll betray you. They'll fail you...maybe even hurt you, as I suspect you've been hurt before. Someone hurt you badly, and now, you think you always have to be in control."

She shook her head, blinking back tears. He couldn't know that. He couldn't know about her childhood and the pain she'd endured.

His dark gaze captured hers, and he gently cupped her chin, not letting her look away from the knowledge in his eyes. "I won't betray you. I won't hurt you. I will never fail you. You can trust *me*."

She sucked in a shuddering breath that sounded a whole lot like a sob. He'd stripped her soul bare in a so few words.

"You don't want control, do you?" he continued. "You want nothing more than for me to rip off what's left of your clothes and fuck you until you scream. Don't you? This turns you on. You don't want it to, but it does."

She couldn't deny it.

"Please stop."

"And you want to know why you feel this way?" he continued, ignoring her plea. "Because, for once, you have no power. You don't want control. You don't want responsibility. You want to let go."

She nodded. He knew everything. If he knew this, he'd seen to the deepest part of her being. She hadn't even told Keera about this secret resentment.

"Say it," he prompted.

"I don't want control," she admitted.

"Do you trust me to give you what you want?"

Did she? Her eyes closed for a second before she looked directly into his eyes. He'd already taken control. He'd already gained her trust by understanding her needs and filling them. He'd patiently brought her to this unbelievably dark place in herself, and he hadn't fallen on her like a ravening beast when he'd entered the dungeon, though judging from the enormous bulge in his pants, he really wanted to.

There was no question. Her words would only give him the permission her body had already granted. "Yes."

"Will you give over your control to me, bending to my

will?" He held up his hand when she started to reply. "Before you answer, know that if you say yes, this will be the last time you have power in this room."

She knew that wasn't true. She'd read enough to know that the submissive truly held the power in the relationship, however subtle it might be. She had to choose to give him the dominance over her. She had to allow his pleasure by giving her submission. She stood looking over a narrow precipice. She could jump to the other side, risking dire consequences but perhaps finding the deep pleasure she craved. Or she could dance away, run from this adventure and pretend this had never happened.

You can give over power or walk away and forever wonder what could have happened?

She wanted to know!

Steel spiked through her, and she straightened her shoulders, firm in her decision even as terror of the unknown slammed her heart against her ribs. She stared into his eyes, unwavering. "Yes."

His lips turned up ever so slightly. "Then give me what I want."

She hesitated, momentarily unsure what he wanted from her.

"You're in complete control," she affirmed.

"Master. When we are in this dungeon, you will call me Master," he prompted. He reached in his pocket and withdrew a key.

She swallowed. "Master."

Reaching above their heads, he unlocked the shackles and pulled her tight to his hard chest when she would have fallen. His fierce heartbeat thudded rapidly against her breast, revealing she wasn't the only one excited by their play. Her arms screamed as blood rushed back into them. Weakly, she leaned on his strength until he righted her.

He pushed the filmy garment from her shoulders, and it fluttered to the floor leaving her naked in his embrace. Strangely, it was her soul that felt more vulnerable. He pulled back slightly, again seeming to look deep inside her and connect with complete knowledge of her desires.

"On. Your. Knees."

Jessica stared up at him in surprise. Was he joking? Kneel? She'd said she'd give him control, but kneel before him? She was reasonably sure she could walk, perhaps even run, now that the effects of the gel had dissipated. This was her opportunity to make a break for it.

And miss one of the most intriguing experiences in her life.

She'd promised to bend to his will…

He didn't say a word. Watching her, he moved a few steps away and deprived her of the comfort that had made her feel so safe. His scowl darkened while he waited for her to make her decision. He seemed to know so much about her. He likely knew exactly what was going through her head right now. He was probably poised to pounce on her if she bolted.

She wouldn't. He made her feel secure in a way she never had before. What had he said? He wouldn't betray her? She could trust him?

He was right. She wanted this. She wanted him to have control. She wanted to forget everything that lay outside this dungeon—at least for now.

"Jessica?" he prompted, his voice dangerously soft.

Her head bowed, Jess closed the distance parting them. She needed him to know she wasn't scared—not of him anyway. He heart thundered in her chest, and she sank to her knees right at his feet. Whatever happened, good or bad, her decision had already been made. She'd

Brynn Paulin

given over control. She had to follow through.

He didn't step away, and her breasts pressed to his powerful thighs. Eye-level with his protruding, strained fly, she decided she didn't mind the view from here. He wanted her, possibly as badly as she wanted him. If that were true, they'd crash against each other in desperation when they finally came together. It would be wild, out-of-control sex.

She hoped he hurried.

"Hands behind your back," he instructed.

She nodded although she wasn't sure she could do as he ordered. Her arms burned and barely responded to her brain's orders to move. Realizing her predicament, he moved behind her then crouched down and eased her hands into position, helping her twine her numb fingers together at the small of her back. His large hands rubbed up and down her tingling limbs.

"You'll be fine in a moment," he assured her as he stood then returned to his position before her. His thumb stroked along her cheek. "You were chained longer than I'd wanted."

Still, *he* had ordered her chained, Jessica interpreted, filling in his unspoken words.

Before she lingered on the realization, he wedged his boot between her thighs and nudged them apart. "Never together," he told her. "Sit back on your ankles." Once she was situated, with arms behind her, knees wide apart, her ass resting on her heels, he gently tilted her head forward.

She studied the toes of his black boots. They were a lot like the kind she pictured most bikers wearing. With his leather pants, they looked incredibly hot. Oh God, who was she kidding? Everything about this situation seemed hot to her. At the moment, he could be wearing a hotdog suit, and she'd probably find him amazing. His strong presence, not his attire, sank into her, drawing her and molding her reactions.

An odd magic had woven around them in this place. It pulled forward parts of her being that had never seen the light. She'd hidden so many of her feelings since childhood, locking them away in her own private dungeon. It seemed fitting that they'd surface here in *this* dungeon, yet struck her as odd that it had been a stranger identifying her deep-seated needs.

This position spiked up that need about a hundred-and-twelve notches. Spread open, waiting. The cool air rising through the stone floor mingled with the heat pouring from her core. Frankly, she was surprised steam wasn't billowing around her.

Holy crap! She was really into this.

"Remember this position," he commanded. "When you are with me, when I tell you to go to your knees, this is what I want."

She nodded, completely compliant.

How long would he make her wait before he took her?

She might have to figure out how to make this more than a one-time deal. Much more. That might not be easy, though. She couldn't imagine trusting anyone else with this power over her. If he hadn't already proven worthy of her trust, she wouldn't be kneeling here either.

She watched the Dom again. No, she couldn't trust anyone the way she was trusting him right now. Maybe, it was the mask and the façade of anonymity. Who knew? He probably did. He seemed to know her and what she wanted better than she did.

"You have been particularly disobedient and willful tonight."

"I—"

"Silence," he barked, startling her with his raised voice.

Her eyes went wide, but she held her tongue.

"I have warned you many times, yet you continued to fight me."

She shook her head. If he hit her, she'd flip out. She'd heard about that stuff. Some aspects of BDSM intrigued her, but the thought of being beaten into submission sure as hell didn't. She trusted him, just not that much.

In contrast, her body throbbed at the prospect of him exerting further dominance over her. Curiosity and the thought of exploring this new opportunity kept her in place. That and her desire to please him.

"Look at me." The center of her fantasy threaded his fingers through her bound hair and pulled her head back. "I will not have my slave disobeying me."

Whoa! Wait a second! Slave? Her breathing accelerated, and she sank her teeth into her bottom lip.

"Do you understand what I'm saying? You belong to me." He enunciated each word clearly. "All of you. I'm claiming you. From here on, you are mine. You are my responsibility, and you will give me your complete obedience. I'll see to your needs, and I'll teach you how to obey me and bring me pleasure. I'll discipline you if need be. You will trust me in all things."

Give complete trust? *For tonight only, right?* The dungeon master was deep into this. She almost believed he meant forever, not just for this scene. She took a deep breath. She wasn't so sure about this, even for one night.

Her head turned marginally to the right. She stopped herself before she totally denied his claim. Her quivering body spoke of her acceptance. Only her mind refused to embrace his assertion. She dipped her chin to hide her thoughts.

He made an amused sound in his throat. "No, I didn't think you'd so easily agree. You will though. In time. You will learn."

"I don't even know your name!" she blurted.

His hand slashed through the air, dismissing her excuse. "Names aren't important. You know what you need to know about me. You will address me as Master when we're here. I will answer. Your trust and obedience aren't dependent on my name." His lips quirked. "You're not big on obedience to someone else though, are you? Unless it feeds your power."

How did he know these things about her?

He tipped her head up, making her look at him again. "Now, my disobedient slave, it's time for your next lesson."

His announcement prickled fear over her skin, her heartbeat throbbing in her throat. She cautioned herself to stay calm. He'd promised not to hurt her, and she was here for the adventure...no matter what happened.

"Safe word?" she blurted out.

"Smart girl," he praised her then dashed her spirit by shaking his head. "But no safe word. If I push you too far, you need only say 'stop, now' in a firm voice, and I'll stop. It will never get that far. I'll stop before I breach your hard limits."

"Should we...negotiate?"

His lips quirked as if he were trying not to laugh at her. "No, my little control freak."

"But—"

His look stopped her.

"Your first lesson was to trust me. You must understand that I know your needs, and I will care for them. Did I care for you?"

She couldn't deny it. She also couldn't deny that the thought of him taking care of her filled her with an unaccustomed sense of wellbeing. She relaxed, confident that everything would be okay.

She *could* trust him.

"Yes, Master." The term didn't sound as foreign rolling off her tongue as she'd thought it might. It actually felt…comfortable.

He pulled her to her feet and led her to the low bench she'd noticed when she'd entered.

Oh crap.

She'd seen a spanking bench before, curiosity sending her to the internet after reading about one in a book. This wasn't one. It was more of a narrow ottoman to give her midsection support.

"On your knees," he said, his tone back to the intense, quiet command from earlier. Why did it make her feel safe with him? Everything about him screamed danger. How far would he go in his discipline and training? What would she do because of the feelings he evoked within her?

She glanced at the bench. "Please…"

He shook his head. "*Now*, Jessica."

Trust, she reminded herself. *You promised to give him control and trust him.*

She complied with his order, and he wrapped his fingers around her upper arm to steady her. His care heightened her growing faith in him even as he pushed her so that she leaned over the low, cushioned bench. Despite telling herself to remain calm, every muscle in her body tensed. Her chest pressed into the padded surface while her fingers clenched at the small of her back, her ass a little higher than her shoulders. She dropped her face onto the edge of the seat. Damn it. She didn't want to be here. She didn't want to trust him. Yet, she desired nothing more.

He left for a moment. She closed her eyes, listening to the silence around them right now, feeling the slight coolness of the air, letting the moment calm her.

She looked up when he returned, and he set three

items on the seat beside her head. She swallowed hard in fear. Cuffs, a gag and a whip—at least, that's what she figured it was. Long, wide strips of knotted leather were bound together in a black handle. A cord wound around it, no doubt providing a better grip. Was this the flogger he'd mentioned?

Her cleft immediately flooded, aroused by the forbidden desire. Treacherous body. She could have stupid fantasies all she wanted, but she wasn't sticking around here to be whipped by that. She unclasped her hands and levered herself upward.

Chapter Six

Ryan had anticipated Jessica's fear. He'd been testing her.

Splaying his hand on the middle of her back, he held her in place. He couldn't let her run out now, just when they were making progress. If she left, she'd reinforce the internal walls she'd erected to sustain her control. He'd never be able to breach them again.

She probably thought he was breaking all the rules of BDSM right now…all the things she'd read in her silly little books. With no safe word, contracts or negotiations, he knew he had her off balance, but it was the way of things in his group.

"Lesson one, trust. Lesson two, obedience and discipline. Return to your position." He emphasized each word. Right now, he knew her head would be screaming that she was crazy yet her body would obey. He bit back a smile when she obediently sank back against the spanking bench and laced her fingers behind her back.

She might not be trained or experienced, but she was particularly responsive to his voice inflections. The way she so easily fell into her submissive role and followed his commands pleased him more than any of his past subs ever had. Her anxious and sometimes apprehensive mien separated her from those before her. Their main objective had been the game. Sure, they'd been aroused, but they hadn't locked onto anything except how Ryan's performance would enhance their pleasure. They were into the scene but not the lifestyle.

That wasn't what Jessica was all about. He'd known that since the day he met her. When she truly surrendered, she'd give everything to him.

He drew his finger over the crease of Jessica's ass.

"You're mine, Jessica. All of you. Your mouth, your breasts, you pussy, this sweet ass. Every part of you. By the end of this weekend, you'll be mine, body and soul."

Jessica trembled with instant reaction. She was deeply aroused. This wasn't the calculated arousal of the women he'd known before her. She'd been born to be his. Now that they were together, they'd become a mutually beneficial alliance. She was the other half of his coin. The s to his D. They were made to coexist and were incomplete without the other. He'd recognized that soon after meeting her, as well. Being apart from her, knowing someone else could be enjoying her because he hadn't yet claimed her, had eaten at him and occasionally kept him awake at night. Between sessions with his hand, he'd plotted ways to get her on her knees before him without scaring her and chasing her away forever. Patience and going slow had been of the utmost importance with his skittish kitten.

She'd soon realize she belonged at his side. He'd introduce her to new worlds.

With practiced speed, he fastened the cuffs around her wrists then stepped back to survey his work. The other items remained where he'd left them. His body instantly tightened and his throat grew dry at the sight of Jessica stretched over the bench, completely open to him. Even in the dim light, her cream glistened on her bare folds. Long stretches of soft, pale skin begged for his mouth, his hands and his flogger. If he knelt behind her and lifted her slightly, he could drive his cock straight to her core.

He shifted his stance, trying to adjust the pressure behind his fly.

"How do you feel right now?" he rasped. Did her position make her as hot as seeing her this way made him?

"God, don't make me talk," she begged, her voice muffled against the seat.

He knelt and leaned over her. His lips grazed her ear.

"You will obey me. Answer me when I question you. How do you feel, kitten?" he repeated.

His hands slipped beneath her to cup her breasts. He knew they'd still ache a little from the gel Bobby had put on them since the emollient hadn't been wiped from them. She gasped as he pinched her nipples. He tugged them, rolled them then pinched them harder. Later in bed, he'd lick those delicious points until she begged for release then he'd lick them some more. Judging by the way she squirmed, he'd bet he could make her come just by tormenting the rigid tips.

"How do you feel?" He needed her talking so she didn't drift off into sub-space. While they played this game, there was always the chance she'd move into that alternate state of mind because of her intense reactions. He needed her here, fully participating of everything they did.

"Helpless," she admitted.

"Do you?" he asked. "Why?"

"Cuffed, kneeling and pressed between a bench and a man I don't know?" A tremor rocked through her, rippling against his chest as he leaned over her. She shifted beneath him, her ass brushing his tormented cock. Damn, he wanted to rip open his pants and just take her.

He promised himself he'd be inside her soon. When *she* was ready. He'd grown up with that rule—monitor the submissive at all times, no exceptions. The sect shunned the use of a safe word, believing a worthy Dom was always in control—of himself and his slave. A worthy Dom recognized his sub's state of mind, identifying acceptance or stress. A worthy Dom knew when he was pushing limits and he knew when he'd ventured too far, the latter being a cause for immediate cessation of activity.

An unworthy man did not play and was not allowed within the ranks of the sect.

Ryan studied Jessica. Right now, she was in a mild state of acceptance. She definitely needed to be further along before he took her. He wanted her begging for him.

He took a deep breath. Damn, her scent and that dripping cleft beckoned for him to sink to the balls in her sheath, but the woman beneath him was far too stiff.

"I think you're still fighting to be in control," he observed. Moving his hands from beneath her, he trailed a fingertip down her back. She arched into it, moaning. Good. Before long, she'd completely surrender to her hedonistic side. Where the body went, the mind would follow.

"No," she denied. "You're in control."

"Glad to know it." He turned his wicked hand and slid it inside the crease of her ass. The cheeks squeezed together as he teased at the tight flesh. "Have you ever been taken here?"

"No."

"Mmm. It will be my complete pleasure then. How do you think it will feel to have my cock inside you here?"

He dipped down to moisten his fingers in her pussy then returned to her ass. Slowly, he worked one tip inside her to the first knuckle. The snug passage was still well-lubed from Bobby and Finn's earlier ministrations to prepare her.

Her muscles clenched around his finger as she reacted to the thought of him taking her. "It will hurt. You're too big," she argued. Obviously, she remembered the replica of his cock and how it had stretched her pussy.

"You think so? We'll see."

"No."

"Trust me," he admonished firmly.

She sighed, spreading her knees a bit farther and canting her hips. "Yes, Master."

"That toy..." he started. "It wasn't an exact copy of my cock, by the way. I didn't lie. It is from me, but...without modifications."

She turned her head, and he saw her brow furrow. "Modifications?"

"Piercings."

Her eyes widened, her lips forming an O. "What...what kind of piercings? Will they hurt me?"

"No, kitten. You'll love them. They'll drive you out of your mind."

"Okay," she said slowly. She swallowed then licked her bottom lip before drawing it between her teeth. Damn, he wanted to taste her mouth and bite that lip.

"You'll feel every millimeter of me when I push in you." His finger mimicked a slow drive inside her. Forceful tremors shook her while he screwed the digit in and out of her ass in a slow, measured rhythm. When she'd loosened enough, he added another. This time, she rocked into the gentle thrusts.

God, she was beautiful.

"What kind of piercings?" she whispered.

"Jacob's ladder. Mine is five horizontal piercings up the underside of the shaft. And an apadravya. That's a single piercing through the head. It goes from the top to the underside. All six are barbells. No rings."

"Why would you do that?" she breathed.

He leaned close to her ear again then nipped the lobe. "To give my submissive more pleasure than she can imagine. You will scream for me, kitten. After me, no other man will ever be enough. Now, enough stalling. I told you to tell me how you're feeling," he reminded. "Go on. You said helpless—which I don't believe, by the way."

It would take more than what he'd done to Jessica to make her helpless. She could eviscerate anyone with that sharp tongue of hers. Anyone but him. He saw through her guise. Whether she knew it or not, he was her perfect match and probably one of the only people she couldn't cow into doing exactly what she wanted. Right now, she wasn't afraid, not even close to it. If she were scared, she wouldn't be lying docilely beneath him, enjoying this. And that was good. He didn't want her terrorized into compliance. He wanted her true submission.

Jessica tried to think through the myriad reactions, physical *and* emotional, overtaking her. How could she describe the delicious sensations filling her? Her ass had always been a taboo spot. She'd never let anyone touch her there, yet here was this stranger shoving his fingers in and out of her. And it felt so good. Too good.

She couldn't imagine anything more. Frankly, the thought of his cock plunging into this virgin territory petrified her.

"I'm not sure," she admitted. "I feel unsure, I mean."

"You can be sure of me. I won't fail you. Not tonight, tomorrow or ever."

"This is just for tonight."

"We'll address that later. Now…do you like what you feel? Take deep breaths. Focus on your body, not your thoughts. Deep breaths…"

His mesmerizing voice crawled along her spine, nestling in below her heart. She homed in on the tone, the quiet resonance of it echoing through her, the rhythmic drives of his fingers. Suddenly, a million answers roared to mind, all of them relating to how badly she wanted him inside her. *I need you. Anywhere. Any way you want.*

She couldn't say that.

"Um…"

"Be honest with me. You must always be completely honest. For both our sakes."

What was he? A freaking mind reader?

"It's weird. Um…good." Good? It was wonderful. Great. If she got much more aroused, she'd have a puddle beneath her. Why hadn't she done this before? Why hadn't she given up her control? Obviously, the right man had never come along.

Could she have a standing appointment with this Dom? He said he'd never let her down. He'd intimated that he wanted more with her. Was that part of a script? A thread of sadness cinched around her heart. She wanted a genuine connection, not someone doing his job.

"Not good enough, kitten."

"It feels good, but I need more than sex," she blurted out. Oh God, why did she say that? She pressed her face into the bench, mortified by her emotional neediness.

She should know better than to express that. Her deep emotional needs wouldn't ever be met. Life had taught her that. Not by her parents who'd expected her to be their emotional support—and still did. Not by past lovers who'd wanted her to make all the decisions in their relationships. She'd never met a guy who wasn't little more than a man-child. She couldn't remember a time when anyone had taken care of her for any reason beyond obligation. Those times had been grudging at best. She'd learned to take what she could get as intimacy.

But it wasn't intimacy. She knew she didn't know how to ask for or accept it. She'd pushed away friends the few times they'd tried to get close. Keera was the only one who'd somewhat infiltrated the shell Jessica kept around herself.

His free hand petted over her hair, almost as if he understood her needs. "You want to know you'll be taken care of. You desire a deep connection to someone—to me." His lips grazed her ear. "I told you…you're mine, Jessica," he whispered. "Not just your body. All of you. Fully give yourself to me, and I will always take care of you. Emotionally as well as physically."

He added a third finger to her ass, spreading her further. She yelped in surprise though the intrusion wasn't painful.

"Easy," he murmured. His thumb stretched down to rasp over her clit. Ever so slowly, he continued stretching her, while working in and out. His other hand stroked over her shivering body. "Just relax," he instructed. "Stop tensing. Stop thinking. Just feel. Feel me filling you. Feel me surrounding you." His lips pressed to the center of her back, and she trembled. "Feel me owning you."

She tried to relax but found it damned difficult with his continual flicking over her sensitive nub. With her eyes closed, everything disappeared—everything but his hands on her skin, his fingers in her, his body bent over her, his murmured words against her temple. Nothing distracted her from riding the waves of sensation.

"It's so good," she said through her teeth. She could barely stand it. Her need was too strong. A need purely for him. This was nothing like the lame love making of her previous lovers. No wondered she'd stopped finding time for sex. If they'd been like this man, she'd have found it hard to leave their beds.

"You're good to continue?"

She nodded, without opening her eyes. "Yes, Master."

He pumped his fingers deeper. Suddenly, she felt a strange drag of stiff fabric over her skin. Her lids popped open, and she turned her head. Dread settled over her. The flogger was gone. It hadn't been fabric moving. It was leather. Oh fuck, maybe she wasn't ready to move on.

"Relax," he said. "I told you punishment was coming."

"Don't hit me," she pleaded, unable to keep the tremble from her voice.

The whip pulled over her again, the ends splaying out across her back. "I don't hit. Hitting, which is much different from spanking, only satisfies an abuser. A flogger is completely different. It brings pleasure to both Master and slave."

"And pain..."

"At first, perhaps." The thick, cord-wrapped handle of the flogger dragged over her ass while he continued his fingers' assault on her tiny opening. "Many couples use spanking as part of their sex play—even those who consider themselves vanilla. The position, the pain, the dominance of one over the other... All enhance the encounter." The thick handle slipped into her drenched folds, rasping across the tender flesh. "Now, the flogger is different from that. This is not for play, Jessica. This is because you were willful and disobedient."

She pressed her lips together before she protested, claiming she hadn't known.

"Today, the flogger is a tool of punishment," he went on. "Yes, it will bring some pain. Still, in the end, it will bring you pleasure."

She doubted that.

Jessica gasped as the smooth end of the corded grip nudged past the lips of her open pussy. Each ridge of leather caught on her tender walls, sending a riot of sensations to her womb. She pressed her face into the bench overwhelmed by the feeling of the handle tormenting her sheath while his fingers alternately filled her ass. She moaned when he pulled his hand free, but she had little time to ponder it as he drilled the handle in and out of her. His knuckles knocked against her clit with each stroke.

Her inner walls pawed at the corded rod, amplifying the reactions shooting through her. Release coiled inside her, drawing tighter and tighter until she danced at the edge of explosion.

She jerked when he suddenly pulled it away then draped the flogger across her back and over her bound hands, the damp end cradled against her ass.

"Don't move," he ordered. "The flogger will shift if you disobey."

Taking deep breaths while her body rattled its protest against being left on the brink, she listened to him move around the room. How long would he leave her here in this torment?

She heard water running, followed by silence. Straining her ears, she listened and anticipated his approach. When nothing came, she started to lift her head. A leather tail shifted, and she froze then carefully planted her forehead in the cushion again.

"Naughty, slave," he admonished.

Oh no, he was watching.

"I'm sorry, Master," she replied, her voice muffled by the seat.

"Um-hmm."

Not seeing him, not knowing what he doing, was killing her. And he didn't seem to be in a big hurry to return to her, either. Didn't he need to fuck her as much as she needed to be fucked? For that matter, *would* he ever fuck her? Was this some mental torment to take her to the edge then leave her there without ever giving her what she desired?

He'd said he'd fill her needs. He'd better or that hapless pedestrian was in trouble again. It wasn't easy to kneel here, effectively being put on display. She tried to forget about her vulnerable position, but damn it, it turned her on. How had she not known this about herself? She'd always had submission-like fantasies. Still, she'd never thought she'd actually *want* to be in the center of one in real life.

Though she'd been listening for him, she startled when he returned and moved aside the flogger. The man walked as silently as a cat.

"Don't move," he reminded her. A moment later, her cuffs were separated, and he repositioned her so her arms draped over the other side of the bench and down to the floor. A metallic click announced one wrist had been attached to a ring driven into the cement. She yanked at it and found there was no give.

"You can leave me loose," she told him. "I won't move."

It wasn't true. She was worried about what was coming. She wanted to be able to dart for the door if need be. If she ran screaming for the exit of Pleasure Palace with the dungeon master on her heels, would people help her or help him? Would they think it was just a game and look away?

"I like you this way. Besides, I think maybe you might need a little help." His strong fingers closed around the other wrist, and he dragged it to join the other. The lock clicked into place as he fastened the cuff to the same loop as the first.

"Lift up a little," he told her.

She couldn't move. Her breaths came in shuddering pants as she pressed her face into the cushion of the bench. She couldn't do this. She couldn't let him punish her. She needed to leave. For the first time since entering the dungeon, she felt truly helpless. He'd ripped away her bravado and left her exposed to him. He could do anything, and she couldn't stop him.

"Kitten?" he prompted when she didn't move.

What had he said earlier? Breathe? Why couldn't she catch her breath?

"Jessica?" he said, a bit louder.

"I'm scared," she mumbled, his voice pulling her back from the edge of panic. He'd told her to be completely honest. She hoped it didn't backfire on her. "Help me."

To her surprise, he stroked his palm over her head again, trailing his fingers down to the end of her braid then repeating the same path. The silence was broken only by their breathing. He didn't rush, and his patience calmed her more than anything he could have said. When her breath synced with his, copying the slow, deep inhalations and long releases of air, he gently lifted her middle and slid the bench from beneath her.

"Elbows down," he told her. At the same time, he guided her into position. Her arms stretched out in front of her, and her ass pushed up in the air as she knelt. He stroked his hand over it and onto her bowed back. "I will always take care of you," he promised. "You have only to ask."

Her eyes burned, and she was glad he couldn't see her face and the tears that threatened to escape. Had anyone ever given a fuck about what she felt...about her wellbeing? How ridiculous was it that it had taken getting chained up in a BDSM dungeon to find someone who cared about her needs? Even if it was just for this scene.

"Thank you, Master," she said, her broken words barely a whisper as she forced them past the knot in her throat.

"My sweet kitten." He stroked her back once more, before his fingers clasped one of her butt cheeks and squeezed. "This is what you wanted. Total release from responsibility. Total surrender. Total loss of control and power." His tone hardened as they moved past his soothing and back to the order of business. But now, she was ready, and her fear didn't return. "You are entirely mine. At my mercy."

Her pussy spasmed, filling with warm moisture. Her skin felt flushed from the heat racing along her chest and into her face. Oh God! Why did she have to be so aroused by the idea of being completely at his whim?

He slid a small, thin pillow beneath her head. "I don't want you to hurt yourself against the cement when you jerk. You're scared right now—"

No, she was so far from scared right now. Perhaps, a little apprehensive…but he'd stimulated the dark recesses of her being and she wanted this. She wanted whatever he would dole out. Not that she'd say as much. Her excitement embarrassed her.

"—but in a few moments, you'll learn that with the punishment comes pleasure. Your body will experience things you've never imagined, and you'll never want to leave here. You'll crave more. You'll yearn for me to do more."

She couldn't imagine it, yet she'd never imagined being this aroused before. Heck, she'd never imagined any of this, any of her secret dreams, coming to fruition.

From out of the blue, her thoughts conjured her fantasy from this morning, kneeling before Master Ryan.

Had it only been this morning? Would the Master in her daydream have gone this far? Until recently, she couldn't have pictured her boss as a Dom with her on her knees before him. But more and more as of late, her illicit thoughts had turned that way. Now, she had no problem seeing it.

Would Ryan come here…do this…be her secret Dom? With her head turned against the pillow, she looked at her current Master from the corner of her eye. She couldn't make out his eye color in this dim lighting, nor could she see his hair with the head covering. From the small amount of body hair showing, she suspected it was dark brown…possibly black. Ryan had black hair.

Jesus, what was she thinking? This was not Ryan. Sure, he hid a rock-hard, powerfully muscled body beneath his suits, but she'd seen it, in part, the few times she'd witnessed him in casual wear. This man had tattoos and piercings, too. That didn't seem to be something her staid boss would have…especially the piercings. She couldn't imagine Ryan hiding those beneath his custom-made trousers.

The Dom moved from her line of sight, and she sighed, closing her eyes again. When she thought of Ryan, her remaining anxiety dissipated quite a bit. She trusted him. She trusted this man, too. With a few moments of care, he'd earned it.

The silence was different now. Butterflies took off in her stomach again as she anticipated what he'd do to her. It was an excitement she hadn't felt in years…if ever.

The waiting was the worst part. Her captor—when she thought about it, that's what he really was—didn't seem inclined to want to get on with things. It was a head game. He was fucking with her. Putting her in this ridiculous, revealing, unfortunately arousing position. Watching her without really touching. Making her feel totally helpless without her usual control. And she loved it. But what was this all about? Playing with her?

Please...don't let him just be toying with me. If he built her up and didn't deliver, she'd... Well, she didn't know what she'd do. All she knew was she needed to fuck almost more than she needed to breathe right now. Even the air touching her exposed pussy drove her need higher.

She shifted, adjusting the weight on her knees and flexing her inner muscles. If she rushed home, her vibrator would help with this relentless need. That would be safer than being here. She could control that. She wouldn't make any stops—except... Darn it, she needed batteries. She'd just have to make do without the vibrating function. She was vibrating enough to do the job anyway.

"If I ask really nicely and tell you I'm done playing and I want to go home, would you let me go, please?" she bargained.

"No."

"I'm serious. I know you get paid to do this whole thing... I'm sorry. I'm done. I won't ask that my friend's money get refunded. Really, I'd just like to go home."

He sighed, and a moment later, his boots appeared in the corner of her vision. His heels tipped up as he hunkered down beside her and touched her cheek. "Poor Jessica, so confused by all this."

"Stop patronizing me, and unlock the cuffs!"

"Hmm. And here, I thought we were beyond this. Are you taking back the gift you gave me?" He leaned down so his mouth was near hers, and he stared directly into her eyes. His stormy gaze pierced her as if it were lightning arrowing to her core. "I'm not getting paid," he rumbled. "I'm here for you. Only for you. Because of you."

"Do I know you?" she gasped, thoughts of leaving

evaporating under the fire of her shock. Still, a heavy sensation fisted low in her pelvis, warming her, tingling to her folds. Dear God, was it possible he wasn't a stranger? That she *knew* him? That—

Stabbing his fingers through her braided hair, he angled her head and covered her lips. His tongue speared into her mouth, taking possession of it as easily as he'd possessed the rest of her. Jessica groaned, melting toward the cement and only held up by his iron-like arm under her middle. Ravenously, she met him, tasting him and feeling the open need in his urgent kiss. She breathed in his spicy scent, absorbed his cinnamon taste and lost herself to him as he consumed her soul.

"Still want to leave?" he asked against her mouth, ignoring her question. His uneven breathing filled her as she struggled to take in air.

"No," she whispered.

"Shall we continue?" He pulled back and stood. "Or do I let you go, and we both fruitlessly try to forget this ever happened?"

She turned back to her original head-down position.

"If you don't work for Pleasure Palace…" Why was that even hotter? "Then I'm chained up and naked with a random stranger." She wasn't so sure of that status anymore. After what they'd done, could she consider him *a stranger*?

"Whether I worked here or not, it doesn't change how well you know me…or don't know me."

"Having you work here… That's different. It was almost therapeutic, like sex counseling. This is…"

"Wrong? Sinful? Exciting? Arousing? Exactly what you've dreamed of since you were old enough to understand sex?"

Her fingers clasped the loop of metal holding her cuffs. This scene was all the things he'd listed and more.

There was way too much truth in his observation.

"Yes," she reluctantly admitted.

"Does that scare you?" His deep, sexy almost familiar voice sank through her. He could take her to the verge of orgasm with his confident, commanding tone alone. Every word proved he had complete control of this situation. Every syllable whispered, *you know him.*

And as she focused on him, she didn't care. Right now, he was proving to be the answer to her darkest desires. If he'd been driven to make this stand for her...

"I won't endanger you, Jessica," he assured her when she didn't answer his question.

She loved how he said her name as if that alone confirmed his claim on her. *Named and claimed by my Master.* She bit her lip and shivered.

"You're completely safe with me."

"Yes...Master. Thank you."

So this was it. Again, she was presented with a decision. He was, in not so many words, offering exactly what she'd asked for. With a word, she could go. The alternative? She could explore this unknown lifestyle. With him. She wanted both. Fear urged her to run; excitement told her to stay. Her mental pendulum swung back and forth like a wind chime caught in a tornado. She should reassert that she wanted to leave, yet she didn't actually want to. Not really. She wanted to see what would happened. Wasn't it true that the only real reason she wanted to leave was because she was scared of the flogger? Jessica Rush, wasn't afraid of anything!

"I want to go on," she said firmly, tightening her fingers on the ring.

She yelped as the flogger thudded against her ass before she could beg him not to hurt her. Much. Deep down, if she examined her hidden fantasies, all those dominations, all the captures, all the force, this was in there, too.

"Let it out," he said. "Scream if you must. Personally, it makes me hotter, knowing the frenzy that will take you."

Tears welled in her eyes, and the sting spread against her buttocks. Frenzy? Hah!

"Again," she whispered. The flogger fell, the leather biting into her tender flesh, and she bucked unable to hold back a loud cry. He didn't give her time to react before another stroke caught her thighs, another on her back, on the crease where her leg met her ass so perilously close to her needy cleft.

Her mind went fuzzy as she anticipated another blow and the backslap as the ends ricocheted and connected again. She angled her hips toward it. He ignored her silent plea and let it fall on her upper back.

"Please, oh please," she begged, widening her knees and dropping her shoulders to the floor. This time he gave in to her, but the extra strength in the strike made it clear it was his decision and his alone. No amount of angling or begging would sway him from his mission of total power.

As searing tendrils of pleasure twisted into her, she didn't care that he now had full control. He could have it. All of it. For as long as he wanted.

Chapter Seven

Ryan watched Jessica's body quiver as he doled out the promised flogging. He'd purposely chosen a medium-weight flogger to give her an intense experience without the risk of really hurting her. He'd meant to count how many strokes he'd given, but instead, he'd lost track, just watching her body and listening to how her cries had segued from pain to intense pleasure. She rocked toward him wanting more. Witnessing her initiation into the pleasures of submission aroused him more than anything so far tonight. His cock throbbed behind his zipper and a thin line of moisture rolled down the center of his back. His pulse pounded through him, and he forced himself to take deep, calming breaths.

He weighed his options.

He could go on, deny his own release and give her the orgasm she deserved as a reward for offering over her total submission. Or he could drop his fly and plow his rock-hard cock as deep into her as it would go. Either way, their pleasure would continue, and she'd get her orgasm that way, too.

Wouldn't it be better if they were together in the climax? He needed her walls surrounding him, squeezing his dick until he could barely move. He wanted to feel her reactions to him, not just witness them.

Still, Jessica could take a few more strokes. He didn't think either of them could bear much more than that, though. Sweat had broken out on his brow and not from exertion. Just working Jessica, whose body also glistened with her perspiration, drove his temperature to unnaturally high levels.

Drawing back, he angled the flogger, letting the tails fly down toward her delicate folds. Jessica jerked, and he knew one had connected. He suddenly had the urge to kiss it better while he drove her straight over the edge with his mouth.

He'd never had a submissive affect him like this. Each thud of the flogger jerked his cock, pulling her soul toward him and the waiting oblivion of release.

"Again," she begged, her body sagging with the extreme pleasure attacking it. She felt his discipline everywhere—he'd seen to that—and now, it overwhelmed her. She cried out passionately even when the tails weren't connecting with her. Her hips rocked in search of someone to fill her.

Him.

Not one more stroke. He flung the flogger aside and reached for his zipper. He shoved down his pants just far enough to expose his cock. Jessica looked over her shoulder, her face tearstained and her eyes dazed.

"Oh thank heaven," she whispered when she saw what he was doing. Quickly, he rolled on a condom and knelt behind her. Grasping her hips, he drove into her with one powerful stroke, experiencing the heaven he'd wanted for so long. He felt each of his piercings raking over her delicate inner flesh and knew she'd feel the intense pleasure of it, too.

"Yes!" Jessica shrieked, straightening her arms and shoving back into him. Her molten passage branded him, the burning honey of her extreme arousal coating him and dripping down to his tight balls. He moved just enough to relieve some of the pressure of her clutching walls on his dick, but found he needed that tight squeeze more than he needed to breathe. Urgently, he rammed back inside, giving everything over to her. She thought she was helpless? Her writhing body had the power to give or refuse what he'd desired for agonizing months.

Reaching between them, he rasped his thumb over her exposed nub. He circled it, pinched and her cries echoed off the stone walls and back into his ever-tightening body.

"That's right, my kitten. Purr for me. Tell your Master how much you need him." He wouldn't last long, and he wanted her flying with him when he finally erupted inside her. His words would give her the mind-fuck she needed to accompany the possession of his cock.

"I need you. God, I need you!" she sobbed.

She bucked under him almost throwing off his wild rhythm as he pistoned in and out of her pussy. Her "Yes!" and "oh God!" alternated with "Please!" and drove him on. Her fleshy walls convulsed around him.

"No! No! Oh God!" she screamed, going rigid while he continued to pull her back onto his erection.

The tight grip of her pussy closed around him. He drove on, fighting his release until the last moment when she was spent in his arms, a ball of vibrating nerve endings. Knowing it would drive her to another orgasm, he dragged his fingers over her clit again, coaxing another explosion.

"No…" she moaned.

"Take it," he rasped, knowing it would complete this

scene in her head. She needed it. She needed his total command over her. "Yes, squeeze my cock. Milk it. Oh kitten, yes…"

She made a strangled sound, and her body shuddered beneath him. Another wave of release tore through her, even stronger than before. She shook violently in his arms, her release flooding around him even as her pussy convulsed again. The waves of her climax pulled him with along it, washing over him and dragging him under into sweet, achingly perfect oblivion. Urgently, he made one last drive and blasted inside her.

"Mine!" he bellowed, filling her. She was his, *his and only his*, and he never intended to let her forget it.

* * * *

Jessica slowly became aware she was curled on the cool stone floor with a very male body wrapped around her. Sometime during her haze, he'd released the cuffs holding her. Her arms were crossed over her chest with his covering them.

"You did well," he murmured. "I am proud of you, kitten."

She nuzzled her head back against him, warmed by the praise. It pleased her inordinately that she'd satisfied him. "Thank you for convincing me not to run."

"Hmm," he replied. He sounded distracted as he pulled back slightly. She winced when he touched his fingers to her back. The result of flogger didn't feel so good now, yet she still had a strange sensual satisfaction from it. She smiled, despite the pain. Over the next few days, this would be a constant reminder of the intensely perfect time she'd spent in the Pleasure Palace dungeon. Every time she moved, the dungeon master would be with her.

Rising, he carefully lifted her in his arms. He kicked the pillow toward the bench then set her on her feet before it.

"On your knees. On the pillow," he told her. "Then lean over the bench."

She immediately complied, though she couldn't stifle her groan. She didn't know if she could take more quite yet.

At moments, he'd been somewhat kind, but now, he was almost tender while still commanding her. He smoothed his fingers over her brow. "We won't do anything else right now," he promised, somehow guessing her thoughts. Why should she be surprised? He'd seemed to know them all along.

She didn't move from her position as he left her and crossed the room. She heard him open cupboards and run water, but she didn't look at him. Taking slow, measured breaths, she leaned her head on her crossed arms. The dichotomy between her emotions earlier and now made her head spin. Where she'd been scared before, overly agitated, now she'd come to a serene oasis of peace.

"Master?" she asked, figuring she'd better continue to use the title, especially since she still didn't know his name and she didn't know what else to call him. She had a feeling he still wouldn't tell her, either. Not tonight. "Can I ask you a question?"

"Ask me anything."

"How did you...um... When did you..."

He returned to her side and sat on the bench beside her, a square bowl on his lap. He'd completely removed his pants while he'd been away from her, and she got her first look at the piercings on his far-from flaccid cock. A shiver went through her, centering in her core, as she remembered the sensation of each barbell running along her inner walls.

Taking a steadying gulp of air she focused on her question. What had it been… of yes…

"How did I get to be a Dom?" he asked for her.

She flinched as he dabbed a warm, damp cloth over her bruised skin. "Yes. I'd imagine you don't just wake up one day and say 'I think I might like to be a Dom. All I need is a submissive'. There has to be some process."

"There wasn't really." He dabbed cool cream onto her back and ass, carefully rubbing it in to each mark. "I was raised in a D/s family. My father is a Dom, and my mother's a sub."

That surprised her. She'd never thought of this lifestyle in a family setting. "How does that work? I mean with kids and all?"

"It was subtle. My mom didn't run around naked, wearing chains and leather. We never saw our father do anything that any other dad wouldn't do. Sometimes, they'd disappear to their room, even in the middle of the day." He shrugged, continuing his ministrations, and she felt herself slipping further and further beneath the spell of his voice. Warmth filled her as the intimacy of the moment twined around them, binding them together.

"My father is always in charge, and Mom mostly complies with what he says," he went on. "That doesn't mean she's weak. She's extremely strong and successful in her own right. Just as you are. I have complete respect for her." He lifted Jessica's chin so she looked into his eyes. She still wished she could see their color, but even this close, the dim lighting obscured a clear view. His thumb smoothed over her swollen bottom lip. "And believe it or not, I have complete respect for you, too. Submitting doesn't make you weak. You have to be very strong to do it."

She'd never thought of herself as particularly strong. Actually, she spent every day trying to prove herself.

Maybe, she didn't need to do that as much as she'd always thought.

"My screams weren't very strong."

"That's a matter of opinion. While I used the flogger on you, you didn't swear at me. You didn't cry and beg me to let you go. You let your body adjust and take it and sink into pleasure. I know men who can't handle as much. You were beautiful."

"I bet you say that to all your submissives."

"There aren't others. I don't share, I don't cheat, and I don't do polyamorous relationships. If I had another partner, I wouldn't be here with you."

Bending over, he kissed one of the stripes crossing her shoulder blades. The buzzing threads of awareness started in her middle again. Again? She wanted him again? She couldn't possibly. The new need building low in her belly argued that her body wasn't nearly as broken and exhausted as she might think. She moaned and dropped her head back to her arms. No, she couldn't take more. Physically or mentally. She liked his hands on her body, but she was done in right now.

Then his firm fingers moved to her ass. Oh man. It felt good. He seemed to know just how spent she was, though. Gently, he worked the cream into the marks, unknowingly easing her desire. Was it crazy that she wanted him to take her to bed somewhere and press her into a firm mattress? Wouldn't Keera have a field day with this? She'd say, "I told you so. I told you that you'd have a good time at Pleasure Palace."

Okay, so Jess should have had more faith. How could she? Giving up control had never gone well for her.

With this man rubbing his hands down her thighs, her weak faith was growing fast. So was her need for more of him.

Silence fell between them, the only sound their

breathing and sporadic groans from her as he occasionally touched spots more sore than others. It wasn't long before her body had practically dissolved into jelly. He had her so relaxed that, if not for her increased awareness of him, she could have fallen asleep. Overall, she just felt...*good.*

She couldn't rouse the energy to move when he left her once more. Again, she heard water, and she wondered if he wasn't the cleanest Dom in the world. She smiled, turning her head to watch him. For a guy, he had a graceful gait. He really did move like a cat, his large frame moving in a lazy assured roll as he walked.

The scarf tied around his head had hiked up a little in the back and short strands of hair peeked out. In the dim light, she couldn't tell if it was brown or black, just dark. It didn't trigger specific recognition, though. She knew a ton of muscular well-built, dark-haired guys—she worked in construction for God's sake. He could be anyone,—and she was swiftly coming to the conclusion she *did* know this man. There was a familiarity about him...about the things he said and how well he seemed to know her. Why else would he be here, *for her* as he'd said, if he wasn't getting paid?

That realization, that she must know him, should have troubled her. It didn't. She only hoped he'd introduce himself later, without the mask. Maybe, they could continue this in the bright light of real life with no illusion separating them. As much as she wanted that, she decided not to push the issue now.

Her brows furrowed when he turned toward her and her gaze dropped to his tattoos. Perhaps, she didn't know him after all. She couldn't think of a single man in her life that she hadn't seen without a shirt or at least with sleeves short enough to reveal the wide band of ink on her dungeon master's biceps.

So…she was back to square one.

"What do your tattoos signify? Can I ask that?" she inquired when he returned and sat beside her. At his silent urging with his large, warm hand, she sat back on her heels, wrists at the small of her back. She winced only slightly when her ass connected with her ankles. "They look like some sort of words."

"Hmm…well, in a way they are."

He cleaned the inside of her thighs with the new cloth he'd brought, wiping away her sticky cream. The way he cared for her made her all shuddery inside. She looked into his mesmerizing eyes, enveloped in his intense gaze. Her lips parted.

She wanted him again. Her eyes dropped closed on a tiny moan as the warm cloth pressed to her folds. She heard the wet slap of the cloth on the cement as he tossed it away then cupped the back of her neck, pulling her to him. His mouth covered hers, feasting at her parted lips and sending tremors shooting through her once again. She lifted up at his urging, meeting him chest-to-chest and feeling his jutting erection against her belly. Being pressed to him, complying to his will this way, filled her empty spaces as nothing ever had. He tilted her head and drove his tongue in for more. She sucked at it, taking his taste, showing him what she wanted to do to his cock if she ever had the chance. Oh, and the thought of taking his thick pieced erection into her mouth, exploring every inch of it and the barbells running along it, made her moan with a need that rose from deep inside her.

They were both gasping for breath when he pulled back.

"Tattoos?" she managed, grasping for some level ground, for sanity. She wanted to know everything she could about him, but maybe, that wasn't allowed in this lifestyle. Maybe, he was supposed to be shrouded in mystery to up the intensity of the game. She frowned, not liking that idea.

For some reason, she was sure he'd tell her. Perhaps after another flash-fire round of passion.

Every action, every look, every little word seemed to be a match set to a drought-stricken forest. Everything spoken between them fed that blaze. Right now, she didn't care about the stripes across her back or that they'd fucked until she'd collapsed, mere minutes ago. She needed him again.

"Every man in my family has them. We belong to a larger sect and the ink is part of the induction ritual. So are the piercings. At eighteen, if this is the lifestyle a man chooses and if he's a Dom, he goes to see Uncle Tony to get the marks and the metal." He pointed to the tribal tattoo at his navel, partially blocked by the tip of his erection. "This one basically says 'control your belly'. It's a reminder of my vow to always control myself during any situation, sexual or otherwise, that involves my sub."

She had to admit, he'd exhibited more control than she could have. She'd been writhing and begging, and given the chance, she would have pounced on him without a second thought. Though, she had to admit, he'd brought that out in her. She'd never been so desperately needy for any other men.

He held out his arm, displaying the band of black figures on it. "This one says 'keeper of the temple'." He touched her forehead. "And 'owner of the treasure'." He cupped her mound, and she tilted into him, making a wanton sound when his finger slowly dragged over her clit. Pulling away, he flattened his hand between her breasts. "And 'protector of the spirit'."

She swallowed wondering if eventually, she'd get a mark that said temple, treasure and spirit. Even if this was really just for tonight as she still suspected, she'd look into it. She was all those things. Even if he didn't permanently claim her, he'd touched those parts of her, marking her as indelibly as any tattoo could.

"What now?" she asked. She didn't want this to be over yet.

"How does your back feel? There was lidocaine in the cream."

"I'm okay." She would have said the same even if she felt every bruise. "I'd like to continue."

He was silent for a moment, and from the corner of her eye she could see him studying her. "I don't think you can. Not without injury or making you ache so much you regret this tomorrow."

"But—"

"Don't argue with your Master. I'd hate to end this evening with a spanking on that well-flogged ass."

"All right," she said sadly, caving to his damnable voice of reason.

"I didn't say we were finished. We're just finished for right now."

"We didn't even try—"

"Another time. I promise."

* * * *

Jess had never been so exhausted and energized at the same time. It was nearly eleven by the time she let herself into her house. She locked the door, threw her keys in the dish on the table beside the door and set her purse beside it. Keera tended to give her a hard time about her "everything in its place" mentality, but it had always served Jess well. While growing up, Jess had learned quickly that her parents had no time and zero inclination to help her find things in the chaos of their apartments.

Thankfully, she'd always had her own space and from the time she was old enough to comprehend her situation, she'd created a haven for herself, a place she cared for where she could always find her things. After the first time her parents had been evicted and she'd come home to find everything on the lawn, she'd learned to carry her most treasured possessions with her, as well. She'd been seven.

Twenty-odd years later, that memory lingered with her. Sure, she was a bit OCD about her bills, putting everything in its place and taking care of herself, in general, but in her experience, if she didn't, no one else would.

But her Dom claimed he would—and so far that had proved true. It was too soon to put all her faith in him though.

Hugging herself, she giggled at the thought of calling anyone "Master", but she couldn't imagine him as anything else—at least, not while in that dungeon where he'd broken through her barriers and in the end made her feel so…cherished.

Cherished? Her brow furrowed. Yes, there were instances when he'd been so tender and completely into her, too. And *in* her. Her grin widened as she remembered the sensation of his cock, with all that metal, piercing her.

Unbelievable. She'd never experienced anything like it. Signing in pleasure, she fell backward onto her couch then winced with a gasp at her aching backside. Her Master had thoroughly marked it as his, and she couldn't be happier.

Did that make her weird and twisted? She supposed not; she'd read plenty about it and knew it was normal in some relationships, but…

She needed to talk to Keera and get her take on things.

Her friend seemed to have a more varied sexual scope than Jess did.

Jess glanced at her watch. It was too late to call Keera now. She was either at the party, with her man or asleep right now. Jess decided to just text her friend and hope she'd see the message in the morning.

After retrieving her phone from her purse, she sent a message: *Weird night. Would love to talk to you about it. Call me in AM?* then headed upstairs to her bedroom for a long, hot bath then bed.

It wasn't until she was neck-deep in bubbles that she thought about her Pleasure Palace experience again. After she'd been cleaned up, her Master had returned her clothes and they'd talked while she'd dressed. That had seemed weird, and she'd wished he'd leave her in privacy to dress. He'd seemed aware of her discomfort and had raised an eyebrow at her when she'd held her clothes in front of herself and delayed.

"I've seen you naked, kitten. I've probably seen you more intimately than anyone else ever has, and I intend to get even more familiar with all of your body. I've been *inside* you. I think you can get dressed in front of me without being embarrassed."

She'd glanced at the floor. When he put it like that, it did seem silly. "Yes, Master."

While she'd gotten dressed, he leaned against the counter where he kept his tools and watched her, his muscular arms crossed over his beautiful chest. "You'll come back," he said. It was a statement, not a request. "We'll continue your lessons then."

Lessons?

"My schedule precludes me meeting again before Wednesday. Can you be here then?"

He's giving me a choice? "I…well, I think so. I have to check my schedule."

He'd nodded. "Okay, here's the plan: if you can make it, arrive here just as you did today. Give them your name and they will bring you to me. Instructions will be noted with your name in the files at reception. I put a card in your pants pocket with the number to the office. If you can't be here on Wednesday, call that number and follow the same procedure of giving your name and they'll contact me."

She'd finished dressing about then, and he'd pushed away from where he was leaning. Taking her hand, he led her to the front of the club where a security guard had waited. Her Dom cupped her face, running his thumbs over her face, and leaned forward. She'd though he would kiss her, but his lips pressed to her forehead.

"Goodbye, kitten. Until next time."

Jess had shivered at the promise in his deep, rumbling voice. And she'd known she'd go back, no matter what she might have to rearrange on Wednesday.

The security guard had walked her to her car and stood nearby until she'd gotten in. "The rules," he'd reported when she'd told him she was fine and he could go. Truthfully, she kind of liked the feeling of security, of being taken care of, that gave her.

At a stoplight on the way home, she'd pulled out the card and flutters had bombarded her at the note written on it in small precise letters.

Jessica Mine,

That's right—You Are Mine. I will see you on Wednesday. Until then, you are not to touch yourself for pleasure without my permission, and you are not to let another man touch you. I don't share.

M. R.

M. R? She pondered his signature now as she soaked in the tub. Were those his initials? Did the M stand for Master? Was R the initial for his first of last name? Did the Doms have special made-up names at the club? And dear God…his note just made her want think about him and touch herself more. He'd probably known it would have that effect.

She groaned as she sank just a little lower in the tub and crossed her arms over her middle, fisting her hands. Her pussy tingled with need—and she could do *nothing* about it. She was a terrible liar, and if he asked her, he'd know if she wasn't telling him the truth. Even now he was in control, and damn, if that didn't make her even hotter. Suddenly, Wednesday seemed incredibly far away.

Chapter Eight

To Jessica's surprise, she had two text messages in the morning. One was Keera practically demanding to know what had happened last night and telling Jess she'd be over at ten, lattes and pastries in hand. The second was from an unknown number, but she knew immediately who it was from.

Kitten, I hope you behaved last night. I'd like to see you before Wednesday and have freed some time for tomorrow. Would you care to meet me for dinner and entertainment at Pleasure Palace at 5?

Delight exploded through her, and she didn't hesitate before responding that she'd be there. She was still wearing a silly grin when Keera burst into the house for their breakfast.

"Tell me," her friend cried, dropping the food on the table in the breakfast nook where sun poured through the windows. "Don't leave out a thing."

Jess pressed her lips together knowing she certainly *would be* leaving out a few things…or ten.

She reached for her coffee, but Keera pulled it from

her reach. "Speak!"

"Arf. Give me my damn coffee."

"So crabby. Someone need a spanking?" Keera teased.

Jess stared at her speechless and felt color blazing into her cheeks. Her friend's eyes widened and her mouth dropped open.

"Holy fuck, Jess… Did you…? You didn't ditch me last night, did you? You were there at Pleasure Palace, just not at the party." Her stare filled with glee and she went to clap her hands before she realized she was holding the paper cup. She set it down and clapped in excitement. Jess snatched up her drink, hiding behind it as she sipped and Keera demanded details. "Tell me!" Keera insisted. "God, your obsessive control freak must be *freaking* out right now."

"Um, a little," she admitted.

"So what happened?"

"You had nothing to do with it?" By the time Jess had left last night, she'd suspected "her friend" they'd referred to hadn't been Keera.

"Uh…*no*! Spill it, bitch. I want details!"

"Maybe I don't want to share," she hedged.

"Right, which is why you begged me to come over here this morning."

Jess didn't dispute the claim, though she'd only said to call. "Pfpht, we have breakfast together every Saturday."

Staring at Jess in silence, Keera tore a chunk off her cinnamon roll, clearly not believing her friend.

"Okay, fine," Jess laughed. Though she was embarrassed, she'd known she would tell Keera. They shared just about everything, though Keera was closed fisted about her secret boyfriend, only sharing scant details, and if the subject of her past came up...? Well, clams weren't as closed up. Everything else? Fair game.

"Maybe, I shouldn't tell you anything," she went on, "since you won't tell me anything about your boyfriend."

"You mean my Dom, who I meet up with at Pleasure Palace—when we're not going other places, that is."

"Really?" Jess breathed in disbelief, a sense of relief filling her.

"Yeah, really," Keera replied, serious for once.

"Last night, when I got there, this cute disgruntled goth girl opened the door—"

"That's Francesca. She's... Well, I think she's been hurt before and a lot of what she puts on is just a front, so don't take it personally if she's a bitch to you."

"I kinda thought she was funny, after the fact—you know...when I wasn't being freaked out."

"So..." Keera circled her hand in a go-on-with-it motion.

"She said my friend had arranged a special package for me. I thought it was like a massage or a spa treatment or something. Something to relax me before the party. Then these two guys came in..." Blushing furiously and sometimes having to stop and gulp down a bit of coffee before being able to go on, Jess explained what had happened right up to getting chained up in the dungeon and the Dom coming in. "I still don't know who he is."

"And?" Keera demanded, her eyes wide with the need to know more.

"And, I'm not fucking telling you that part! He's a Dom, and I don't easily give up control, but he's in control now. So if you have your own Dom, I'm sure you can guess."

Keera smirked. "Was it good."

Good? Just the thought of more had her tingling. "Yeah."

"Are you seeing him again?"

"Tomorrow night."

"Good. And Jess?"

"Yeah?"

"Don't try to control this. Just let it happen. Pleasure Palace doesn't let just any Joe's hairy dick in there just because he claims to be a Dom. You're safe."

"Joe's hairy dick? Nice mouth, Keer."

Keera winked. "Some people—well, one in particular—like my naughty mouth."

Jess held up a hand. "No! Stop!" she cried and her friend laughed, stuffing another chunk of her roll in her mouth.

"Speaking of dicks—"

"We weren't."

"Weren't we?" Keera raised an eyebrow, and Jess knew their conversation was going south. "Is he pierced?"

Jess grabbed the bag, deciding it was time to retrieve her own pastry. She plunked it onto a napkin then licked the gooey sweetness off her fingers. Her silence was her only answer.

"He is, isn't he?" Keera sighed. "An apa and a ladder like my guy? There's nothing like that, is there? All those metal ridges pushing in—"

She choked on her roll. "Fuck, Keera! Stop!" she begged, coughing.

Keera smirked again, apparently delighted by their entire breakfast conversation. "So, I have an idea. Let's go shopping today. You might not know his name now, but I bet you will soon. We need to sex-up your wardrobe."

* * * *

And they did. Jessica shook her head as she recalled the day before. Keera knew all the places to go to "sex-up" Jess' wardrobe as she put it. Jess had been terrified Keera would try to shove clothes at her that she's never wear in public, and there had been some seriously sexy lingerie, but for the most part, the additions were subtle. Clothes that fit better, closer to her body. Heels. Fabrics that were less utilitarian and more feminine. Dresses and a pair of suits that hugged her curves. A sexy little black dress for going out, as well as another in red. Lace-topped thigh-high stockings rather than pantyhose—Keera assured her she'd feel sexy in them, even if no one else saw them.

The whole spree had made a huge gouge in Jess' savings, but as she dressed for her evening with her Dom, she couldn't feel guilty over the expenditure. Keera had been right about the clothes. The way they made Jess feel, as if she really were sexy, couldn't be compared. The purchases wouldn't cripple her budget, she just better make the clothes last awhile.

Smiling, she slipped on matching navy-blue bra and booty panties that were like silk against her skin then pushed her feet into her heels. Her grin widened as she stood before her cheval mirror and took in her reflection. She'd never thought her curves were particularly rocking but right now… Holy crap, she was hot. She wished she could stand before her Dom in this. What would he think? Would it bring *him* to his knees? She kind of liked that thought, even if she knew it would never happen.

She kicked off the shoes then finished getting dressed in a silky blouse and faded jeans that clung to her curves. In his text earlier, he'd told her not to worry about what she wore; he'd provide clothes for the evening when she arrived.

Jess glanced at her watch then put on her shoes again. She had a half hour to get there by the designated time, so she'd better get her ass in gear. She rushed through the house and out to the car, grabbing her purse on the way. Thankfully, there was no traffic to slow her along the drive and she arrived with ten minutes to spare.

The same goth girl answered the door today, this time wearing a floor-length black dress with a plunging neckline and a slit to the top of her super-pale thigh. Jess had never seen such flawless white skin. Somehow, despite the show of skin, the girl—Francesca, Keera had said—managed to look like a young Morticia Addams.

Her sleek black hair hung in a curtain to her waist, and a hank of it glided over her shoulder as she tilted her head to look at Jess, one side of her mouth lifting.

"So…you came back. A glutton for punishment, eh?"

Jess stared at her, her mouth dropping open. "I…uh…"

Francesca giggled, ruining her façade. "That was a joke. Lighten up. Come on, my big brother is waiting anxiously for you."

"Your brother?"

"Oops," the girl gasped, covering her lips with her black-tipped fingertips, the glee in her eyes telling that her admission hadn't been a mistake at all. Obviously, she was a bratty little sister. Jessica loved it.

"You have anything else to share?" Jess asked.

"Better not. The walls have ears and all…" Francesca winked. "I don't want to earn my own whipping. I'll leave that to you."

"Gee, thanks."

"Oh, your pleasure."

Jess shook her head as Francesca fell back into her bored, put-upon demeanor and led her down the hallway. She opened a door to a room much like the one Jess had been brought to the last time.

"Someone will be in to prep you soon. Have fun. I let…*him* know you're here." With that, she gave Jess a little push inside then slammed the door. Definitely a brat.

Butterflies that had been fluttering in Jess' belly took off in a full-fledged storm. Her body buzzed with anticipation of seeing her Dom again and the possibilities for the night to come. She shook her ice-cold hands as nerves stole her heat.

"Hi."

Jess looked up as a statuesque blonde stepped into the room, wearing khaki pants and a cute black scrub top with red lipstick kisses all over it—not the sexy wear Jessica would have expected here. "Hi," she replied, trying to smile through her nerves.

The woman grinned, her entire manner friendly and kind. "I'm Vanessa, and I've been assigned to be your personal technician whenever you visit." She winked. "Because I'm the best. Your Dom has set up a special treat for you, so we'd best get started. Thank goodness you're a little early because I only have three hours for everything. We'll start with the massage, body scrub and any waxing then the manicure and pedicure followed by hair, makeup and getting dressed."

"Seriously?" Had she died and gone to BDSM heaven? She hadn't been that well-behaved.

"Welcome to having a wealthy Dom who likes to spoil his subs."

Subs? Jessica frowned. "Does he have more than one?"

"Oh! No, no," Vanessa replied. "I mean…whenever he has one. And he hasn't in a while."

The tech showed her into a small dressing room. "Everything off. There's a spa robe hanging on the hook. Put your things in that overnight bag on the bench and it will be ready for you at the desk when you leave."

"I won't change before I go?"

"Oh no, honey. Whatever you wear goes with you. He purchased it for you."

"Oh, I see." Jess nodded and didn't really understand at all. She felt like she'd been dropped into some strange fairytale.

Vanessa put a hand on Jess' shoulder. "Just roll with it and enjoy. I know it's overwhelming but trust me, he's gifting you for gifting him with submission. You've given him something special and this is his way of letting you know."

Warmth washed through Jess. He appreciated her; she'd truly given him something. She was his treasure. She took a deep breath through her emotions. "Let's do this."

Suddenly, she needed to see him even more than she had before.

Vanessa pampered her in all the ways she'd mentioned, relaxing Jess and making her feel even more beautiful than she'd felt earlier when she'd stood in front of the mirror in her new lingerie.

Now, she stood in front of another mirror, dressed in a red, silk slip dress that came to the top of her thighs and barely covered her bare pussy. Matching red, four-inch heels lengthened her legs, but she knew her Master would still be taller than her. Underneath the dress, a lace and bone bustier supported her but didn't cover her breasts, leaving them accessible to her Dom. Her hair had been styled into a fancy twist, and a black sequined mask covered the top portion of her face and wrapped up on one side. It curved into her hair like four splayed fingers. A fifth, like a thumb, curled just below her cheekbone.

A matching choker wrapped her neck, the initials MR in the front in red. That, the scrap of fabric showing his ownership—that he *owned* her—made her wet, her sex clenching with the need for more of his claiming. Her nipples pressed against the soft fabric over then, showing just how aroused she was.

"He's here," Vanessa said. She turned Jess, and there in the doorway to the spa stood her Master. Jessica gasped at the sight of him, but the light squeeze of her assistant's hand regained her attention. "Knees," the woman whispered, the sound barely a breath.

Immediately, Jessica dropped down to the soft carpet, bowing her head and assuming the position he'd taught her the last time she'd been here, not caring that it exposed her pussy. At the moment, she'd do anything for him. Suddenly, she wondered if this was part of how this whole thing worked. He gave; she gave; they both got what they wanted. It was a strange compromise, but made sense in a way she hadn't considered before now. Still, she knew not all D/s relationships worked like this. They all had different versions of give and take. This way was just…theirs.

It warmed her to think there could be a "theirs", though she didn't even know his name. She didn't need to. She was him. That was all that mattered here.

"Master," she whispered when he stopped before her. It surprised her how easily she called him that, without feeling weird or silly. To her…it was just his name and his title of respect and didn't seem so strange at all. Not here with him. She wondered though how it would feel somewhere else.

"Kitten, you're beautiful." He squatted before her, and his generous, hard, bulge was in her line of vision. His lips moved to her ear, his hand skimming along her thigh to center. "My lovely, exquisite treasure," he murmured for her hearing alone, just before his finger dragged over her wet folds.

Jessica whimpered, so aroused by him she didn't care that someone else was in the room.

"Vanessa, leave us," he said.

"Yes, Sir."

Jess assumed the woman had followed the order, but she didn't worry about it and she didn't look, her attention on his fingers alone as they pushed inside her.

"Do you need to come, little one?" he asked.

"Yes. Please, Master," she moaned.

"Have you touched yourself?"

"No. I followed your order."

"Good girl," he said, increasing the drives into her and adding his thumb to flick over her clit. Warm sensations wove through her, piling one atop another until she was on the verge of coming and her walls starting to convulse on his fingers. He pulled his hand away. "That's enough."

A tiny sound escaped her though she tried to hold it back. Her entire body screamed for release. She needed it.

He stood and held out his hand for her. Only when she took it did she feel the wetness and realize it was the one he'd had inside her. Now, she'd smell the musky scent of her arousal whenever her hand came near her face.

"A bit of instruction, kitten. Walk just behind me and to the right. You are to be polite to other Doms, but you do not need to defer to them, and you definitely don't need to obey any of them." His hand cupped her chin and he lifted her chin so she looked into his eyes. "You are mine, and the only one you need concern yourself with is me."

"Yes, Master," she whispered, her throat feeling a little dry. She hadn't considered being around other people. And having him declare once again that she was his, especially after how he'd had her pampered today, just…moved her.

With a nod, he released her and turned toward the door. She followed him in silence, two steps behind him and slightly to his right as instructed. From her position, she freely roamed her gaze over him. He wore slim-cut black pants that looked tailored to his body. His perfect ass and powerful thighs mesmerized her as she watched them move beneath the expensive trousers. His shirt was a silky red fabric that perfectly matched her dress. On his feet were polished dress shoes, and the only thing askew about his appearance was the mask and head covering, though she supposed since she too was wearing a mask, that might just be a thing in the club's public areas. She'd heard they were incredibly discreet about members' identities. Perhaps, this was part of that.

He led her down a wide, brightly lit hallway that was very un-dungeon-like. The walls and wainscoting were painted white and large black-and-white photos of isolated figures and various body parts lined the way. It was all quite tasteful and artsy. Had she not known better, she would have thought she was far from a BDSM club. Apparently, there was a lot she didn't know.

"Welcome, Sir," her Dom was greeted at the double doors at the end of the passage. The blonde hostess, in a short black skirt and a red corset with black embellishments, led them to a table near a wall on the far side of the subtly lit room. Candles flickered on each table and concealed lights illuminated the red walls.

When they stopped, Jessica noticed the table had only one chair. She glanced up at her companion, biting the side of her lip in consternation. Okay, she could guess what was happening here. The chair was for him.

Sitting, he confirmed her thought.

"The cushion is for you to kneel on," he said, indication the plush, red pillow near his seat.

She nodded. "Yes, Sir." Glancing around as she lowered herself to her knees, she noticed she wasn't the only one who'd be kneeling beside a Dom.

"Move closer to me," he ordered quietly when she was settled a foot from his knees.

Her brows drew together. If she moved much closer, she'd be in his lap.

At her hesitation, he leaned forward and tapped the collar around her neck. "Who's initials are these?"

She drew in a breath. "I don't know. I don't know your name."

Now, where had that come from? She didn't want to be mouthy with him, but it just popped out.

His quiet growl raked over her. "Fine," he rumbled. "Who do you belong to?"

"You, Sir," she replied, thinking it better than her fist inclination—a snappy retort of *myself.*

"That's right. Now, get your ass closer to me."

This time, she obeyed, following his crooked fingers until her breast pressed to his leg.

"Better," he said.

"Not really," she replied, the proximity to his groin making her uncomfortably needy, especially since she was still worked up over his play earlier.

His thumb pulled over her lip and she smelled her scent on him. "Such a naughty mouth," he commented. "You really want a spanking, don't you, little kitten?"

She bit into her lip, narrowly missing his finger. Yes, she did want a spanking, the memory of her last "punishment" warming her core. Swallowing, she stared up at him, though she kept her face slightly averted.

"Perhaps," he said while parting his legs and cupping her chin, pulling her so she leaned up and toward him, "we need to better occupy your mouth."

Her eyes went wide as he flicked open the button on his pants and his hand went to his zipper. She couldn't do *that* here. With people *watching!*

"But—" Her word was cut off as he pulled her mouth

to his thick cock, the tip with its metal pushing between her lips. She groaned at the taste of him, her protests evaporating and moisture forming in her pussy as she widened her lips to take him deeper. She moaned at the feel of his piercings running back and forth along her tongue as she sucked. Eagerly, she flicked her tongue along them, exploring him and trying to bring him pleasure. Despite her naturally mouthy behavior, she appreciated being with him and all he'd done for her. She *wanted* to please him.

And that was the crux of this whole experience. Her submission gave both of them pleasure. She didn't have to prove anything. She didn't have to be the best at anything or perform sort of professional miracles like the ones she pulled off daily at work. She made him happy by her obedience, by simply giving him herself, by letting him worry about things and by just letting go.

She knotted her hands behind her, glad they held her dress in place and she wasn't flashing her ass at the room. Despite her realization about her submission, she belonged only to her Dom. That was one thing she was sure she *did* have to protect—that she shared herself only with him.

"Oh God, fuck," he swore as she sucked him. He curled forward a little, creating an intimate circle with her. "Your mouth…oh, fuck, kitten. Yes, suck it. You're going to make me come in that sweet, naughty little mouth. Does that make you happy?"

She moaned around him again and took him a little deeper. There was no way she could take all of him. She just didn't have that skill and no recent experience. For him, she'd try; she'd learn.

His hand smoothed over her head, and his fingers caught in the hair at the nape of her heck, tugging her back until she was forced to release his cock. Before she could question anything, he pulled her up onto his lap, facing away from him, her legs straddling his.

"Master," she cried softly as his cock pushed through her sodden folds and deep inside her. He was going to fuck her, right here, in a roomful of people! He turned her head and kissed her as he thrust into her, the piercing raking along her sensitive flesh. Pulling back, he murmured, "I want you to ride me. Directly across from us is another Dom. He seems quite taken with you. Turn and look at him."

Her cheeks burned as she complied and met the eyes of the other man. She knew he couldn't see anything, because her Master was keeping her covered, still she felt completely exposed.

"Put your hand back on my hips and ride me, kitten," her Dom ordered against her ear. "Don't argue," he added when she was about to protest. "Ride me and keep watching him."

Her skin burning, she did as he said, using him as leverage to lift and lower her lips. Her eyes never left the man watching them. His hand rubbed over his crotch as he stared, and Jessica felt her walls tightening around the cock plowing inside her as the illicitness of it all overtook her. While she watched, the other man opened his pants and fisted his erection. She stared at his hand as it worked up and down his length, his thumb sweeping over his tip. When she flicked her gaze up, his eyes bored into hers. She gasped, her breathing ragged at the scene that had captured her.

God, *she*…straight-laced Jessica Rush was fucking a man in public, putting on a show for another guy.

Her Dom pressed his mouth to her back, his breath warming her skin as she rode him. He nipped and licked across her shoulder blade, kissed down her neck, sank his teeth into her shoulder—

"Ah!" she gasped. She bit her lip, trying to hold back her cries as her orgasm overtook her. His hand came to her throat, squeezing lightly, while she jerked and fought to keep silent in the quiet room. "Give it to me," he demanded. "Give me your screams."

Her wail seemed to echo in the quiet room while her body convulsed, her pussy clamping onto her Master's cock.

"Fuck," he rasped in her ear. "Oh, fuck, Jessica. Your hot little pussy is going to kill me. God, I can't—oh fuck." His hand on her hip tightened as he stiffened beneath her. She heard the man across from them groan and watched his cum leak over the side of his hand, and another orgasm exploded through her. This time, her Dom's mouth captured her screams as she jolted on his still-rigid erection. He consumed her, his tongue darting in to taste her while her body bowed in his arms.

"Well done," he whispered against her lips when she sagged against him. Cradling her against his body, he turned in his chair, putting his back to the other man before he helped Jessica off his cock and tucked himself back inside his pants. He pulled her against him again, keeping her on his lap rather than telling her to move back to the cushion. She was glad, since she was sure she didn't have the strength to support herself at the moment.

It wasn't until he lifted a champagne flute to her lips that she realized their food and drink had been brought to the table while they'd put on that show. She took a sip of the bubbly alcohol.

Her eyes widened at the full, fruity flavor. "I've never had champagne like this."

"It's a demi-sec. A favorite of mine I was introduced to while on a trip to England. They keep it on hand here for me. You like it?"

"Yes. May I have another sip," she met his eyes,

"Master?"

He lifted the flute to her lips again, watching her sip. A droplet rolled over her lip as he pulled away the glass, and he dove in to capture it with his mouth before he kissed her again.

Jess groaned against his lips, her arousal building again, though in truth, it had barely subsided after her orgasms. She just wanted more and more of him. She leaned into him, her fingers curling in the front of his shirt and feeling the plates of hard muscle beneath it. He was so powerful, both in muscle and personality. She had no doubt he'd dominate a roomful of people in whatever he did away from this place.

"Let's eat," he said after a moment.

"Okay," she breathed. Whatever he wanted… "Should I kneel again?"

"No, I quite like you perched here. Don't move."

"Okay."

She felt him moving as he reached around her, and moments later, he brought a piece of buttered roll to her lips. She took a bit and when a few crumbs dropped to her chest, he dipped his head to capture them. Jess watched him while she chewed, wondering if she'd ever had a stranger dinner than this, where there was one plate, one set of cutlery and one glass each for water and champagne. She sat docilely on his lap, her hands in her lap, while he fed both of them. There was plenty of playtime—for him—and discussion between bites.

"Do you have any questions for me?" he asked as his thumb grazed over her nipple, playing with it through the silky fabric of her dress.

"Some."

"Ask. Pretend we're on a date…at Applebees or something. What would you ask me?"

She chortled then pressed her face into his shoulder

while she laughed so the sound didn't disturb the other diners—though when she thought about it, they'd already heard her loud orgasm.

"What's so funny?" he asked, his tone amused.

"I was just thinking of us, at Applebees."

"Hey, I eat there sometimes. We'll go sometime."

"When you finally tell me who you are?" She wished she could figure it out, and she hoped he didn't think she was an idiot because she hadn't yet. Without seeing all of his face... And she got the feeling he was disguising his voice, speaking in a tone and volume he wouldn't normally.

"Yes," he replied. "After I tell you."

"Will it be soon?"

"Yes."

"Tonight?"

"No."

Jessica frowned. She didn't like secrets or feeling as if she was being made a fool of.

"Stop," he rasped against her ear. "You're letting in your insecurities and they have no place here. My reason for secrecy has nothing to do with hurting you in any way. I want your trust without the complication of identity."

She narrowed her eyes. "I know you, don't I?"

"Yes."

"Am I going to be pissed off?"

He lifted the champagne flute to her lips once more. "Drink," he ordered when she hesitated. She sighed, recognizing his delay tactic, but he didn't move the glass and after a moment, she complied with his wish. He took a sip, too, before setting aside the flute.

"Yes," he replied finally. "You'll probably be annoyed with me."

"Just annoyed?"

"I'm hoping we'll get past it quickly. I've wanted you for a long time, kitten. I haven't been with anyone since the day I met you."

She drew back, staring at him. "And how long ago was that?" she gasped.

"A while. Next question."

She growled. "What do you do when you're not here?"

"Work, run, spend time with my family," he chuckled, "play the cello, actually. My parents insisted all us kids learn an instrument."

"I want to hear you play."

"Someday…"

She grimaced, understanding his reply but wanting it now.

"Dessert?" he asked. "Tiramisu?"

"My favorite. Yes, please!"

"I know." He looked over her shoulder and made a motion with his hand. A moment later, the dessert was placed on the table, the other dishes cleared away and their champagne filled.

"Okay…so…what do you do for work?" she asked.

He grinned. "Try this," he said, lifting a fork laden with the confection. "I've never had better. I think you'll like it."

"You're not going to answer?"

"Nope," he replied.

Jess sighed, giving up her quest for identity information. "Fine. Okay, let's see… You've been to England. Do you like to travel?"

"Yes, a lot. Do you?"

"Yes, but I rarely do—unless it's around the state for work. Where have you been?"

"All over the States, including Alaska and Hawaii. I want to go to Alaska again next year—with you, if you're willing. I traveled Europe after high school. It's a family thing. All of us have."

"Wow, that's a nice tradition. So…who is all of us?"

"My siblings and me," he hedged and offered more tiramisu.

Damn it. She thought she might catch him on that one. She swallowed, enjoying the sweet, liquor-laced flavor. He was right; this was the best she'd ever had. She watched his firm lips as he took a bite.

Impulsively, she leaned forward and kissed him, tasting him. She never would have done that with another man, but this situation, the scenes they'd played out… It all fast-forwarded the intimacy of their relationship. She hoped with everything in her that she'd be able to get past his revelation when he finally made it. Right then as he deepened the kiss, lifting his hand to cup the back of her head and hold her in place as he took over, she promised herself that she'd try—she'd do whatever she needed to in order to understand when he finally told her his identity.

"That's probably not something I was supposed to do," she whispered when they parted.

"In the bedroom while in a scene, in the playroom? No, you shouldn't. But here, like this, it's perfectly acceptable to me. I won't make you guess what's right and wrong. I'll tell you, and if you make a mistake, because I haven't instructed you properly, I'll correct you the first time, without repercussion on you."

"Thank you, Master," she said, bowing her head slightly in deference.

He lifted his chin, his lips brushing hers. "I love kissing you."

"I love kissing *you.*"

"Good. Would you like more dessert?"

She shook her head. All she wanted was him.

"I don't have a scene planned for tonight," he said. "My intention was only dinner together and getting to know one another better. So that you'll feel more comfortable with me."

"I do feel comfortable with you."

"Good."

"I have to be up early tomorrow, but I don't really want our night to end."

"What do you want?"

She shrugged, heat rushing into her face. What she wanted embarrassed her, and she wasn't sure she could tell him.

"Be honest, Jessica. Don't ever be afraid to tell me what you need. I will always take care of you." He touched the place where the tattoo banded his arm. "It's my sacred oath."

The breath left her as she realized how connected that made them. Okay…she could do this. "Do you still want to see me on Wednesday?"

"Yes."

"That's…um…a long time away."

"An eternity," he sighed.

"I was wondering if…well…maybe, could you… Oh God!" She covered her face with her hand. "Will you…um—"

He pulled away her fingers and made her look at him. "Will I…spank you? Make you remember me until then?"

She nodded, biting her lip. Geez, why was she being such a wuss about this? She was a confident woman— except…not so much with him. She was still too out of her element.

"It will be my pleasure," he said and stood, setting her on her feet in the process. He tilted his gaze and caught her stare again. "But remember this, little kitten. This is not a punishment. This is for you, because it's what you want."

She swallowed, her throat dry, and nodded. "Thank you, Master."

Chapter Nine

Jessica shifted in her seat, trying to find a more comfortable position without alerting Ryan to her discomfort. He'd arrived bright and early at her house this morning with her favorite Starbucks and a smile.

"Ready to go?" he'd asked.

"Sure," she'd said, letting him take her overnight bag while she carried her handbag. She was so thankful for the advances of tablet technology that allowed her to travel without her laptop. So much more convenient.

She'd settled in the passenger seat while he'd stowed her bag in the truck, and she'd immediately realized she'd made an error in judgment last night. While she would definitely think of her Dom all day due to her well-paddled backside, the trip across state with her straight-laced boss would be far from easy.

Last night had been bliss. After their meal, her Dom had taken her back to his playroom—he'd corrected her when she'd called it his dungeon. She'd found it was actually two rooms, the second much like a bedroom. He'd bent her over the side of the king-sized bed, her ass in the air, and lifted her skirt.

"I think perhaps rather than a spanking with my hand, I should use a paddle. What do you think?"

"Whatever you think is best, Master," she'd replied, though she was a bit scared of a paddle. Butterflies had bombarded her insides in a flurry of nerves.

"Perfect answer, kitten." He'd stroked his hand over the back of her head and down her back. *"You're absolutely perfect,"* he whispered. *"I knew you would be."*

Immediately, her nerves evaporated as warmth spread through her. She'd pleased him. How had she been so unaware of her submissive side until now? She smiled into her arms as she waited for him.

He sat beside her, and when she peeked over at him, she saw a wood paddle on his lap. It didn't look too scary, the flat surface no bigger than his hand. She could do this.

"Here's what we're going to do," he said. *"We'll go until you reach orgasm or you decide you've had enough, at which time, I want you to say Alaska. Can you remember that?"*

"Yes. Alaska."

"At that point, I'll stop the paddling, and you will kneel. I want you to suck my cock again, but this time, I'm coming in your mouth. Understand?"

She licked her lips. She liked the sound of that. *"Yes, Master. I look forward to it."*

He stroked her head again. *"You're such a good girl."*

Now, remembering, she shifted again in her seat again. She hadn't needed to safe word. He'd brought her to a screaming orgasm, so violent her pussy had flooded and she'd felt it rolling onto her leg as she eagerly knelt before him and worshipped that magnificent cock until he'd spurted down her throat with a tortured cry of completion.

"Are you okay?" her boss asked, snatching her away from the memory.

She looked over at him with a bland smile. He'd die if he knew. "Yes, I'm fine. Why?"

"You keep squirming around."

"Oh, well...I...um... I have an achy back today." And achy back*side* anyway. She kind of wished she had some of the numbing cream her Dom had put on her after the paddling. It had certainly helped for her ride home last night, but by the time she was heading to bed the twinges had started. By this morning, underwear and pantyhose had been out of the question. She'd decided to go commando under her suit skirt, opting for thigh-high stockings as well. Pants would have been a better option for the site, but again, they were out of the question.

"I'm good at backrubs," he offered then added quickly. "Purely platonic."

She chuckled. "Thanks. I'll keep that in mind." Opening her purse, she pulled out a couple ibuprofen then downed them with a swig of her coffee—her favorite. She grinned at Ryan remembering what she liked. When she glanced over at him, his brow was furrowed.

"Are you okay?" she offered back.

"Hmm?" he asked distractedly. "Yes. Yeah, I'm fine. Just thinking."

"Work?"

"No. Just thinking of something that happened this weekend, wondering if I miss-stepped. You know how it is." He waved his hand, dismissing his thought. "Relationship crap."

She hadn't realized he had a girlfriend. "Call her later. I'm sure she'll forgive you, if you need it."

He smiled. "I hope so. She's the one, you know?"

Well, that ruled him out as her Dom. Thank God! That

could be awkward. Seriously, how would that work at the office? *I'm sorry, Master, but I think your idea is full of shit and here are all the reasons why.* Still, she'd better shove him out of her fantasies. She wasn't dreaming of another woman's man. Besides, she had her own guy now. Sort of. Maybe...

"Congratulations. I'm happy for you."

He tapped his fingers on the steering wheel. "As long as it all works out. So, tell me about this site. What's been going on? Honestly."

"It's been a battle. I'm winning...but still. I've been reporting my issues with the on-site construction manager; so you know about that."

"I've read your reports, but give me the un-spun truth about what's going on. No sugar coating."

She sighed quietly, not wanting to seem as if she couldn't handle the site problems for this mall project, but knowing Ryan expected the unadulterated truth. "Clive is positive he knows better than anyone else what needs to be done. God forbid he consult me or follow the schedule or, I don't know, consider that we might have a budget for the project or codes to meet. He's incredibly good at pissing off our contractors. If he'd behaved like this earlier in the project, I would have requested he be fired. I didn't start having issues with him until we were halfway into the construction. Firing him at that point would have crippled our timeline, so I've just had to stay on top of him. Every day. It's exhausting, and I really don't want to work with him again after this."

"You won't."

Her head whipped around to look at him. What did that mean?

"Why?"

"Because if he's an incompetent douche, I don't want him on my team—that stays in this car by the way."

"You don't want me to tell anyone you called him that?"

"Uh, no."

"Don't worry." She waved her hand, indicating the car. "This is Vegas."

"Great then, here's the thing. I gave you this project because I knew you were the only one who could handle him. He's been a problem before. This is his last chance."

"Does he know?"

"He knows. It's probably why he behaved until that far in. He'll likely panic when he sees me with you today."

"Why? You always do site visits."

"Trust me on this one. He doesn't want to see me."

"So, I'll need to replace him three-quarters through the project?"

Ryan nodded. "Probably."

"A little warning would have been nice."

"I'm giving it to you now."

She blew out a breath and looked out the side window. Sometimes, Ryan really pissed her off. "What if I asked you not to fire him? We're managing."

"I'll consider it, but I don't like that you're putting in extra hours babysitting him. And we'd better not find he's pulling shoddy work."

"So far everything's been at code, on spec and polished.

"All right. Give me the rundown on the subcontractors."

For the next hour and a half, Jess relayed progress, issues and wins for each part of the project. Though she reported general project updates to Ryan on a regular basis, these were minutia that were left out of the overview and items he normally didn't need to hear about to know the project was running well.

* * * *

His woman had a brilliant mind and stunned him with her efficiency. Ryan just wanted to sneak Jessica away somewhere and show her how appreciated she was, but that would be totally inappropriate for the job. Even if she knew he was her Dom.

He intended to tell her today. It was part of his plan— get her away from home, alone and without a way to escape, and make her listen and understand. It might all blow up in his face.

So far the day had gone well. Jess was in her element while dealing with the crew, and she knew the project inside and out. It did disturb him, however, that the men seemed to defer to him while talking, and he wasn't sure if it was because she was a woman or because they knew he was her boss, though she was in charge of the project. More than once, he'd redirected queries and the relayed information to Jess. Once corrected, the men dealt with her in, what he assumed, was their regular deferential manner, and she seemed grateful.

When they broke for lunch and they could speak privately, she confirmed that.

"Thank you for the redirects," she said as they settled into a booth at, of all places, Applebees since it was closest to the jobsite. He couldn't help but be amused and had seen her small smile when he'd suggested it. "I was contemplating how to do it without sounding like a petulant brat demanding attention."

He shook his head. "This field is still very much a man's world. It's always a fine line you're walking, isn't it?"

"I suppose so, but I love my job. Most of the people are awesome, but you already know that. To me, knowing we're making something important to the community, that these beautiful building will be full of life from the businesses and consumers going into them…it fulfilling work. I mean, this mall will be a center for the city and an attraction for those visiting here—and *we* made it."

Her excitement and joy over the project filled him, and he couldn't help smiling as the same feelings overwhelmed him. "This is why you were the best person for this development." He reached out and touched her hand. She startled away and he realized his mistake. Well, fuck. Right. She didn't realize their intimate relationship…yet. Tonight, he reminded himself. It couldn't happen soon enough.

"Sorry," he said quickly. "I was just excited about telling you… You know, we're bidding on a new project for later this year. It will slightly overlap this one, but we want you in on the discussions. With the timing of it and your enthusiasm, you're the best fit for it."

She tilted her head with a small smile. "Tell me. It's not often I see you so excited about something. You're so laid back."

Oh kitten, you have no idea how excited I am all *the time when I'm with you.* Sitting back, he launched into an overview of the health club project Theo had brought him last week. Over the past few days, he and his brother, and occasionally their father, had brainstormed and planned their full proposal to Fit-Life. His brother Max would come into things soon, as he drew up initial designs. Key to the discussions so far had been which personnel to utilize and who would be in what position. Jessica's name had come up repeatedly, and it pleased him to know she was so well thought of in the company. It wasn't just him and his desire for her.

Since he was taking this trip with her, and he was her boss, he'd been tasked with feeling out her confidence in taking on the monumental job. So until their food arrived, he shared what he could, without revealing sensitive information best discussed in the privacy of the Cress offices.

"They want us to do several facilities around home, and if those go well, they'll expand across the state. They have quite a presence on the West coast and the surrounding states, but little in the Midwest or the East coast. This is a huge opportunity for us."

"Oh my God," she breathed. "And you're considering me to head it up?"

"You're the most qualified person on our staff. It makes sense. You'll be supervising others at your level, so it will mean a promotion to Senior Project Manager. What do you think?"

"I think I'd absolutely love a chance at it."

"It's not a done deal of course, but Theo and my dad wanted your 'in' before we proceeded much further. As the head of the project, your input will be needed at all stages. You might need to travel out to the Fit-Life offices a time or two."

She shrugged. "I don't see why that would be a problem."

"I didn't figure it would be." Best of all, with the project taking place in their area over the next year, she wouldn't be traveling overnight, taking her away from him. That would be one of the best perks of winning the bid. Thank God, they were really the only ones in the running right now.

"We should go check into the hotel after we're done here. What else do you need to do at the worksite today?"

"I need to meet with the electrician this afternoon. They're having some challenges with the wiring for the reclining seating in the theater and there's another issue with the carousel in the food court. I also need to review some signage changes for one of the tenants. I'm ending the day with a status meeting with Clive."

"I want to sit in."

"I figured you would." She played with the straw in her glass, pushing at ice cubes. "I've got my tablet with me, and I can check my email for a few minutes, give you some privacy, if you want to call your girlfriend before we head over to the hotel."

Girlfriend? Oh right…their discussion this morning.

"No, I'll be talking to her tonight. We need to clear up a few things, and it'll take some time."

"Oh…well…okay." Her brow furrowed, but she didn't look up at him, and Ryan wondered what she was hiding by not looking at him.

Confusion bubbled inside Jess. Why the hell did she care whether or not Ryan had a girlfriend? He deserved someone. So what if she'd been fantasizing about him for ages? Didn't she have someone else to occupy her now, someone who obviously cared about her and wanted to have a future. He'd made that clear last night.

Guilt mixed into her muddled emotions. She shouldn't be thinking of Ryan in any way other than as her boss, but when they sat here like this, discussing ideas, when they worked together with such synergy and similar thought processes, as they had today, she wondered how they'd mesh in a personal relationship. What would it feel like in his arms? To have his mouth on her?

She bit her lip. God, she was screwed up. Why was she still thinking like this after she'd started something with a Dom at Pleasure Palace? After the way he'd blown her mind yesterday, she shouldn't be thinking of anyone else. But she was. She needed more than a sexual relationship. She wanted to whole package—hot sex, tenderness, compatibility, stimulating conversations, a partnership, a sense of worth outside of her submission…

"What are you thinking?" Ryan asked.

"Nothing." She grimaced as she looked up at him. *I'm wondering what you'd be like in bed.* "Just thinking of something that happened last night. A personal thing, so don't ask."

"You don't look very happy about it."

She sighed, shrugging. "I'm not...*unhappy.*"

"But..."

"It's kind of hard to explain."

"We've known each other awhile, Jess. I consider us to be friends. Really, with the size of company, practically family. If something's bothering you, you can talk to me."

She stared at him, sizing him up. Could she talk about this? They always seemed closer to one another when they weren't in the office, as if the wall fell when they left the Cress building. But no, she couldn't discuss this with him. Well, not deeper than on a surface level, anyway.

"I don't think so, Ryan. Not about this. It's a sex thing."

"I've had sex before—"

She laughed. "Family" or not, there was no freaking way. "No. Just no," she choked out, shaking her head. "I'm not discussing sex with you. Besides, what I meant was: the relationship is a sex thing—you know, sex only. I was just thinking about... Well, it's not really what I want. I need more than that, you know?"

"I know," he replied quietly, staring intently into her eyes. A shiver ran down her back as a vague recognition ran through her. Something she couldn't quite grasp but was right there beyond her reach. Something that maybe...she didn't want to know?

Her heart started to slam in her chest.

"Ry-Ryan?" she stuttered, her voice sounding odd to

her hearing as blood rushed past her ears, making everything seem as if she were underwater.

His chin tilted. "Of course, you need more than sex. I've know that all along, kitten. I promise I'll give you everything you need—now, that you know."

Even before he confirmed his identity, Ryan watched the blood drain from Jessica's face as she realized he was her Dom from Pleasure Palace.

"M. R.," she murmured, as if not hearing him. As if just making the connection between his name and the initials that stood for Master Ryan. Her eyes widened, filling with tears, as she gasped for breath. "No... Oh... *No!*"

She surged to her feet.

"Jessica, stop," he ordered, but she ignored him and dashed from the restaurant. Fuck! His submissive, the woman he loved—yes, loved—had just run out on him.

"Fuck!" he cursed, repeating his thoughts and gaining the disapproving glares of nearby diners. Ryan didn't care what they thought. He flagged down the waiter to settle their bill.

By the time he'd paid and rushed after Jess, she'd disappeared. He checked the car, though he was sure she wouldn't be there. Looking around, panic starting to rise, he tried to decide his next move.

Pulling out his cell, he dialed her number. When she didn't answer, he hung up and dialed again. And again. And again, until he started going directly to voicemail and he knew she'd turned off her phone. He jammed the cell into his pocket, swearing roundly and getting pissed.

He drove his hands through his hair. Fuck, fuck, fuck!

Not knowing what else to do, he started walking. There were a hell of a lot of retail businesses along this road. She could be in any of them.

When his phone started ringing, he dove for it and yanked it from his pocket. "Jessica?" he exclaimed.

"What the fuck did you do?" his brother snapped.

"Theo," Ryan sighed. "Look, I can't talk. I need to—"

"I know, you idiot. She just called Keera, hysterically sobbing. Keera, of course, came right to me. Seriously, you *idiot*, you couldn't have handled this better?"

"Stop calling me an idiot."

"You prefer fuckwit? Because, man, you couldn't have fucked things up worse."

"Do you know where she is?" Ryan demanded.

He heard Theo muffle the phone and ask, "Did she say where she's going?" Ryan couldn't hear Keera's response, but Theo said, "Then ask her. Look, fuck the friend loyalty. It isn't safe for her to be wandering a strange city on her own while she's distraught. Ask her where she is and if you need to come and get her."

A moment later, Theo returned to the call. "There must be a small park of some sort near you. She's there."

"Thank you."

"Just un-fuck this, okay? We can't afford to lose one of our best employees because you wanted to screw her."

"It's more than that, and you know it."

"Whatever. Just fix it."

Ryan hung up without responding. Park. Where was the park? He looked around and didn't see anything remotely resembling one and no signs to indicate a direction.

Using the map feature on his phone, he pulled up an overview of the area. Damn…how had she gotten that far so quickly? It looked as if the park was ten minutes from here, on foot…in the other direction. Making an about-face, he jogged toward it and his woman, not caring that he probably looked strange running down the sidewalk in his business attire.

Thankfully, the park was small by most standards, just a small pond with a nearby picnic area, a playground, a large grassy area for kids to run, two baseball diamonds and a walking path around it all. He easily located Jessica on one of the benches near the water, where some ducks swam, oblivious to everything.

She was bent forward, her face buried in her hands. Her shoulders shook, and he knew she was crying. Shit. Was it so bad to find out he was her Dom? And he *was* hers. She belonged to him; there was no fucking way around that. He wasn't giving her up. This situation… Yeah, it was a mess, but he'd fix it.

Quietly, he sat beside her. He wanted to yank her into his arms, but instead, he leaned forward, resting his elbows in his knees, and waited for her.

"Go away," she begged, somehow knowing it was him. "I'm too…*angry* to talk to you right now—or ever."

"No, baby. Not happening."

"Please…just—"

"No. We need to talk."

"All those things…" She sniffled, more in control than he'd thought. Fat tears still rolled down her face, but she wasn't sobbing. "Everything I did…*with you.* How are we supposed to work together? How do I even face you? How can I do my job and remember what happened between us and… I'll have to quit—"

"Kitten—"

"Don't call me that!"

"It's who you are. All fight and claws and curiosity and so damn cuddly yet so in need of human touch that you break my heart. You're over-thinking this and coming to all the wrong conclusions. Look at me." Knowing she'd need help, he cupped her chin and turned her tearstained face toward him.

"This is humiliating," she whispered, closing her eyes.

"Why?" he whispered back.

"You know why." She looked at him, and the regret in her eyes pierced straight through him, yanking out his soul. "The things I let you do… The things I *asked* you to do."

"That doesn't matter. You're mine, and that's between us and only us."

"How can you ever respect me or take me seriously at work?"

"Oh baby…because I love you. Do you have any idea how long I've wanted you? I wasn't lying when I told you there's been no one since I met you. It's been you and only you. So we have BDSM in our relationship? Plenty of people do, and they function in society just like everyone else. You've seen my parents together. You've seen how my dad values my mom's opinions, how she's his equal partner in the business, even though she doesn't want any sort of title. Being my dad's submissive doesn't change her important role in other aspects of their lives or his deep respect for her. Your submission to me doesn't change how we work together, how *I* respect *you*. You're phenomenal at your job and invaluable to me. I don't want anything to change there." He grinned. "I'll still boss you around, because, well, I'm your boss and I'm always that way. And you'll still call me on bullshit, because that's part of what *you* do."

Jess stared at Ryan. The moment she'd seen his piercing gaze and made the connection between him and her Dom at Pleasure Palace, her world had exploded. She hadn't been able to breathe as chunks of her being had seemed to fall away, revealing the vulnerable, damaged woman she hid from the world. Even her Dom had only seen a small part of her. He didn't know the trauma her parents had put her through year after year, how unstable her childhood had been and how her parents loved to blame their issues on her—their child and scapegoat. Few knew how she'd stopped talking to them the day they'd blamed their last eviction—that she knew of anyway—on her and her college expenses, which was complete crap since she'd paid for everything her extensive scholarships hadn't covered. She'd bought her own food and clothing and anything else she might need since she'd started earning money at sixteen. Ryan didn't know how they regularly asked her for money or how her relatives rallied around them, casting her as the ungrateful, selfish daughter who'd destroyed their lives.

Though Jess had Keera, she'd truly had no one to lean on until she'd opened up just a little and let her Dom in. And he was Ryan. Her boss. Allowing him in had destroyed everything she'd worked so hard to build. Had he been laughing at her the whole time? Taking pleasure in winning control from the known control freak?

Vaguely, she'd heard him say her name as she'd fled the restaurant, but she hadn't been able to think, couldn't respond. She couldn't stop and face him then—she didn't even want to face him now. At the time, she'd just needed to run and hide and figure out what had happened and how to breathe again. Everything. She'd lost everything because of stupid fantasies, the need for affection and the overwhelming desire to belong to someone.

I love you. Suddenly, those words pierced through her hysteria and echoed in the emptiness that had hollowed her out. *I love you, I love you, I love you...*

After a moment, she realized the phrase wasn't just echoing in her head. He was whispering it into her hair as he rocked her. How had she gotten into his arms? Onto his lap? She was clinging to him, her face buried in his chest, her fingers knotted in his white dress shirt. He rubbed a hand up and down her back while he soothed her, and she finally started to quiet, though her breathing still hitched every few moments from the intensity of her breakdown. She'd never cried this hard, never, not through everything she'd experienced.

"Don't be angry with me," he murmured against her temple.

Not be angry? The revelation had humiliated her—he'd humiliated her. Was he laughing at her the whole time? This was devastating.

"I know I should have told you outright—I *know* I should have—but I just couldn't. I couldn't, Jessica. I'm your boss, and I live a D/s lifestyle—and I wasn't sure of you and how you'd take it all. I needed you in the frame of mind first. I needed to know you'd accept me. I love you, kitten. I have for a while."

He loved her? Oh God…he *loved* her? Small, tingling tendrils of warmth pierced her ice-cold limbs, slowly infusing her with a tentative peace she'd never experienced.

"I love you, too," she mumbled into his chest.

He pulled back so he could look into her face, and she witnessed rare vulnerability in his eyes. And she knew…He thought she might reject him and his declaration. He swallowed as she studied him through tear-blurred vision. "Say it again," he begged.

"I love you."

"Oh kitten." His mouth was on hers, claiming it with a fervor that swept away everything but his lips on hers, his tongue claiming her, his arms around her so tight she never could have squirmed away. She never wanted to.

"Master," she whispered back to him, trying it out now that she knew his identity. He groaned, and it echoed through her, affirming his place in her life. She was his. His hand curved around her hip, holding her close as she sat across his lap and reminding her of her panty-free condition. Every move she made reminded her of how he'd "mastered" her yesterday.

Lifting away, he looked down at her and ran his fingers over her bound-to-be mottled cheeks. Lord, she probably looked a wreck.

"That's only for in private," he said.

"This is pretty private."

"Not private enough. You only call me that at Pleasure Palace. Otherwise, it's Sir, if you must. Or just plain Ryan. God, I want you so much right now. I want to bury my cock in you, knowing you're mine and that you finally know exactly who I am—that I'm your master and you belong to me. No masks. Face-to-face, with full knowledge. I want to hear you cry out my name as you come, over and over."

The knot of pleasure and desire tightened in her middle. His. She was his. "You're mine, too," she said.

"Damn right, I am," he growled and took her mouth again, so hard she knew her lips would be bruised from it. One arm remained banded around her back, holding her close, while the other moved between them and he cupped her breast. His fingers rolled her nipple through her clothes. "I haven't paid nearly enough attention to these," he said. He kissed his way down her neck then bit her shoulder while he tormented the tip. His cock was hard against her hip. "Tonight, I'm going to kiss and lick and bite them until you come."

She didn't think it would take much on his part to get her there. Tonight couldn't come soon enough. They certainly wouldn't need two rooms at the hotel. She supposed they'd discuss that after they left the site.

"Ryan, how am I going to meet with the electrician? I'm a mess."

"You're beautiful."

She rolled her eyes, feeling stronger and more like herself, though she was barely starting to adjust to her new reality.

"Did you just roll your eyes at me?"

"No…" she said in faux-innocence, blinking at him as if she'd never consider such a thing.

"You are naughty."

"Are you going to spank me?" she asked playfully.

"Probably. Unless you're too sore. But I like the feel of my hand on your ass. So…" he said, changing the subject. "We need to talk about your job."

She stiffened. Here it came. She'd known this was too good to be true.

His hand slid along her leg, stopping just above her hemline. His thumb rubbed over her sensitive inner thigh, just above her knee. A tremor ran through her and she wanted him to explore higher. She didn't want to talk. He stilled, perhaps sensing the direction of her thoughts.

"Do you remember what I told you before about my parents and the dynamics between them? Could you hear me? You were crying pretty hard."

She had been, but when she focused on those moments, his words were there. "Yes," she said, nodding.

"I don't know what they do in the bedroom, and Jesus, I don't want to know, but outside the bedroom, there's mutual respect, trust and admiration. I want that same sort of thing for us. I want us to work together just as we always have. You can't worry that I'll disagree with you on issues and take it out on you afterhours when we're alone. That's not how this works."

That was a relief, since they disagreed frequently. She was in the field more often than he was; in the trenches, so to speak. Because of that she was more in touch with the projects and knew what would work and what wouldn't.

"Okay..." The word drew out as she let him know she was absorbing what he said yet sensed he wasn't finished.

"I will never lie to you, and I'm sorry I lied to you by withholding my identity before. That's not a great start for us, and believe me when I say the guilt over it ate at me. I wanted to tell you. I've never lied to you about anything else. I won't. We need trust between us. You can believe what I say. As part of that...please trust me when I tell you you're beautiful. God, Jess, your curves, your soft skin, your incredible mouth, your gorgeous green eyes and wild red hair..." He chuckled. "When you let it out of its tight pins, anyway. To me, every bit of you is perfect, and I want to kill any man who looks at you, including my brothers."

"Your brothers?" she repeated in disbelief.

"Trust me. They've noticed you, but they know you're mine. They would never move in on you."

Okay... She'd have to digest that later. There were so many things to address there. But right now...

"Last night—" she started, remembering Ryan encouraging her—touching her—while the man watched them.

His hand tightened on her thigh. "That other Dom across the dining room? I had to show him you were mine. Only mine. My perfect little kitten, claws and hiss and all. You purr only for me."

Her panties got wet only for him, too. They would be now if she were wearing any. She wasn't perfect, and she knew it, but if she was perfect for him...? She bit her lip, accepting it with a nod.

"Now," he grinned then made a sorry-to-say-this face, "you do have mascara streaked down your cheeks, and even though it doesn't make you any less lovely, I know how you are." He pulled a handkerchief from inside his suit jacket and handed it to her.

"You carry a real handkerchief?" she asked, running her thumb over the linen. His initials were embroidered in red in one corner. RMC—not MR. Ryan Mason Cress.

"I'm told it's the best thing for drying my woman's tears," he said. He took it from her, drying her face and gently wiping away the black smears. "Hopefully, I won't need it often, but it's another way I'll take care of you."

She shook her head. "You're so much more than I ever imagined."

"I promise, there's a lot more I want to show you." He tapped her nose. "Better?"

She nodded. "I'm sorry I panicked and freaked out."

He shook his head. "It wasn't how I wanted to tell you. At freaking Applebees." He muttered the last in disgust, and Jess laughed until he yanked her against him and covered her mouth with his once more.

Chapter Ten

"Look, sweetheart, do you want the wiring done or not?"

Jessica narrowed her eyes at Clive Honeycutt. Her meeting with the electrician had been uneventful, but this meeting with the site manager hadn't gone nearly as well. He'd gotten belligerent on several issues already, including the failure to meet safety requirements and several code violations.

She gritted her teeth at his nasty tone, but kept her face as blank as possible. "What I want is for the electrical to be done without the threat of the complex burning down soon after."

"You're being melodramatic."

"No, Clive, I'm not. It's a safety issue, and what you want to do won't meet code. Our electrician knows it. If you try to force the issue, he'll quit and pull all his staff."

"They have a contract—"

"To do the job to our standards, following legal requirements. We're not paying extra because you want to change the specs or because we need to bring in a new contractor. And if we get fined by the city, it's coming out of your pay."

"You don't have to be such a bitch about it. It's one little thing."

"It's an entire wing of the mall, Clive," she replied calmly, not giving him the satisfaction of reacting to his name calling. "Try to remember this is a jobsite, not a bar, and keep your language in check."

He sneered. "If you can't handle it, sweetheart, then you shouldn't be here, trying to be one of the boys."

"Enough!" Ryan growled, slamming his hand on the table.

He'd been sitting quietly to the side after making it clear Jess was in charge. Until now, he'd been scrolling through his phone, and she hadn't even thought he was really listening. She supposed that was a ploy to keep Clive from deferring to him and ignoring her. As much good as that had done.

"I don't care who you're speaking to," Ryan continued, pinning Clive with a glare Jess never wanted to receive. "Your behavior is unacceptable. You know you're wrong on these issues, and they need to be fixed now. Stop trying to sidestep it with sexist comments."

"She shouldn't be in this job, and you know it. Who'd she sleep with to get it? You? One of the other Cress kids? She has no business being here, and she knows jack-shit about running a construction project. She gets her panties in a twist over everything."

Ryan's jaw clenched, and Jess knew he wanted to punch this guy. "Jessica is more than qualified for her position with Cress Construction, and she's one of the best in the field. You on the other hand, I'm not so sure. It's only because of her that you haven't been relieved of your position on this job. I think perhaps you should go home for the day, and we will finish this discussion tomorrow morning before we head back. At that time, I'll expect you to apologize to Jessica for your out-of-line comments."

Clive rolled his eyes and slammed his binder closed before storming from the construction trailer. Ryan followed him out the door, while Jess gathered her things, her own anger simmering. Not at Clive but at Ryan.

She'd had the situation under control. Clive would have settled down after a few more minutes then they would have hashed through things. She'd dealt with him enough to know his MO. He bullied, and if she didn't cave, he conceded to her instructions. Ryan stepping in had just acerbated the issue. He couldn't do that. He couldn't jump in and protect her from flack on jobsites. Yes, they were a couple, but he wouldn't have done that to a male project managers—

Yes, he would have, she realized. She took a deep breath and closed her eyes. Ryan was their boss. If Clive had been nasty to any of Ryan's employees, Ryan would have intervened and taken Clive down a peg or two. She couldn't take this personally or think it had anything to do with their relationship.

God, this day had been a roller coaster. A good morning, the disaster at lunch, Ryan's declaration of love, a productive afternoon on the site and now, this... The ups and downs were giving her a headache. At the moment, dread hollowed out her gut, making her a little nauseated when she thought of the repercussions of the day. Though the trip had been a success until this meeting, she'd lost confidence in Clive and wasn't sure he wouldn't deliberately sabotage the project from spite then try to blame someone else—possibly, even her.

"I feel like I'm going to have to watch everything he does from here out, as if I wasn't already watching every little thing," Jess said, once they'd settled into the car and were heading for the hotel.

Ryan shook his head, and his hands tightened on the steering wheel, his knuckles going white. "No, you won't. Tomorrow, Theo and Keera will drive over and have a discussion with him. He's been on probation to improve his behavior—something he's obviously chosen to ignore the past few months. I'll need any notes from your discussions with him, so I can pass them along. As head of personnel, Keera will need to review them before the meeting."

Jess could tell there was so much more he wanted to say, but wasn't.

"So…what you're saying? That he's going to be fired?"

"Yes."

"Because of me? Just like that?"

"More like because he's an ass who won't do his job, and things would probably continue on a downslide until the end of the project, no matter what you do. He used to be a good guy. I don't know what the fuck has happened to him over the past two years. Whatever it is, it doesn't give him carte blanche to be an incompetent jerk."

"Maybe you should talk to him about it…"

"Do you *want* to keep working with him?" Ryan snapped in disbelief, his gaze jerking to her momentarily before refocusing on the road.

"No. I just don't like the idea of firing anyone, and I'm concerned about bringing in someone new, as well as security issues."

He reached over and squeezed her fingers. "You have a soft heart, baby." He drew her hand over to rest on his leg, and she flexed into the hard muscles, remembering the feel of him between her much softer thighs. He growled, and his grip tightened. "I'm sure you can get Ron Westfall up to speed pretty quickly. He's new, but he's just finished up the supermarket project in Kalamazoo and impressed us all with his work. He'd be ideal to take over here. I want you used to working with him. When you start the health club project, I want him to be a key player."

They continued discussing the job as Ryan steered the car toward the hotel Cress always booked for employees making site visits. Jessica's nerves ramped up with each of the all-too-short miles they covered. A knot of apprehension clutched at her middle.

Now that she knew his identity, what would happen? How would things go? In part, she'd enjoyed the anonymity of their previous status. That security had been false, of course. Ryan had always known exactly who *he* was...who *she* was.

His warm fingers enveloped hers. "It's all right," he said, his words a quiet balm on her frayed nerves. "The same rules apply now as before. I'll never harm you, kitten. You're mine, only mine, and I'll always protect you. Always take care of you. Physically and spiritually."

"Thank you," she replied, unsure what else to say. She had a million questions but was unable to verbalize a single one. Though Ryan's assurances should make her feel better, a turbulent uneasiness roiled in her belly. Ryan was her boss. How could they make this work?"

"Baby..." he cajoled. "I don't plan to pounce on you and wrestle you into cuffs—though now that I say it out loud, that sounds like it could be fun. But maybe we can save that for a different day, for someplace with far more privacy than a hotel room."

She grinned, as humor broke through her worries. "No, I don't suppose you'd want someone busting in on that, huh?"

"Uh, *no*."

Now, she laughed at his emphatic response. She could

just imagine the horror for her, the submissive, and for security rushing into the room. Oh, the humiliation.

Her...the submissive. Jess bit her lip as the terminology sank in. Did she really think of herself that way? Sort of, she supposed. If they continued on, she would be his. His submissive. It seemed so foreign to everything she'd strived to be her entire life.

Ryan squeezed her fingers. "You're thinking very loudly."

"I have a lot to think about."

"More than before, when you were having blind encounters with a Dom whose identity you didn't know?"

"You make it sound so sordid."

He shook his head. "I'm just saying that this should be easier."

"Oh, no, it's not," she laughed. "Knowing you opens a whole new batch of issues. You're my boss. Now, my job is involved...my security. Everything I've worked to achieve."

"I'm very good at compartmentalizing."

"Mm-hmm," she scoffed.

Ryan sighed, and she felt his irritation growing. Geez, she hadn't wanted to piss him off. She just wasn't sure of this whole...situation.

"Look, I'd say to consider this Vegas. You know...what happens in Vegas stays in Vegas, but I don't want that. I want you in my life. I've wanted you in my life for a long time, Jessica. Can't we at least try?"

And by "we" she knew he meant "you". Couldn't *she* try to make this work? Did she want to or not? God! She needed a minute to think. She hadn't had a moment away from him or work since she'd discovered he was *The* Dom from Pleasure Palace.

"I...Ryan...I just need...time."

"Time?" he repeated, so quietly she almost didn't hear

him.

Gah! Now, she'd hurt him. She'd been more sure when they'd been in the park. She'd told him she loved him. She did, didn't she? Yes…she'd come to love him over all the years and projects they'd worked on together.

She tightened her hold on him when he moved to pull away. "I'm just…scared," she whispered.

"Oh, kitten. You're safe with me. I promise. Just trust me."

"I *do* trust you."

He pulled into a parking spot at the hotel, and she was startled that they'd arrived so quickly. She'd been completely caught up in her fears and hadn't paid attention to the road once they'd started talking.

Ryan unfastened his seatbelt and reached over to release hers then pull her into his lap. His hand cupped her cheek and he settled his warm lips over hers, tasting and comforting her. The sheer tenderness assured her he cared for her, that he cherished her. Her head yelled that it was all too fast, but her heart quietly thumped the reminder that this had been such a long time coming. It was right. She'd belonged to him a lot longer than she wanted to admit. Why else had she fantasized about him? Why else did she care so deeply what he thought, far beyond what she should have cared about her boss' opinion? Why else had she avoided relationships with other men? If she were truthful with herself, she'd admit that she'd compared them to her straight-laced, enigmatic boss and none of them had ever measured up.

"Yes," she said against his lips.

She felt him smile. "Yes, what?"

"Yes, I'll try…Master Ryan," She smiled, teasing him with the title, feeling more confident while secure in his arms.

He growled. "I do like the sound of that." He nipped

at her bottom lip, pulling it gently. "You've been driving me crazy with this lip. Whenever you think, you bite it. It makes me think of what I want to do to you."

"What do you want to do to me?"

"Taste every inch of your body. Bite it. Claim it. Show you that you're mine."

Jess shivered, her core quivering at the idea of him inside her again. He hadn't said he'd fuck her, but she knew. Wherever he planned to start, that's where he'd end up…with that amazing pierced cock buried deep within her.

"You like the thought of that, kitten?" His wicked, knowing smile said he already knew.

"Yes," she breathed.

"Let's go check in."

She stifled a groan. She wanted more of him. *Now.*

"Soon, baby," he murmured in her ear as he slid from the car and set her on her feet. "I don't want an audience for what I have in mind. Besides, I have plans for our evening, plans that start out in public then end up with you moaning beneath me."

"You're going to kill me."

"Mmm…no, I want you very much alive." He kissed the sensitive skin behind her ear then nipped at her earlobe. "But maybe…a little death later. Or maybe a few."

A few orgasms? Sign her up! "Could we skip right to the private part of the night?" she asked, perhaps a little too eager now that she was settling into the idea of sex with him…her boss. Oh God! She was insane. Her emotions and thoughts were all over the place. Scared. Excited. Anxious. Needy. Every time she thought she had a handle on things, it seemed to slip away from her.

His eyes narrowed slightly…thoughtfully. "Whatever it is you just thought, that's the reason we're going out tonight. You need to see that we're more than boss and employee. We're more than what happens in the bedroom. I want the whole relationship."

She swallowed past the rock forming in her through. He was so damn...*sweet*. "Okay. I..." She took a deep breath. "I want that, too."

Wanting him was the one thing that remained constant in her rollercoaster of reactions to this situation. She wanted him; she wanted to find out what they could have together.

She was terrified.

"I want to see what we can have," she whispered, mostly trying to convince her rational self. That part of her was none-too-pleased, but she forced herself to ignore that little nagging voice.

"Good." He grabbed their bags, and they headed inside to check in.

The chain hotel's lobby was large but rather run-of-the-mill. Clean, with a fireplace and comfortable seating. Functional and far from swanky. They catered to traveling businesspeople and didn't need any particular bells and whistles to attract customers. Jess had been here several times before now, always by herself. Anthony, the cute blue-eyed, sun-streaked-blond desk clerk, recognized her as she and Ryan walked to the desk.

"Ms. Rush, it's good to see you again," Anthony greeted her, smiling. "You're looking as beautiful as ever."

"Thanks, Tony," she replied as she pulled out her loyalty card and handed it to him. "I bet you say that to all the girls."

He pressed his hand over his chest. "My mama taught me not to lie—especially to such pretty ladies." He winked.

"Oh you," she laughed, rolling her eyes. "How're

things? How's your mom? Better from the flu?"

"Yeah, she's doing great. Everything's great. I'm deep in my new semester of classes."

"This is your last year, right? Then off to med school?"

"As long as I score high enough on the MCAT next month—Hey, do you have a reservation? I don't see your name in the system."

"It's in my name," Ryan cut in icily. His arm slide around her waist, pulling her close to his side in an unmistakable sign of ownership. When she glanced up at him, his glacial gaze assessed the other man.

Oh, Ryan did not like Tony talking to her, did not like that Tony obviously knew her.

"O-okay. And that's…"

"Ryan Cress. You should have one king room reserved for us."

Tony click on his keyboard. He focused on the screen, but looked uncomfortable under Ryan's stare. Annoyed, she shifted to step away, but Ryan tightened his hold. His lips pressed to his ear.

"Mine," he whispered. "Don't forget that."

She rolled her eyes. This was what she was in for. She'd agreed to *try* to be the sub to this Dom, to see where a relationship would go and what it would entail. But she'd also agreed with the understanding that this wasn't a 24/7 D/s arrangement. With that knowledge, the part of her that struggled to always maintain control clawed its way to the forefront of her thoughts.

"Tony, do you have any other rooms available?" she asked. It was rather highhanded of Ryan to assume she'd sleep in the same room with him. When they'd left her house this morning she'd had no idea of their intimate relationship.

The clerk frowned. He shook his head. "No…" he said

slowly. "Without a reservation… There's a big pharmaceutical convention in town this week and all the hotels are booked. I don't even have overflow options right now."

"Oh…well, thanks." She made a face and watched as he handed Ryan the small card folder holding the room keys.

"Can I help with anything else?"

"No," Ryan cut in before she could say a word.

Tony forced a smile. "Okay. Um… The elevators are around that corner to the left." He pointed. "Have a good stay."

With his bag over his shoulder, and wheeling her bag with the hand on that same side, he kept his arm firmly around her as he guided her to the elevator. She pressed the call button, butterflies bombarding her middle at Ryan's implacable demeanor.

"Like I'd let you stay in another fucking room," he growled as they waited.

"You were assuming an awful lot to book only one room." She swallowed hard, trying to maintain her outward composure while her insides were ready to melt into whatever he wanted. She wasn't a marshmallow; she never had been and that was what had attracted him. Wasn't it? She wished she was more sure of what he really wanted, what he really saw in her.

"I'd *assumed* my woman—the one who begged to skip right to the bedroom scene when we were out in the parking lot a few minutes ago—would want to be with me. I fully intended to get everything out in the open today. Just…not as it happened. One way or another I planned to have you in my bed."

"And if I'd refused?"

He made a small triumphant sound that denied her idea that she might win if that argument had occurred.

She realized too late that her question revealed that she indeed intended to sleep with him tonight. Well, fuck. So much for not revealing her hand.

They remained silent as they rode the elevator to the sixth floor and walked to the room. Ryan unlocked their door then waited for her to enter. Moments later, they stood shrouded in dim shadows. The curtains were drawn and no lights had been left on to welcome them.

Jess looked up at him as he dropped their bags beside the door. An instant later, she was in his arms, crushed to his hard chest as he plundered her mouth.

"Oh God," she gasped against his lips.

"You're mine, Jessica. Mine," he growled. His hand went beneath her ass, lifting her, and her legs automatically went around his hips. Her skirt hiked up as she pushed closer to him. She groaned as his fingers dug into the flesh of her sore behind, reminding her of the attention he'd given it last night. That ache did nothing to dull her need. In truth, it only amplified her desire to have him fuck her.

He ground against her center as he ravaged her mouth with tongue, teeth and lips. His hands flexed as if he knew exactly how the touch pushed the bite of pain through her, a pain that was quickly morphing into that strange pleasure that put her right on the edge of coming. Her mind went blank to anything but this man, what he did to her and what she could give in return.

He glanced down at where he ground into her. "You're not wearing panties."

"No."

"Why?" he demanded, his voice tight and that muscle ticking in his cheek. "You knew you'd be around the work crew all day—all men."

"I...I thought they'd... I couldn't stand the idea of them against my skin all day. The rub of my skirt was bad enough." Why was he suddenly so angry with her? "It's not as if anyone but you would see beneath my skirt."

"Are you in a lot of pain? I have cream with me. You should have said something. I would have—"

"Ryan, this morning you were just my boss. Then later, we were busy. Besides…it's not a bad pain so much as…well, an arousing reminder. It's… It's one of the best things. Feeling you. Afterward."

She bit her lip at the confession, and he growled, dipping his head forward. Gently, he sank his teeth into the abused flesh and pulled it free from the clasp of her own teeth. He sucked her lip into his mouth and laved it with his tongue before he kissed her fully once more.

It felt as if she were flying as he took command and kissed her with such demand, such dominance, she felt as if she were burning in his flame. It wasn't until her back hit the mattress that she realized, he'd been carrying her. He wedged himself between her thighs, pulling one of her legs up around his him as he ground into her. His other hand pinned her wrists over her head.

Jess moaned. How could she have had doubts about this? About him?

He kissed across her jaw then scraped his teeth over the skin behind her ear before trailing his mouth down her neck. His tongue dipped into the hollow at the base. She trembled at the unaccustomed pressure before he nudged aside the edge of her shirt and bit her collar bone.

"Ah," she cried out, bucking beneath him. His pelvis pressed harder into her, and she swore she could almost feel the ridges from his piercings. She wanted to feel them again. Rubbing over her clit. Pushing inside her.

She pulled at her wrists, wanting to unfasten his pants. His fingers tightened.

"Please," she begged. "Please, I need you."

"Hmm," Ryan hummed, a low sound of pleasure. Releasing her leg, he moved his hand between them. Her skirt was pushed up around her waist now, giving him unimpeded access to her pussy. He traced her crease, and she cried out again, shaking under him. "You're so wet, kitten," he murmured, as his fingers pushed inside.

"For you. Just for you. I need you. Please."

"Not yet." Abandoning her pussy, he reached up and yanked at her shirt. Her buttons went flying as he exposed her lacy, flesh-colored bra. Dragging down a cup, he clamped his lips around one nipple then returned to his torment of her needy core. His finger circled her clit while he circled his tongue over her crinkled areola, randomly flicking the tip and drawing hard.

Her sex contracted with each vigorous suck, cries escaping her in ragged pants. Her back arched on the bed as she tried to get closer to him. She fought her climax as it bore down on her, faster than it ever had.

"Don't come," he ordered.

"I can't...I..."

"Don't."

Her fingernails bit into her palms as she tried to hold it off while he continued his sensual assault on her body. Cool air wafted over her rigid nipple as he left it. Using his teeth, he pulled down the other cup and repeated his sucking, licking and biting. Her fists tightened, but the nails digging into her palms only reminded her that his big hand held her prisoner. That she was at his mercy.

He adjusted his hand so his thumb now circled her clit. Two fingers pushed inside her, pumping in and out and mimicking what she wanted his cock to do. The penetration marginally soothed her, and she was able to get control of her release. Still, she was barely holding back with paper-thin will.

"Please...Ryan..." she begged.

He pinched her clit. Hard. Pain lanced through her, but instead of cooling her, it ignited a climax she couldn't stop. Her scream echoed through the room. She went rigid beneath him in an arch of agonized ecstasy. Colors rushed before her vision. Her skin was on fire.

He was staring down at her when she returned to herself. Both hands were planted on the mattress, neither touching her.

"Feeling better?"

Was that a trace of disappointment in his voice?

"I'm sorry," she whispered. Despite her orgasm, her body still throbbed. She felt empty. She needed him. Her hands lifted to reach for him, but she dropped them back to the bed, deciding that would be a bad idea. He didn't seem receptive to her touch right now.

"I'm not angry." Dipping his head down, he pressed his lips to her forehead. Then he rose and stood beside the bed. He held out a hand to her. "I sometimes forget how much training you still need. Come on. Up with you."

His fingers closed around hers and he pulled her upright. She stood staring at him when he released her. Her wrists automatically pushed behind her to cross over her rear. He trailed the back of a fingertip over the slope of her breast then back up and over her nipple.

Jessica stifled a groaned. Her hands fisted and she bit the inside of her lip to keep from begging him for more.

"Stay there," he said then headed for his bag. He returned with a smaller black bag that he placed on the bed and unzipped. Toiletries? Her eyes widened when she spied the contents. So...he carried a portable dungeon. "Turn," he said as he straightened with metal handcuffs in his fist.

Immediately, she complied though discomfort quivered through her. Though he'd restrained her several times before now, it still made her uncomfortable. The part of her always wanting control didn't like the helpless feeling of being restricted by cuffs or whatever he chose to use. She bit back her sigh as the cool metal circled her wrists.

"Tell me about the boy downstairs."

She lifted a shoulder. "I don't really know him. He's just checked me in and out so many times that he's familiar with me. Cute kid. In college. Still lives with mom. He's no one to worry about."

His knuckle trailed down her spine and even through her shirt it seemed to burn her. "Is there someone I should worry about?"

She shook her head. "No. There's only you."

"Good." He slid a blindfold over her eyes, stealing her sight, and she startled, not realizing he'd moved to grab anything else. Taking her forearm, he guided her a few feet away. "Kneel."

He steadied her as she bent her knees and followed his command. He held her upright when she would have rested back on her ankles.

"Move forward slightly."

She scooched her knees then groaned as her bare breasts came in contact with bare wood.

Ryan stroked his hand over her hair. "I'm going to take a shower. And you are going to stay right here and have some corner time. Do. Not. Move."

"Yes, Sir," she whispered, feeling very much like an admonished schoolgirl—save for her exposed breasts and her skirt being hiked up around her waist. Her position was both humiliating and arousing. More the latter, she had to admit. If she stayed with him, if she explored this relationship as they'd discussed then sensual discipline would come into play.

"One more thing, I think."

She felt something hard nudge at her opening. Slowly,

he slid the long, hard length into her. It seemed surprisingly light, and a moment later, she head a click and it started buzzing. It wasn't just inside her. A bit of it flicked over her clit. Oh God… She'd be jerking into climax in minutes!

"Close your legs, now, and hold it in place," he said. He kissed her temple then she felt him stand. "Come as many times as you must, kitten. But try not to. Remember to stay in this position and keep it inside you. I'll be back after my shower, and I'll leave the door open, so I can hear you."

Though she couldn't see due to the blindfold, Jessica squeezed her eyes shut and she vaguely heard the water come on in the bathroom. She wanted to take a shower too. With him. With, maybe, a little shower sex mixed in. Still, her on her knees, Ryan dominating her, it was straight from her fantasies. But…could…

God! She could barely think with the incessant, hard buzzing against her clit, but she had to. Thinking was the only way to keep from orgasming, though she was pretty sure it was a foregone conclusion no matter what.

The pulse in her throat throbbed and the sound of her blood rushing past her ears nearly drowned out the pounding rhythm of the water. Her skin burned as it flushed with her arousal, and her pussy… Had she ever been wetter? Her folds flooded with moisture and she squeezed her legs a little harder to hold in the vibe and stave off her climax. The sensations intensified. No!

Fuck! What had she been thinking before? Right. Fantasies. Like a porn movie, flashes of her most vivid dreams filled her thoughts. They were in Ryan's office, both dressed in their stiff business attire and her skirt was up around her waist—much like now, she realized. Only, in her mind, she was bent over his lap and he was spanking her bare ass. Yeah…she really wanted him to spank her.

A jolt went through her, landing within her clit with an electric shock. A choked cry escaped her as tendrils of sensation fingered into her limbs and her breasts. The cool wood against her rock-hard nipples was nearly unbearable. She breathed harshly, trying to push back the release barreling toward her like a speeding train.

Suddenly, she felt Ryan pressed to her back.

"Good girl," he murmured against her ear. His naked skin was a balm as he kneed apart her legs and reached down to pull away the vibrator. In one swift move, he turned her so her shoulder was next to the smooth wood instead of her chest. His hand at her nape, he pushed her forward. She had only a moment to register the thick head of his cock and that glorious piercing in the tip before he surged forward and into her so hard, her knees scooted across the floor a few inches. The burn did little to dull her passion as she rocked back into him, taking and meeting every drive. Thankfully, something smooth and smelling of Ryan protected her cheek that was also on the floor. His shirt? Whatever…

She loved how his smell enveloped her as he took her with a ferocity she'd yet to experience from him. As if he were claiming her. Branding her. Or perhaps, as if he'd waited too long to be inside her and the separation had made him mindless. She could think of little but *her* need for him.

One of his hands clamped onto her hip, holding her where he wanted her while the other slipped beneath her. He ran his fingers around her nipple, tracing it, rolling the tip before suddenly, he pinched—hard—and pulled.

"Ah! God…please… Oh, please, Sir," she cried as she bucked beneath him, overwhelmed by his fucking and his attention to her breasts, his hand now moving to the other breast.

"I love your tits, kitten. So perfect for my hands." He filled his palm with one, cupping it as he spoke. Slowly, he squeezed. "I could spend all night buried in them."

"Yes. Please," she whimpered.

"You want that? You want me to fuck your breasts?"

"Whatever you want, Sir." Whatever he wanted... She just wanted to come. His Jacob's ladder ran up and down her inner walls, almost too much to bear. She felt herself starting to squeeze around him and fisted her hands, trying to make it stop.

"Oh, no, kitten. No easy answers like that. I asked what *you* want."

What? What did he ask her? Oh, right... Fucking her breasts. "Yes..." she breathed. "I think I might like that."

Would he let her come first?

"I want you to come. Come now. Now!"

"Yes!" she cried. She relaxed her grip on control and a dam burst inside her, exploding into shuddering reaction.

"Fuck..." Ryan gasped, surging hard into her and holding still. Together, frozen in the moment, Jessica felt invisible ties binding around them. No matter what happened, part of her would always be his, and...yeah...she'd always have part of him with her, too.

Breathing heavily, they collapsed together on the carpet and Ryan pulled her close. He murmured praise and endearments in her ear. "I love you, kitten. I fucking love you. We're going to be so good together."

God, she hoped so. They had the sex part down anyway. It was the relationship part that worried her. Business relationship? Check...good. Personal relationship? Well...she had zero experience with successfully navigating those waters.

"Love you, too," she replied, deciding on honesty. She really did love him. She had for a long time. If this didn't work out, it might kill her.

They lay there for a while, basking in the warmth of their feelings and the closeness of their still-connected bodies. Ryan couldn't seem to stop touching her. His hands ran over her shoulders and arms, her hips and thighs. He kissed her neck and upper back, and she sensed he was easing her down from the pinnacle they'd reached, taking care of her. Comfortable bliss surrounded her and drew her deeper into his web. Turning her face into his shirt, still bunched beneath her, she smiled. He'd captured her as surely as a spider did a fly. She doubted she'd ever escape—and she didn't want to.

"Let's take that shower," he whispered, pressing a lingering his to her nape then pulling away. He lifted her up into his arms and drew off her mask. It dropped unheeded to the floor.

"Didn't you just—"

All at once, she realized he wasn't wet—not from showering anyway. He was a little sweaty.

"No. I was watching you."

Oh… Well, what did she say to that? Heat filled her cheeks as she imagined what he'd seen.

"You were fucking hot."

Jess bit her lip. She was? Hot?

He leaned in and used his teeth to free her abused lip. His tongue laved over it. "Yes, you. Submitting to me. Learning about that side of yourself. In the throes of rapture but trying so hard to control your orgasm. Because you want to please me. You…trying to please *me*. It's beautiful."

"Oh…"

He was the beautiful one. As he set her on her feet beside the shower, she drank him in. Her Dom, all broad, hard muscle and tanned skin. The tattoos marking his arms and belly gave him an air of danger she hadn't recognized when she'd seen him in only his suits. It had always been there…in his demeanor and pervading authority. Now…well, she could name it now. Yet, she knew he would never harm her. Hadn't he promised her as much right from the start?

A shudder ran through her. He might not physically harm her, but she sensed her emotional wellbeing was marching to the block. He had the power to eviscerate her. He could leave her as nothing.

Ryan turned her to face away from him then released the cuffs. He ran his hands over her shoulders and arms to massage the muscles.

"Feel okay?" he asked.

"Yes," she answered. No. Not really. The further they got from the scene in the bedroom, the more her uncertainty about this situation poked at her and she felt as helpless as a fly pinned to a board. There was no getting away from this captivating man, and truly, from the deepest part of her, she didn't want to. She just didn't see how this would all work.

He frowned, peering closely at her.

"I'm fine," she insisted.

"Jessica?"

"Yes?"

His hands rested lightly beside her jaw and he used his thumbs to lift her head and make her look into his eyes. "This relationship won't work if you're not honest with me."

Hell…

She released a chagrined breath. "I'm used to working through things on my own—"

"That won't work here."

"I understand that. I'm just so…scattered. I'm all over the place. Embarrassed—though not so much anymore— scared, worried, thrilled, excited, worried again… I can't seem to get a handle on things. I don't like that. I usually have more control of my emotions."

His slow, thought-filled nod seemed to signal his understanding. "I haven't given you the firm foundation you need in order to feel secure. Will you be patient with me and let me show you how the relationship can work between us? Give me the rest of the week at least—no kink, no sex, just us being together. Please?"

They were standing here naked, about to take a shower and he was offering to forego sex? He wasn't begging her to give them a chance; he was negotiating, a win in his sights.

"No."

"No?" He took a step back, his hands dropping from her.

She shook her head. Time to be brave. Did she want this or not?

"No," she repeated. "I'm not saying no relationship. I'm saying... Well, pulling everything apart won't show me how things can be. I agree to the week as a trial period—an all-inclusive trial period. I need the whole picture before I make a decision. With one caveat."

"Go ahead." His face gave nothing away. They could have been settling a business deal in a boardroom, not standing naked and navigating the future of their relationship.

Here goes nothing...

"On Friday, if I decide I can't do this, it all ends. No repercussions, no reminders or comments, no bargaining for something more...nothing. I'll do my job and you'll do yours and we'll be all business."

His jaw tightened, his body otherwise still as he regarded her, no doubt digesting her terms.

"So...if I agree to include everything and... Say I discipline you on Friday and you're angry with me. Everything's just over. Seems dangerous for me."

She could see his point. "I trust that you'd help me understand why I was being disciplined and you'd keep it in the right context—personal not business. If you don't, I don't want that sort of relationship. And if I can't accept it, even after you've made the reason clear, then I shouldn't be in that relationship anyway."

He smiled, admiration in his gray eyes. "Are you sure you've never negotiated something like this before now?"

"Never have."

He held out his hand. "Ms. Rush, I accept your terms."

She slipped her fingers into his. "And I accept yours, Sir."

He brought her knuckles up to his mouth and pressed his lips to them. "You won't regret this; I promise you. Now…let's shower then I think some dinner and dancing are in order."

Chapter Eleven

Jessica grinned as her assistant, Glenna, brought in an arrangement of roses and set them on the credenza. She knew the woman was dying to know who they were from since Jess never got flowers at work, but she wasn't going to indulge the curiosity. She knew word about her and Ryan would get out eventually, but they'd both decided on the way home today that they would keep the whole thing mostly under wraps for now. While there was no policy against them dating, it seemed best until Jess made her final decision about their relationship.

As soon as Glenna left, Jess hopped up from her desk and plucked the sealed—thank God—card from the flowers.

Here's hoping for "yes". Thank you for every moment so far. You are my treasure. ~~ R

"Fuck me," she whispered as a tremor shot through her. The man could practically give her an orgasm with a few words. Gathering herself, she fanned herself with the card as she returned to her desk. She stowed it safely in her handbag then pulled out her phone. Pulling up Ryan's number, she sent him a text.

Jessica: *Beautiful*
Ryan: *Not as beautiful as you. I miss you.*

She chuckled, shaking her head.

Jessica: *We've only been back for an hour. Which reminds me...how did you manage the flowers?*
Ryan: *Kitten, I can't share my secrets.*
Jessica: *Is this an "if I tell you I'd have to kill you" thing? Wouldn't want that.*
Ryan: *A little death?*

That question could lead to sexting and she definitely wasn't doing that at work.

Jessica: *Thank you for the flowers. Getting back to my reports now.*
Ryan: *LOL. Coward.*

Rather than reply, she locked her phone and turned back to her spreadsheet. She'd barely finished the third update when the phone on her desk rang.

"Jessica Rush," she answered, cradling the phone between her ear and shoulder as she finished her next update.

"Jessica, this is Marcy. Mr. Cress is requesting that you come to his office." Marcy was Ryan's assistant so she didn't need to ask which Cress wanted to see her. Depending on the day, there could be six of them in the office.

"Thanks. I'll be right over."

Though she didn't figure this was business, Jess grabbed her iPad and leather portfolio then headed over to her *boss'* office.

Ryan's brother, Max, was standing at Marcy's desk when Jessica got there a few minutes later. The girl barely looked over. "You can go right in," she told Jess. She immediately refocused on the design Max was drawing on her palm. Ryan's younger brother was a designer and one of the biggest flirts Jessica had ever encountered, and most of the women in the office, young and old, just ate it up.

Shaking her head, Jess headed into her meeting. Ryan stood as she entered.

"Lock the door," he said in a quiet tone as soon as she'd closed it.

Oh... she'd been right. Not a business meeting.

The lock silently clicked into place.

She set her things on the shelf beside the entrance before turning to Ryan. He'd rounded the desk and she walked right into his arms. It felt so good to have them close around her, holding her tight to his chest.

"I missed you."

"We've only been back an hour," she laughed, hugging him back just as intensely. She breathed him in. His deep woodsy scent filled her with calm. Everything was perfect when she was right here.

"I know. I just found out I have meetings to cover until eight tonight. They start in about fifteen minutes. They're Theo's, but since he's out in the field, dealing with the Clive situation, they're mine today."

"Sucks to be king," she mumbled.

He laughed. "Yeah."

"Knowing that...I miss you, too. So I guess I'll see you tomorrow then."

After the meeting with Theo and Keera earlier, they'd

headed back here to the office. They'd planned that Ryan would take her home this evening, since he'd picked her up there yesterday and they'd have dinner afterward.

"I can just catch a cab home. No big deal," she added.

"No, I can ask Max or Josh to take you."

"Ryan, you don't need—"

"I want to," he interrupted. "You're mine to take care of, remember?"

"At least, this week," she sighed.

"Hey," he leaned back and lifted her chin so she looked at him, "I'm planning for a lot longer than that." His mouth covered hers and she went on her toes to meet him fully. His arms tightened and he groaned into her. "God, Kitten. How have I gone so long without you?"

"Good hand skills?"

He swatted her ass, and she jumped. "Cheeky," he laughed.

Her teeth sank into her lip as she smiled.

"Come over tonight—and stay over," he said. "I'll make us a late dinner."

"Spend the night?"

"Yes." His hands smoothed down her arms and he caught her hands in his. "I want to be with you."

She wanted to be with him, too. She'd only spent one night in his arms, but she wasn't looking forward to a night alone.

Jess nodded. "Okay, I'll be there. Just text me when I should head over."

* * * *

She'd never been to Ryan's home, but when she pulled up, it took her breath away. It was a two-story combination of classic and modern set in an L-shape. She couldn't quite take in the size because of the way it had been set on the lot, but from the driveway, it was overwhelming and she was pretty sure her whole house would fit in the garage. The structure merged Tudor and Shingle styles and featured two large chimneys and walls of cream-colored brick, stone and siding. Massive windows overlooked an extensive porch and an expansive, manicured lawn.

For a moment, she just sat and stared at the place. She'd known the Cresses were wealthy, but criminy… And this was just Ryan's place.

Though Cress Construction specialized in commercial projects, she'd heard that Max had designed his brother's house. If that was true, his talent was wasted on malls, supermarkets and gas stations. She'd seen some of the remarkable offices he'd designed though, so he had some creative outlet.

She couldn't wait to see the inside of Ryan's house. She'd been an architecture geek in college and in part, it had led her to this career. She loved buildings and all the special details that made them special—like the rounded turrets to either side of what had to be the great room and the gabled dormer windows in several of the upstairs rooms.

Leaving her car in the circular drive and grabbing her bag, she headed for the front door where Ryan waited with his arms crossed over his chest and a grin playing over his lips.

"Hey, Kitten. Like the house, do you?"

And he'd caught her gawking. *Classy, Jess.* Thankfully, he knew her obsession with architecture. "Uh, yeah. I think I've got a bit of a girl hard-on going on. This place is unbelievable, Ryan."

"Come on. I'll give you the tour."

Taking her bag from her, he led her inside the house. His fingers grasped hers as they walked past the spacious great room, lined with windows and featuring open exposed polish beams overhead. A fire burned in the fireplace in the corner, giving the place a warm, homey scent, but she didn't have time to enjoy or take-in any of it as he led her through the house. Briefly, she spied a state of the art kitchen, a large dining room, an office closed off from traffic by glass walls, and a sunken family room that overlooked the backyard. The stairway was near the last room and Ryan hustled her up it.

"You're not very good at this tour thing," she commented as they reached the second floor.

"I didn't say where we'd start," he replied. He released her hand then slid his arm around her. His lips pressed to her temple briefly as they walked. "There are five bedrooms on this floor."

"Five," she repeated in disbelief.

"And that bathroom." He nodded toward an open door. "But there are also shared baths between two bedrooms on each side of the hallway. And here," he opened a door at the end of the hallway, "is the master suite. My room."

He set the bag just inside the room and flipped on the light to reveal the expanse. The bed was dark wood with a hunter-green comforter covering it. A pair of chairs with matching upholstery were arranged near one of the windows with a built-in seat. Two open doors revealed a large closet and a sumptuous bath. A third door, opposite them, was closed.

"Another closet?" she asked.

"No."

"Red room of pain?" she quipped, referring to a popular book that had featured such a room.

"It's not red."

"Oh…" Well, geez. So much for joking.

"Do you want to see it?" A gleam of anticipation lit

his eyes, but she wasn't buying in.

"No. Later, maybe?"

"Later…today?" he clarified. "Or later…on another day? Or later…never."

"Sometime. Just not… I don't think I'm ready today. You promised to warm up dinner, not warm up me."

"Fair enough. Though I do enjoy warming your ass."

She bit her lip. She liked that, too, and he knew it. "Fair enough," she echoed. "Later."

"Today?" he asked, his gray eyes turning predatory.

"Yes. For the spanking," she quickly added. "No for the not-so-red room of pain."

"Deal. Now that you've had the quick tour, dinner's ready."

"So quick?"

"My housekeeper left pot roast and vegetables in the slow cooker."

"A housekeeper, huh? You're turning more and more into Mr. Christian Grey at every turn. How screwed up was your childhood?"

Ryan laughed. "Not screwed up at all. A bit more aware of certain alternate lifestyle proclivities once I was ready to be sexually active, maybe, but I actually think that helped keep my curiosity about the mysteries of fucking at bay."

"A late bloomer, then?" she asked, feeling more and more comfortable with him by the minute. If this was what being with him would entail—this easy bantering with the kinky fuckery in the bedroom—she could certainly deal with it.

"Sixteen—if you're asking about my first time, that is."

"I was."

"You?"

"I was twenty-one. Does your housekeeper live in?"

she asked, changing the subject. Though she'd teased him about having one, she couldn't imagine him not having someone with a place this size. "She doesn't have a little French maid uniform and run around serving you drinks when you're alone for the evening, right?"

He bit the side of his mouth, obviously trying not to laugh. "No. She's in her late forties and probably wouldn't be caught dead in a French maid outfit—unless it was at home for her husband of almost thirty years. She's only here for a few hours every morning during the week—a little longer on Fridays since she does my grocery shopping that day. A cleaning crew comes in one morning a week to dust and spruce up things."

"Fancy," she murmured under her breath.

He looped his arms loosely around her waist and pulled her closer. "And what do you think of French maid costumes."

She shook her head. "No. Not happening."

Ryan nudged her toward the bed and before she knew it, she was sprawled on the mattress, his body over hers. Their legs tangled as he kissed her jaw. "Oh, I don't know…" he whispered. "I can picture you in one with frilly little white panties peeking out and just begging me to spank your ass. Maybe, I'll have to see what I can do about that."

"Ryan…"

His groin circled against hers and his thick, hard cock pressed into her.

"Dinner," she reminded him.

"It'll wait." He nipped her earlobe and his hot breath warmed her skin there. "I'm picturing you bent forward like you're maybe dusting something… Mmm, yeah, and I come up behind you." Suddenly, he knelt up then left the bed. "Come here," he said, beckoning her to join him. Before she knew it, he'd turned her to face away from him and bent her to lean over the edge, propped on her straight arms. "Yeah, like this," he said and pressed his erection against her ass. His fingers moved around her to the button on her jeans, opening it then sliding down her zipper.

Jess bit her lip, knowing he'd find her soaked for him if he went for her pussy.

He didn't. His hands moved to her hips. "And I'd push the panties down your hips like this," he went on, slowly shoving her jeans and cheeky boy shorts down her thighs. He kissed the back of her neck then between her shoulders and down her spine, the thin fabric of her shirt little barrier from his hot mouth. The fabric wadded at her knees, binding her as he knelt behind her. "Then I'd—"

"Ryan!" she cried when his mouth pressed to her pussy, the position completely foreign to her. She'd never had a man lick her this way.

"God, you taste good," he groaned. He clasped her hips, holding her in place when she tried to squirm away from the pleasure. "Stay still, kitten. This pussy is mine and I want it right now."

She moaned, her head dropping to the blankets as he licked and sucked. "Yes, Sir," she gasped. She couldn't help but roll her hips into him, needing more of the pleasure he doled out so lavishly.

"I didn't actually intend on taking you tonight," he confessed, the words coming out as growls as he consumed her.

"Why not?" she breathed. "I...I don't think I can stand much longer." Her legs were wobbling, her knees weakening as her orgasm blazed toward her.

"Try. And don't you come yet. Do you hear me, kitten?"

"Yes...Sir," she rasped, mentally grappling for anything to keep her anchored.

"I wasn't going to take you," he went on, "because I wanted to just hold you, get you more comfortable with me…like we talked about yesterday."

"We agreed to take the 'No sex' off the table."

"Yeah, we did, but I figured tonight… Well, I guess that plan won't happen. Maybe later, after I fuck you hard."

"Okay, Sir. A do-over later."

He smacked her ass and she moaned at the biting pain. She loved when he spanked her. "Are you laughing at me?" he demanded. She still heard the joy in his tone. He was as amused by this as she was.

"No, Sir. I'd never laugh at you."

"Liar," he laughed. "Fuck, I love that you're mine."

"I am." There was no stopping the breathy, blissful tone. Belonging to Ryan. God…

She jerked as his teeth caught her clit, her sharp cry echoing off the beige walls.

"You ready to come?"

"Yes! Please, yes. Can I come, Sir?"

She felt his groan against her folds. "Come, kitten. Let me hear you purr."

And she did. She shook while he kept licking and sucking. He released one of her hips and thrust two fingers into her convulsing passage, finger-fucking her while her climax went on and on. When she collapsed into the blankets, he followed the motion, never letting her pussy a millimeter from his lips.

"Fuck me," she muttered into the blanket, a curse not an invitation, when she'd become boneless and he'd finally sat back on his heels, giving her a reprieve.

Behind her, Ryan chuckled. "Well, actually, I'd rather you were on your knees, taking care of this, my little slave."

She turned her head enough to look over her shoulder

and see him stand. He'd opened his pants and was stroking his cock. She hurried to move and knelt before him, her pants still around her knees. She eyed the metal that gave her so much pleasure, thinking of it running over her tongue.

"Open," he ordered, and she parted her lips, waiting for his length to slide between. She moaned her approval and thanks as he pushed inside. Her eyes closed momentarily in pleasure. She loved the taste and feel of him. Opening her eyes, she looked up at him then raised her hand, her question in her eyes.

"Yes," he hissed. "Use your hands. Touch me. I want to feel your fingers on me."

Wrapping her fingers around his base, she jacked him in time with her descents down his cock. Her thumb pressed into each of the Jacob's ladder piercings, seeking to give him as much sensation as possible.

His hands pushed into her hair, fisting and guiding her up and down.

"Fuck, yeah," he muttered. It wasn't long before he was shaking much as she had earlier. "Jess...I'm gonna come," he warned.

"Mmm," she hummed while taking him deep again.

"You need to stop if you...don't...want..."

She shook her head, sucking harder again.

He cursed as he erupted and his warm seed shot into her mouth. She swallowed, not wanting to lose a bit of his gift to her—his loss of control.

"Damn, baby," he muttered when she released him. He dropped to his knees. His mouth was on hers in a moment. She tasted herself, and wondered if he tasted himself on her lips. His arms wrapped around her and held her flush to him, her head tipped back as he kissed her.

They were both breathing heavily when he sank back

to sit on his heels, pulling her onto his lap. "Dinner?" he asked.

"I'm kind of full."

"Smartass," he laughed.

She grinned. This, this thing between them, it might just work.

* * * *

"So Theo told me Clive was belligerent, bordering on violent, when he was escorted from the job site this afternoon." Ryan kissed her temple then her shoulder.

They were curled up on his couch, their legs tangled and her lying against his chest while he stroked his hand along her upper arm and back.

After their play upstairs, they hadn't dressed. She'd pulled on her panties and taken off the blouse she had over her cotton cami, while he'd left on his sexy black boxer briefs and a T-shirt that hugged his body and showed off his muscular torso. Thankfully, the fire was warm. She loved this intimacy with him, barely anything between them as they cuddled and talked.

"His threats worry me," Ryan confessed, his tone almost distracted, and she wondered if he was replaying the things the ex-manager had said. "Most of his anger was directed at you. Watch your back, would you? I don't like the idea of him out there. He's a loose cannon, but since he hasn't made a direct threat or done something to warrant bringing in the authorities, there's nothing I can do to keep you safe other than watch you 24/7."

"You're not planning to do that, right? Geez, tell me you're not going to go all Fifty Shades on me and hire a bodyguard."

"No, baby. Don't worry."

"Do you think I'm in danger?"

"I hope not. Honestly, I think the best thing is to just be careful right now. I don't know why your Mr. Grey hired a bodyguard for his girl, but this is real life and a disgruntled ex-employee doesn't call for overkill."

"He's not my Mr. Grey."

"You've mentioned him a few times, Ms. Rush. How many times have you read that damn book?"

"Once... Well, parts of it twice. I was curious."

"Hmm..." He kissed her temple. "I hear it's not all that accurate."

"I wouldn't know," she replied. "I'm all new to this. Have you read it?"

"No."

"I've read some stuff on the subject, though. BDSM stuff. On websites, other romance books." She shrugged. "What I got was that...how people practice it is different from person to person."

"True."

Jess grinned, relief flowing through her. Though she still felt as if she knew nothing about the lifestyle, she'd gotten something right.

"I mentioned the sect I belong to—do you remember that?"

"Yes. Your tattoos and piercings are part of that."

"Right. There's more to it than that. Like you said, there's a range of play and methods. Our sect, however, is kind of a...governing body. We have guidelines to adhere to."

"Like a cult? I'm not going to be handing out flyers door-to-door, am I? Getting people to join the Church of Holy Spank."

"Such a smart mouth," he growled. "I think you're going to need to visit the Church of Holy Spank later."

"Spank me, Master, for I've been very bad," she quipped.

He shook his head. "*No,* it's not a cult. You can get out if you want to. It's a subculture society, though. And there are rules, structure, records… They educate people and instill a rather strict standard of conduct. I have to admit, my family is a bit fringe as far as they're concerned. Most people in the group practice the lifestyle 24/7. We don't."

"And this strict group…they let you get away with that?"

"They don't really have a choice. Our family was one of the four that founded the group in the 1800s when we came to the States."

"Wait… The 1800s?"

"BDSM isn't new, kitten."

She made an irritated sound at him. "I *know* that. It just surprises me. You've been around this long and no one knows about it."

"First rule of fight club…"

She laughed. "Whatever. Seriously, how is it a secret?"

"Those who are in, also have family in. The perks of being part of it are worth the secrecy, plus our families are…let's say…interlocked. We hold shares in each other's businesses and interests. Enough to be trouble if secrets aren't kept. There's some intermarriage. Besides, we're all very private people. I know some of the others, because we're friends and whatnot, but only the Keeper of the Records knows everyone."

She pulled back so she could look at him. "I still don't get how it remains a secret."

"Most people don't walk around advertising they're in the life, sweetness."

"I get that."

"Fine. Think of it this way. You have a billion dollars; it's always replenishing. The only stipulation to keeping it is that you don't tell anyone about it."

"You're telling me."

He closed his eyes, sighed then opened his eyes again and pinned her with a glare. "You don't tell anyone unless you trust them implicitly and want to share the billion dollars with them. Really, no one talks about it because there's nothing to tell. It's like saying you can trace your roots back to the Mayflower. None of us see it as anything earth shattering. It's just our...family."

She still didn't get it, but whatever. The people in Ryan's sect must have some rigid moral code not shared by the rest of the world. Of course, they were pretty big on discipline...

"At fourteen, we start getting training—"

"*Fourteen?*"

He laughed. "Nothing sexual and certainly nothing hands on. The concepts of Dominant and submissive are introduced—as personality types only. Rules of behavior and self-control are trained into each of us. Those of us who are dominant learn to treasure the submissives, to know they're a precious gift. The submissive training is quite similar...yet, quite different, as well. Same concepts; different direction."

Her head was spinning. Shaking it slowly, she settled against his chest again and stared into the flicking flames in the fireplace. He'd thrown some additive in with the logs and she saw occasional streaks on blue or green as the bits burned.

"Too much?" he asked.

"It's a lot to get my head around."

He kissed the top of her head. "In time, it won't seem so strange. Just trust me to take care of you."

She reached up and clasped his fingers where they rested on her shoulder. "I do."

"Decide to say yes to us," he whispered, telling her

the answer he wants from her on Friday, decision day.
Yes or no to Ryan and Jessica day.

Jess didn't say anything. She just snuggled deeper into
him, determined not to jump the gun and yell *yes, yes,
yes!*

His arm tightened around her. "I understand."

"I like this. I really do. It's more than I could ever
have dreamed of between us, but you know I'm not one
to jump the gun."

"I know, baby. Believe it or not, I appreciate that.
When you say yes, I'll know it's not a whim, that you're
really in."

She shook her head, chuckling. "You're pretty sure of
yourself, Sir."

He growled and sat up. He pulled her to straddle him
then pushed his hands into her hair, cupping her head and
pulling her down for a kiss. His lips brushed hers. "I'm
pretty sure of us, kitten. Nothing has ever felt so right."

As she sank into his embrace, opening for him, she
had to agree. Nothing in her life had ever felt so right, so
much as if it were perfect and she belonged, and that
terrified her.

"Let's go to bed," he said when they were both
breathless. "We have to be to work early, and I want to
hold you tonight."

"It might take a while to go to sleep." She grinned,
hopeful for his cock buried deep inside her until the wee
hours of morning.

He shook his head. "No sex, little kitten. Just being
together today."

She groaned, pouting just a little. "Fine."

"Who's in charge here?" he asked, running his thumb
along her bottom lip. She sucked the lip into her mouth
and bit into it.

Her sigh signaled her compliance. "You are."

"That's right. I am, and I will do what's best for us. You need a frame of reference to base your decision on. If we're all sex all the time, you'll have unrealistic expectations."

She gasped in mock disbelief. "You're not a sex god! Oh no…" She made to climb off his lap. "I'm out of here."

He yanked her back to him then lifted her into his arms and carried her toward the steps. "I wouldn't go that far. You can still revere me as your sex god."

"Such an ego," she mumbled into his neck.

"Let's go to bed, brat."

"Spanking?" she asked, optimistic for the outcome. It still shocked her that she liked his hand on her ass so much.

"No."

"But you said…"

"Fair enough. I did. But tell me this: will you be satisfied with just that and not having me fucking you until you can't move afterward?"

"No, but—"

"I don't want to leave you that needy, baby. That would be a true punishment and not making love to you tonight will be hard enough."

She'd kind of relished the idea of feeling him tomorrow while she sat, but she understood. He was right, and though she didn't like it, she agreed with his intentions and her already high opinion of him raised a few more notches. Her decision was forming fast— submitting to him wouldn't be a mistake. It would be perfect.

Chapter Twelve

Jessica didn't like this.

Sitting in the conference room with seven other people, she listened as Ryan gave report on upcoming projects, listened to the other project managers give statuses on their sites then gave back feedback. She was last on the agenda, the other five project managers reporting before her while Ryan's assistant took notes.

Ryan was aware of most of her updates, but he wouldn't like what she'd discovered first thing this morning on her call with Ron. He'd done a thorough check on supplies, materials and fixtures yesterday and the discrepancies were monumental—enough that someone might lose their job. Someone like her. She'd been charged with overseeing this job, the company had put faith in her, and despite all her oversight, this had happened.

Failure echoed hollowly inside her. She'd gotten off the call with Ron just in time to rush here and hadn't had time to do more than jot notes and run to the conference room.

Alec Heller, the manager beside her, nudged his elbow into her arm and her gaze whipped to him. He nodded toward Ryan.

"Ms. Rush?" Ryan said, and she got the feeling it wasn't the first time he'd said her name. Shit. That just made this worse. In competence and inattentiveness. Vicious kamikaze butterflies slammed around her belly, making her feel a bit nauseated. Her extremities turned cold as her nerves amped up and she met Ryan's implacable stare.

"You have a report?" he asked.

"Yes, though I don't have anything written up to give all of you," she answered, standing to address the room. Usually, she came in prepped with charts and spreadsheets. She looked at the other project managers. "You may have heard that Clive Honeycutt was removed from the Overland Mall project and fired."

"About damn time," Alec muttered. "The guy is a giant-ass prick."

Jessica smiled at him.

"Ms. Rush. Your point," Ryan growled. Oh, so he didn't like her being friendly toward another man, no matter how innocent. Despite her nerves, that bolstered her a little.

"I've just gotten off the phone with Ron Westfall, who's taken over on that project. Our inventory doesn't match records. We have shortages, and worse, many of the fixtures have been switched out for lower quality versions—that's not what was delivered and accounted for. In some cases, the items are obviously used."

"Salvage?" Ryan asked, surprise clear in his voice. She nodded. "Yes."

"Action plan," he snapped and she fought back a shiver. He was pissed, and from his glacial stare, she suspected his anger was at her.

"I… I-I just found out minutes before this meeting."
She took a deep breath to steady her voice. *Be strong,
Jessica. Don't let them see you crack. Do that later.
Alone.* "Ron is faxing over his initial inventory then
doing a deeper more thorough check. I'm checking
against procurement orders and verifying shipments with
our suppliers. I should have a full picture before the end
of the day. At that point, a police report will need to be
filed. I also suggest that other sites he's worked on be
checked. This can't be the first time he's done this."

She hoped that anyway. Though it would mean more
loss for the company, she wouldn't be the only one
duped.

Ryan nodded, his level of ire unshifted. His lips were
a thin line and that telltale muscle throbbed near his eye.
"I'll need copies of your findings, a detailed spreadsheet
of discrepancies and copies of any police reporting so I
can submit it to our adjustors."

"Yes, Sir."

Heat flared in his eyes, but was quickly extinguished.
"Marcy," he turned toward his assistant, "run me a full
report of any projects Clive has worked on for the past
two years. Call those clients and schedule a follow-up
walk-thru on all of them to take place immediately. If
anyone questions it, tell them know it's part of our
warranty procedure detailed in the contract, item 14.5."

"Will do," she replied.

Jessica closed her planner, not wanting to see her
damning notes. "I should head over to the site to help
with—"

"No," Ryan interrupted. Her gaze shot to his. "We
need you here, as the hub point as information is
submitted and checked," he answered before she could
ask why.

Meaning, he didn't trust her out there anymore and

needed to keep her under his watchful eye. Her stomach dropped. The churning butterflies stopped, leaving her with a deathlike emptiness like none she'd ever felt.

"Yes, Sir," she replied, struggling to get her response above a whisper.

Ryan gathered his things and left the room without a word. The other project managers were looking around, a couple staring at her, but no one said a word. Taking a deep breath to steel herself, she gathered her things and headed out in Ryan's heels.

She'd expected him to be waiting for her, ready to read her the riot act, but he was nowhere to be seen. He'd probably call her to his office later. At least, he hadn't told her to clear out her things. He'd assigned her more work. Granted, it was to clean up this mess, but he hadn't fired her. Yet.

Fuck. Just when things had been going so well.

At her office, she told Glenna she was setting her phone to send over all calls and requested that nothing be put through that was unrelated to Overland Mall. Her assistant appeared concerned, probably because Jess had never done that before, but nodded.

She closed her door behind her and quietly flipped the lock. Sliding down her door, she dropped her things to the floor then pressed her forehead to her knees and gave in to the quiet sobs she'd been holding back for what seemed like hours.

She'd failed. She'd tried so hard, but she'd failed...

The noise of the outer office filter through to her, but she ignored it.

Her cell phone buzzed, but she ignored it, too. She couldn't deal with anyone or anything right this moment. She had to pull it together before that, and that meant getting this out. Jess shook her head, the very thought of allowing herself to feel sorry for herself, even for a few minutes, pulling her out of indulging in her misery. She had to deal with this. She'd just fall apart later. At home.

The rattle of her door handle startled her, and she stumbled to her feet. Hurriedly, she gathered her things from the floor and dropped them on the desk. Whoever had tried her doorknob knocked lightly on the wood. She dashed her hand over her face to scrub away her stupid tears. There was no way to hide what had happened, though.

Dreading facing even her assistant, she opened the door, but it wasn't Glenna. Ryan stood there. His breath sucked in and he pushed inside her office, closing the door behind him.

"You've been crying."

Apparently, she was in love with a rocket scientist. She grimaced. "Yeah."

"Kitten, it'll be all right."

"Yeah…it's just great that I'm a giant fucking failure."

"Watch your language," he growled.

She swiped at a stray tear and turned to head back to her desk. Ryan yanked her against him, her back to his chest. His face buried in her neck. "You are *not* a failure. As you so nicely pointed out in the meeting, he's probably done this before."

"You're so pissed at me."

"No…I'm pissed at him. I'm angry *for* you and I needed to go meet with Theo and my dad. This could start a real shit storm."

"I'm sorry."

"Hey…" He turned her, leaned back and lifted her chin so she was forced to look at him. "This is not your fault."

"If you hadn't fired him…"

"Yeah, he might have gotten away with this like he

might have on other jobs. It's over. We'll get it fixed and thank fuck he's only been on-site manager for a few jobs." His thumbs stroked her jaw. "It'll be okay, baby. Just do your job the outstanding way you always do and we'll get this cleaned up." He leaned his forehead to hers. "No one's lost faith in you. If anyone can pull this out, you can. You're our top project manager for a reason, and it has nothing to do with me wanting to fuck you. My brother and dad would cut off my dick before they let that be my reason."

She couldn't hold back her snort as his assertion pierced through her mood.

"Oh, you think that's funny? You wouldn't like it so much if you were going to bed with a eunuch."

"I'm not in love with your cock."

He pulled her close, enfolding her in his tight embrace, making her feel as if nothing could get to her in his protective hold. "No, but you like it a lot."

She made a noncommittal sound, burrowing into him.

"Brat," he laughed. "Feeling better?"

"A little." Some of her peace in the moment faded away as he reminded her what had brought them here.

"I love you, too, by the way."

"Ryan…" she whispered. She looked up at him, and he kissed her hard. In a breath, he had her pushed up against her office door and she fought to keep silent as he plundered. Glenna did *not* need to hear her getting it on with her boss.

He pressed into her, and she barely suppressed her moan as the ridge of his erection ground into her center. She'd never been so grateful for pants. But was he really going to make her come? Here?

"Put your legs around me," he whispered.

"Yes, Sir." His hands went under her ass as she followed his direction.

"You know, I wanted to drag you out of that conference room and fuck you every time you said that."

"Said…what?" she panted. Her thoughts scattered as he moved against her, bringing her closer and closer to orgasm—through their clothes!

"Whenever you said 'Yes, Sir.' I wanted to strip you and have you on your knees."

The first quivers trembled through her body and she bit his shoulder.

"Fuck," he breathed. "Are you going to come, kitten?"

She nodded, never releasing her mouth's grip on him.

One hand slipped between them and he tweaked her nipple through her blouse. "Do it. Come for me. Show me again who you belong to."

She choked out a gasp, unable to stop the sound as her body obeyed him. "Yes…Sir," she panted. Her legs tightened around him as she canted her hips into his powerful body, wishing she could have his cock, but knowing he'd probably never fuck her here. He still seemed bent on making her feel good…oh, so good.

"Such a good girl," he murmured, lowering her onto unsteady legs. She sagged against the door while he continued to kiss her, slowly receding until their foreheads leaned together and they just stared at one another.

"Did you need something? When you came in here?" she asked when she could somewhat gather her thoughts.

"I got what I came for."

Her brows rose. "That?"

"I just wanted to check on you. I could tell you were upset, but I couldn't do anything about it earlier."

"Oh… Well, you helped, so…thank you."

"Always a pleasure, baby." He shifted, adjusting. "Except for this."

"I could…"

"No. If we go there, we'll go too far. I'll survive. I might need to jerk off a time or three in my office—"

The phone ringing on her desk interrupted him. Apparently, Glenna thought this one should come through. "I better get that."

"Okay. Just keep me updated on the Clive thing, all right."

Before she could answer, he stroked his thumb along her bottom lip, deep longing in his gaze then he was gone. She dove for the phone before it went to voicemail. The ring indicated it was an outside call.

"Cress Construction. This is Jessica."

"Is this…Jessica Rush?"

"Yes," she said, straightening at the cool female. Absently, she smoothed her hand over her hair. "Yes, this is."

"Good afternoon, Ms. Rush. This is Stephanie Wells calling from Mr. Sissek's office at Sissek Construction."

Sissek Construction? Why were they calling her?

"Mr. Sissek would like to discuss the possibility of interviewing you for a job with our company. We're familiar with your work, and quite frankly, we'd like you to work for us."

"A job? What position is he offering?" Jess didn't particularly want to leave Cress Construction, and thereby Ryan, but with the latest developments on the mall project, she wasn't so sure she shouldn't keep her options open. If she said yes though, it would be the end of things with Ryan. Sissek Construction was direct competition. But if this Clive fiasco ended her job here, it would still be the end. Losing the career she'd worked so hard to get wasn't an option.

"It would be a project management position, much like you have now. We need someone willing to travel and who's not afraid to go head-to-head with the crew to

get the job done. We're expanding into work on the East
Coast and are looking for the right person to cover New
York and Connecticut as our regional project manager."

Jess' eyes widened. That sounded like a whole lot
more than the position she had now. It sounded like a
really good opportunity. "That sounds like a wonderful
opportunity," she hedged. "It's definitely something I'd
have to consider before jumping into it."

Stephanie chuckled. "Completely understandable. Can
you get back to us by the end of the week?"

"Yes. Of course." Apparently, Friday would be more
than Ryan and Jessica day. It would determine multiple
directions for her life. Taking down the Stephanie's
information in her planner, she thanked the woman for
the opportunity then disconnected and sank into her desk
chair.

Holy crap. This day was a complete roller coaster
worth of up and downs.

* * * *

"So, why did I get a job reference call for you from
Sissek Construction today?"

"What?" Jess exclaimed, staring at her best friend.
She'd intended to tell Keera all about everything that had
happened, including Sissek, but apparently, they'd
jumped the gun.

After a long day of sorting through the Clive mess and
the stunning losses, as well as making a preliminary
action plan for remediation of the problem, she and Keera
had decided to meet up for coffee at a tiny café about a
mile from the Cress building. Jess would have liked
something stronger and more numbing than coffee, but
that would wait until later. With Sissek adding to her
stress, she might drink something harder than white wine,

too. An entire liquor store sounded good after this day—and she wasn't actually much of a drinker.

"Yeah. You didn't tell me you were looking for another job, friend."

"I…*wasn't*. I'm not. Damn it. If Ryan finds out about this—"

"I'm not going to run to him with it."

"Or tell Theo? Ryan told me that's how he tracked me down on Monday. You went to Theo."

"I was worried and…well, Theo and I…"

"He's your secret guy?"

"Yeah." Keera's smile said far more than that simple word. Jess had known her friend was head over heels, but she looked…downright *in love*. "He wants to tell everyone, but I'm not really ready. At least, I wasn't. I think I'm just about there."

"I know why I'm not screaming to the world about me and Ryan—I mean…it's too new, and with this freaking Clive mess, I just want to wait. But what's your excuse?"

"Besides the fact I'm fucking the president of the company?"

Jess narrowed her eyes at her friend. "Really? You expect me to believe that's your only reason. Come on…"

"Okay, fine. I've had some problems in the past. Problems with family that have kept me from digging in roots. I'm starting to feel comfortable here, comfortable with Theo—like my past won't fuck up my future anymore, you know?"

Jess snorted. "Trust me, I get the family and the past' factor. I've been letting it screw up my life for years, but Ryan…" She trailed off, carefully choosing her words since she wasn't sure what Keera knew about the Cress family. Ryan had never said his brothers were in the lifestyle, just that his parents were. "I have always kept things clutched close because of my past. Ryan doesn't let me do that. He gets inside to the real me and demands that part of me."

Keera nodded in apparent understanding. "Very dominant? Very into discipline and, um, traditional tattoos and piercings?" Now, she was biting back a smile—unsuccessfully. "Likes when you're tied up?"

In the middle of sipping her coffee, Jess choked. She hadn't expected that line of questioning. "Um...yes."

Her friend shrugged. "Stands to reason. I mean, Theo owns the Palace."

"What?" Jess exclaimed then leaned forward and repeated in a whisper, "What?"

"Oh yeah. I guess there's a big club over on the other side of the state that caters to the...um, *lifestyle*, but there was nothing here, so he built one. Kind of impressive to me, if you must know. He was only twenty-two and fresh out of college, but that boy knows what he wants, and well..." She chuckled and took a sip of her latte. "He's rather demanding about what he wants, too. It would stand to reason his brother is much the same way. I believe all the brothers have shares in that business."

"So they're all," Jess looked around to see if anyone was listening. No one was nearby, "Doms?"

"From what I understand. I don't know from personal experience, though. Theo's rather over-the-top possessive. 'No one fucking touches you. You're mine,' and all that. I swear if he could put me in one of those Middle Eastern robe-and-veil combos, my face would never see the light of day again. I won't lie, sometimes I flirt with other guys just to get under his collar. His reaction is definitely worth it."

"You don't!"

"Well, not often. I enjoy being able to sit comfortably from time to time. It's just when he's been so bowled under by work that I know he needs a break—I'm his perfect outlet. I pretend I've been neglected and I'm bored and looking at the available male pickings, and he comes running. I'd never cheat on him, and I'm ninety-nine percent sure that he knows that."

Jess shook her head. She couldn't imagine doing that to Ryan, but then Keera was far different from her and she and Theo had been together for a while. Keera had been with her "secret guy" for at least six months now.

As if cued by her thoughts of Ryan, Jess' phone buzzed.

"Being summoned to the master's chambers?" Keera laughed as Jess glanced at the screen.

Ryan: Where are you? Your car's still at the office, but I know you left a while ago.

"You mind if I text him back," she asked her friend.

"Oh you'd better. Those boys might have amazing control, but they tend to go ballistic when they can't find what's," her voice dropped an octave, "*theirs.* Before I left the office, I told Theo where I was going. I expect he'll show up here within the hour."

Jessica: I'm at the coffee shop around the corner with Keera. We're catching up and stuff.
Ryan: I see. Come to my place after.

Jess tilted her head and raised her brows. Maybe, it was the stress of the day. Maybe, it was just that, well, fuck, she hated being commanded. In the bedroom was one thing, but this was clearly outside a scene and outside the bedroom—though from what she'd observed "bedroom" was rather subjective. It seemed to be far less a place than a mood.

"Oh, she's pursing her lips," Keera laughed. "What's he done?"

She held out her phone so Keera could read the message.

"Typical. Asking isn't really their thing."

That seemed to be true.

"Theo just says, 'I'll see you at *blank* place at *blank* time.' It's annoying, but you get used to it and learn to negotiate it."

Jess sighed and clicked to reply.

Jessica: *Why?*

Ryan: *WHY?*

Hmm...he didn't seem to like that. Defiant amusement prickled inside her.

Jessica: *I asked you first.*

Ryan: *Jessica...*

Jessica: *Yes?*

Ryan: *I know where you live. I know where you work. I know where you are RIGHT NOW. Your smartass is not safe.*

Jessica: *I seem to recall I have freewill.*

She could see he was typing. Not waiting for the response, she set down the phone then ignored the subsequent buzzing.

"You know you're courting a spanking," Keera warned after a few minutes and several notifications.

"I hope so."

"They're not all pleasant. When Theo's feeling particularly peeved with me, he'll get me all worked up then leave me that way. That's not as great as it might seem."

"Telling my secrets," Theo half-growled, coming up beside them. He sank onto the wide bench with Keera and slung his arm around her shoulders, drawing her close. He pressed a kiss to the top of her head, and Keera snuggled into him. "Hey, baby," he murmured against her temple.

She made a content sound. "Not telling secrets; just giving Jess a warning."

"Speaking of…" He pinned Jess with a look, glanced pointedly at her phone on the table then returned his stare to her eyes. "Did your phone break in the past few minutes? Lose service? Battery die?"

Of course, the thing buzzed again right then.

Jess tried not to flinch. She held his stare, refusing to cave. Ryan could not summarily order her—no, imperiously *summon* her—to his house, expecting her to fall onto his bed with legs wide-open. And Theo wouldn't intimidate her into action, either. It didn't matter that she really did want Ryan, and she really *did* want to do whatever he suggested and go to his house. After her rough day, she felt puckish and contrary. She was just done. She wanted a glass of wine and a hot bubble bath.

Theo chuckled and shook his head. "Whatever. It's your punishment. Don't say we didn't try to warn you. My little brother isn't as patient as I am."

Jess glanced at Keera in time to see her friend roll her eyes in apparent disagreement.

A shiver worked through her—less at Theo's implied threat than the thought of what Ryan might do. "I think I'll be off. I'll see you tomorrow, Keer. Night, sir."

Gathering her things, she slung her purse over her shoulder and picked up her phone. She couldn't help it. She glanced at the screen.

Ryan: Why are you being difficult? I thought we were past this.

Ryan: What the hell are you on about? You have

freewill, kitten. You can obey me or you can choose punishment.

Ryan: Fine, Ms. Rush, I get your point. I'd like to remind you that YOU got off this afternoon. I've been walking around with a spike in my pants all day. I was suggesting we finish what we started...

Ryan: Are you going to make me come there and drag you off to my house?

Ryan: Jessica. Answer me.

Ryan: I hope you have a good laugh. You won't be laughing later.

She sucked in a breath, just imagining.

Jessica: *Not laughing. I'm tired. I just need to go home and relax.*

She heard the notification ring—not from her phone—just before an iron-like hand clamped around her upper arm. Without a word, Ryan herded her toward his SUV parked on the curb.

"Ryan!"

"No, you had a chance to talk earlier. You chose not to. Now, get in the fucking car."

"But—"

He opened the door and strong-armed her into the seat, somehow managing it without the least bit of shoving. "Put on your seatbelt. Don't you dare try to get out, either. I have no problem turning you over my knee right here and spanking you for anyone on the sidewalk to see."

Her eyes went wide. He wouldn't! *You know he would. And you asked for it. You knew he'd react like this.*

Ryan was sliding into the driver's side before it

occurred to her to move.

"Put on your seatbelt," he ground out. Was he gritting his teeth. Wow, he really was riled up by this. Theo hadn't been kidding.

"I just want to go home," she replied in a small voice. She didn't have it in her to deal with this…him…*anything*…right now.

"We *are* going home." Since she hadn't moved, he reached over and snapped her belt into place then pulled it tight to make sure she was secure.

"I want to go to *my* house."

He didn't say a word as he pulled from the curb. She had a feeling they weren't heading toward her place.

"Some people would call this kidnapping."

The hard look he shot her before turning his eyes back to the road should have shut her up. It didn't. *Now*, she wanted to talk. Go figure. Guh! What was wrong with her?

"You know we're still in the probationary, deciding period and you're pissing me off."

"Really? That's where you want to go with this?"

"Well…um…"

"I warned you about respect, in *and* out of scenes, Jessica. This display is out of line."

She made a disbelieving sound. *He* was out of line. "I don't appreciate you just deciding what we're going to do and where we're going to be—"

"Don't you?" he interrupted, his tone clearly implying that he thought she *did* appreciate those things. "Overseeing things all day exhausts you. I'm taking care of this, our non-work life."

Damn it. Point to Cress. A very grudging point.

She didn't want to admit he was right, though, and opted for silence as she stared out the window. They'd left the city now and the populous streets had given way

to rural roads and fields, any homes wide spread and far from traffic. She loved that about this area. One had only to drive a few miles before being back to open, natural land.

"Are you taking me home tonight?" she asked quietly, her mood calming a bit as she watched the landscape speed past. The solitude, even with Ryan beside her, allowed peace to supplant some of the stress of the day.

"Wasn't planning on it."

"I'll need clothes for work tomorrow."

"Kitten, stop worrying. You know I'll take care of you." He sounded calmer now, too. Maybe, this *was* what they both needed, or maybe, he'd picked up on her change of mood and that had helped.

"Okay." She leaned her head on the window. "This has been such a long day."

He took her hand. "I know, baby." His thumb ran along the top of her fingers. "You did a great job with all your reporting and investigation. I know we're far from finished with this, but you made great leaps in the progress."

"Thank you. I feel like such a failure for letting this happen."

"Hey," he coaxed. "Clive is a bully and a criminal. You can't control that, and this isn't your fault. We'll deal with it. Our legal team is already on top of pressing charges, and your information will be key to that."

"Okay. I just…" She took a deep breath then huffed it out. "I just don't want anyone to think I'm skating by or that I'm getting away with something because I'm with you."

"Is that what earlier was about?"

"Probably. I don't know. I'm just…jumbled I guess. And this is…very new."

"It is. And it isn't."

She glanced at him, askance.

"Baby, you've been deferring to me for a few years now. This is just a different level—a more intimate level."

Well, she supposed that was true.

"What do you have planned for me tonight after my—what did you call it?—display?"

"Dinner. Then…the little room off my bedroom. Maybe, not in that order."

"Oh, a shower? I could use a long one."

"Smartass. You're going to get a long one," he muttered.

She pressed her lips together and stared out the window again, hiding her amusement and, damn it, anticipation.

Chapter Thirteen

It turned out to be "not in that order." After he'd parked in the four-stall garage, Ryan didn't wait for her to get out of the SUV. Rounding the vehicle to her side, he lifted her into his arms then headed inside. He didn't stop until he reached his bedroom. The bed had been made since this morning—his maid was always on top of things and never asked questions, thank God—but the comforter had been pulled back and the bed stood ready and waiting.

Carefully, he laid her on the soft sheets.

"I thought you were taking me to your dungeon," she commented, lifting up on her elbows.

"I figured we'd start here."

"I'm beginning to think I'll never see next door. Despite your promise, you never showed me last night, either."

"Eager?"

She shrugged. "Maybe. I'm curious about what a Dom like you has in his house as opposed to the dungeon at Pleasure Palace."

"Enough to keep you happy."

"I don't need a dungeon for that," she whispered.

He leaned over her, pushing her back into the pillows as he kissed her. Damn, he loved this woman. She couldn't be more perfect, even when she was pissing him the fuck off. "Neither do I."

He was glad she didn't seem scared by his chosen way of living. He had plenty of experience with women rejecting him for his practice of BDSM. Though Jessica seemed to enjoy this scene, he still feared she might end up rejecting him, too, at the end of the week. He didn't know how he'd take that. Everyone outside the lifestyle thought Doms were always strong, almost impervious to life's arrows. He was human, just like any other man. Jessica had given him her control. Nevertheless, she still had the ability to eviscerate him with a few words.

One word in particular. Goodbye.

As he leaned over her, she looked up at him with huge green eyes. Excitement swirled in them without a lick of fear. He knew he'd manage to win her over completely. Though things had been tense earlier, there might be hope for him yet.

"So, slave," he said, purposely reminding her of her current position and plunging them fully into the scene. "We're going to play a little game."

She shifted sinuously on the sheets, looking for all the world like Aphrodite come to seduce the mere mortal man. He wanted to tear off her clothes and sink into her body like the mad man she turned him into with a bat of her eyes and a tiny, naughty smile.

"Is this a game I'm destined to lose?" she asked.

"Depends on your point of view." The way she was taunting him, he'd definitely see that she'd lose but they'd both won. "This game is called, 'Can Jessica stay still?' Ever heard of it?'"

"No but I don't like the sound of it." The aroused edge to her words belied her statement. This wouldn't take long. She was already squirming with desire.

"Now, in this game, I don't cuff you."

She took a shaky breath. "Uh-huh…"

"And I get to try out some of my favorite toys on you."

"What happens when I lose?"

She didn't say *if*. Strange, since it wasn't like her to give up easily. Losing in this particular game must not seem like a bad thing to the ever-competitive Jessica Rush.

Her legs shifted apart inviting him inside. Soon enough. He needed to get her undressed then he had a short list of toys that would be introduced to her lovely pussy. Then he'd fuck her. Long and hard.

The game would be better if she tried to fight the need to move. Time to up the ante.

"If you lose, get to claim my prize—and I'm not telling you what it is ahead of time. If you win…what do you want?"

She licked her bottom lip then sank her teeth into it "This doesn't seem fair," she hedged. "Do I get a chance to see if *you* will stay still?"

"Is the name of this game called 'Can Your Master Stay Still'?"

She shook her head. "What constitutes a move?"

"Anything more than a gentle tremor."

"Shit."

He shook his head, clicking his tongue at her as he pulled off her heels. His hands slid up her legs to the closure of her pants. "Do I need to wash my slave's mouth out with something?"

Her gaze never leaving him, she lifted her hips so he

could pull down the slacks, panties and her nylons. Her eyes had narrowed, growing dark as summer leaves. "Depends on what you want to use."

"Not what you're suggesting…yet. Perhaps, another tactic. Generally, a flogging makes a slave less sassy."

She smirked. "Am I an ordinary slave?"

He finished removing her blouse and bra before answering. God, he wanted to lick those pert little nipples. He grinned inwardly. During the game… She'd never stay still for that.

"No, you're far from ordinary," He finally said then held up a hand to forestall whatever mouthy response was about to spring forth from her. "The game starts now. Moving your mouth to speak is considered movement."

Jesus, he loved playing with her and sparring with her. Years and years of this would be wonderful. She had to choose him.

Jessica pressed her lush lips together, but he ignored it. Opening the drawer beside the bed, he withdrew a few of his favorite tools and realized he'd left the ball gag in the other room. He needed it to amplify her reactions. He'd need to go get it.

He held up a blindfold. "Did I mention that you don't get to see what I'm going to do?"

She growled her displeasure, fury burning in those fiery green eyes as he slipped it over them and eased the elastic bands behind her head. She liked looking at him—something that aroused him as much as it seemed to arouse her. She obviously had things to say about him blindfolding her but didn't want to lose. Her frustration level would have her literally shaking for release soon.

Leaving her waiting he went into his playroom retrieve the ball gag. She might as well get used to it. Some situations required its use, including some rooms at Pleasure Palace that weren't soundproofed. The dining room scene they'd shared being an exception, he didn't want to share Jessica's cries with anyone else. They belong to *him*.

Quickly, he discarded his clothes, not wanting them in the way later then he returned to the bedroom. Standing beside the bed, he looked at her, lying there waiting for him. Her nipples were hard buds and a fine covering of goose bumps had raised across her arms. She tensed, waiting, knowing he stood there, but she didn't say a word. He noticed her fingers curling slightly into the mattress beneath her hands, but ignored the slight movement. That wasn't the break in stillness he sought.

His fingers squeezed around the gag. He wanted to see the dark-blue ball pressed between her lush lips, stretching them as wide as his cock would when he fucked her mouth. There went his control again—drawn far too thin. He had more restraint over himself than this. He'd spent years building it. He wouldn't allow this beautiful little brat to steal it in minutes.

Ryan closed his eyes and took a calming breath. He had to regain himself before he touched her. Rounding the bad, he went to his supplies, considering what else he could use to taunt her. He pulled out a small vibrating egg and a two-sided whip. He didn't intend to use the leather portion on her, but the other end was tipped with feathers. Jessica wouldn't hold out long against them.

Then he nodded, deciding exactly the thing that would drive her insane. Returning to his playroom he opened a refrigerated drawer and removed a heavy, glass dildo and a tube of gel. Perfect.

Jessica hadn't moved when he returned. Good. She was invested in winning the competition—not that she had a prayer. Nevertheless, he needed her to at least try. He wanted to watch her fight her reactions to him and lose. She'd discover she had no power here either. He wanted to remind her of the joy of submission to him. Only him.

Setting the dildo and the lube on the bed, he pressed the ball to her lips.

"Open your mouth," he instructed.

She sucked in a breath through her nose, not moving her mouth.

"I'm not trying to trick you. If I tell you to move, I won't hold it against you," he added.

Her brow furrowed, and he guessed she was deciding if he was telling the truth. He frowned. She knew him better than to think he'd lie. Then slowly, she opened. He pushed the ball between her teeth and fastened the leather strap. His cock jerked. Seeing Jessica bound before him, seeing her modeling his preferred paraphernalia made him hotter than the summer sun. Her in leather cuffs and nipple clamps would drive him right over the edge—in the best of ways.

Not long ago, he'd thought he'd never see her like this…naked in his bed…waiting for him…pert breasts rising and falling on each excited breath. The overwhelming need to reveal his desires and see where it led had distracted him on too many occasions.

He watched her breathe shallowly, being so careful not to move…as if she might actually win. He almost laughed. As if that would happen. He played dirty. It was his specialty and marked him as a master, in more ways than one.

He didn't move for nearly a minute, letting her anticipation rise and knowing her tension rose with every moment.

"It also won't count against you if I move you," he told her, and she startled slightly. His smile was purely wicked as he anticipated the next activities.

At some point, her fingers had clenched into the

sheets at her hips, and now, he gently unfolded them. Her tight, closed up position gave her a false sense of security. He wanted her open and vulnerable with nothing impeding him.

Sliding his hands down her arms, he pulled them over her head and crossed her wrists just above her crown. Dragging his fingertips along the sensitive flesh on the inside of her arms, he made a path down her body. Deliberately, he raked all ten fingers over her tempting breasts then headed over her torso and hips until he reached her tightly compressed thighs.

He traced a line along the crease, from mound to knees. "You are a very naughty slave." Wedging his fingers between, he grabbed her legs and forced them apart. "Never together during a scene," he growled. Parted like this, he could see the glistening folds of her bare pussy. She was so slick for him. He needed to taste her, to lap up that sweet nectar.

Not in his plan... Not yet, anyway.

"Luckily," he continued, grabbing the icy cold dildo. "I know just the thing for disobedient slaves." He dragged the tip along her naked folds and watched her shake as the frigid glass tormented her clit. Pulling it away, he coated it with equally cold lube. "You know...your tight little ass is too small and untried to take me right now."

She made a small sound of disagreement, and her face scrunched as she fought to stay still.

"But," he said as he slide his lubed fingers against her nether opening, "there are other things that are the perfect size." He pushed a digit inside to open her a bit. Her flesh was burning against his colder skin.

She shrieked behind the gag, almost lifting her head from the pillow, when he pressed the dildo against her anus a few moments later. This was one of his favorites toys. The length and modest width made it a good choice for vaginal activity while the deep groove toward the base made it perfect for this.

Agitated, she clenched her muscles, trying to get away without actually moving. He kept the dildo pushed to her while he waited for her to exhale then he forced the tip inside her momentarily relaxed body. She made agitated sounds in her throat, protesting the invasion.

During other play, he might have worried and become more vigilant to her reaction. This was different. With her hands unbound, she could easily reach down and deck him if he really pushed her beyond her limits. Doggedly, he continued the invasion until the entire length of the icy shaft was lodged inside her. He checked to be sure it was seated properly and let go, watching her buck as the chill invaded her heated tissues.

Her muffled, unchecked cries yanked at his cock, begging him to fuck her. Leaning forward, he gave in and sucked her clit into his mouth then nipped the sensitive flesh. Her taste flooded his mouth. Languidly, he dragged his tongue through her tangy cream. Looping his arms under her thighs, he captured them and held her open as he pressed his hands over her pubic bone and helped her to stay still though it was a battle she'd already lost.

Taking his time, he lapped at her folds. Greedily, he took his fill of her, working from the back of her swollen cleft to the front containing her most sensitive flesh. Her protests segued into throaty moans that vibrated through him. He did this to her. He turned her into this warm, sensual creature. She was his.

Grasping her ass, he lifted her and drove his tongue into her supple sheath. It immediately convulsed. He continued his jabbing thrusts, circling her clit with his thumb, while her body jerked into an orgasmic rhythm. Her muscles clenched, and she arched up into him, flooding his mouth with her heady, tangy-sweet taste.

Her pleasure entwined with his, drawing him into her sensations. Shaky with the need to be inside her, he knelt between her legs and grabbed the two-sided whip. He dragged the feather lightly over her in a path from belly to chin, taking the time to flick left and right then briefly around both her nipples. She trembled as it tickled her over-sensitized skin, and she tried to roll away from it.

Laughing, he pushed the blindfold from her eyes and gazed down at her. "You're not very good at staying still, kitten. You lost, by the way."

Her brows drew together, her ire clear in her stare. If the gag hadn't prevented it, he had a feeling her sharp little tongue would be lashing him with her thoughts of his game. Though she'd come, she was far from languid and pliant.

She pointedly slid her gaze away from him.

"None of that," he chided. "I won fair and square."

Her eyebrows shot up and her chin lowered as she looked at him in disbelief. She had an expressive face, and damned if it wasn't as sassy as that mouth of hers. She'd make his life a challenge—a very welcome challenge, too. He didn't want someone who'd kiss his feet. Maybe, his ass from time to time, but that was another thing.

"Now, I get to claim my prize."

Though he'd known he'd win, he'd been more interested in the game and hadn't decided beforehand what he wanted as a prize. He'd have to punt. "So what shall it be?"

She shrugged, but he could see the interest in her eyes. She wasn't as un-invested in the prize as she pretended to be. Good thing since, in the end, she *was* the prize.

He trailed his fingers lightly over her shoulder. "A tattoo? No? I think you'd look good with your nipple pierced. No?" He lowered his voice and let a slow, deviously pleased smile curve his lips. "Oh, I know what I want…"

Slowly, he removed the now-warm dildo. She groaned as the slight ridges caught on her tight flesh. He'd like to leave it in her longer. It wasn't flexible enough for what he wanted from her, though. Next, he removed the gag and tossed it aside. Then without a word or a hint, he turned and walked away.

* * * *

Confused, Jessica dampened her lips and watched him. He sank into one of the large wingchairs near the window. Slouching, his chin resting on his hand, he looked like an extremely bored king surveying his kingdom. A naked king. And she was his only subject.

He pointed to a spot between his sprawled legs.

"On your knees," he growled.

Her stomach fluttered, reacting to those promising words. Excited by the prospect of pleasing him in one of her favorite ways, she hurried to comply. Carefully, she knelt with knees parted and her ass resting on her ankles as she crossed her hands behind her.

"Sir," she said, head bowed as she surveyed him through her lashes. Reaching to the side, he removed a strip of brown leather from the table. Her eyes went wide as he leaned toward her.

"I want you to wear this—no speaking!" he ordered when she started to open her mouth. "You've given yourself to me, you lost our bet, and now, I'm claiming my prize. You get to be my pet."

She swallowed hard as he looped the leather around her neck and fastened it. While her body tensed and reacted to the screaming voices inside her, she tried to remain calm. She trusted him. She'd promised to give over this power to him for the time being. This was just another part of that. But he'd just put a collar on her. A collar!

Her outraged senses protested, even as she told herself this was just part of the scene. He couldn't do this. She shouldn't let him. She couldn't breathe. Could he see what this was doing to her, how terrified this simple step made her.

He tipped up her chin with two fingers. "Relax, kitten. You're mine, and I want you to know it."

She started to shake her head and he caught her with those same fingers. "No," she whispered. This was too much. She couldn't—

"Yes," he countered and leaned forward until they were eye to eye. "You. Are. Mine. I won you fair and square."

Fair?

Somehow, she managed to hold in the question. His damn game had been anything but fair and he knew it.

"Yes, Sir," she managed, though every ion of her being screamed for her to just get up and run away. That plea increased to deafening levels when he withdrew a longer strip of leather a moment later. Deftly, he fastened it to the D-ring beneath her chin.

"I wouldn't want you to run away," he explained.

She tried to swallow around the intolerable tightness closing her throat. On her knees before him, leashed and at his mercy... How many more humiliations would she endure tonight? Every time she thought she had her footing, he pushed her further. There wasn't much farther she could go before he shoved her right over the cliff of no return. Would he push her too far? They didn't even have a safe word.

Because he knew and he'd promised... Her eyes

trained on the tattoo around his biceps. *Keeper of temple, owner of the treasure, protector of the spirit...*

He wouldn't hurt her. She had to hold firm to that.

Once again, he leaned back, this time giving a gentle tug on the leash. "Now, for my prize—"

This wasn't his prize?

"I want to watch you pleasuring yourself."

Her stomach knotted. She'd never masturbated in front of anyone. She couldn't do this. Years of Midwest morality crashed down on her, reminding her of all the lectures she'd ever gotten about what good girls did and didn't do. Good girls don't touch themselves. Not that she'd ever paid attention to that. Her battery operated friends were the only stress relievers she'd had some days...before this *thing* with Ryan.

And a good girl wouldn't find herself willingly in this situation, would she? But she had.

"Wouldn't you rather I pleasure you with my mouth, Sir?"

He chuckled. "Maybe later. But that's not what I want right now."

"O...kay."

Her teeth sank into her bottom lip, and she took a deep breath. Maybe if she closed her eyes, she could pretend he wasn't here watching her. It wasn't as if he hadn't seen all of her. Hell, he'd *licked* all of her. Besides...

An erotic thrill teased her exposed cleft. This was another one of her secret fantasies—touching herself while someone else watched. Alone in the dark, she'd kicked off her blankets and thought of this as her fingers had reached for her waiting pussy.

Her lids dropped as she moved her hands from behind her back then started to slide them up her thighs.

"And you will look at me."

Damn it. So much for blocking out everything and

pretending she was alone in her room. Slowly, she raised her chin and looked up into his slumberous eyes. The bright rays of sunset glared into this part of the room, bathing them in nearly blinding light that made this all somewhat surreal and dreamlike. Ryan's gray-eyed stare seemed to glow silver—molten impassioned silver—as he stared down at her, his lust oh-so-evident.

"Start with your breasts," he rasped, leaning against the back of the chair. His cock jerked, and he reached for it, circling the wide girth with his strong fingers. Mesmerized, she watched him run his fist up and down the shaft. "Touch them in a way that arouses you."

Hesitantly, she raised her hands and cupped her breasts. Her fingers teased over the taut peaks, tracing the wrinkled areolas. Faint strands of bliss inched through her, and she sighed. Her breathing raced as her hands tightened, molding the mounds.

"Pinch them."

Raising her eyes, she met his gaze and followed his command, immediate pleasure pain streaked through her straight to her waiting womb.

"Harder."

Jess whimpered. She caught the tips between her thumb and forefinger, pinching hard. Her head tossed back, pulling at the restraint at her neck. Her strangled cry echoed around them as her hips jerked, her ass lifting away from her heels as she straightened.

"That's it," he murmured. "That's what I was waiting for. Do it again."

Pushing her breasts into her palms, she complied. Her fingers squeezed together and twisted slightly, drawing another cry. She couldn't believe she was doing this in front of him. Then…she just didn't care. Every touch was about pleasure—*their* pleasure.

"Now, touch yourself with one hand."

Immediately, she pushed her hand down her belly and into her drenched folds. She licked her lips as she watched a droplet appear on the head of his cock. She wanted to taste him the way he'd tasted her. She almost groaned in protest when he smoothed it into the flushed flesh. That pre-cum was hers.

Fine. Well, she hoped he enjoyed the show and came all over his hand. Releasing her other breast, she leaned back on one hand, going as far as she could with the leash wrapped around his fisted hand. She parted her mound with her fingers. She wanted him to see them plunging inside. But not yet.

Her hips swiveled as she rubbed her clit, the tight little knot of nerves pricking tremors along her limbs. Here it was. His dark, desire-filled stare had her so aroused it took next to nothing to bring on the tide.

Her cries came in earnest now, growing in intensity as she plowed two fingers into her channel and scraped them over her g-spot. *Oh. God. Yes.* She might have screamed it aloud as she reached deep, surging through gushing folds, but she wasn't sure.

Suddenly, he yanked on the leash pulling her toward him before her release could fully take her.

"Come here," he commanded roughly, half dragging her as she scrambled to comply. Her legs shuddered, barely holding her. Ryan lifted her onto his lap, draping one of her legs over the armrest, while the other sprawled toward the floor. He steadied her with an arm behind her back. She clasped his knee and continued to work her slippery passage, since he hadn't told her to stop. Her head turned into his shoulder as she moaned. This entire scene sent fire leaping through her veins. She'd never felt quite so decadent or sensual.

Leaving the leash dangling down her chest and between her legs, he grabbed her hand and pulled it to his lips. He stared into her eyes while he sucked the juice from her fingers. His tongue worked between them, drinking in every drop of nectar.

"I want to see you come," he told her. "Can you come with your fingers?"

"Sometimes," she answered, her voice a husky shadow of normal. Right now, she was sure she could find her release by looking into his eyes alone. They seemed to stare straight to her core and make love to her with just their sultry, knowing look.

He reached into a drawer in the table beside them, where he'd had the collar, and removed a vibrator with an extra protrusion to stimulate her clit. It seemed similar to hers at home. This was almost familiar territory. Oh baby, she could definitely come with this!

He handed it to her. "Use this."

Without waiting for her to start, he caught up the leash, wrapping the excess length around his hand before he gripped her thigh to hold her legs wide. His cock knocked persistently at her hip. He'd grown more aroused while he'd watched her performance, and she felt the damp evidence painting her skin. She wanted to forget the vibrator, turn to straddle him and sink onto his burning-hot erection. The toy was great, but it was nothing compared to wrapping around a real man and touching all that warm skin.

She couldn't turn, though. He held her tight in his firm grip, and he'd commanded something else. It was her duty to comply, no matter her desire.

Breathing shallowly, she pushed the vibrator slowly inside her pussy and flicked the switch to the lowest setting. A steady pulse worked across her cleft. Mmm…yeah. This was good. A deep groan rasped up her throat. Losing herself in the sensation, she rocked the vibe in and out of her clenching sheath pretending it was his cock again.

"Turn it higher." He sounded…breathless. Was this turning him on as much as her?

"Yes, Sir," she gasped as she obediently followed his wish. She was really getting into this D/s thing. "Oh!"

Jess' cries crescendoed as she surrendered to the toy. The pounding vibrations raked over her. It was too much. She had to pull it away; she couldn't take more.

Ryan's hand trapped hers, holding the vibrator in place.

"Take it," he grated.

"I can't. I can't!" Her body twisted, straining for more, trying to escape. Heat swept through her as she writhed. Sharp, almost painful tremors gripped her entire body as she screamed her climax, knowing he really would shove her over that cliff of no return. She'd never recover from this.

"You can." His mouth covered hers, capturing her keening wails from the strongest orgasm she'd ever experienced splintering through her. Her jerks almost threw her from his lap, but he held her firm and kept her safe. His tongue attacked hers with claiming ferocity while she twisted and wrapped her free arm around his neck.

She barely felt him move as he stood and strode to the bed with her in his arms. He yanked the toy from her clasping body and tossed it aside. Immediately, he replaced it with his cock, stretching her wider, slamming even deeper, each ridge from his piercings torturing her over-sensitized folds. Trapping her hands over her head, he again caught her gaze. "Mine," he repeated with each upstroke. "Mine, mine, mine…"

She struggled to meet him each time, until he slowed. "Yours," she replied on a breathless whisper. "Yours. I'm yours."

"I intended to take my time this round," he said against her neck while he sucked at her pulse. "You're so damned hot!"

"I've never been so hot before," she managed. Each excruciatingly long slide took forever, and her urgent movements weren't fulfilled. Like this, the slow thrusts emphasized his girth as he parted her clutching tissues. On each measured stroke, her body closed then had to readjust as he returned. Her belly tightened, readying for the new release coiling inside her womb.

"Don't come yet," he whispered, trailing his mouth to her breast. He sucked the peak deep inside his mouth. His tongue rasped over the hardened nipple.

And she wasn't supposed to come? How the hell?

She tried to draw her focus away from her pussy and the exquisite sensation of his cock plunging in and out of it. Away from the deep draws of his wicked mouth on her nipples. Away from... *Oh God!*

Work. She still had, uh, *work*, yes work, waiting at home for her. Reports...lots and lots of—

Oh, fuck, he felt so good!

She panted trying to hold off—

"Now, Jessica!"

"Yes!" She exploded around him, clamping down on his cock and hampering his continued digging thrusts.

"So...tight..." he grunted through his teeth. With one deep stab, he rolled, pulling her to straddle him. Fighting through her release, she rode him, the leash slapping against her chest as he grasped her hips. Reaching up, he wrapped it around one of her breasts then kept the end in his hand as he reclaimed his grip at her waist.

She glanced down at the black leather, surprised at how aroused she was to be his slave for the moment. Totally his to control and direct. She didn't have to prove herself to him. She only needed to obey and react. Gazing down at the fire burning in Ryan's eyes, she knew she'd pleased him. She almost heard the clank as the chains of discontent that had bound her for so long fell away. Freedom. Because she was his.

"Thank you," she whispered, unable to articulate everything she was feeling even when he tilted his head, waiting for her to clarify what she was thanking him for. Leaning forward, she brushed her lips over his and rode him with everything in her. She wanted him to explode as hard as she had, and in that, she was giving him the gift of herself, everything she had. She wouldn't tell him yet, but her decision was pretty much made. She wanted him. She wanted *this*. For as long as it lasted.

Tremors immediately started through her as the angle hit her hot spot, setting her off. Adjusting, she kept on, unwilling to slow before he found his pleasure, too. In moments, his fingers tightened, and he shoved her up and down on his shaft with more force. She might be on top, but he was in control. She sat up, palming her breast as he worked her.

"Oh, yes. Oh…fuck…kitten. I'm…oh—"

He surged up into her with a ragged bellow, banging into her trigger point. Jessica let go, riding the riptide pulling through her. They both froze, captivated by the moment as they tried to catch their breath. Captured in this moment, she knew she could stay here forever.

Gently, he tugged her down into his embrace. His lips feathered over hers. She couldn't stop her smile as she gazed at him, pure happiness and contentment flooding through her. This was where she belonged—here, in Ryan's embrace.

"Well done, love."

She snuggled into him, pleased with herself, pleased to be in his arms, pleased that she'd satisfied him. With that knowledge came a sense of power that surprised her.

This was what they meant—part of it anyway. This was a submissive's power.

A buzz broke into her scattered, muzzy thoughts, but she focused on the mixed sensations of his formidable arms holding her as if he'd never let go and the slight possessive pull at her neck. His lips pressed to her hair. She must look a mess by now. She couldn't rouse enough energy to even care.

Her brow furrowed as the buzz went on then she laughed.

"Ryan, I think the vibrator's screwing the floor." She couldn't help her giggles as absolute giddiness filled her spirit. Today had sucked, but right now, she didn't think she could be happier.

Chapter Fourteen

Jessica woke slowly, disoriented by the light shining in her eyes. Where the heck was she? She blinked then squinched open one eye. Mmm...yeah. She was in Ryan's bed. They hadn't closed the shades last night and morning light flooded through the large windows. She bit her lip. She loved the pure sunlight. It had always filled her with so much happiness. Probably because her childhood had seemed so...dreary. It was likely a mood, rather than a true occurrence, but it still colored her memories.

She wouldn't think of that now. She'd rather think of better things...like last night. After their game, she'd slipped on Ryan's button-down shirt and he'd pulled on a well-worn pair of jeans. Together, they'd gone downstairs and made dinner. Good food, good wine, good company... After eating, they'd curled up on his large couch again and cuddled while watching a movie, though there'd been a lot more kissing and touching—everywhere—than there'd been actually movie viewing. She wasn't sure it had even finished when Ryan had gathered her into his arms and carried her back up here to his enormous bed where he'd made sweet, oh-so-tender love to her before they'd collapsed together, breathing heavily from the power of it—both emotional and physical. How was it possible that that he touched her soul with each touch, every whispered or growled command, all his sweet nothings spoken into her heart? God, she was falling hard for that man.

Speaking of… Usually, he was wrapped around her while they slept. Stretching, she found herself alone, the sheets where he'd been were cool. Where was he? Pushing up on her elbows, she scanned the room and listened for any sign of him. Nothing. Of course, with the size of this house and the quality of the construction, it was unlikely that sound would travel far. Still, he clearly wasn't in the next room taking a shower. Another glace showed it was a few minutes past six. Ugh! Time to get up. She collapsed back into the mattress, feeling lethargic. There was something in that man's DNA that drugged her whenever they had sex. Getting up the next morning always seemed impossible.

With another groan, she rolled toward the side of the bed and forced herself to her feet. Staggering a little, she headed for his magnificent bathroom and the shower that could accommodate a dozen, rather than just her—though, she and Ryan had used the space quite effectively last time they were here together. She sighed as she remembered the sensation of his hands and mouth on her as multiple shower heads had pulsed against her body. She'd been overwhelmed by unbelievable pleasure by the time he'd slid into her body and taken her over the edge into oblivion.

Geez…if she kept up this way, she'd be late for work. Master Ryan wouldn't like that—especially since he'd need to drive her and they needed to stop at her house so she had something to wear into the office. She grinned at her irreverent titling of him this morning. Yes, he was *Master Ryan* but she doubted she'd ever call him that with a straight face—not outside the dungeon at Pleasure Palace. Still, the knowledge that they had a lot awaiting them this morning before even going into the office propelled her into action. First, she had to get clean then she needed to search out her clothes from yesterday, though the thought of putting on the same underwear for a second day running made her cringe. She grinned. So she'd skip them. Problem solved.

She had washed her hair and was running her hands over her body, sudsing up with the unisex, citrus body wash she'd found on the shower's shelf when a second pair of hands started sliding over her skin, too. Lips nibbled at her neck and she tilted her head to give him better access.

"Mmm, good morning," she murmured then gasped as he cupped her breasts and plucked at her nipples. "I missed you when I woke up."

"I went for a run then started coffee and mixed up stuff for breakfast. Just need to cook it when we get downstairs."

"Overachiever," she teased.

"Got to take care of my woman."

A deep, throaty sound of pleasure answered him as she melted against him, letting him have his way. He guided her to the seat built into the side of the enclosure. With his hand between her shoulder blades, he urged her to bend.

"Brace your hands, baby."

"Yes, Sir," she breathed. She expected him to surge into her, but instead, he ran his hands over her ass then down her thighs. Glancing back, she watched him crouch and slide his palms to her ankles. Circling them, he pulled her feet farther apart and didn't let go.

Jessica screamed as his mouth pressed into her folds, his lips unerringly finding her clit and drawing. He licked and nipped until her legs wobbled and he didn't let up even then. The angle seemed so much more illicit than when he went down on her while she lay on her back spread open for him. And the sensation… Her back arched as the lightning spiked through her pelvis and into her thighs. Her fingers clenched on the seat and she wondered how long she'd be able to hold on to the smooth surface, slippery from condensation.

"Ry…I'm…I'm…gonna…Oh!" Her arms buckled then she found herself half-lying across the seat, panting as he continued holding her open, devouring her with that devilish mouth. Already, another orgasm built on the last. She'd never survive this man.

"I love you…I love you…" she whisper-chanted. "I love you…oh…*God*!" Changing positions, lifting her feet right off the floor to accommodate him, he plunged into her.

"Mine. You're mine, kitten," he growled through his teeth.

Was there even a question? "Yes," she cried, bracing her arms against the wall at the back of the seat to give herself leverage while he fucked her. "Yes, I'm yours. Only yours."

"Fuck, yeah, you're only mine. Fuck…baby. You feel so good," he groaned. To her surprise, he pulled out.

"No," she protested in displeasure.

"Hang on. Just hang on." He tugged her up into his arms then pressed her against the wall. Her legs circled his waist, welcoming him, holding him to her as he thrust inside her pussy again. He covered her mouth with his, drinking in her jubilant cry as his hips began their pummeling rhythm. She tasted herself on his lips and it drove her wild, knowing it was there because of the constant pleasure and attraction between them, because he lusted for her—for every part of her—as much as she did him.

"Fuck," he swore again as she started to tighten around his girth, squeezing his release from him as waves of release erupted through her again. With one last, deep drive, he lost himself in her. Afterward, he leaned against her, panting into her neck as she kept her arms and legs firmly around him, hugging him with her whole being. She never wanted this intimacy between them to end.

"I love you, kitten," he murmured into her skin before he kissed that spot with a light sucking-licking caress. "Never doubt that. I fucking love you. Forever."

She grinned, feeling forever—a forever she never dreamed—looming ahead of her. "I fucking love you forever, too."

* * * *

Ryan watched Jessica sipping her coffee. They'd finished the French toast, scrambled eggs and mixed fruit he'd prepared and now sat together in the breakfast nook that overlooked the backyard. Unaware he was admiring her, she watched the deer and two fawns that frequently ate from the bushes in his yard. If they didn't get moving they'd be late for work, but he couldn't bear to interrupt this moment. It was the peaceful moments like this that assured him this chemistry between them wouldn't flash out. They worked well together. They fucked well together. They relaxed well together.

As a submissive, Jessica pleased him, but to his surprise, that was the least of his attraction to her. Yeah, her lush body made him hard at every turn. Her curves drove him mad, and the thought of anyone else touching her… He took a sip of his coffee to keep in his growl. He'd kill any fucker who tried to take what was his. That violent realization both startled him and frightened him a bit. He'd never been this…obsessed with any other woman. Submissives and women came and went with little care on his part. In the past relationships were just fucking and sexual pleasures, not this full picture opening before him as he got in deeper with Jessica.

After their shower, she'd slipped on his shirt again, mentioning that she wanted the freedom from her work clothes just a bit longer.

As if reading his thought she turned toward him, her long, curling hair, sweeping around her shoulders. "We need to start moving so we can stop at my place. I'm not wearing the same clothes to work as yesterday. That's way too much like a walk of shame."

"Ashamed of me?"

She snorted. "You know I'm not."

Good. He wanted the world to know they were together. He wanted to make it clear far and wide that she was *his*, but he had to respect her limitations. Decision day was tomorrow. Her yes or no on the relationship. All signs pointed to yes, but he still felt as if he walked a tightrope. Would he make a misstep and plummet into a life without her? The possibility felt as ominous as death. Probably, a little melodramatic, but she made him feel melodramatic and willing to do anything to keep her.

"Would it completely freak you out if I had clothes here for you to wear?"

"Are you trying to tell me you're a crossdresser?"

He gave her a look.

"Okay, not that. I'm fine with it, I guess. Knowing you, you were anticipating something like this morning happening. Am I right?"

"Yeah."

"And these are clothes I can wear to work? Not something Pleasure Palace-y."

"Completely work appropriate. Promise," he confirmed. This was going better than he'd expected. He'd anticipated a fight or irritation on her part.

"You don't have special lotion you want me to put on or something."

"Do I need to get out the hose?" God, he loved this woman.

"I like your hose."

"Unfortunately, *that* we don't have time for. I have a meeting this morning at eight-thirty. You may have heard of it, since you're supposed to attend."

She laughed, getting up from the table then rinsing her cup and placing it in the dishwasher where she'd already put their breakfast dishes. "It's not like they can have the meeting without you. I'm sure people would welcome one less meeting."

"Are you saying we have too many meetings?"

"I wouldn't dare!"

"Brat. C'mon. I'll show you the clothes and you can pick what you want."

"More than one thing to pick from? Now, you're getting creepy," she teased.

He glanced at his imaginary watch. "I'm sure we still have time for a spanking."

Laughing, she dashed out of the kitchen then jogged up the steps. "You need to catch me first."

Running after her, he scooped her up halfway up the stairs and carried her into the bedroom. She was giggling as he sank onto the edge of the bed and turned her over his lap. He yanked up the tail of the shirt to expose her bare ass. His hand clapped down on the firm flesh. She cried out as he watched red blood on her skin.

"More?" he asked. "Does my naughty girl need

more?"

"More," she gasped, her love of spankings so evident. She was just so…fucking…perfect. His cock grew hard, wanting to fuck her while she was on her knees, her well-spanked ass in the air. Hell, he would be in agony all morning.

His hand clapped down on her rear a few more times. These weren't playful strikes; he didn't go easy on her, knowing that wasn't what she wanted or what she required. His kitten wanted to feel him today.

"Sir," she cried, and he knew she was nearing her edge. Every blow was turning to pure pleasure and dragging her nearer and nearer to climax. If he stopped and reached down, he just knew he'd find her drenched with her arousal.

Grinning, he smacked her bright-red ass once more, this time keeping the strike much lighter. He followed it with another much lighter still. If he was walking around rock-hard, she wasn't coming. *Lessons, kitten. Lessons.* It would make tonight—or maybe lunchtime—even more explosive.

She looked up at him in confusion as he slid her to her knees before him. Without a word or explanation he got up and headed for the closet.

"Come," he threw over his shoulder then added with a point, "here."

He wasn't looking at her but clearly heard her frustrated sigh.

"Yes, Sir," she ground out.

He cupped her head, tangling his fingers in her hair, once she stood beside him. His lips pressed to her temple. "I promise, you'll come hard later. But now…let's get dressed. We need to leave in fifteen minutes, if we're going get there anywhere near eight."

"Okay," she whispered with grudging understanding.

"Who's in control, baby?"

Her lips pursed and her face squinched as she looked away, clearly fighting to keep a snarky retort from escaping. "You are," she finally said.

"Right. Now, here. There are a few things for you." He pointed toward the back of the walk-in where five dresses hung then indicated the built-in drawers in the shelving beside them. "There are a couple pairs of panties and bras in the drawer there. I only picked up a few things, since I figured you'd rather choose your own things. We can go shopping over the weekend."

She glanced at him with her brow furrowed. "I…have clothes, nice clothes, at home."

He drew her close and kissed her again. "I know, kitten, but I like buying things for you. A woman can never have too many clothes, right?"

"I don't know about that…"

She wasn't frivolous and didn't have a new outfit every day of the month, and he liked that about her. She had quality things, but from what he'd observed, didn't go overboard. Just one more things she was pragmatic about, but he wanted to pamper her.

When she didn't move, he cupped her face and tipped his forehead to hers, looking into her eyes. "Let me spoil you. It makes me happy."

And that was the key word: happy. She wanted to please him. It was intrinsic to her make up, and he knew he was playing a little dirty to use it against her.

She bit her plump bottom lip and nodded. "Yes, Sir."

* * * *

Jessica gathered her long hair into one hand and lifted it off her neck as she stared at her computer. She wasn't used to wearing her hair down—it seemed far too unruly when it wasn't constrained with clips and pins and out of her way—but Ryan had specifically requested she wear it down for him. He loved the way it curled down her back, especially when he buried his hands in it while he kissed her—or whatever he was up to at any given moment when they were getting intimate.

Her body still buzzed from their encounter this morning—their unfinished encounter, damn him! And every time she moved, she remembered his hands on her, how she'd almost come, how she'd been teetering on the edge when he'd stopped and put her on her knees. If she didn't know it was expressly forbidden and that somehow, she didn't know how, he'd figure it out, she'd just take herself down to the restroom and finish business.

While it might help in the moment, though, the idea seemed hollow. She wanted Ryan with her. She'd thought he might come in and share "lunch" with her, but he'd been called into a meeting with his father and Theo that was supposed to last until mid-afternoon. The company was branching out, developing new properties rather than just contracting out to other businesses, and the trio left the premises this morning to visit some properties they were looking at utilizing.

Just as well. She needed to run out to get her prescription refilled or Ryan would need to sheathe-up before playing. She didn't imagine that plan would make him happy. Maybe, she'd stop by Victoria's Secret while she was out and find him some sexy lingerie to enjoy— while she was wearing it, of course. As much as she'd teased him earlier, Ryan was man through and through and she couldn't picture him in anything the least bit girly—well, not without giggling like crazy, anyway.

Quickly, she finished rereading the police report filed against Clive. When the authorities caught up with him, he'd certainly need a lawyer. With only a few of the properties surveyed, they were at nearly a half million in fraud and theft. Another stab of guilt shot through her, but she tried to remind herself he'd pulled the wool over more eyes than just hers. Thank God, she wouldn't need to deal with him ever again, unless she had to testify against him. Even then she wouldn't have direct contact with him.

She closed her computer and gathered her purse. It was a little after lunch hour, so maybe, she could get in and out of the pharmacy quickly. As she headed out, she let Glenna know she might be a little longer than an hour then headed out to where she'd left her car yesterday. Time for a little shopping. Tonight, she planned to get him worked up with her wispy lingerie then whisper her future intentions to Ryan while he was busy fucking her. She planned to say yes to submitting to him, to kneeling before him, to letting him command her. She was his.

* * * *

"Hello, bitch."

Jessica's blood ran cold at the growled words. She'd just opened her car door and tossed her Victoria's Secret bags into the backseat. She'd been smiling, deep in thought about Ryan's reaction to the scraps she'd picked up, when the nasty greeting had been spat at her.

Closing the door, she turned toward the man who'd made her life hell the past week. Obviously, he'd followed her.

"Clive." She wanted to look around and see if anyone else was in the lot. The mall wasn't busy this time of day during the workweek, but it wasn't deserted by any means. "What do you want?"

He shrugged a shoulder, leering at her. "My pound of flesh? Some of what that Cress prick is getting? How much cash does it take for you to spread your legs?"

Her mouth dropped open in outrage. Fear turned her skin to ice as she backed away, but there was nowhere to go. She'd parked at the edge of the parking lot. A cement barrier and a hell of a drop off blocked her escape. Could she go over the hood of her car, get a running start before he came after her on that side?

"Because I've got money, probably more than enough for a whore like you."

"Stolen money," she retorted before she thought better of it.

That gave him pause. For a second. "You know about that, huh? Does it really matter to you how I got rich?"

He pressed closer, trapping her against the car when she tried to move away. His heavily muscled, tattooed arms caged her in. His hot, alcohol-laden breath filled her face as she shrank back from him. There was nowhere to go.

She shoved against him, and desperately wondered if she could get to one of the heels she wore and bash him with it. Could she get in a good hit before he stopped her? She had to try.

"Get away from me, Clive!"

He grabbed the collar of her dress and jerked her forward as she tried to reach for her shoe. Though he didn't seem to notice, but with one leg lifted, she was dragged off balance and thrown into him. He didn't budge, and she thought she might vomit from the proximity. He hadn't showered anytime recently. The strong alcohol smell had masked it somewhat before, but close up… She fought back from him. Just as quickly as he'd yanked her forward, he slammed her backward into the car.

Her head collided with the vehicles frame. Stars flew before her eyes, and she did the only thing she could. She screamed—she tried to anyway. Like a nightmare, her throat had closed and as hard as she tried to force a yell through it, there was nothing but a croak. Desperately, she fought him, shoving, hitting, clawing, anything she could to get free.

"Thing is," he panted as he continued slamming her, "I don't want to fuck you, bitch. I want to kill you."

Her vision blurred. Everything was going gray… She tasted blood. Her struggles weakened, but she refused to stop. If she stopped, he would kill her.

"Help!" she screamed again, the sound stronger this time, but it wasn't soon enough. She felt herself fading, her body feeling both hot and cold at the same time, and the pain. So much pain.

"Hey!" she heard as the world faded. Her last impression was falling as two dark figures rushed toward her.

Chapter Fifteen

Where the fuck was she?

Ryan was rapidly going insane. Ominous, hollow dread ravaged his gut. Something was wrong. Very wrong.

"Is she back? Have you heard from her?" he demanded.

Glenna shook her head. "Nothing. She had a meeting with Rockford Paving at four, but never showed."

It was a few minutes after five. "Are you sure she didn't say where she was going?"

"She just said she might be a few minutes late coming back." Glenna wrinkled her brown and looked away, as if she'd thought of something but wasn't sure whether or not to speak.

"What?" he demanded, not caring that he was being a crazed dick. "Just spit it out."

"Ryan..." Theo cautioned. He'd been glued to Ryan since they'd figured out Jessica was missing. Concern shown in his eyes, reflecting the worry Ryan felt.

"Do you..." Glenna stopped and took a breath,

seeming to gather herself. "Do you think she'd just…quit? With no notice?"

"No. Why would you ask that?"

"Well…"

God, this hesitant woman would be the death of him. Ryan bit back another demand. He knew he was scaring her. He'd been on a tear for the past few hours, ever since he'd been unable to reach or find Jessica. If anything had happened to her…

Jesus. He couldn't even consider it.

"Yesterday," Glenna finally said. "She got a phone call from Sissek Construction."

"Do you know why?"

She shook her head. "Jessica didn't say."

Jess hadn't mentioned anything about them to him, either. That bothered him. Why was their competition contacting one of his Project Managers?

He turned to Theo. "Have you talked to Keera? Has she seen Jess?"

Theo gave him a look, as if to ask, "and when do you think I would have talked to her. I've been with you." Keera was in a seminar off-site today and had her phone turned off. Still, Jess' best friend was Ryan's best hope right now.

"I left her a message and asked her to call me immediately when the class is over. Should be any minute—" His phone rang, cutting him off. "There she is now." He took several steps away from Glenna's desk in order to gain some privacy but Ryan stayed at his shoulder.

"Hey, baby," Theo answered.

Ryan heard Keera's cheerful, tinkling voice come over the line, though he couldn't hear her actual words.

"That, too," Theo said, leading Ryan to guess Keera had asked something about Theo missing her. "Look, have you heard from Jessica."

There was a long pause then he heard Keera speak again, the tone completely different.

"No, he didn't do anything," Theo replied. "She left for lunch, told Glenna she might be a few minutes late but never came back."

This time, Keera's panicked response of *What!* was clear then she started a torrent of words Ryan couldn't quite pick out.

"Baby, calm down," Theo cut in. "I'm sure she's fine and there's a reasonable explanation for this. Are you...somewhere safe?"

He nodded while he listened.

"I'm going back to my office," Ryan growled. "Maybe, she left a message while I was gone." He was about to call the police, but he wasn't so sure how far he'd get with that.

His assistant was gone when he got to his work suite, probably on her way home since it was quarter after now. When he got to his desk, his phone flashed with a message. Hopeful, he dialed in, but disappointment came moments later. It was the contact from the health club chain. Important, but not as important as other things right now.

Fuck! Where was she? He took a few deep breaths to calm down and dialed her home phone, listening to it ring until her voicemail kicked on. Hanging up, he dialed her cell with the same results.

"Ryan," his dad said from the doorway as he rapped on the doorframe with his knuckles. Concern shown in his eyes. Word of Jessica's absence and Ryan's reaction had obviously flown to all levels of the company. So much for keeping this relationship a secret—fuck that anyway. And he'd never had any intention of keeping from his family. They all knew. Now, all the employees probably would soon, as well.

"Dad," he replied.

"Have you heard from her?"

Ryan shook his head, and Declan nodded as if expecting that answer. How could he not? Ryan was sure every bit of his being screamed that he was completely freaked out.

"I made some calls," Declan said, coming farther into the room. He held out a piece of paper torn off a notepad. "This is the number for Detective Ian Fillion with the local PD. He's in the sect."

That would explain the phone calls. His dad had called the Keeper of the Records to find someone connected to them that they could call. Someone who'd help them when it wasn't necessarily "policy" of the law enforcement.

"Thank you," he said, feeling a bit of relief and able to take a deep breath for the first time in hours. His chest was still overly tight, panicked, but there was...hope...again.

"Let me know when you hear anything. I'm heading home to your mom, but I'll keep my cell beside me."

Ryan nodded. He'd seen the need before, it being common in the sect. Whenever something like this happened, something bad the Dom could envision happening to him or to his sub, the innate desire to be with his sub was unquenchable. It was the bond between them, even stronger than that of mere marriage. The symbiotic connection unified the sub and Dom in a way unparalleled by anything else. Ryan felt it already with Jessica. No doubt, Theo would be at Keera's side as soon as possible, too—of course, that would have happened anyway. Theo had it bad for her. Ryan was surprised his brother hadn't collared her yet, though Theo claimed it would be soon.

As soon as his dad exited Ryan's office, Ryan picked up his phone. Quickly, he jabbed in the numbers written on the paper.

"Detective Fillion," the man answered.

"Ian Fillion?" Ryan clarified to be sure.

"Yes."

"This is Ryan Cress. I'm from—"

"The sect," the man finished. "I recognize your name. What's going on?"

A succinctly as he could, Ryan explained what was happening, each word rousing his worry once more.

"Okay, hang on," Fillion said.

Ryan heard him typing, no doubt accessing the department's system and looking to see if there was a record of anything happening. God, Ryan prayed not. While he wanted to find her, and *now*, he couldn't bear the thought of her hurt…or worse.

Fillion made an unhappy, thinking sound, and Ryan gritted his teeth to keep from pouncing on it.

"Does Ms. Rush have any family nearby?" the detective asked.

"No, she estranged from them. She just has her best friend, those here at work, me and my family."

"And you're…"

Ryan didn't hesitate to answer since Ian was in his alternative community. "Her Dom. And her boyfriend." In the lifestyle, the two things were occasionally exclusive from one another, and he wanted it clear he and Jessica shared the whole picture—at least, he hoped they did. Tomorrow was still decision day…

"Okay. Can you meet me at Faith Community Health downtown?"

"The hospital? What happened to her?" Ryan was already on his feet and running for the door. Theo spotted him and was on Ryan's heels as Ryan listened.

"I don't have all the details, but I'll get them by the time you meet me. The initial report is that she was attacked. I may have some questions for you."

Which meant he was a suspect…or a possible person of interest…or whatever the current fucking buzzword being used was. "Fine. I'll answer anything you need. Is she…" He swallowed, feeling as if his insides were being ripped out. "How bad is she?"

"I don't know yet. She was unconscious when she was transported."

No…baby, you've got to be okay.

"I'll meet you there. I'm about fifteen minutes away."

"I'll meet you in the front lobby."

"Thanks." Ryan turned to Theo as he hung up. His brother had his phone to his ear. Obviously, he'd called Keera or one of their parents when he'd seen Ryan on the run. "She's at the hospital," Ryan told him. "Someone attacked her while she was out. The detective couldn't tell me anything else…except she was unconscious when they took her there."

Oh God…someone had attacked her. She'd been alone all this time. He couldn't get to her fast enough.

Theo finished relaying the information then shoved the phone in his pocket. He grabbed Ryan's arm. "C'mon. I'll drive. You're too worked up."

"I'm fine."

"No, you're not. You don't need to end up in the hospital, too. Jessica needs you."

His older brother was right. "I have to call Mom and Dad," he muttered.

"Keera's doing it."

Theo circled to the driver's side of his Beemer, clicking his fob to unlock the doors for them as he walked. Moments later, they were speeding down the street toward the hospital.

Detective Fillion met them in the lobby. He looked between Ryan and Theo and accurately determined which brother was Ryan. Ryan figured it was probably because he looked about ready to lose his shit.

Fillion held up a hand to stop questions. "She's okay. I haven't been up to see her, and they're still waiting for her to be fully conscious. She's bruised and has a concussion, but otherwise, they say she's okay. He was slamming her against the vehicle, but she escaped without neck or spine damage. The doctor I spoke with says Ms. Rush will be able to go home today, if she regains consciousness soon,."

"But she's got a concussion."

"Bro, they send people home the day after heart surgery. C'mon..." Theo remind him.

Right. Okay... Ryan wanted Jessica safe at home and in his arms anyway.

"Where was she? When this happened, I mean?"

"At the Vistaview mall. There were a couple witnesses. Two teenage boys ran in when they saw what the attacker was doing. They got a good look and were able to describe him as muscular and tattooed." He touched his arm where he would have a similar tattoo to Ryan and Theo. "You can understand my hesitation about this until I saw you."

"I would never harm her!" Ryan exclaimed.

Fillion didn't reassure him, but of course, he wouldn't know the full nature of Ryan and Jessica's relationship. He wouldn't know if Ryan was a complete sadistic asshole. People fell through the cracks, even in the sect. Sanctions could be made, but good behavior wasn't a guarantee.

"We got them with an artist and have a sketch." He gave a grim smile. "You don't match."

"Can I see it?"

"Yes. You might be able to help us with this." He pulled out a tablet then opened an app. A moment later, he flipped the display to show the brothers. Ryan's eyes widened, and he glanced at Theo.

Fuck.

"You know this man?" the detective asked.

"Yeah. Clive Honeycutt. He was fired off one of Jessica's projects on Tuesday. We've since filed a police report and criminal charges have been brought up for theft."

"We'll be adding assault to that. The kids mentioned him yelling about murdering her, but the DA's office will need to decide on the level of charges."

"Can I see her?" Ryan asked. He wanted Clive put away, but he needed to be with his woman. He needed to touch her, to reassure himself.

"Yeah. Like I said, I already talked to her doctor. I'm sure she'll be back in to see Ms. Rush and talk to you soon." He gave Ryan directions to the room. When Ryan turned to Theo, Theo shook his head.

"I want to talk to the detective for a minute. Keera's on her way, too. I'll wait for her out here."

With a nod, Ryan headed toward Jessica's room, feeling both relieved and sickened by the situation. His worry had dissipated slightly, but not enough to be comfortable.

As he entered, he found her lying motionless on the hospital bed. She still wore the red dress she'd put on that morning, but now, it was ripped, the neckline gaping and showing her bra. For some reason, they hadn't changed her into a gown, and it seemed odd to him, but whatever… Looking around, he spied her purse and shoes in a bag in the corner of the room.

"Jessica, kitten," he said softly, stumbling toward her. God, she was so still. His only comfort was the gentle rise and fall of chest. Her lip was swollen, and mottled color ran up the right side of her head. From what Fillion had described, most of the damage from the attack would be to her posterior anyway.

Rage sizzled inside him as he gazed at her. He tried to push it down and maintain a cool demeanor, not wanting her to see murder in his eyes when she woke. But if Clive Honeycutt were before him, the man would be dead.

Taking her hand, he ran his thumb along her skin and noticed the bruising on her knuckles and fingers. Several of her carefully kept nails were broken. His girl had put up a hell of a fight. Glancing over at the hand that rested on her abdomen, he noticed the same damage. That arm had an IV needle in it.

Gently, he touched her face then dropped a kiss on her forehead. "I love you, baby. You're safe now. I'll take care of you." Straightening, he reached over and adjusted her dress to fully cover her chest. "I'll take care of you," he repeated. "You have my sacred vow." He leaned his forehead on her shoulder, barely able to breathe through the terror and rage warring inside him.

She was his treasure. His to protect.

"Mr. Cress." Startled, he looked up to meet the perusal of a tall, blonde woman just entering the hospital room. "Detective Fillion told me you were on your way. I'm Dr. Manning. I've been treating your...submissive," she told him, adding the last sotto voce. Ah...so she was in the community, as well. He was always surprised to find how widespread the sect really was.

"My girlfriend," he added.

She nodded and closed the door to give them privacy. "Ms. Rush has been under my observation since arriving. While she's been shaken up, we didn't note more than mild brain trauma, caused by the attack. The CT scan didn't reveal anything of major concern. When she's ready to go, I'll prescribe some medication for pain and nausea. You may find that she displays some disorientation, nausea, vomiting, dizziness, temporary optical distortion, ringing in the ears. She'll probably want to sleep a lot, and that's okay. Just keep a watchful eye on her. At the far end of the spectrum, she may have some memory loss, but we won't know the extent of her symptoms until she wakes."

"Why isn't she awake?" The list of possible problems was overwhelming, but no matter what Jessica woke to, he wasn't leaving her side.

"Partly, the medication." She nodded toward the IV. "Partly, because her body's been through a trauma. She's not ready to come back fully. I don't expect she'll be under much longer. She was conscious, on-and-off, for short periods earlier, but never long enough for us to get any real information from her—like who to contact. Is your first name Ryan?"

"Yes."

"She was asking for you, but we didn't know how to contact you."

He made a face. "I'm putting my name in her phone as *contact in case of emergency*."

"Good idea. So...she needs to take it easy for a couple days. No screens. They just irritate the recovery process. That would be no phones, tablet, TV, movies and the like. Especially, no video games, though, I guess that might not be her thing."

"No, they're not."

"She should relax and limit her interaction with other people—nothing to over-stimulate her brain. And in your case...no *play* for a few days, at least. Definitely nothing that would have her in an odd position or have her head below her heart. Got me?"

"Got it," he replied. Did she think he was an idiot? He

was more likely to wrap Jessica in a bubble.

Dr. Manning peered at him, her eyes narrowing as if reading his thoughts. "And after a few days, don't try to coddle her. Doms like you seem to be cut from the same cloth. You're freaked and want to wrap her in cotton wool. Don't. It's the last thing she'll want. Let her take the lead and let you know what she feels up to."

"Noted. Thank you. I appreciate the advice." He looked at Jessica. "You're right. I'm freaked out."

"Not surprising, seeing as your *treasure* was attacked by some madman."

"I'll keep her safe."

"I don't doubt it." She reached into her coat pocket and drew out a business card. "I've written my cell number on the back of this. If you or anyone else in our circumstance need a doctor or if you have questions about Ms. Rush after you've left the hospital, please call me. I'll be back to check on her in a bit."

Before he could thank her, Dr. Manning turned on her heel and left the room.

Deflating, he sank into the chair beside the bed. Taking, Jess' hand in his, he leaned his head against the side of the bed and waited.

"Ry?"

He looked up to find his brother and Keera.

"How is she?"

Ryan shrugged, standing. Though he hadn't done this to her, there was nothing he could do to fix it either. He felt defeated and helpless. He needed to do something, but there was nothing he could do but be here for his woman. Quickly, quietly, he relayed the doctor's information, leaving out the bits about the play. While his brother and Keera practiced the same, he didn't find it necessary to relay that part of Dr. Manning's cautions.

Tears streamed down Keera's cheeks as she gazed at

Jessica. "You're sure she's okay?"

"They did tests. I fucking hate that she's not awake, but they assure me she's all right and will recover fine." Hopefully, she hadn't lost her memory of him. In the whole scheme of things, he knew that was selfish, but he couldn't stand the idea of her not knowing him and the love between them.

Theo pulled Keera in to his chest. His hand cupped the back of her head as she buried her face in his shirt. "Shh, baby. Jess'll be okay. Hush now."

He met Ryan's gaze, and Ryan saw the same raw emotions there that assailed him. Clive could have just as easily come after Keera since Theo had been the axe and Keera the personnel supervisor overseeing Clive's termination.

"The police have a video from the mall's surveillance. It didn't have the best shot of his face, so the sketch confirms the identity. It was definitely Clive. I've seen him enough times to recognize him."

"You saw…the attack?"

Theo closed his eyes momentarily then glanced down at Keera before meeting Ryan's stare again. He gave a single nod, his ashen face reflecting his horror.

Whatever had been recorded, it had been bad. Of course, it had—Jessica was unconscious, beaten up and lying in a hospital bed. God, he needed to nail Clive's ass to a wall.

His free hand clenched.

"We're going to leave now that we've seen you two. Call us if you need anything. Stay home with her tomorrow. If you must, you can work from your home office." He handed Ryan his car keys. "We'll come over and collect the Beemer tomorrow and bring you your car. Max or Josh will help get Jess' car to your place, too." He paused. "She's going to stay with you, right?"

"Yeah." Even if she didn't choose in favor of the relationship with him, she was staying until he knew she would be safe. Hell, he had plenty of other bedrooms, if she insisted.

"Smart," Theo agreed. "Have her come up with a list of what she might need from her house, and Keera and I will be sure to get it to your place."

Ryan had a feeling Keera would be staying with Theo until he deemed her safe, as well. His brother was nothing if not overly protective. There would be no more "coffee dates" without one of the four brothers nearby. Jessica had been joking about a bodyguard the other night, but this was no joke. Things had become deadly serious.

Theo gave him a one-armed hug then Keera squeezed him tight before they both departed. Ryan sank back into the chair and waited.

* * * *

Jessica stirred then moaned as pain radiated down her skull and into her neck and shoulders. Agony throbbed behind her eyes—it was everywhere, but mostly behind her eyes, trying to press them out of her skull.

"Baby…"

Slowly, she turned her head. "Ryan," she whispered, trying to grasp what was happening, why she was in so much pain. "What happened? Why am I…here? Where am I?"

"Shh," he soothed. "Do you remember anything about what happened today?"

"I was…at work. I needed to go to the pharmacy to get my prescription. Then…I went to the mall to get…" He breath caught. "Clive," she rasped. "He grabbed me. He…he…"

"It's okay, baby. You're safe. I won't let anything

happen to you. You're safe," he repeated, trying to calm her. Leaning close, he brushed aside the tears that had started rolling down her cheeks. "You don't have to talk about it right now."

"He said he was going to kill me."

"He's not touching you. I swear. He's *not* touching you." He bent then lifted her hand the couple inches to his lips. Pain filled his gaze as he straightened. She wanted to reach out and pull him to her, to make him feel better, but the overhead lights hurt and just watching him move was starting to make her dizzy.

"Can you turn down the lights?" she asked. She tried to look around, but her vision kept blurring, making her dizzier.

Ryan reached for the control beside her, and a moment later, the light went out, the room's illumination now coming from the lamps on the periphery. "I just called for the nurse, too. You're in the hospital," he said. "You've been mostly unconscious for a few hours. You've woken a couple times, but you've been really out of it. Terrified the crap out of me," he confessed.

A disembodied female voice came through the speaker, interrupting whatever he might have said next. Ryan let the person know Jessica had woken.

"I'm okay," Jessica assured him, hating that he'd worried.

"You will be."

Before she could ask him what he meant, a white-coated woman walked into the room, her non-nonsense stride full of authority. "Ms. Rush, welcome back to us," she said. "I'm Dr. Manning. Do you know where you are?"

"Yes. Hospital."

"And you remember what happened?"

"Yes. I was attacked at the mall."

"Do you know who this is standing beside me?"

"My…boss. Ryan."

The doctor tilted her head, glanced at Ryan then looked back at Jess. "And can you tell me who the president is?"

Jessica blinked at her. What did that have to do with anything? "Bill Clinton."

The doctor patted Jessica's hand then glanced at Ryan. "So, there's a little bit of memory loss. There's no telling quite the extent, but my guess is that it'll be spotty and will clear up within the next few hours. We'll check again before you two leave. If there's…a problem, we'll discuss it then."

Memory loss? What the hell was this woman talking about? She was fine. She sure as hell remembered the attack in pure Technicolor quality.

"Overall, how are you feeling, Jessica?" Dr. Manning asked.

"Lots of pain."

"We'll get you something for that. Nausea?"

"A little. The room feels like it's rolling around and things are a little blurry—but not always."

"Normal symptoms," the doctor assured her. "We ran some tests while you were out, and everything looked good. You have a concussion though, and that will cause a range of side effects. I've brought Ryan up to speed on everything so he can worry about you. You should close your eyes and try to relax. Rest a bit more if you can."

"Okay." She nodded then regretted it. Closing her eyes, she groaned.

"Stay still," Dr. Manning murmured, her voice nearer as she leaned closer. Cool, feminine fingers stroked over Jessica's skin checking her. The touch was strangely comforting, but she just wanted Ryan's arms around her. Then the hands were gone. When she opened her eyes slightly, trying to keep out the bit of light that was still too much, she saw the doctor had turned to Ryan. She patted his arm. "She'll be all right. Hang in there. I'll be back in a little bit."

Then Jess and Ryan were alone. She watched him as he moved closer to her side, his manner almost…*hesitant?* Why?

He leaned his hip against the mattress and trailed his fingers over her wrist. "You called me your boss."

"You are."

"Do you…remember me as anything else?"

For a split-second she considered messing with him, but the idea was gone almost before it formed. He was traumatized enough by this happening to her. They hadn't really discussed their relationship status and she definitely wasn't comfortable breaking out the Dom/sub status to the doctor.

She turned, though she couldn't move much without pain radiating through her, and stretched her free hand over to lightly caress his forearm. He was worried for her, but she just wanted to comfort *him*.

"I love you," she whispered.

"Oh, kitten, I love you, too."

"I'm fine, okay? Banged up, but fine."

He scowled. "You weren't fine when you were unconscious for hours this afternoon. And you have a concussion. You're not *fine*."

"Ryan…"

"I can't stand that this happened to you. I can't stand that it could have been worse!"

"But it wasn't worse," she assured him.

"And thank God for that. I want to kill him, Jessica. So help me, if he was here right now… My anger has never been this out of control. I've always been so *in* control."

The pain in his eyes, the intensity of his emotions, pierced her. If she'd had any questions about committing to him, they would have evaporated right then. It had become increasingly clear to her over the past week that she did want to be with him, she *did* want to submit to him and live this life, but she'd held her tongue, knowing he wouldn't accept her decision before the time they'd chosen. For the same reason, she kept it inside now, as well.

"He won't touch me—he won't get the chance. I'll be more careful."

"Damn right he won't touch you. Until this is cleared up, you're staying with me and you're not leaving the office alone."

"You... I... What? You can't just take over my life and tell me what to do. I can take care of myself, and—"

"I can and I am. I don't care that you're so damn independent and determined to do everything on your own. Regardless of what you decide about us, I won't take risks with your safety. If this is a deal breaker, so be it. If that's the price of keeping you safe, I'll pay it."

She pressed her lips together and stared at him. The reality of the attack, the pain and side-effects of the concussion and the bruising to the rest of her body, and the utter confusion over her situation and her relationship with Ryan weighed on her. The world was still shifting from clear to unclear as she tried to focus on him, and she took shallow breaths to counteract her nausea. Her skin felt clammy, and she shivered, even the slight movement too much. Apparently, her vehement reaction to Ryan's words was too much in her state.

"I..." She took another shallow breath. She'd have to deal with his version of keeping her in *captivity* later. Right now, incredible fatigue dragged her toward sleep again. "I need to...sleep. Will you stay here?" Though she didn't want the protection he proposed, if one could call it protection, she didn't want to be alone right now, either.

"Baby, no one, not even you, could make me leave your side. I'll be right here. Just sleep. I'll keep you safe."

Chapter Sixteen

Jessica stretched as she came awake, feeling all the bruised places from the attack yesterday. Without opening her eyes, she snuggled back into the pillows. It was Friday, her decision day, and she was in Ryan's bed. Thick blankets covered her, keeping her warm and enveloping her in his scent, but she was alone. She reached out an hand toward his side of the bed, checking if he'd just moved away from her, but he wasn't there.

He had been in bed with her earlier. It had been late when the hospital had finally released her. She and Ryan hadn't spoken much after he'd announced she'd be staying at his place for the foreseeable future, and she'd mostly slept, not wanting to talk...or argue. At one point, she'd relayed the events at the mall to the police detective who'd come in, and if Ryan had been brooding before, his mood turned much darker, definitely murderous, at hearing the complete details from her point of view.

When they'd returned to his place, they still hadn't spoken much. He'd undressed her with care, helped her into bed then climbed in behind her. He'd held her tight to his body all night, his nose pressed into her neck. The desperation in his embrace said what he'd tried to say in words, what she hadn't accepted before. He had to protect her. He couldn't bear this. She meant everything to him.

Slowly, she opened her eyes to see if he was somewhere else in the room, though the silence, much like yesterday, told her he wasn't here. Today, the room was dim. He'd drawn the shades, probably so the bright sun wouldn't bother her eyes, and the door was closed. She groaned as she sat up. Okay, this pain and dizziness would get old fast. Thankfully, she felt better now than she had last night, so hopefully, the achiness would pass quickly. She wanted to get on with her life…and her decisions.

The world spun a little, seeming to tilt sideways then right itself, as she stood and looked around for her clothes. The ripped dress was gone, and she figured Ryan had thrown it away. Last night, he'd pulled off his shirt and made her wear that over her torn clothes as they'd left the hospital. Thankfully, he'd worn a T-shirt under it or she would have started her own protest. She might be his, but he was hers, too, and no one got to ogle her man's bare chest—not anymore. He was taken.

She grinned. She really had made her decision, and without much thinking on it, either. Coming to the conclusion organically just felt…right. She couldn't wait to tell him. She knew he had to be worried, especially after his highhandedness last night. But she understood his reasons, even if she completely disagreed and would do her best to change his mind. Not all their life took place in the bedroom, and she didn't need to submit to him in everything.

Determined, she went to the closet where he'd hung the clothes he'd purchased for her. Her brow furrowed.

There seemed to be more today than… Wait a minute. Those were her clothes, from her house…and why were they hanging in *his* closet? It wasn't all her things, but certainly plenty of them.

She closed her eyes and pressed two fingers to the center of her forehead, rubbing as she tried to control her irritation. She didn't like that someone had been in her house collecting things. It probably wasn't Ryan. She couldn't picture him leaving her alone, not after the way he'd been yesterday. Then who? One of his brothers. She frowned, not liking that idea at all.

Determined to discuss it with him—and discuss might include some arguing—she selected a pair of skinny jeans, a loose blouse she'd wear untucked over it, cheeky panties and a matching lacy bra. In the bathroom, she discovered her toiletries, including her favorite shampoo, body wash and perfume. Deciding against a shower, since she wasn't completely steady on her feet, she sponge-bathed then pulled her hair back in a loose ponytail that she immediately loosened even more then pulled out completely. She settled on a cloth headband, to keep her hair somewhat constrained without putting strain on her throbbing head.

Well, she looked almost human. Time to find Ryan.

She gripped the handrail hard as she started downstairs, taking slow steps. Halfway, she sank down and sat to wait for the world to completely right itself. She closed her eyes, still gripping the handrail, now above her, as if it would keep her steady. This pain and constant dizziness was annoying.

"What the fuck?"

She raised her head, meeting Ryan's outrage as he raced toward her. Then she was up in his arms before she thought to spit out words. Her face planted in his chest.

"If you'd just given me a second, I would have been

fine," she mumbled.

"A second for what? To fall down the stairs? That would have been just great. And stop fucking saying you're fine. You're not fine!"

"Jesus, calm down."

He growled, but she noticed he was taking her to the ground floor, so she didn't complain anymore.

"Couch or table?" he asked.

"I'm hungry." Maybe, that was why she'd gotten dizzy earlier. Well… Part of it anyhow. Low blood sugar since it had been so long since she'd last eaten.

"Okay, kitchen then," he said, turning that way with her still in his arms.

"I can walk."

"I'm sure you can." But he didn't put her down, and she stayed firmly wrapped in his arms as he strode toward the breakfast nook that overlooked the backyard. "I was coming to get you from upstairs, Ms. Impatience," he went on. "I made Spanish omelets and toast. Hope that's okay."

She nodded. "Coffee?"

"Of course." He left her and walked over to the counter. In moments, he was back with a mug, doctored to perfection, and a plate with her food. He returned with his own plate and drink a few seconds later. "Did you want something besides coffee? Orange juice? Water?"

"No, this is fine." She took a bite of the omelet he'd made and closed her eyes in delight as the delicious flavor of the egg concoction exploded over her tongue. "Mmm…you're a good cook. French toast yesterday; omelets today…"

"I'm good at breakfast foods and grilling. Take me beyond that, and we're in dangerous territory."

She grinned. "I'm a passing-good cook. Not so good at grilling though. I manage to char everything."

"Noted. So…Dr. Manning said no screens today and nothing overly cognitive. That leaves out most everything we'd usually do."

She smirked at him. "Sex?"

He chuckled. "Nope. Not allowed to do that for a few days, either—I'm sure you wouldn't really feel up to it anyway."

"I don't know about that."

He shook his head. "Cuddling maybe. I think we know each other pretty well, but maybe, we can just relax together and get to know each other even better. It will be helpful if…"

Ryan trailed off, but she could guess what he was about to say. "If I choose to say yes to us entering fully into this relationship?" she finished for him.

"Yeah. I know today was supposed to be the day you were telling me yes or no, but I don't expect that now. I can wait until you're feeling better and not as confused from the concussion."

She snorted.

His mouth dropped open. "Are you laughing at me?"

"No…" She drew out the word, shaking her head slowly with wide, faux-innocent eyes. "But if I were, today seems to be the day to do that since it seems you won't touch me. I'm not confused, by the way. My head hurts, and my vision is wonky from time to time. The knock on my head is still making me a little dizzy at unexpected moments, but that's all. I'm definitely not confused."

"You still shouldn't be making big decisions with the meds they've given you. Which reminds me…"

She almost growled as he got up and went to the counter. Turning, he came back with a amber-colored prescription bottle.

"You should probably take one of these."

"I'd rather take Tylenol or something."

"These are safe for you to take."

"They'll make me sleepy," she argued.

"Are you always so difficult about everything?"

"You know me pretty well. You tell me."

He glared at her, shaking his head. "If it weren't on the list of things we *can't* do, I'd turn you over my knee and spank you right now."

She took a bite of her food, barely holding back her smile. "Rain check?"

"You seem a little too eager for punishment."

"But you make it so good," she shot back. Sparring with him made her feel a lot better. Human again. "I don't feel bad enough for prescription-strength pills, *and* I'm not confused. Pretty much, I'd already made my decision yesterday morning, *before* any of this happened. I'd planned to tell you last night and put us both out of our misery. I'm not at all confused about that."

Ryan sucked in a breath then a naughty smile curved his lips—a naughty smile that did things to her middle. Her pussy convulsed as his eyes spoke of possessing her in illicit ways that would make her scream for him.

"You're mine," he growled.

"I have been. I don't think there was really much of a question. I want you—all of you—and I want to give this a go."

He nodded. Leaning toward her, he buried his fingers in her hair, gently cupping her head, and kissed her. "Thank you, kitten. You won't regret this."

* * * *

Jessica wasn't regretting being with Ryan at all, but almost a week and a half later, he was pissing her off. He'd let—yes, *let*—her come back to work on the

Monday after Clive's assault, but there'd been no sex, kinky or otherwise, since that Thursday morning before the attack had happened. By Saturday, she'd been feeling pretty good, most of her side effects gone and she'd even known who the president was. She'd been ready to get intimate with her Dom but had understood about waiting the few requisite days for her body to heal. She'd *thought* Monday night would see them resuming activities. Not so much.

And now it was the next Monday. She'd been patient; she really had. They were together practically constantly, their time in the office being the only break in that. Even then, he was mere yards away. The tension of needing him was twisting tighter and tighter, and she had no way to escape. With the Clive threat, taking a run outdoors—alone—wasn't remotely an option. Ryan wasn't even thrilled with the time she'd spent on his treadmill, trying to run off her need. He'd deemed the activity to be too much if longer than fifteen minutes.

There had been so much talking, getting to know each other's likes, dislikes and rhythms. It had been almost as if he'd been courting her, though she lived at his house and slept beside him every night. With sex out of the picture, emotional intimacy had grown between them. It was perfect.

And she might kill him soon.

Because the sex was always at the periphery of their relationship, in integral part of who they were. Yes, she welcomed their bonding, but she needed the full union with him. All the feelings and all the fucking.

She'd had enough of him holding back.

Today, Ryan was in a meeting until lunch, and she was ready to act. She'd put two seductions into play over the past six days but been shot down both times. Now, it was time to get his attention in a way he couldn't avoid.

At noon, she strolled over to his office suite. Marcy was just getting ready to leave for her break.

"Ms. Rush, how are you feeling?" she asked.

"I'm great, Marcy. Thank you. Is Mr. Cress back yet?"

"No. He should be here any minute though. Do you want to wait in his office?"

Good. That would give her time.

Ryan hadn't exactly apprised Marcy of his relationship with Jessica, but rumors had flown when she'd been missing and Ryan had lost his shit over it. He'd been rather attentive since then, always checking on her. It wasn't hard to see they were together. Then his poor assistant had walked in on them kissing the other day, neither of them locking the door nor apparently hearing her knock. Jess had been on his lap, her arms around his neck. There'd been no mistaking the moment.

After that, Jess was sure the entire office knew of the relationship, since Marcy was a bit of a gossip about non-business matters. Ryan wasn't concerned, but it bothered Jess a little. She didn't want people to think she hadn't earned her position, rather than sleeping her way into it, but there were no rules against them being a couple and she loved him, so she'd deal.

"Yes, I would. I'll text him and let him know I'm here. Have a nice lunch."

Marcy nodded and headed toward the elevators. Once Jess was sure the woman was gone, she headed into Ryan's office and locked the door. He carried a keycard ID that unlocked it, so she didn't worry about him getting inside.

Pulling out her phone, she texted him then undressed, removing her dress, bra and panties, but leaving on her stockings and heels. Even as she stripped, part of her argued. This was so unlike her. Perhaps, she had more of a head injury than anyone had thought. No. She just needed him, and a grand gesture might be the only way to get past his over-protective wall.

Her nipples hardened as she rounded his desk and settled into his desk chair with one leg hooked over the side while she leaned into the opposite corner. She positioned one arm to drape over her raised thigh while her other rested on the chair armrest. Then she closed her eyes and waited.

"Jesus," Ryan whispered a moment after she heard the door lock click. "You are so fucking lucky that I got your text message to come to my office alone. If anyone else had seen you…"

She regarded him through her lashes. "Desperate times and all that. I'm tired of waiting while you treat me like china, Sir. I swear to God…if you stop things between us again, like you have the last few times, I'm finding someone else to help me out. Maybe then, you'll—"

"Like hell!" he growled, as he pulled her from the chair by the shoulders, dragging her to stand before him—and he was correct there. She wouldn't go to anyone else. His finger tightened. "You're mine."

"Then prove it."

"I should spank you for this—"

"*Please…*"

"Have you ever heard the term topping from the bottom?"

"Yes."

"And should you?"

She bowed her head. "No. I'm sorry. I just…need you so badly," she finished in a small voice. It was no act. She felt bad for pushing him, and she didn't want to disappoint him in any way, but he had to know she was feeling better. The abstinence he'd imposed was ridiculous.

"Hmm," he responded, and she felt his gaze on her. Then his hand swept up her side, skimming over her ribs and cupping her breasts. Goose bumps lifted in the wake of his touch, making her shiver.

"Yes," she breathed, her head tipping back. She bit her lip to keep from moaning loudly as he pulled at a nipple. Arching her back, she pushed into the touch, wanting more, so much more.

"You are so responsive."

"I need you. So much. I love your hands on me. Only *your* hands, Sir."

"Damn right, only my hands," he growled. He nuzzled her neck roughly then sank his teeth into her shoulder. "Are you sure you're up to this?" he asked. "Last chance, because once we start, we're not stopping."

She knew that wasn't true. If he saw she was distressed, he'd assess her and stop if necessary. "Yes, I'm sure," she said emphatically. "*Please.*"

"Fine. Good. Then…" He paused, and she was pretty sure it was dramatic effect; equally sure he knew exactly what he wanted from her. "Get on your knees. Now." He gave her shoulder a rough shove, but not so rough she stumbled. Assuming her position, she waited while he circled her. Through her lashes, she saw the way his cock tented his pants. Good.

He stopped at his desk and opened one of the side drawers. She didn't look to see what he was getting out and heard it slide shut a few seconds later. Wordlessly, he moved to stand before her. He lifted her chin with two fingers. "I have something for you. Though…" He shook his head in consternation. "You don't deserve gifts for disobedience."

She would have tipped her chin forward in shame if he hadn't been holding it upright. When it came to their sexual relationship, nothing seemed as important to her as pleasing him. She craved it in a way she'd never craved anything before. Certainly, she'd never felt this way with any other man.

"I'm sorry," she repeated, genuinely contrite.

His hand slipped back to stroke her hair. "You're forgiven, kitten. I understand. I may have been a little too…protective since the attack. I plan to remedy that in a moment—after you've accepted my gift."

Her gaze shifted to the blue box in his other hand.

He held it out to her. "Open it."

"Yes, Sir." She took it from him, hesitating as if it were a poisonous snake. The rectangular box felt heavy in her hand. A necklace? A bracelet? A…collar? No. Not from a jeweler.

Holding her breath, she snapped open the lid to find a gleaming gold chain with a large teardrop-shaped loop in the front. The piece was both simple and unusual, and something she could wear on any occasion.

"It's beautiful," she murmured, running her finger over it. Glancing at him and seeing the tension in his face, she knew this was no ordinary necklace.

"Not all collars look like collars," he said. "Jessica, will you wear this one for me? Will you give everything over to me?" He pressed his finger to her lips to keep her from immediately answering. "Your heart, your body, your soul? Your submission? Will you be completely mine? Think about it before you answer."

Think about it… He wanted everything. She wanted to give him everything, too. This was so much more than her simple agreement to be with him back on "decision day". This was—at least, it seemed like it was—more. So much more. It wasn't a ring or a proposal, but it was definitely more permanent than the agreement they'd exchanged.

"Yes… Yes, Sir. I would be honored to." Tears burned her eyes. The little girl who'd been alone, the teenager no one had wanted, who'd been forced to take care of herself, the woman who'd fought so hard for so long to belong… She was now the one desired by this wonderful man. Not only that, he considered it his purpose in life to take care of her. She wasn't on her own anymore. She was his, and she'd cherish him for as long as they were together.

He took the case from her and removed the necklace before dropping the box on his desk. She lifted her hair and held her breath as he slipped the collar around her neck. It snapped shut with a distinct click that shot a shiver down her spine. The metal felt cold on her skin where he'd draped it around her.

His triumphant smile filled her, and Ryan curled his hands over her shoulders. "Mine."

His.

"Yours," she agreed.

"Well done, my love."

Her hand lifted to the loop, remembering the ring on the collar she'd worn the night of their bet. It seemed so long ago now.

"It's stronger than you'd think," he said, as if reading her thoughts. Contemplatively, he fingered the heavy gold. "The clasp is reinforced, and I can attach a lead to this loop if I want to, and it wouldn't break. But that's not my purpose today. You agreed to be mine, and I wanted my collar on you."

"What do you expect of me?" she asked. They should have already had this conversation. She should have thought to ask *before* he'd put the collar on her. But with everything that had happened they'd never really discussed all the requirements of her submission. For the past week and a half, he'd avoided it as if the conversation would lead to the act. Oh, she had a good idea from fleeting comments here and there and from what they'd already done, but actually faced with his collar, she needed to know more.

This was no sex game. Accepting this visible symbol of his ownership was giving up a measure of the independence and power she'd fought so hard to claim. This was allowing him to take care of her, trusting him to do what no one else had. Giving him control...

"I'm not asking you to give up your life," he said. "You will, of course, live with me. I think that's a given."

"I already live with you."

He grimaced. "Even after Clive is in custody, I need you to stay. I want you in my bed every night."

"I want to be in your bed, too," she replied. No need to leave him out on a limb all by himself. He was her support, she could lend acceptance.

Relief filled his eyes, but surely, he'd known she would say that.

"In public, I'll expect you to go toe-to-toe with me, just as you always have," he went on. "In private, especially in the bedroom, you will regard me as your master. You will defer to me."

"Yes, Sir."

"Still, in public, you will never forget who you belong to, even if our relationship isn't made public."

What did he mean, their relationship wouldn't be public? Wouldn't he claim her in a way people could see? Would they be a secret?

"You'll let me select what you wear. I'll choose your wardrobe, and you'll pick from that every day."

"Will you wear your leather pants, then?" she asked.

"Only at home or at the club. Aside from that, you'll still make plans, spend time with your friends and family, but you'll check with me first—especially when it comes to your family."

That sounded normal. Even if they had a vanilla relationship, that would be a polite *modus operandi*. She nodded her understanding as she listened to his guidelines.

"Of course, my family will know what you are to me. However, you will not discuss the full nature of our relationship with anyone unless I give you permission." He chuckled. "That seems to go without saying. I've trusted you on that point for a few weeks already, as it is."

"And I won't talk about it. No one else needs to know what we do in private." Again, it struck her that even if they were in that so-called vanilla relationship, discretion would be the case.

"And at all times, you will remember you're mine. I will have your respect. I will have your complete devotion. And you will have mine. The world *will* know you belong to me, even if they don't know the extent of how."

No problem with me. She almost smiled, but he was being too serious and this all seemed so…official and formal. With an effort, she tamped down the signs of the happiness bubbling inside her.

"One last thing… Be very clear on this. I'm not asking you to be a mindless sycophant. You are an exceptional and extraordinary woman. I don't want to change that about you. You'll always be the friction that drives me farther at work. Even when we're alone, I'll want your opinion. I'll expect discussion and for you to speak your mind, even if you don't think I'll agree with your conclusions. Outside the bedroom especially. In the bedroom, I will always be your master."

She glanced around his office, refraining from raising her eyebrows. "Bedroom" was apparently a situational term for him because this was very much a D/s situation at the moment. This was far from a bedroom. Still, there was no doubt who was in charge.

"And if my opinion is this?" she pushed. She turned and bent forward on her elbows, ass in the air and shoulders to the carpet. She swayed slightly, tempting him. Her whole point in waiting naked in his office was to get him to finally fuck her.

Eyes half-closed, she reached down and glided her fingers across her clit. With her head turned, cheek to the carpet, she watched Ryan's nostrils flare. He dropped down behind her.

"Topping from the bottom," he muttered.

"I *need* you."

"You're aware you'll be punished when we get home?" he rasped, bending over her.

God, she hoped so. He'd been so careful around her for too long.

The crisp fabric of his suit rubbed against her over-sensitized skin, and he bit her shoulder. She moaned in pleasure. He dragged his nails down between her shoulder blades, scraping lightly over her spine. Then drawing back, he smacked her ass. Jessica yelped.

"Yes, Sir."

"You want me to *fuck* you?"

She shivered at the hard rasp of "fuck", the desperate neediness in his tone. *Yes, yes, yes, yes, yes. Fuck me until I can't walk straight. Yes.*

"Yes, please…Sir, please," she begged.

"You're naughty to distract me like this, but I can't stop wanting you—even when you're so willful. I want to possess you and know you're mine for my pleasure. I want to show you who you belong to."

She touched at the gold necklace he'd put on her.

"For how long?" she blurted, unable to suppress the

wounded girl inside her. "How long do you want me?"

"Forever. You're mine. You're fucking mine. I'm not letting you go."

She blinked in surprise and craned her head to stare at him. "Not just a few months?"

"No." His brow furrowed. "Is that…all you want?"

Was that a faint tinge of hurt in his voice?

"Of course not! No, Ryan…of course not. No…"

"Good," he breathed. "That could have been a fight."

"No fight."

He wanted forever? With her as his submissive, taking his instruction, receiving his punishments, sharing his pleasure, living by his side? Tough gig. The happiness she'd been pushing back bubbled inside her. She needed him so much. She needed him as her Dom. She needed to belong to him, to be possessed by him. She'd give him everything, and he'd keep her compulsion for control from overwhelming her ever again.

Jessica met his eyes again. "I love you."

Gently, he pulled her upright then kissed her, worshiping at her lips, reminding her that she was indeed his treasure and he'd guard her and care for her always. As he saw fit. She could trust him and give him her power.

Sitting back, he looped his finger through the necklace and pulled her forward. "I love you, too. Now…I want your mouth on me."

"How romantic," she quipped.

"You're so mouthy. You definitely need something between those lips."

"Yes, Sir," she replied, running her tongue along her bottom lip.

He stood, and she knelt up, opening her mouth and waiting.

"So perfect," he murmured. He reached for his belt.

Quickly, he unbuckled then yanked open his pants, pulling his cock free. She loved being naked before him, ready to serve him while he was nearly fully clothed. God, she loved belonging to him. Was this what she could expect from their time together? She trembled in happiness.

His thumb ran along her open lips, before sinking inside. She sucked eagerly at it, showing him what she wanted, that she desired serving and pleasuring him. He groaned, and she watched his cock jerk in reaction to the tiny bite she gave the pad of his thumb. Pre-cum formed on his glans. She wanted to lick it and taste him more than she wanted to breathe.

He looked the picture of arrogant, businessman perfection in his tailored suit and starched shirt. But the thick, metal-studded cock protruding toward her told the real story. Ryan was a sophisticated bad boy, the big bad wolf wrapped in the trappings of civility.

He ran his hand along his fully erect shaft, staring down at her in dark hunger, lust burning in his gray eyes. His thumb caught the pre-cum she craved and smoothed it around the head. She sucked in a breath, forcing back a cry of protest. Her tongue shot over her bottom lip before she sucked that lip between her teeth and swallowed hard. Her breasts rose and fell rapidly

"You want this?" he asked, his voice pure grating demand. Ryan was gone. This was Master R, the dungeon master, the commander of her fate.

She nodded. Hell, yes, she wanted his cock. She clenched her fingers where they were knotted behind her. "Yes, Sir."

"Then beg for it. Tell me how much you want it, slave."

Oh, God, she wasn't sure she could get any wetter. Every time he talked like that, her body reacted, and she knew, if he touched her, he'd find her soaked.

"Please…" she breathed. "Please, I want it. I want you."

One side of his mouth drew up. "Oh, I think you can do better than that."

Her teeth sank into her lip again. He was really going to make her beg explicitly? Well, she had come into his office, stripped naked and waited for him. She could talk dirty to the man she loved.

"I want to suck your cock. I want to lick it, to feel every inch of it sliding over my tongue. Please can I have it? Can I taste you? Will you fuck my mouth the way I want you to fuck my pussy? Own it like the rest of me? *Please, Sir…*"

He stroked his hand over her hair. "That's a good girl." Suddenly, his fingers fisted, pulling her head back. "And whose are you?"

"Yours," she gasped. "Only yours. Please…let me have your cock."

By the heat in his gaze as he looked down at her, she knew she was saying the right things. She stared into his eyes, lifted her chin and slowly opened her mouth to take him. He groaned, stepping closer. His hand wrapped around his cock, and he traced her bottom lip with the head. Quickly, she flicked out her tongue to taste him.

"Yes," he sighed, pushing in a bit, and she sucked her lips around him. "Oh, God, yes."

The hand fisting her hair opened, palming the back of her head and pulling her toward him as he pushed deeper. She breathed through her nose determined to take him as far as he wanted to go. As he neared the back of her mouth, she tilted her head back, opening further for him as she sucked.

"Fuck," he grunted, and she would have smiled if her mouth wasn't full of him. Her eyes watered a little, but she didn't gag and she felt exceedingly proud of herself for that. Ryan wiped away an escaping tear and smiled down at her. "Such a good girl. Use your hand, baby. Take me only as far as comfortable."

She nodded and pulled free. "Can you sit down?"

Wordlessly, he sank into his desk chair, and she crawled to him then bent over his cock again.

"Feels so good," he gasped. When she glanced up at him, watching him through her lashes, he had his head tilted back against the chair, his eyes closed.

She kept her gaze on him, loving the sight of his pleasure-pained face as she sucked up and down his shaft. She cupped his balls, rolling them in her fingers and tugging slightly. His lips parted, his breaths panting from him harshly as she dragged him to the very edge of his climax. She didn't want him to come in her mouth, she wanted him to fuck her, but if this was what he wanted...

"No. Don't. You have to stop," he groaned as if reading her thoughts.

Before she could react, he'd dragged her off his cock and into his lap. She straddled him, her knees on either side of his hips, his shaft at her opening. Ever so slowly, he pushed upward and breached her tight opening with his metal adorned erection. She gasped loudly, and he paused.

"Baby, you've gotta be quiet," he whispered. "My office isn't soundproofed." He yanked her forward, pressing his mouth to her ear. "And your screams are mine. Just mine. No one else gets to hear them."

Jess shivered, overcome by his intensity. "I'll be quiet," she half-sobbed.

He jabbed up into her and buried himself fully, and Jess cried out, barely muffling the sound in his shoulder in time to keep her cry from echoing around the room.

He grasped her hips, propelling her up and down his

shaft as he thrust. If she'd thought for a moment that she'd be in control in this position, she'd been dead wrong.

"If you're not quiet," he panted, "I'll need to spank you later—and there will be no coming. I'll take you to the edge all night and never let you fall."

"No," she begged.

"Then you'd better figure out how to keep silent, slave."

She whimpered. Her face pressed into his neck as she moved with him, riding him. Her nails dug into the back of the chair as she grasped it for balance and used it as an outlet for her struggle.

When he leaned her backward, supporting her back with his hands as he captured a nipple, she exploded around him. Her pussy convulsed over and over, squeezing his cock almost painfully as he kept driving. She clapped both hand over her mouth. "Oh God, oh God, I can't...*I can't*..." she chanted.

"Fuck! Oh...*fuck*," Ryan growled with one last deep drive inside her. He pulled her against him, kissing her frantically, until the pulsing stopped and he slumped backward into his chair with her clasped against his chest. "Fuck..." he whispered again, almost reverently.

"Thank you," she murmured into his sweaty neck. "I needed you so bad."

"I think...maybe, we should take the afternoon off," he suggested.

That sounded like such a good idea. "We can't. We both have work to do. Besides, if we do, everyone will know what we're leaving to do."

"And what will we be doing?" he teased.

"Fucking." Her brow furrowed. "That's what you meant, isn't it?"

"Damn right."

His brow furrowed, and he turned serious. "Are you okay? I was rough."

"I'm perfect."

"Yes. You are."

Just then, the buzzer on his office phone went off. Apparently, Marcy was back from lunch already.

"Mr. Cress, your father asked that you come up to his office in fifteen minutes."

He grimaced. "Thank you, Marcy. Let him know I'll be there. I just need to finish my meeting with Ms. Rush then I'll head right up."

"Foiled again," Jess laughed after he disconnected. "No more playtime."

"Don't worry, kitten. Your ass will be mine later."

"But I was quiet and—"

"Yes, you did well," he interrupted. He caressed her cheek with the back of his fingers then cupped her face with both hands. "And I'll let you come tonight. Over and over. I'm well aware of how you love your spankings."

She bit her lip and smiled. Hopefully, tonight would mark a new, wonderful beginning. Her submission to him and lots of sex *and* togetherness for them both.

Chapter Seventeen

"Bad news," Ryan announced as he walked into her office several hours later. Jessica looked up from the work she was wrapping up before shutting down for the day. Since the first time she'd hooked up with Ryan at Pleasure Palace weeks ago, she'd taken work home less and less often. Remarkably, it hadn't impacted her productivity.

"What bad news?" she asked. Was there another Clive development or some other problem at the worksite? She frowned, dreading the report.

"We've been summoned to family dinner at my parents' house."

"Family dinner?" That would be new for her. Her family had never done that and she'd never been to one at a friend's, either. "Do you guys do that often?"

"Once a week. We've skipped the last few."

Her eyes widened. "You didn't tell me. I don't want to piss off your mom and dad—"

"They know it was all me and that it wasn't your fault. Well, except last time. We were supposed to go to their house the day Clive attacked you. Instead, part of us ended up at the hospital and the rest decided not to get together. Everyone was worried about you."

She knew he was telling her the truth. Keera and every member of his family had come to see her in the couple days following her release from the hospital, all of them bringing her flowers and checking to see how she was doing. Ryan's mother, Melody, had called her frequently since to see how she was settling in. As a group, they'd welcomed her into their fold, even before Ryan had officially claimed her. She touched the necklace around her neck. Maybe, they'd known his intentions all along, and the collar was just a technicality.

"Did they know that you planned to…" She glanced at the open door and realized she didn't know if anyone else was in earshot. She tapped the necklace. "To do this?"

"Yes. Theo and my parents did anyway. And if you think they could keep that to themselves, you'd be wrong. Once one of them knows, they all know."

Jess nodded, unsurprised. She'd always known they were close knit. Coming into the group from the outside was intimidating.

"Are you just about ready to go?" he asked, changing the subject. "We're supposed to be there in an hour, and I want to go home and change first."

"Me, too," she agreed, shoving her tablet and phone into her handbag then standing to join him. "Let's go."

"Wait. First…" His fingers lifted her chin. She glanced worriedly to the side. They were standing in front of her open doorway. Anyone passing would see them kissing. Until now, they hadn't kept their relationship a secret, but they also hadn't been public about it.

"Hey," he whispered against her lips. "Focus on me. Don't worry about anyone else."

His mouth covered hers, and she moaned softly,

sinking into the pleasure he offered. She was his, so whatever he wanted... When his lips parted hers and he deepened the kiss, she melted forward, fisting her fingers in his crisp shirt.

"Are you guys going to miss dinner again?"

"Fuck off, Max," Ryan said against her lips before taking her mouth again.

His brother chuckled. "It's your hide. See you later—I might save you some dessert. I hear Mom made tiramisu...lots of booze in it."

"Fuck *off*, Max," Ryan growled again. "Go away."

"This might be why I was worried about the doorway," she murmured.

"Yeah, well nobody but my damn brothers would dare comment or interrupt."

She laughed and pressed her face into his shirt. "Maybe, we should go so they don't have more to tease you about."

"Right." His sarcasm lay thick in his voice. He slung his arm around her shoulders to lead her toward the elevator. "Like they'd need anything. You don't have siblings, so you don't know this, but anything is material for their comedy routines. I'm sure you'll hear childhood secrets tonight."

"Really? Can't wait."

He dropped a kiss on her nose. His arm looped farther around her neck and he touched the loop on the necklace. "And you wonder why I didn't bring you around them for dinner before now? I didn't want you running when they started in...Now, it's too late." They stepped into the elevator. He pressed the garage button then pressed his mouth to her ear. "Because you're mine now, and it's too late to run."

* * * *

"So, Jessica, Tell us about your family."

Jess paused with her wineglass halfway to her lips and stared at Ryan's mom like a deer in the headlights. The question had been posed in a kind, truly interested tone. Melody Cress had been nothing but welcoming since Jess had walked in the door. Everyone had accepted her as Ryan's woman. She'd never felt so much as if she belonged.

"I…" She rubbed the back of her neck as her skin heated.

"It's okay, baby," Ryan murmured beside her. He squeezed her thigh.

"They're not really in the picture," Jess admitted.

"You don't get along?" Declan asked.

She shifted her gaze to Ryan's dad and shook her head. "They're kind of…deadbeats, I'd guess you'd call them." God, would he think she was some sort of gold digger now? It had never occurred to her to lie. Maybe, she should have. "I mean," she hurried to say, "they left me on my own a lot while growing up. I've taken care of myself my entire life. We, um, grew apart."

Declan's eyes narrowed as if he were assessing her. He rubbed his chin thoughtfully as he regarded her, and she wondered what he saw, what he was thinking of her. She glanced over at Ryan, wondering how soon they could leave. In minutes, she'd gone from feeling welcomed to feeling…not unwelcomed so much. Just an outsider.

"Well," Declan said, drawing her attention back to him. "You belong to a family now. We're all here for you. No more having to stand on your own."

"Oh, Christ, here comes the 'a sheath of branches is stronger than one' speech," Theo muttered.

"Theophilus Cress," Melody admonished. "Respect your father."

"Yes, ma'am," he replied. Beside him, Keera snickered, but her laugh died as he leaned over and whispered in her ear. Color flooded her cheeks, and Jess could only imagine what Theo had said.

"Theophilus?" she said, drawing attention from her friend.

"Oh yeah," Ryan's sister, laughed drily from across the stable. She still managed to sound snarky, despite the humor in her eyes. The goth pixie from Jessica's first time at Pleasure Palace sported a wide hot-pink stripe down one side of her black hair today. Despite her heavy makeup, her face appeared porcelain-like and flawless. Her blood-red lips curved into a smirk as she launched into baby-sister mode and spilled secrets. "I'm the only one with a normal name—"

"Francesca…" Melody interrupted in warning.

"Right," she splayed both hands to indicate herself. "Francesca, Italian."

"Francesca," her mom repeated with more warning.

"Hey, Ma, you picked them."

Declan patted Melody's hand. "Let her be. It'll come out sooner or later."

Clearly, Francesca was the indulged baby of the family. Jessica loved the way she picked on her older brothers, just a little bratty but obviously loving them all. She just loved to give them crap. When Jess had been hurt though, she'd shown up the next day in jeans, a T-shirt, long hair in twin braids hanging over her shoulders, declaring she was ready to help out in any way needed. By then, Jess had been feeling steadier and Francesca had convinced her brother to let them take a "boy-free" walk around the backyard.

"So…" Francesca drew out the syllable. "My oldest brother there is Theophilus. It's Greek. Mom was on a bit of an ancient languages kick before me. Max is Maximus.

Ancient Roman. And Josh is Josiah. Hebrew."

Jess turned to Ryan. "You're the only brother who got
off without an ancient name?"

"Oh did he?" his sister asked. "Ryan, how is it that
you spell your legal name?"

"You are such a brat," he growled.

"Isn't she?" Max agreed. The affection was clear in
both their voices.

"At least, she wasn't giving me shit at work today,"
Ryan replied.

Josh huffed a scoffing laughing. "She would have
been if she'd been there. I'm pretty sure there's a reason
Dad won't let her work at the office."

"Boys," Melody cut in.

"I don't want to work in that boring-ass office,"
Francesca argued. "Ick!"

"Yeah, because you're so much better suited to a sex
club," Theo muttered.

Jess looked at him in confusion. But Francesca
worked for him? If he didn't want her there, then why
employ her?

"You shouldn't have lost that bet," Ryan told him.

"How the fuck was I supposed to know she actually
knows Anthony White?"

"The movie star?" Keera asked. When Francesca
nodded, she added, "Can you introduce me?"

"Why?" Theo demanded.

"Have you *seen* him?"

"And…?" he growled.

"He's *so* hot!"

Theo pushed back his chair then pulled Keera from
hers. "We'll be right back."

"I think I like family dinner," Jess laughed to Ryan as
her friend and Theo disappeared from the room, Keera
complaining about still eating her dessert.

"This is nothing."

"And...how do you spell your name?" she asked.

"Oh I like her," Josh cut in. "Can I have her? You'd like me a lot better than him, Jess. I can hack into all your enemies' accounts and make their lives hell."

"I only have one real enemy," she replied. "No one can find him."

"Trust me. I'm working on it," he said darkly. "No one messes with my family and gets away with it."

Warmth flooded through her. She was family? Thank you seemed inappropriate yet not enough. She just smiled and gave him a nod, hoping he could see her gratitude.

Ryan threaded his fingers through hers. "It's R-A-Y-Y-A-N," he said, finally answering the question and redirecting the conversation again. "It's Arabic. And no, my mom wasn't on drugs. She's...eccentric."

"I prefer 'special'," Declan said, kissing his wife's hand. His enduring love shone in his eyes as he gazed at her, and Jess hoped that she'd have the same when she was their age. Would she still be with Ryan? Would she someday be gathered around a table with her husband and their kids?

"When are you going to contact the Keeper of the Records?" Declan asked. "Now that you've collared a submissive, you need to inform the sect's leaders."

"The sect?" Jessica echoed.

"He hasn't told you about the group we belong to?" Ryan's father asked in confusion. He glanced askance at Ryan.

"He...he has," she offered quickly. "We've talked a little about it and he's explained things. I just didn't know Ryan needed to...um, *report* our relationship."

"I don't," Ryan cut in. He narrowed his eyes and glanced around the table. "And I'm not going to. They can mind their own business."

"One of us taking a partner *is* their business."

Francesca shot to her feet. If possible, she looked even paler than she'd already been with the skin-lightening makeup. "I agree with Ryan. The world would be a far better place if they'd just mind their own damn business. We can choose our own damn partners!"

Before anyone could say a word, she stormed from the room. A few moments later a door slammed. Uncomfortable silence oppressed those remaining at the table.

"I'll go talk to her," Melody said quietly then she left the room, too. Jess watched her follow Francesca and remembered the conversation she'd had with Ryan's sister when she'd come to visit. Cesca, as she actually preferred to be called, had been in an arranged partnership with a man from their sect. A betrothal of sorts. She'd gone to live with him across state, fallen in love with him, but the lifestyles they practiced were too dissimilar. While her family practiced partial D/s— basically only in the bedroom—he'd been raised with 24/7 mindset. There were no off times. The Dom was always in charge of everything and the submissive always obeyed him, in every aspect of life. Independent Cesca had baulked and the relationship had fallen apart.

Frankly, Jessica was sure she couldn't deal with that sort of lifestyle either. If Ryan had wanted that…well, they might not be together now, despite her love for him.

"Ryan," Declan cajoled, his voice pulling Jess back to the now.

"I don't want to talk about it, Dad," Ryan interrupted. "Only permanent partners have to be reported. Until then, my choices aren't their business. My relationship with Jess doesn't need to be inked into their ledgers."

Only permanent partners… He'd said forever, but… Apparently, that term was a subjective as bedroom. He didn't really mean it. He'd meant until he was finished with her. God, she was an idiot!

Her fingers fisted in her lap and she took a deep, calming breaths. Okay, he didn't want to claim her. That was it, wasn't it? He didn't see a need to report this relationship—this *temporary* relationship—to whatever governing body they were discussing. He saw them as a fling, and she'd been stupid to believe she belonged and that she finally had a place. *Stupid, stupid, stupid!*

Her hand shook slightly as she reached for her wine glass and drained it. Ryan was busy having a glare-off with his dad, but Theo was watching her. His eyes shone with concern. "Are you okay?" he mouthed.

She nodded, pressing her lips together then attempting a smile. A pathetic one she was sure. Uncomfortable, she looked away.

God, how could she have been such an idiot? Of course, she didn't belong here or with him. She'd never belonged anywhere. She'd never really been wanted. And this was why it was better that she just took care of herself. Like always.

* * * *

Somehow, Jess managed to make it through the rest of dinner, which in truth had disintegrated quickly after the sect discussion. She wanted to ask Ryan to take her home—to *her* home—but knew that wouldn't happen. His misguided sense of responsibility for her would make him take her to his place so he could protect her or whatever.

"Well, that was a clusterfuck," Ryan muttered once they were settled in the car and he'd pulled from the driveway.

"It was fine," she whispered. She stared out the side

window, not wanting to see him, even in her peripheral vision . She couldn't look at him until she felt under control again. Tears burned in her eyes, threatening her tenuous hold on her emotions, and she just didn't think she'd be able to stop them once they started. She'd lain herself open to him for weeks now, giving Ryan all of her. Everything. Fuck! She knew better. When had she ever really been welcome and wanted? Never…

"What part of it was fine?" he countered, rueful as he drove. "When my family decided your first dinner with us was a perfect time to display all our weirdness? When my sister stormed off? When my dad start in on my *duties*?"

"Dessert was good."

He snorted. "Yeah. I could have used more of the alcohol in it to dull the pain." He took her hand, and she almost sobbed. She didn't want him to touch her. Didn't he have any idea how much he'd hurt her tonight? Obviously, he didn't. He'd probably think she was an naïve idiot if he knew that she'd believed they were more than they were.

Woodenly, she let him hold her hand, his thumb caressing her wrist.

"What's wrong?" he asked when the silence had stretched into minutes.

Okay, he wasn't so oblivious to her mood…

She sighed. "I want to go to my house."

"What? Why?"

Because I'm a stupid girl who fell in love with you and thought forever really meant forever. Because being with you right now is ripping out what's left of my soul.

She shrugged. "I haven't been there in a while. And, uh, I could use some alone time. I'll be fine. I'll lock myself inside and set the alarm. There are things I need to do there. Laundry, bills, cleaning…"

"At ten at night? Bullshit. What's going on?"

"Ryan, I just need some space."

"You didn't want *space* earlier. If I remember correctly, you were begging for my cock."

She squeezed her eyes shut, shamed by her foolishness. "I was caught up in the moment. Now, I'd really like—"

"No. We still don't know where Clive is and it's not safe. I want you with me."

"Do you?" And what about after Clive was in custody? Would she be welcome then? For how long?

"Yes. What the fuck do you mean by that? Of course, I do." Irritation laced his tone, but something she couldn't quite place tinged the edges. Concern? Confusion?

Whatever. He'd made his position clear.

"You know, I'm not some toy you can play with until you're bored."

"Play with..." he echoed quietly, as if unable to believe what he was hearing. "Where the hell is this coming from? Have I ever treated you badly? For fuck's sake, Jessica. I asked you to move in with me."

"No, you didn't ask. You *told* me you wanted me there with you."

"So..." he ventured. "Is that what this is? You want me to...ask?"

"No."

He swerved to the side of the road. "Jessica," he bit out. "Look at me."

"I—"

"Look at me. Now."

She drew in a breath, shaking her head slightly, then turned her face toward him. Slowly, she opened her eyes. The night's shadows and the illumination from a nearby streetlight threw his face into sharp angles. His gray eyes appeared black as his stare pierced her.

"*What* is going on?" he demanded. "What happened between this afternoon in my office and now? What's causing you to want to run? Dinner wasn't *that* bad."

"I just realized we want different things."

"Bullshit. Tell me the truth."

That was the truth. They did want different things. He wanted short-term sex; she wanted a long-term relationship. "It *is* the truth," she insisted. "Just take me to my h—"

"No," he interrupted. "You're coming home with me. To *our* home. End of discussion."

"Ryan—"

"Are you going to explain yourself?"

"Explain myself?" she exclaimed in outrage. "I want to go home. You're the one being bullheaded."

"So you're going to drop the blame in my lap?"

"That's where it belongs."

He shoved his hands through his hair then stared out the windshield, gripping the steering wheel so hard she could see his knuckles whitening despite the darkness around them. "What the fuck did I do?"

"Nothing," she growled. God! Why couldn't she just tell him…explain that she'd realized she wasn't in the position she'd envisioned? She hadn't found her forever after all. It was humiliating to realize she'd been so wrong. Yes, he wanted to be with her…for the time being, however long that was. Could that be enough?

No. She'd been there before. Always waiting for the shoe to drop, always wondering when the rug would be pulled out from under her. The gnawing tension would eat her up inside, destroying any peace she'd found and coloring everything to a dull gray while it leeched away any happiness.

"It's nothing," she repeated with less venom, sounding almost listless. Nothing? It was *everything*. "I just need to get my head back in the right place. It's been a long day."

"Baby…" Ryan pulled her into his strong arms, not questioning her explanation. Tears sprang to her eyes again, as his hand stroked over her hair and he kissed her temple. Disconsolate, she accepted the comfort, though he had no idea that he was comforting her in her decision to leave him…to leave this situation…to leave Cress and everything she'd built since she'd gotten there. This could very well be one of the last times in his arms.

He just held her. His lips pressed to her temple, and he murmured soothing sounds while she shook. His shirt was soaked by the time she pulled back and scrubbed her eyes and cheeks with the back of her hand. He cupped her face.

"Are you okay?" he asked.

No… "Yes."

Ryan studied her for a moment then nodded. He didn't look convinced, but he pulled back onto the road then drove them to his house. They traveled in silence. Undressed in silence. Climbed into bed in silence.

He drew her into his arms, and she curled into his chest. His lips pressed to her hair. "We'll talk about everything in the morning, kitten. Just rest. It'll all be okay."

But she knew it wouldn't. It couldn't be. They both wanted very different things.

"Will you make love to me? Please?" She needed him. One last time, she needed him, over her, in her, loving her in the way only he could.

As he rolled her under him, she opened herself to him and gave him everything one last time.

* * * *

"Jess?"

Ryan bolted upright, searching the shadows for his woman. She wasn't in bed beside him, and the sheets were cold. Scanning the dim interior of his room, he saw he was alone. Worry echoed inside him as he flipped on the bedside light then climbed out of bed.

"Jess," he called again, louder this time. The house was dark as he emerged into the hallway. He ran downstairs to the equally dark lower level, calling her name again. She wasn't there. The rooms resonated with emptiness.

Already knowing what he'd find, he dashed to the garage then sagged against the doorframe, staring at the empty space where her car should be. It was gone.

What the fuck? What the actual fuck? She'd been upset last night but... She'd settled. He'd thought she was all right—at least, all right enough to stay with him until they talked through things in the morning. He'd sensed something still bothering her, but had known she wasn't up to hashing things out right then.

He straightened, thinking of everything that had happened last night. There was something he wasn't seeing. An invisible piece of the puzzle. Jess was hiding her real feelings from him. That realization drove home just how new they really were. Not too new to build something permanent though. When he got his hands on her, he'd sure as hell make her believe it. She'd tell him what was wrong, and he'd show her they were right.

Turning to head back into the house, he slammed the door. Damn it! This was unacceptable. She was his and she should be upstairs in his arms right now.

After storming to his room, worry dogging every step and twining with his anger, he snatched his phone from where he'd left it on the bedside table. It was while he punched in her number that he saw the glint of gold. Staring at it, he paused mid-dial. His hand dropped to his side and the phone fell from his numb fingers.

His collar, the collar she'd just accepted from him, lay on her pillow, obviously arranged into a perfect circle so he'd easily find it. She'd left it there for him to discover, so there would be no mistake. She was leaving him.

Oh, but there was a mistake. A huge mistake. If Jess thought she was leaving him, she was sorely mistaken. She was his. And he wasn't giving her up. Ever.

Scooping up the phone, he finished dialing. The call went directly to voicemail.

"Where are you?" he demanded. "You are not leaving me, Jessica. Get your ass back here. You. Are not. Leaving. Me. You're mine, kitten, and I will come for you no matter where you go."

Not satisfied with that, he opened a text message.

Call me. Whatever's going through your head right now...we need to talk about it. I love you, and I know you love me. Tell me where you are and I'll come to you.

Not expecting an immediate answer since his call had gone to voicemail, he headed for his closet to get dressed. He'd go to her house and confront her there.

But Jessica wasn't at her house, and she didn't show up while he waited.

She wasn't at work.

And she didn't answer her fucking cell phone.

By three o'clock, Ryan was out of his mind again, sure something had happened to her, and filled with impotent rage because there wasn't a damn thing he could do about any of it.

Chapter Eighteen

Sitting alone in her car, Jess stared at the floor of the passenger seat, her vision unfocused as she contemplated yesterday, the day so far and what she had to do now.

She'd left Ryan. Tears filled her eyes for the millionth time since she'd slipped from bed in the early hours of morning. She blinked them back as her hand pressed over her mouth. Oh God…she'd left him. Lying in his arms, so secure in his embrace, knowing it was all a lie, she'd made her decision. End things now; save herself from even deeper hurt later. She'd felt actual physical pain when she'd extricated herself from his grasp, knowing it would be the last time she'd feel his strong hold around her. Taking off his collar had just about killed her.

So many of her things were in his closet, but she'd left them all. She was used to losing things. Her favorite clothes were a small loss in the scheme of things. She'd replace them. It wouldn't be the first time.

She'd called in sick before the office had opened, not quite able to make herself quit on the spot. Cowardly, but she needed her ducks in a row before facing Ryan with her resignation then moving forward.

At eight sharp, she'd called Sissek Construction and Planning to see if they were still interested in speaking with her about employment. Earl Sissek had asked her to come in for an interview at ten. And now…now she had a job with them if she wanted it. Apparently, her reputation had proceeded her. Nice to know. She'd told them she'd consider their offer and get back to them by the end of the week. That had irritated Mr. Sissek. But she needed to think over his offer, and he'd conceded to her timeline.

That had been hours ago. She'd driven aimlessly, and for a few minutes, actually considered a trip out of town to visit her parents while she thought through things. She hated this, the indecision. Since childhood, she'd been in control and kept a clear direction for her life. One man and a few weeks had changed that all. Now, she even waffled about going to see her mother and father, two deadbeats she'd vowed to avoid at all costs. There wouldn't be any comfort or peace there. Seeing them would just cement her reasons for being in command of herself and her destiny. Seeing her would rev up their requests for money.

She leaned her head on the steering wheel, closing her eyes and holding it tight. She thumped her forehead against it a few times. What to do… What to do…

She needed to go home. She'd have to face Ryan. Maybe, she should call him and smooth the way over a phone line first. When she'd left, she'd thought she might never see him again. Of course, that had been her overwrought emotions speaking. Slightly more in control, she knew she had to face Ryan. She'd need to talk to him and tell him this was over. He wouldn't be happy, but judging by his argument with his father last night, he'd get over it.; He wasn't invested—not like she'd been. Or was…

The truth was if he declared his undying, eternal devotion…if he vowed that forever really was forever and not until he was finished with her, she'd be committed to him.

She blew a harsh breath through her teeth. No… That was fairytales speaking. She didn't even need that much from him. He'd said he loved her, and that was enough, if he was committed to her for more than the short-term. No one could claim forever; no one could look into the future and see what perils lay ahead. She just didn't want to be with a man who was already planning his exit strategy. And last night, that's what she'd heard. Ryan already foreseeing their ending.

She had to explain that to him. It had been childish of her to hold it all in and hide her insecurities. It wasn't fair to end their relationship without making it clear why she wouldn't go forward with it. The games were fun, but she needed more than that.

Pulling out her phone, she powered it up. She dreaded what she'd find. Ryan wouldn't have been happy to wake up alone this morning. She stared at the apple on a white background until it blinked to her lock screen. Opening the phone, she found several texts from Keera and one from Ryan. She read it, shaking as she absorbed the emotions in it. Her determination wavered. Quickly, she went to her calls. She had two an hour since four this morning. Jesus, he must have woken minutes after she'd left. There were only two voicemails. The second, from this afternoon, started with a frustrated growl.

"Where the fuck are you?" he demanded. "Answer your God-damn phone! Call me. I'm *worried* about you."

He sounded far more pissed off than worried, but that was her fault. She'd let things lie unfinished. Shaking, but refusing to cry anymore, she started her car and started for home. When she was almost there, she dialed Ryan.

"Where are you?" he demanded as way of greeting.

"I'm…" She swallowed. Fuck, this was hard. "I'm on my way home. We should talk…face-to-face. If you want to—" She stopped suddenly as she turned onto her street and saw his car in her drive. "Oh…you're already here."

So much for re-gathering herself.

"Yeah." He hung up, and she saw him stand from where he'd been sitting in her porch swing. Trepidation clawing at her, she parked beside his car and got out to face her soon-to-be former lover.

"Where have you…"

His question dropped off as he took in her dress, a plum-colored sheath that ended mid-calf but had a off-center slit to just above her knee. The square-cut neckline revealed barely a hint of cleavage. She'd picked up the garment and the matching heels earlier today, not wanting to return to her house.

"…been?" he finally finished after a long perusal. "You're awfully dressed up for a sick day."

"We both know I wasn't sick." Not with an illness anyway. She skirted him to unlock her front door.

"Where were you?"

"Ryan, I'm allowed to have a personal life…and it was personal." She needed to talk to him about their relationship, not the interview. That would be gasoline on the already raging fire.

He eyed her critically, and though his anger was evident, so was his worry. "Are you actually sick? Did you go to the doctor?"

And he just wasn't getting the hint to back off. Of course, as a couple, they'd shared everything recently. There had been no secrets. He hadn't allowed any. He'd demanded everything from her. But they weren't a couple, were they? He'd made that clear last night.

"If you must know, no, I didn't go to a doctor. I had

an interview."

He stared at her, hurt, shock and disappointment pouring from him. He stepped toward her and she a stepped back.

"Another job?" Ryan advanced on her, not letting her escape. Her back pressed to the wall and his hands pressed beside her shoulders, his chest rising and falling with ragged breaths. His incredulous gaze burned into her, branding her as a traitor. "You're actually leaving me?"

Cold fear washed over Ryan. All those months, he'd waited to claim her, and now, he was going to lose her. And he didn't even know why. He'd worked so hard to get them here...and the waiting. The waiting had been excruciating.

No. No, he wasn't letting this bullshit happen.

"It's not as if we're a permanent thing, Ryan. You made that perfectly clear last night."

"What are you talking about?"

She ignore him and crossed her arms defensively over her chest, obviously trying to distance herself even though he had her trapped up against the wall of her small house. She didn't meet his eye, instead staring at his shoulder.

"Yes, I'm considering another job."

"You're thinking of leaving Cress Construction?" Obviously, that's what she'd just said but he had a hard time comprehending it. Fine. She didn't need to work for Cress for them to be together, but was she planning to go to the competition? That sent a message loud and clear. They both knew she couldn't work for a competitor and still be with him.

"The job I interviewed for today may or may not happen. But yes, I've decided to actively pursue other opportunities."

"Why? I don't know what you think is happening here, but you're sure as hell wrong. Obviously, you're upset about something that happened yesterday. Did you even consider talking to me about it? A relationship—any relationship, not just one like ours—needs communication. *Talk* to *me*."

She stared at him, and though she tried to hide it, he could see she was on the brink of tears and fighting it. She didn't want this any more than he did. So, what the hell?

"Ryan, we want different—"

"No," he growled, shaking his head. They did not want *different* things. For God's sake… "You're not doing this."

"For my career, I need to think about where I'm going…"

She was going the career angle? He raised his eyebrow and leveled an incredulous stare at her. "We both know this isn't about your *career*. But fine. What do you need? A promotion? More money?"

"I'm not a hooker you hired off the corner," she snapped. "You can't buy me. It was a mistake to get involved with you. I knew this would happen."

"You knew what would happen? That I'd fall in love with you? That I'd want you to be mine? That you'd want me? That we'd be perfect together? I don't want you to leave."

Her look of disbelief cut through him. "Right. You don't want me to leave because you're not done with me yet. But this will end, and where will it leave me? Alone. Heartbroken. Used. At odds with my boss? We can't work like that. I can't do that."

"Why are you—" He cut himself off and looked around. Her next door neighbor was watering his lawn and staring at them. A few houses away a couple kids were playing in their yard. "We're not doing this on your porch." He jerked his head toward her front door. "Go inside, and we'll talk about this."

"I'm not asking you in."

"I don't give a fuck. I'm not some damn vampire. I don't need to wait for your invitation—and you *will* let me in. We're not finished with this discussion."

Not letting her close him out, he barged in behind her. She continued glaring at him petulantly, her arms crossed over her chest again.

Never breaking eye contact with her, he closed and locked the door. "I've missed several meetings today while I've tried to track you down."

Her lips pressed together, and she said nothing. Then her eyes slid away, and she shrugged. "Your choice," she finally said.

"Maybe, but you had to know I'd worry about you. I always will. I have this ridiculous, insatiable need for you that—"

"It'll go away."

His fingers flexed at her mouthy interruption. She needed a spanking, and he needed to give her one, but at the moment, he wasn't so sure he could hold himself in check as much as he should. He'd vowed to always be in control, and she was testing him to his limit today.

"It won't *go away*," he grated.

"Right." The sharp syllable was anything but an affirmation. With one word, she was calling him a liar. Again. And he'd had enough.

"On your fucking knees, in the corner, *now*." He pointed. "Perhaps, that will help you listen."

She stiffened. "No."

"No?" he laughed in disbelief, far from amused. "Do it."

"No."

"Jessica…" he warned.

"Ryan…" she replied in equal tone.

His cheeks drew in and his eyes narrowed as he stared at her. Below his eye, a muscle ticked. He pushed an irritated breath out through his nose.

Silence stretched between them, a furious man and his quarrelsome woman facing off. He held her gaze, waiting and forcing back his sardonic grin when her hands drifted behind her back then she angrily dragged them back to her sides. She was his. She would always be his. Her body responded, even when her belligerent attitude fought it.

When the submissive movement happened a second time, he tilted his head and raised an eyebrow.

"Fine!" she growled. She stomped to the place he'd indicated and dropped to her knees, showing her heated displeasure with each move. "Jerk," she whispered, as she placed her hands behind her and pushed her forehead against the corner.

Maybe, he was, but he didn't care. She was his, and he'd fight for her in whatever way she needed him to.

"You want to repeat that, kitten?"

"No," she replied, through clenched teeth.

Fine. He'd deal with her mouth later. Perhaps by fucking it. That brought them both pleasure.

"First of all," he began, leaning his shoulder against the wall opposite her corner. One ankle casually over the other, he crossed his arms as he watched her. "When there's a problem—even if you *think* there's a problem—you need to discuss it with me. Don't go off half-cocked and making assumptions."

"I think you made your position pretty clear," she sniped back.

What the fuck was she talking about? But thank God,

she was talking. He'd heard that corner time could clear a submissive's mind, but this was the first time he was seeing it in action. He'd need to remember this when it came to Jessica's pissed-off, uncommunicative moods.

"Second," he growled, "*What* is the problem? I don't know what's got you so pissed off that you're sneaking away in the night, putting yourself in danger, worrying me and even interviewing for other jobs."

"After last night, it seemed that I'd need to—get another job, I mean."

"Why?"

"You were quite adamant that this...*thing*...isn't permanent, and...and that's fine." Her voice broke on *fine* as she lost her battle for toughness.

He fought the urge to kneel behind her and take her into his arms. She was crying, and it killed him, but they needed to maintain the balance of power. She needed his mastering not his comforting right now.

"And, well...I...I can't work with you, be around you every day, once you decide you're done with...me. So...so it's better if...if..."

"Oh kitten," he sighed, crushed by her sob. He slid to the floor beside her and pulled her into his arms. Forget mastering. She needed his strength supporting her. He rubbed her back, holding her to his chest as she wept. Her face pushed into his neck, fingers curling in his soft shirt. "How did I make you think this?" he asked.

"L-last n-night at d-d-dinner."

Oh shit. The sect talk.

"Baby, listen... The sect gets in our business all the time. Even though my family isn't deep into their rituals and rules—actually, it's because we're not conformists— they try to push their precepts on us. When it comes to our partners, they want to push the 24/7 lifestyle on us and give us all kinds of rules to follow. They want to tell couples how to run their daily *private* lives. My family practices only partial D/s, not the 24/7 variety—as you already know. Since my ancestors were one of the founding families, the sect wants our mates to come from a certain pool of women who've been raised in the culture. And even though you haven't been immersed in our culture since birth, they'll expect certain behavior from you—behavior *I* don't require. I'm trying to shield you from it for as long as possible. I want to protect you as long as possible. I want you to feel secure in your position with me and my expectations of you, before they try to muddle everything else with rules I don't even need you to follow."

"Oh my God," she whispered as his explanation sank in and she apparently realized her misguided actions. Her arms circled him, squeezing him tight...desperately.

"Baby, it's okay," he reassured her, stroking her back. "I'm not letting you go,"

She sniffed. "You should. I'm such a mess. Too screwed up..."

"Never. You're mine. This is a bump."

"More like a cliff. Caused by all the years of the emotional fracking inside me."

"We'll heal all the chasms. I promise. I'm not giving up on us and I'm not letting you give up on us either."

She nodded against his neck. "Ryan," she sighed and he heard her surrender, her relief to be back win his arms—both physical and spiritual. Shifting, he pulled her onto his lap and rocked slightly as they held each other in silence.

"Ryan?"

"Yeah, baby?"

"If the sect is so bad, why don't you break away from them?"

"Because it's not all bad. It's good to have the

associations, to be part of a group that can help you when you needed—specifically in situations arising due to BDSM. Sometimes, if things happen outside of it. The officer who came to see you at the hospital and the doctor who took care of you…both, are part of our group. One phone call put me in touch with Detective Fillion, and it helped me find you that day. Being part of the sect gives us like-minded people to associate with and places to meet. There's a rich sub-culture dating back to the early 1800s. I wouldn't trade that away and keep my descendants from having it."

"Then why—"

"I don't want you to have to deal with it until you're ready. You don't know very much about them, and throwing you into it could be disastrous. I want you to learn what you need to know from *me* not them. I've seen what can happen up close and personal. My sister grew up in our culture. She knew what to expect, and her arrangement imploded. She's never been the same—"

"Arrangement? Like an arranged marriage?"

"Exactly like that. There's something like a courting period beforehand, a betrothal so to speak where she lives with her future partner. My parents were trying to play nice with the sect. My sister, who'd been an All-American cheerleader-type, along with my parents agreed to an arrangement with one of the sect's prominent families. Her man's a good guy—I like him—but things between him and Francesca were explosive. Not in a good way. She couldn't conform to expectations, because she was raised different. You're even further from their expectations. I'll protect you from it however I need to. Right now, until we take the next step, it's not their business. It's *our* business."

"Okay."

"Just okay?" he asked.

She bit the side of her mouth—thinking, embarrassed, irritated? He wasn't sure.

"I'm sorry…um…Sir."

"You deserve a spanking." They both needed the catharsis of it—her to receive and him to give.

"Probably," she agreed.

"It's more than probable."

She sighed. "Okay."

He stood, carrying her with him, then set her on her feet. "Go upstairs, take off your dress, pull down your panties and wait for me," he instructed.

Jessica tipped her head. "Yes, Sir."

* * * *

Waiting, Jess bent over her bed in bra, stockings and heels. Her lacy panties were around her thighs. Her hands were at the small of her back while she leaned over the end of the bed, her torso against the mattress.

With her head turned, she watched Ryan collect her oval, flat-backed hairbrush from her bathroom, the tie of her bathrobe and small stuff animal from her dresser. He pushed the small plush toy between her lips. "You may need to bite into this. Your neighbors' houses are too close, and I don't think your soundproofing is good. I can hear the kids playing outside."

She nodded, beginning to worry how bad this would be. The methodical silence as he moved, as he prepared the scene, unnerved her. Other than gagging her, he gave no clue as to what he planned other than the implements he gathered. The brush, the tie, a small stool… He pushed the stool between her legs. It came to knee high and forced her legs apart. Because of the height, she couldn't even bend them together to protect or stimulate her most sensitive areas. It was wide enough to cause her panties to dig into her thighs.

He bent her arms so her hands were near her elbows and her forearms were parallel. The soft, terry tie slid underneath, and he started binding, wrapping and tying from elbows to wrists. It pulled her shoulders into an awkward, almost painful position and kept her immobile. More so, it restrained her hands in such a way that she couldn't protect her ass. She'd have a rough time getting away if she tried.

For several long moments, he stood regarding her, and she jumped when he finally spoke.

"You understand why you're being punished?"

She nodded.

He bent and removed her gag. "Tell me."

"Worrying you. Running out. Not communicating, thereby letting a misunderstanding cause problems. Being mouthy."

"Putting yourself in danger. Turning off your phone so no one could reach you. Taking off your collar without permission," he added for her. "You understand all these things?"

"Yes, Sir. I'm sorry." She really was, and her apology wasn't offered in an attempt to avoid the punishment. Nothing aside from her heartfelt, dead-serious "Stop" would stop this, and that bore even great consequences she didn't want to contemplate. She'd hurt him. She'd hurt *them*. She'd failed him. The force of that shame made her want whatever he doled out.

She flinched when he sat beside her hip, out of her sightline. Reaching over her, he pressed the gag back to her mouth. Biting down on it, she turned her face into the mattress and waited. His hand ran over her. It wasn't sensual. Instead, the touch was matter-of-fact as he checked her position and made sure she was exactly where he wanted. She felt, rather than saw, him move to reach for the brush then he stood.

Her whole body tensed. Her toes curled. Her fingers clenched. Waiting… Waiting…

The first strike burst fire across her flesh. She gasped at the pain, but Ryan didn't give her time to adjust or to let the pain start morphing toward a stinging pleasure. One hand rested on the small of her back, holding her in place while he rained down blow after blow on her ass, in even measured hits. She lost track of the number as she cried out, desperately trying to squirm away, hot tears streaming down her face. Ryan's preparations, as well as his firm grip kept her in place, helpless but to take her punishment.

She did her best to muffle her cries, to take the spanking bravely, to make him proud of her—could he be? After what she'd done? She wouldn't complain when she couldn't sit tomorrow.

Her body shook as heat started rolling through her. No…that couldn't be right. There was nothing sensual about this. Still, her body was growing hotter, her pussy getting wet. She hoped he couldn't see it.

Suddenly, he stopped and she felt something bounce beside her. She turned her head to see the brush. It was over, but she couldn't stop shaking. Silent sobs hurt her chest as she wilted into the blankets. Ryan's fingers were cool against her skin as he untied her arms. He stretched them out carefully beside her, running his hands over the muscles then smoothing his palms over her shoulders. His lips pressed to the base of her neck then he was gone.

Her eyes widened as she watched him walk to the door. He'd never left her without rubbing numbing lotion into her spanked skin, massaging her muscles and bringing her down from the space he'd pushed her to during their play. Except…this wasn't play, was it?

She took deep breaths, trying to center herself as she

heard him go downstairs. It took several minutes before she was able to push herself to sitting. She immediately flew to her feet. Holy fuck! Looking over her shoulder into her mirror, she saw her ass was beet-red. She still had some of the cream he'd given her after her first weekend with him, so she soothed it over her skin, sucking in a shattered breath at the cool gel on her burning skin.

Afterward, she rifled through her closet and found a silk robe, hoping it wouldn't hurt against her skin. It wasn't comfortable, but she'd live. Not bothering to belt it, she overlapped the edges and held it closed as she headed to the ground floor. She was almost afraid Ryan had left, that he'd been angry enough with her to leave her without another word, but she found him in the living room, slouched in a wingchair and almost absently running his fingers over his obvious erection.

"Ryan?"

He looked up but didn't say anything.

Jess knelt beside his knees and laid her head against his leg. God, she ached, but reaching out to him, showing her devotion to him was more important. She'd endure and be fine. "I really am sorry."

His fingers threaded through her hair. "I know."

"Then why…" She reached up to run her fingers over his fly, but he caught her wrist, holding her away from him.

"I wanted to fuck you more than I want to breathe. But that's hardly a punishment."

"Oh." She sagged a little, knowing she'd really fucked up. Sadness filled her. She didn't want him to suffer because she was being punished. She bit her lip, looking up at him..

He stroked her head, petting her. "It's all right, little kitten. I can live without sex. God knows I abstained from the time you came to work for me until we finally got together."

"I could… Could I suck your cock? I can get you off, at least."

He didn't say a word but widened his legs in a silent invitation. She moved between them and let her robe fall open to display her body while she touched him. He groaned, his eyes turning molten gray as he surveyed her naked breasts and pussy. "Christ, I want you," he murmured.

She wanted him, too. So much.

Her hands rested on his thighs as he yanked open his pants and pulled out his cock. She watched his hand moving up and down his length.

"Please," she whispered, leaning closer.

"I have a better idea," he said. "Go lie on the couch. On your back."

"Yes, Sir." Biting her lip as she wondered what he was thinking, she moved to follow his command. Feeling slightly self-conscious, she rested back, bending her legs up to take some pressure off her reddened rear. Her feet overlapped slightly as she curled her toes and watched him stroke his cock while he watched *her*. The robe fell open around her and she curled an arm up over her head. She worried a fingertip of the other hand while she thought of what she wanted to do with his erection.

"God, you're beautiful," Ryan muttered as he pushed her legs flat and knelt over her, straddling him. His hand never stopped playing over his cock and as the sunlight from her large front window played over him, she had a pretty good idea what he intended to do. He didn't seem to care that they might be seen and she decided to forget that too. The only thing that mattered was Ryan and how she could please him.

She trailed her wet fingertip down, over her neck to

her chest. Holding his heated gaze, she trailed the finger up the slope of her breast and circled the nipple.

"Yes, touch yourself," he growled, his hand moving faster. His breathing had grown harsher. "Pinch it. Pull. Yes, like that. The other one, too."

Shifting, Jessica brought her other hand down. She molded the mounds of her breasts, squeezing up to the tips then pulling. Her neck arched as she tugged and rolled the peaks. Her own breathing stuttered and she felt herself getting wet as she reacted to his molten stare and the sound of his hand flying up and down his cock. When her gaze dropped from his down to his arousal, the pre-cum forming at the tip mesmerized her. He'd swipe it away down the shaft, but more immediately replaced it. She wanted it on her tongue. She wanted it in her. Somehow, she was pretty sure she'd get neither wish.

Ryan groan, and he pitched forward, catching himself on a hand braced beside her shoulder. "*Fuck...*" he breathed, the word a ragged, tortured sound. A plea, an acclamation, gratitude.

"Yes...please..." she whispered. She arched her back, cupping her breasts and pushing them toward him. Her eyes closed as the first scalding streams of his cum spattered across her skin, marking her, claiming her. She was his for his pleasure, however he wanted to take it. Still, an unexpected spasm rocked through her core. It strengthened as he reached down, almost in daze and smeared his release over her chest. He rubbed it into her nipple. The skin puckered further, growing even stiffer as he massaged the tip and it glistened momentarily with the sticky seed.

Why did this turn her on so much?

Her arousal from his touch pushed her right to the edge of her own orgasm. When he repeated the procedure with her other breast, a small, involuntary cry escaped her. She was so close to coming it would take very little to shove her over the cliff. She fisted the edges of the robe where it lay beside her, and fought to keep her hips from lifting up into him, begging to be fucked.

She knew that wouldn't happen. The spanking had been only a part of her punishment. This was the rest. He was keeping himself separate from her. Not fucking her, not letting her give him a blowjob—she doubted he'd even let her touch him. What would tonight be like? He wouldn't leave her here, so what would it be? A wall of pillows between them? They both knew their bodies gravitated toward one another, even in sleep.

Ryan's hand stilled, and she glanced down to see all his release had been rubbed into her. Though she couldn't see it, it seemed as if she'd been indelibly marked. Claimed by him, and that had probably been his intention—to reclaim her and remind her she was his.

He tucked his cock inside his pants then climbed off the couch. "Go get dressed so we can go. Just put on clothes, nothing else."

No shower. Okay, then.

Nodding, she rose and headed upstairs. Little was said between them after that. She'd brought some things from her place, and he carried the bag into the house then upstairs. When he turned into one of the unoccupied bedrooms, her stomach fell.

"I'm sorry," she said, hovering in the doorway. "Please, Ryan, I don't want to sleep away from you."

His jaw tightened and his cheeks drew in slightly. He took a breath then pinned her with his gaze. "I think maybe you need to be. You planned to leave me—you *did* leave me. I can't have you somewhere else on your own because it's not safe, but being alone here with your thoughts…" He shook his head, shrugged then set her bag on the end of the bed. "I'll stay out of your way—"

"No," she pleaded, taking several steps into the room.

He skirted her and headed for the hallway. "If you need anything from my bedroom or bathroom, I'll be downstairs. You should get it now."

His feet thudded on the steps as he jogged down them. She stared after him, her fingers on her bare neck, gasping at the emptiness ripping through her chest. She'd seen the same desolation in his eyes. This was as hard on him as it was on her. Maybe harder. She'd been the one to leave him. He was just giving her what she wanted.

Chapter Nineteen

True to his word, Ryan kept out of her way for the rest of the evening. Feeling like the pariah she was, Jess retired to her room early. Pissed off—with herself or with him, she wasn't entirely sure—she didn't resist the urge to give the door a good slam when she went in to go to bed. Ryan probably didn't hear it anyway. She had no idea where he'd gotten to, but she knew he was in the house somewhere—at least, she thought so. His vehicles were in the garage.

She slept fitfully, hating every moment away from him and castigating herself because she knew it was her fault. She waffled between the need to assure him she was his, that she wouldn't leave him and that she'd realized her mistake and the irritation that he was punishing her like this and that he couldn't understand her position. Apparently, this was the shitty side of a D/s relationship they didn't write about in the novels she'd read. Discipline wasn't all about the sexy fuckery. Sometimes, it was being put in a metaphorical corner.

At three in the morning, knowing sleep wasn't

coming, she climbed out of bed. Her mind and body were both too restless. Unless she calmed, she wouldn't drift off at all before morning. Still dressed in her sleep shorts and tank, she queued up music on her phone then started through her favorite yoga sequence. Eyes closed and focusing on her breathing, she flowed from one pose to the next.

The routine was twenty-ish minutes depending on how long she held each position. She was three-quarters done, breathing through the warrior pose when a noise caused her to open her eyes. A sleep-tussled Ryan stood in the doorway, leaning against the frame and watching her with a slight smile on his lips. Dark circles marred the skin beneath his eyes, and she wondered if he'd been as restless as she had.

Less than gracefully, she stumbled from the position and straightened to face him.

"Hi," she whispered.

He didn't say a word, just strode forward the couple steps separating them, scooped her into his arms then carried her to his bedroom.

"Ryan—"

"Shh… Just sleep. We'll talk tomorrow," he murmured, placing her on the bed. He climbed in and spooned behind her, his arms tight. She closed her eyes, feeling at peace for the first time since yesterday afternoon. Faintly, she heard her music filtering in from the other room. She ignored it. It would shut off at the end of the playlist and nothing—*nothing*—would pry her from Ryan's arms again. The last twenty-four hours had been a hell she would avoid repeating at all costs.

Her hair slid off her shoulder, and his mouth pressed to her skin. One hand worked beneath the hem of her tank and cupped her breast. Jess moaned quietly, relaxing into him and this intimacy. "I love you," she sighed.

"I love you, too, kitten." She felt rather than heard him chuckle behind her. "So much that I can't stand even a night away from you."

She covered the hand on her belly with her own, lacing their fingers. "Neither can I. I could barely breathe all day... God, Ryan—"

"Shh..." he soothed, rolling her onto her back and moving over her. His lips covered hers, and he proceeded to do what he hadn't earlier. Reassuring them both, he made love to her until they collapsed together, still joined, and finally slept.

* * * *

Ryan had left the house by the time Jessica woke the next morning. If she hadn't been cuddled up in his bed, wrapped around his pillow, she would have thought she imagined the sweet lovemaking the night before, but no, she was naked and sated between his sheets. Stretching, she glanced over at the clock and saw it was after eight and he'd brought in her phone.

Leaning up on an elbow, she reached for it and immediately found a message from her man.

Good morning, baby. I hope you slept in. I needed to go into the office to get ready for the site manager meeting this afternoon. I called Max and asked him to bring you into work when you're ready. His number is in your contacts now. Call him when you're set. Don't forget that the meeting is at one. Love you forever.

Jess flopped back into the pillows, smiling. She loved him, too. So much. She'd love to stay here and bask in the feeling, but she was already late for work— apparently, with the boss' blessing—and she needed to get moving. Despite his desire for her to relax, she had work from yesterday and she couldn't afford for her projects to get off schedule. She'd be stuck in the staff meeting today for all their onsite managers. The annual get-together to present new policies, procedures and safety measures, upcoming project information and an overall state of the company would take the entire afternoon.

She'd better get moving. Besides…chances were good she'd get to see her sexy boss in his suit this morning. That thought sent a little flutter through her as she climbed from bed. The tailored lines clinging to his muscular body just did her in— and had long before she'd ever seen him shirtless and wearing those skin-tight leather pants.

She glanced at his playroom, wondering if he wore them in there. All this time and he'd yet to show it to her. She'd tried the door the other day when he'd been coddling her after Clive's attack. Ryan kept the damn thing locked up, and she still didn't know what he hid behind it. That was a matter for another time, she supposed.

With her phone still in her hand, she headed into the closet. She dialed Max on the way. In the time it would take for him to drive from the office, she could shower, dress and have her morning coffee.

"Hey, sis," he answered. "Ready for me to fetch and carry?"

She paused, thrown off by his greeting. "This is Jess."

"Yeah, I know. And the way things are going, Ryan will be dragging you into our crazy family soon. Anyway…are you ready?"

She laughed. "Yes. I'll be set by the time you get here from the office—for the fetching. Nothing the carrying."

"Damn it. There goes the highlight of my day."

She snorted. "Right. I'm sure you'll live. I've seen the girls who orbit you."

He blew out a derisive breath. "None of them could handle me—not like you and Keera do my brothers."

Oh…so that was how the wind blew. He was looking for a sub. She couldn't be surprised. "I'm sure she's out there just wishing you'd hurry up and find her."

"Hmm, I already have actually. She's just not ready for me."

"No one could be really ready for you guys. You're kind of…intense." She pulled out a crimson-colored suit, with a flounce-hemmed skirt that ended just below her knees, and a cream shell to wear beneath the short jacket.

He laughed. "Whatever." She head his muffled voice as he spoke to someone. "Okay, I'm on my way. See you soon."

Going to the built-in drawers, she selected lace and satin lingerie that matched the blouse and gossamer thigh highs. She'd wear the black Louboutin heels she'd bought last year. Ryan hadn't seen them yet, and she hoped they drove him crazy. She grinned, bemused by her thoughts as she chose her clothes and got ready. Ryan, specifically what he'd think about her choices, was never far from her thoughts. She'd never been so caught up with a man. He just…consumed her.

And she'd better get moving because his brother would be here before she knew it. Despite her worry, she was ready, her slightly damp hair tamed into the twist she favored, ten minutes before Max rolled up in his electric-blue sports car—an Aston Martin Vanquish. She only knew that because he'd walked around introducing himself as "Bond. Max Bond" for about a month after he'd gotten it. He'd only stopped when his brothers had started saying "Idiot. You're an idiot" in response. Still, she had to admit, it was a freaking cool, *sexy* car.

To her surprise, he hurried around and opened her door as she skipped down the stairs toward him. "Whoa, you are fucking hot," he breathed.

She giggled. "Thank you, kind sir." A blush burned her cheeks as she realized she probably shouldn't have called him sir. He didn't comment or smirk, and relief spread through her. Max was so flirty, he wouldn't have let that lie if he thought anything of it.

"Are you sure I can't lure you away from my lame brother?"

"He's not lame. Besides, I love him. And what about your Princess Charming? She's out there waiting for you. Remember?"

"Yeah, I should probably get on that," he muttered. His fingers tapped in the steering wheel and she couldn't help thinking how like his brother he was. Handsome…intense beneath his jovial exterior. She wasn't the least attracted to him—not beyond a mild appreciation for his manliness. It was nothing like the single-minded awareness of Ryan.

"You should. She's probably desolate with her need," Jess joked.

"I wish. More like she's oblivious. She thinks of me as her best friend."

"Wait…" Jess turned in her seat to stare at him. "You mean you know who Princess Charming is?"

"Yeah."

"Tell me!"

"No." He immediately turned to a discussion of the weather. When they'd exhausted that subject, he brought up Clive and what kind of progress had been made on finding him and ferreting out the extent of his theft from their projects. Before Jess knew it they were pulling into the Cress parking garage. "Ryan wants to see you before you go to your office," Max told her as they headed into the building and got on the elevator.

Fine with her. "Okay. Thanks for the ride."

"Anytime. Eventually, I'll persuade you to the Max-side."

"Keep dreaming." She patted his arm then kissed his cheek quickly just as the elevator doors opened to their floor.

She heard the growl just before she turned to see Ryan. She smiled brightly, practically diving into his arms. They went around her like steel.

"Jealous much?" Max asked, his amusement evident.

"Of course not," Ryan replied. He kissed her temple. "What's mine is mine and only mine."

Max rolled his eyes and walked away from them.

"How was your morning, baby?" he asked as he led her toward her office. She noticed that he'd dropped all pretenses of discretion as if he wanted everyone to know they were together. There would be little mistaking his arm around her waist, his hand firmly on her hip, while his head tilted toward her while he spoke. His whole demeanor screamed intimacy. He was claiming her this morning.

She leaned into him, accepting it. He said he wanted her "forever", and his family seemed to think she'd soon be part of them—they certainly treated her that way. She'd never felt quite so accepted. "It was good. Thanks for letting me sleep in. How are you feeling? You didn't get much sleep."

"Better now. You look gorgeous, by the way. I'm not sure I should let those guys from the field near you. You're going to cause a riot."

"Stop it," she laughed.

"I'm serious."

"It's all for you, you know?"

His fingers tightened. "And thank God for that."

"Max said you wanted to see me. Did you need something?"

"Not really. Just wanted to see how you were. After yesterday…"

She sighed, still feeling bad about the whole misunderstanding and her behavior. "I'm—"

"Don't," he interrupted. "It's done."

Jess nodded, and her fingers went to her neck. "Can I have my…necklace back?" She wanted to call it her collar, but despite them going public, that part of their life still needed to be under wraps. Heads were popping up over cubicles as they watched and several people watched their progress to her office. She definitely needed to watch what she said.

"Soon enough," he said. He kissed her temple at the door of her office. "I sent you several emails about this afternoon's meeting. Can you review the agenda and see if there's anything you want to add?

"Sure."

"Okay. Well…" He backed away and winked. "I'll see you later then."

And as he walked away and she headed to her desk, she couldn't help her huge smile. So this was love and belonging. There was nothing like it.

She settled into her chair. Task number one: contacting Sissek Construction. She definitely wasn't taking the job. Her place was here at Cress.

* * * *

If one more of the site managers or foremen ogled Jessica, Ryan was going to go postal. The meeting had gone well so far and he should be exhilarated by the success, but inside he was feeling far from it. He seethed from the blatant looks of appreciation continually thrown her way. It had only gotten worse since they'd moved from the sit-down, informational portion of the meeting to this social, team building part. All the men wanted to talk with his woman. Her new site manager, Ron Westfall, had chatted her up for a good long time, while Ryan regretted his suggestion to bring the good-looking man onto the project. As she smiled and laughed, he started planning their evening—her naked and bound in his playroom sounded perfect right now. It wasn't that she was flirting with the guys, but he felt an innate need to reclaim her and remind her she was his.

This jealousy crap was bullshit. He wasn't sure what was up with him. Yeah, he didn't share—he was selfish that way—but generally, these strong negative feelings weren't in his makeup. He knew it was related to yesterday and still being unsettled today. She'd planned to leave him. She'd planned to take another job. Hell, she could still be planning on it. They needed to talk about that and a few other things tonight.

While he brooded and pretended to be engrossed in something Theo was saying to the group they stood with, he watched Max walk over to Jess and place his hand on her shoulder to grab her attention. Ryan growled, and Theo's gaze shot to him.

"Geez, chill," Theo muttered when he saw the direction of Ryan's stare. He leaned close so only Ryan could hear him. "Maybe, you should go join that group, since you're mentally there anyway."

He nodded and walked away without even saying goodbye to those he was with. Theo would smooth things for him; he was great at that. As Ryan walked, Max pulled a paper from his pocket to show Jess. Her eyes widened and she gave him a bright smiled, nodding vigorously.

"Perfect," she said—at least, Ryan thought that was

what he read on her lips, since he was too far away to hear her. Max folded the paper and stuck it back in his pocket. Appearing pleased with himself, Max nodded to the group then walked away. Ryan wasn't sure what his younger brother was even doing at the meeting. As a designer, Max didn't need to be there. Of course, as one of the Cress family, he'd been invited to attend. In fact, their father encouraged it. Though Theo would take over for him, their dad wanted the staff to see his four sons involved in all aspects of the company. Despite that, Ryan was pretty sure his youngest brother, Josh, wouldn't darken the conference room's doorway for even a moment.

As he watched Max leave, Ryan's phone buzzed. He pulled it out to find Jess had texted him. Apparently, she wasn't oblivious to his scowling stares, and when he glanced over at her, he found she'd stepped away from the other men.

Jessica: *Smile. It's almost over. By the way, I declined the Sissek job this morning. Love you.*

Ryan: *I'd smile if every man in the room wasn't determined to flirt with you.*

Jessica: *I'm only interested in one guy here.*

Ryan: *Oh? Does he like whips and chains like me? Mine are calling out your name right now. And tonight, you'll be screaming mine.*

Jessica: *He does and likes to brag about it. I'd really like to see his hot body in leather pants and boots and nothing else. Maybe, get a chance to lick his tattoos...*

Ryan: *Kitten, you are so getting spanked for this hard on.*

Jessica: *Promises, promises.*

He looked up, his dark stare pinning Jessica with his

clear intent. A sweet blush colored her face. She bit her lip then seemed to realize what she'd done and released it. Taking a deep breath, she put her phone in her pocket and glanced away. He followed as she headed toward the refreshment table set up by the catering company they'd hired.

Ryan leaned into her, under the guise of perusing the table's contents, and placed his hand at her waist for balance. "I can't wait to get out of here."

"Same," she whispered.

"What did Max want?"

"What?" Classic Jessica delay tactic. "Oh, he, um, needed to show me something."

"Oh yeah? What?"

"I asked him to design something for me."

"Really? What is it?"

She sighed in frustration. "It's a surprise, okay? You'll find out soon; I promise. Just leave it."

He growled not liking that. His hand tightened then he moved back a step. "Thank you for declining the job," he said suddenly. "That's actually why I came over here. You distract me though."

She chuckled, turning with a bottled water in her hand. "Strange. You have that effect on me too. Maybe, I should have taken that other position."

"Fuck that," he laughed. "You're exactly where you need to be. I'm sure we'll figure out the distraction thing—in fifty years or so."

She stared at him, wide-eyed. He hadn't meant to say that. Not here and not yet. But there it was.

"What are you saying?" she whispered.

"We'll talk about that later, okay? Just... Well, you already know I'm in for the long term. We're permanent, not for the moment."

She nodded, but he saw the shadow pass her eyes

before she quickly hid it behind a bright smile. "I do love the sound of that."

He winked. "I need to get back to socializing. You should too. We only have a half hour left then you're all mine and I'm making good on that promise."

"Promise?"

"Maybe you should review your text messages," he advised as he walked away.

Jessica watched Ryan walk away, his casually tossed out declaration ringing in her ears. *Fifty years or so... Fifty years or so... Permanent.* Forever.

She blew out a breath, her heart racing and her skin flushed as if he'd just fucked her hard. She needed to head over to the restroom and calm down. Maybe run cold water over her wrists to cool off...

He was watching her as she headed for the door, the heat in his gaze almost burning her. His attraction to her would be obvious to anyone but the most oblivious in a fifty mile radius. She threw him a smile just before walking out.

Most people on this floor were in the huge conference/banquet room she'd just left, leaving the hallway deserted as she headed for the ladies room. The pervading silence after the loud chatter felt odd and eerily wrapped around her. Even the two office floors below them, with their sound-deadening panels, weren't this quiet when five o'clock hit and the workers flocked home.

Ignoring the odd unease, she pulled her collar away from her neck and let the cool air waft over her skin. She was just being paranoid since she hadn't been truly alone in weeks, except for the time in her car two days ago. Even then, people were in sight just feet away, going about their daily lives.

She was nearly to her destination when a door along the corridor swung open, and a man stepped from the small conference room. Her eyes widened as she backpedaled a few steps. She sucked in a breath, ready to scream when Clive leveled a gun at her.

"Make a sound, and I'll shoot you and anyone who comes to investigate."

"Why are you here?"

"Why do you think I'm here? You're having this fun little shindig and I had my invite taken away. But since your security is lax because of it, I waltzed right on in to get what I want."

"What do you want?"

His sadistic laugh scraped over her nerve endings. "You, bitch."

"Why?"

"Because you made my life hell for months then got me fired. Now, I'm gonna do time for grand larceny and attempted murder—fucked again because of you. That level of fucking over requires a payback. Lover boy won't want you at all once I'm finished using you up then *marking* you—not that I'm going to let you live. Trust me, you ain't walking away from this. Not this time."

She shook her head, backing up. How far would she make it if she turned and ran? How much danger would she put people in if she dashed back into the room where everyone was congregated? A lot of danger. She didn't doubt Clive would shoot, and his first target would be Ryan if it wasn't her. This was a man with nothing to lose, not since his source of illegal income had been cut off when they'd fired him, and not since his days freedom were numbered due to the discovery of his thievery.

"If you make me go with you…that's kidnapping. You'll only be making things worse."

He smirked at her, raising a mocking brow. "And I

don't intend to stop there. You destroyed my life. I'll destroy yours…then end it." He glanced toward the room she'd left. "It's up to you how many people go down with you."

Her chest tightened, closing, and she could barely breath. Ice cut through her, freezing her limbs. "Don't. Please," she whispered.

"I like you begging. Do you beg for him? That's good practice then," he said, not giving her a chance to answer—not that she would have. Three long strides had him in arms' reach. He grabbed her, yanking her toward him. The gun jabbed into her side as he slung his other arm around her and marched them in the opposite direction, away from people, away from the last safety she'd know.

His hot breath, heavy with alcohol and stale with cigarettes, blew over her cheek. "You'll be begging me all night…maybe longer…until I'm bored with you." His hand snaked up and he squeezed her breast hard. "Oh, I've wanted to see these for a long time."

She pressed her lips together and bit back a cry. There was no stopping the tears that filled her eyes and rolled down her cheeks.

They reached the elevator and Clive jabbed the button. "None of that," he grated, roughly swiping away her tears with the hand that had been assaulting her breast. "Not yet. You'll want those later. Right now, I don't need anyone seeing you crying then deciding to rush in like a bullshit superhero."

He looked around wildly, as if just then remembering that someone else might be in the hallway.

"Fuck!" he exclaimed.

She glanced over her shoulder. Theo was maybe a dozen yards behind them. Clive dove through the opening elevator doors, dragging her with him. They tumbled to the floor, and Clive went to his knees, stabbing the close button then the garage floor button.

"Jessica!" Theo yelled, mere feet away by the time the doors slid closed and the car started its downward decent.

To her surprise, they stopped on the second floor. Clive jumped out, pushing past the person waiting, and dragged Jessica with him. He yanked her forward, adjusting his pace enough to come beside her again with the gun in her ribs. She realized suddenly that he was heading for the stairs. He'd been here enough times over the years to know the building's layout. It had probably helped him get inside in the first place.

He burst through the steel door into the stairwell, and she stumbled on her heels as he dragged her down the cement steps. He righted her just before they both fell then, to her surprise, threw her up into a fireman's hold. Her stomach bounced on his muscular shoulder as he ran down the flight, and she realized she'd never be a match for his strength. Cold dread filled her; still, she fought to get away from him with everything in her. She scratched, punched and kicked at him until he managed to push the gun into her belly.

"Stay still," he yelled, "or you'll make the gun go off."

She froze, unsure whether or not what he said was true but not wanting to risk it. Not here. She'd figure out a way to get away from him.

When he shoved her back to her feet, she stumbled, but he was already pulling her into the lobby and toward the front doors.

Clive skidded to a halt as Ryan stepped in front of them, rage burning in his eyes. At that moment, she was sure he'd kill Clive given the chance.

"Let her go," Ryan demanded, his voice dead calm yet filled with terrifying menace. If it had been directed at her, she might have peed herself. Incongruously, she hoped he never used that tone in the playroom.

Josh and Max flanked their brother a couple feet to his right and left, so as to effectively split her assailant's attention and keep themselves from being easy targets. She had little doubt that if she looked behind her, she'd see Theo. She didn't. There was no way she'd give away his position.

In the distance, sirens wailed. Clive's gun waved wildly. "I'll kill you," he bellowed, backing up a few paces and forcing her to stumble with him.

Ryan looked unfazed. "Let her go. She's not part of this. She followed my orders. I'm the one who had you fired."

How the hell was he so calm?

"She's your girlfriend," Clive countered. "You took everything from me. I'll take her from you."

Ryan looked dismissively at her. "She's not my girlfriend. Jessica just works for me."

She stiffened. He was lying, but damn, that hurt.

"Fuck you!" Clive yelled. "I've been watching. She goes home with you every night. You're a fucking liar!"

Ryan shrugged. "It's a big house." His gaze shifted over Clive's shoulder, and he nodded, seeming to give a signal.

Clive swung around. In a blur, Ryan flew forward, springing his trap and tackling the man. Max grabbed her and dragged her away in the same instant she heard the gun go off. She screamed, fighting to get to Ryan. Josh helped hold her back while Theo had joined the fray, helping to subdue the ex-employee.

When Ryan wrestled away the weapon and it skittered away, she realized the three on the floor were all struggling with no blood to be seen. She calmed slightly and Max pulled her tight into his chest. He seemed to know that if he let up even a tiny bit, she'd run in to help.

Soon police flooded the lobby. Ryan leapt to his feet as the law enforcement took over, and Max turned her into her man's arms. She sobbed into Ryan's chest, trying to get control of herself but unable to calm.

"Shh…" Ryan whispered. "Shh, it's okay, kitten. You're safe now. You're safe. He'll never touch you again."

"I'll kill you, Cress," Clive vowed as he was taken away, securely in cuffs. "I'll kill you and that bitch, too."

"I hope they're getting that all down," Josh said dryly beside them. He drew his fingers along Jess' cheek. "You okay, babe?"

"Ye-ah," she replied, her voice breaking mid-word. She took a few deep, shuddering breaths and looked up at Ryan. "He was…he was going to…to…kill me. After, he—"

"Shh," Ryan murmured again, cupping the back of her head and bringing her back to his chest. Her rock of calm shook slightly beneath her cheek and she knew his emotions weren't far beneath the surface. He just had enough control over them, tenuous as it might be right now, to comfort her first. She knew he'd always be that strength in the storm for her. Hugging him tight, she face-planted into him.

"I love you. I was so scared. I *love* you."

"I love you too, baby. I'll never let anything happen to you. I'll fight for you always. Forever."

Jessica took a deep breath, drawing in his scent, drawing in her future. "Forever," she repeated, closed her eyes and listened to the heart that beat only for her. His spirit, her temple and her treasure.

Epilogue

Ryan: *Where are you?*

Jess smiled and shook her head as she read the text message. Ryan had stopped being quite so protective after Clive had been arrested, but even now, a month later, he got itchy if he didn't know exactly where she was at all time.

Jessica: *I had some errands to run. Are you home?*

Ryan had been on a business trip to the East Coast for the past week, and she'd missed him like crazy. She had a surprise for him too, and she couldn't wait to show him. Hopefully, he liked it.

Ryan: *Yes.*
Jessica: *I'm just locking up my place and I'll be there soon.*
Ryan: *This is your place.*
Jessica: *You know what I mean. The realtor is coming*

*tomorrow and I needed to pack a few more things. You're
sure you want me living there still?*

Ryan: *Do I really need to answer that?*

In some ways, she really did need that from him.
Though she was sure of being with him, that they were
committed, he still hadn't given her back her collar. Now,
that things were more relaxed with her life not being in
danger anymore, he didn't seem in a big rush to move
them forward either.

When she got to Ryan's place forty minutes later,
Bobby and Finn from Pleasure Palace met her at the front
door of the house.

"Uh…hi?" she said as she dropped her purse on the
table inside the door and kicked off her shoes.

"Master R asked us to come and prepare you for the
evening," Finn replied. "We've been waiting."

"Sorry. Master R should have warned me and I would
have been here. Where is he?"

"Soon enough," Bobby replied. "Here. From him."

She took the note and opened it to find Ryan's
handwriting.

Don't be difficult.
Behave.
Obey.
I'll be waiting.
R

"Well," she said, folding the paper and pushing it into
her pocket. "Lead the way, boys."

They took her to the bedroom she shared with Ryan,
and for the first time, she saw the door to the playroom
cracked open. Finally! Excitement raced through her as
she let Bobby and Finn undress her. Minimal prep was

needed since she'd kept waxed since that first day. She let them guide her toward the bed and relaxed as her troubles were once again massaged away. She was limp by the time cool fingers slid into her and her insides started tingling with ravenous need. XT Gel. Fuck. She'd forgotten about that. She moaned as her clit started to throb. Her nipples went rock-hard as the gel was applied to them as well.

Jess stumbled slightly as they lifted her from the bed, placed her on her feet then guided her into the playroom. She stopped, stock-still—or as still as she could while two burly guys were pulling along her noodle-like body. The playroom was a duplicate of Ryan's space at Pleasure Palace. Same furniture, same dim lighting, same faux-rock…same cuffs hanging from the ceiling. Bobby put her in them while she gaped around her. This time he put her ankles in a spreader bar right away. It held her wide and intensified the harsh tingles tightening her dripping pussy.

"Have a good night, Miss," they said, exiting into the bedroom. A few moments later she heard heavy steps down the stairs then nothing but silence.

"I thought you were waiting?" she yelled, taking the belligerent tone she had that first night. "Let me go!"

"Tsk, tsk, tsk," he said from behind her, coming through a door she hadn't seen before, just like on that first night. "So mouthy."

She tried to glare at him but could hardly manage it. This turned her on so much. She didn't need that fucking XT gel in order to be throbbing for Ryan. She wanted him every minute of the day. Being bound for him, knowing he intended to put her through a scene—*finally* in the playroom—just turned her on more. Her eyes ate him up as she took in his form-fitting leather pants, boots and bare chest.

"Maybe, you have something to put in it, Master," she offered, reverting to his Pleasure Palace title.

"Like a gag?"

"Like your cock."

"So naughty." He circled her, his fingers dragging over her body, then froze when he got to her front. With her arms stretched overhead, her breasts lifted, and he was offered a perfect view of her surprise. "What…"

He trailed off as his finger traced over the tattoo she'd had done the morning he'd left for his trip. She bit her lip hoping he'd like it. *Treasure… Temple… Spirit… Everything is yours, Sir* was written in script, curving just below her left breast starting at her sternum.

"Mine," he whispered, then buried his fingers in her hair and dragged her forward for a rough kiss. He consumed her with every bit of the longing and hunger they'd both felt for the last week.

"Yours," she gasped. "For whatever you want. You're in control, and I'll obey you. But…" She bit her lip, breathing heavily.

"But what?"

"Ryan…I might die if you don't fuck me soon. This damn gel!"

He grinned, and she knew he'd ordered that it be used. "What would you give for me to fuck you?"

"Don't play with me," she gritted out.

"That sounds like you're trying to be in control."

She hung her head. "I'm sorry, Sir. Old habits, and…it *hurts…*" She moaned the last word, and it sounded far more like the pleasure it was. Sweet, erotic agony.

"You'd give me…" He tilted his head as if thinking of a prize. "Your submission and your obedience?"

"Always."

"Your body?"

"Yes. Please, yes!"

"Your love?"

"I *love* you," she replied, swaying toward him on the chain holding her hands.

"You'll wear my collar and never take it off again?"

"Yes!" Finally. She'd been wanting it back for weeks, but after he'd told her he'd give it back to her "soon enough", she hadn't asked again.

She groaned as he moved away from her, going to the bank of drawers along the wall. When he returned moments later, she saw the gold in his hand. Her necklace. He lifted it around her neck.

"And never take it off again," he repeated.

"Never," she agreed. "I'm yours."

"Forever."

She nodded. "Forever."

Leaning forward, he pressed his lips to her new tattoo. "I love this. You should have asked before marking the body that belongs to me, but I do love it. Thank you, kitten."

"You're welcome. Now, fuck me. Please, Master."

"You are the naughtiest."

"Spank me? Make me suck your cock?"

Ryan shook his head. "You're going to be the best of trials for the rest of my life." He pulled open his pants, pulling out his hard erection. "I am going to spank you," he said as he stepped into her so the spreader bar was behind his ankles. She lifted her knees around his hips. "Maybe use my flogger. And you are going to suck my cock," he added as he pushed the tip inside her. His fingers traced the crease of her behind. "And I'm going to have this ass tonight, too."

"Oh God," she cried, her head dropping back as he surged inside her. His mouth dropped to her nipple, sucking and licking. His teeth abraded the tip and she screamed with pleasure. She jerked when his fingertip circled her nether opening, pressing but not entering.

He pinched her clit. "Come, baby. Give it to me. Give it to your master."

She bucked in his arms, her entire body overwhelmed by sensation from his touch, the pull of the chains on her arms, the damn gel. Her orgasm washed over her, a tsunami that dragged away anything but the bliss screaming through her and the sensation of his cock still fucking her hard.

"Yes," he rasped. "Squeeze me. So tight. So fucking tight. I'm gonna...*oh*... Fuck, baby. *Fuck*..."

"Why did we wait so long?" he muttered into her neck, long minutes later.

"You were out of town."

"Before I claimed you the first time, smartass."

"The unknown. Fear. You were scared of my overwhelming powers of submission."

"I can't wait to spank this ass."

Jess grinned into his shoulder. He wasn't the only one who couldn't wait for it.

* * * *

Jess yawned as she stared at the spreadsheet on her laptop. Last night had been amazing but long. She ached pleasantly all over, particularly in one formerly unused place, and fatigue dogged her as she tried to stay focused. Four hours sleep just wasn't enough, but neither of them could get enough of the other last night. Ryan had finally pulled the covers over her in their bed and spooned in behind her, his hands like iron on her wrists when she would have started exploring. He'd promised her more today, and she could hardly wait...if she could stay awake.

Maybe another cup of coffee...

She was reaching for her cup when the door to her office opened, and Ryan stepped inside. The lock on her door clicked audibly behind him. One look at him and she knew. This wasn't friend, lover and boss Ryan. This was her dungeon master Ryan in full Dom mode. Her psyche threw a triumphant fist into the air as joy flooded her. Yes!

Jess surged to her feet then came around the desk to face him.

A slow smile curved his full lips. His gray eyes smoldered with a heat she'd always desire.

"On your knees," he growled.

God, she loved those words from him.

"Jessica," he prompted when she didn't move. "Do you want to earn another punishment?"

Another? What had she done now? She had a feeling this was a continuation from last night. They'd never actually finished things.

Without regard for where they were, she knelt before him, her hands behind her back. Her head lowered, she stared at his black wingtip shoes.

Slowly, he circled her. He prodded her knees farther apart with his toes, forcing her slim, black skirt to ride up her thighs. The lacy tops of her stockings peeked from beneath the hem. Much higher and he'd discover she'd forgone panties this morning. Even a thong had seemed too much for her swollen pussy and bruised ass.

"You've been a very bad girl," he told her.

"I haven't," she replied.

"Did I give you permission to speak?"

She shook her head, still bubbling with joy at their play, despite the admonishment. She loved when he was like this, overwhelming her and demanding her obedience.

"You *have* been bad. I've watched you tease every

cock in this office today. They all want you." He caught her hair in his hand and tilted her head back so she was forced to look into his eyes. "But you're mine."

"Yes, Sir." She nodded. *Yes, yes, yes, she was his!* How could he think any differently? This was all part of the game. For one, she'd barely left her office today, let alone flirted.

"So what should your punishment be, hmm?" He released her hair and circled her while myriad possibilities filled her thoughts. Would he flog her again? Surely not *here*. She wasn't sure her body would withstand it, anyway. She'd try though, for him, if he insisted. Heat flooded through her and she fought the urge to squirm.

"No, not after last night," he continued, once again on the same page with her thoughts. "I had intended to take you to dinner tonight. Perhaps, I should take you to Pleasure Palace and let you be dinner for the crowd. Either way, you'll spend tonight shackled to my bed."

Her eyes went wide at the threat, and her pussy went wet—okay…*wetter.* Her fingers clenched where they were joined behind her back. Resolutely, she kept her lips pressed together to keep from uttering a word. She didn't want anyone except Ryan, but she'd given up her power to him. She'd renewed that commitment last night.

Still, she knew if she said the word, he'd stop. He wouldn't force her to let other men touch her. She could stop it. She also knew he was playing with her. Ryan did not share. In the time they'd been together, he'd made that abundantly clear. She trusted that, and she trusted him, which was the only reason, she was on her knees in her office, waiting for his pleasure.

She remained still, biting her lip. Her breathing accelerated. Her heart pounded. Her cleft flooded. She was so wet for him. The scent rose around her, and she was sure he could smell it, too. More than anything, she wanted him pounding into her like he had last night. Or maybe, he could bend her over and impale her from behind. She shivered. So many possibilities and all of them in his hands.

"Stand," he instructed.

As gracefully as she could with her hands laced behind her, she complied, thankful for strong thigh muscles. She kept her feet the requisite shoulder-width apart. In her heels, with her arms in this position, her breasts pushed forward slightly straining the buttons on her blouse. The thick silk concealed enough that it wasn't apparent that she wore a demi-bra which lifted and cupped the underside of her breasts but covered nothing more. The brush of fabric over her nipples had kept her on edge and ready all day.

Ryan flicked open her top button. His finger stroked from the hollow of her neck down to the upper curve of a breast. He nodded when she sucked in a sharp breath. She loved his hands on her.

"So sensitive. Good." Going to her desk, he pulled something from his pocket and set on the surface. She tried to see around his shoulders however couldn't without moving. She didn't dare be *that* disobedient. When he started to turn, she quickly returned her focus to the geometric patterns on the carpet.

"Take off your clothes," he instructed.

She looked around. The office door was locked, but her office, like Ryan's, wasn't soundproofed. Also, nothing obstructed the view from her huge outside window, though she was fairly sure no one could see inside from this far above ground.

"Stop delaying," he ordered sharply.

She swallowed hard. Her fingers went to the buttons on her shirt. Soon. It fluttered to the ground. She released the button on her skirt and pushed it over her hips then let it fall before she stepped from the jumble of clothing.

"Leave them," he said when she bent to pick up the garments.

"Yes, Sir," she replied, straightening. She forced herself to relax and stand calmly before him in only her bra, stockings and heels. Reaching up, she released the clip holding up her hair then shook her head, letting her curls tumble around her shoulders. Unlike yesterday, she didn't have a single mouthy comment to make. Her focus remained the same. Ryan. Everything for Ryan.

His eyes turned smoky as he surveyed her. "You're perfect. This isn't really a punishment, you know. I wouldn't make up some fake offense then discipline you for it."

"I know you wouldn't. I trust you, Ryan. I know this is all…" she shrugged, "part of the game—a game that isn't really a game."

"Right. Today, this is about taking you to the edge."

"A test?"

"Maybe." Taking her hand in his warm fingers, he led her to the desk. He'd lain out a jumble of wires, a remote and a tube of gel. "Do you know what this is?"

She shook her head.

"Let me show you." He picked up the tube then unscrewed the cap. A bit was squeezed onto his fingertip and he turned to her. When he dabbed it beneath each nipple then on her clit, she gasped at the icy cold sensation.

"These are electrodes," he explained, holding up the wires. As she studied the Y-shape formed by the wires, her stomach sank and apprehension filled her. Each end had a small, flat metal tip.

"Like to shock?" she exclaimed, though her voice remained hushed.

"Yes." Ryan watched her, obviously waiting for her protest. She refused to give it. If he was proposing this as something they'd do, she trusted him. He'd push her limits but wouldn't do anything to harm her. With difficulty, she kept still, but she couldn't slow her breathing.

"Have you done this before?" she asked. "I mean…you have experience with this thing."

"Yes."

She swallowed. Her mouth was so dry. "Okay."

Rolling a metal tip between them, he tilted his head and met her eyes. "Answer me aloud. You realize what this is, don't you? You understand what it will do?"

She nodded, belatedly remembering to speak. "Yes…Sir."

"Are you afraid, kitten?"

Afraid? No. Terrified? Yes… "A little."

He pressed a flat-tipped electrode to each of the gel locations then tilted her chin so she looked at him. "You are my treasure. I will care for you always."

Her peace returned. He would treasure her always.

Once again pocketing the remote, he moved to her desk chair and pulled her to straddle him with her knees bent beside his hips. He cupped her ass, pulling her groin to his. She fought back a groan at being so close to his cock, yet so far from it. Her hips rocked into him. She wanted his clothes off so that she could take him inside her and have him fuck her hard while she struggled to keep her screams at bay.

"Caring for you means I must also punish you when you are disobedient."

"I haven't disobeyed. You said this wasn't punishment," she protested. She sucked in a breath, knowing she shouldn't have argued. His stormy gray eyes narrowed slightly as his jaw tightened.

"It's not a punishment; not really. You like the flogger and spankings. You've liked it whenever I'm rough. In the end, I think you'll enjoy this, too. But marking your body, marking what belongs to me without my permission, deserves a response and a reminder of who you belong to, even if I'm pleased with the end result." His thumb ran over the words, a slight smile on his lips. "Next time, if there were one, the result might not be as acceptable."

She nodded. Her cleft flexed at the reminder that she was his. It was the same every time, and she hoped it never changed. She'd never get tired of his possessive side.

Jess squirmed against her arousal and arched closer to him. The wires for his device draped down her abdomen, shifting with each breath and reminding her of their presence. More lay ahead. He had a plan, and she wasn't so sure it would be as pleasant as her other experiences. Rubbing over the hard ridge of his cock… Now, *that* was pleasant. Her pussy opened for him as the small muscles begged to be touched and filled.

Ryan grasped her hips, holding her away from his arousal. "Stay still." As she struggled to obey, he removed the remote from his suit coat. "This has quite a few settings. We'll start with the lowest power. I can choose which electrodes to activate or set it to random."

He showed it to her as he flicked the switch to random. Her eyes went wide at the dial settings. Oh man. Ryan said he start with the lowest, and she trusted him to know what she could handle. If he thought she could take this, she would, even if it pushed her limits. In their time together, he'd never taken her past what she could take. Last night, she'd vowed to submit fully to him. This was part of that.

"Look at me. Don't look away. Don't close your eyes.

Before we start, do you consent to this?"

He was asking her...*permission*?

"Yes."

His chin dropped in a single nod. "Your confidence in me honors me, kitten."

"I love you, and I know you love me."

"You're right. I do." His thumb swept tenderly along the side of her face before he reached down and pulled a ball gag from his pocket—what the hell else did he have in his coat? "You'll need this," he said.

Oh hell, how bad will this be? Sudden, unexpected fear gripped her. She couldn't hide her apprehension. His jaw tightened with determination, and he pushed the ball inside her mouth, quickly fastening the strap.

"If you close your eyes, I'll stop. Immediately. Nod if you understand me."

Against everything that bellowed no and to run away, she complied, giving her affirmative. She just wanted to get it over with.

He flicked a switch on the remote. Setting it on the desk, he grabbed her hands holding them together at the small of her back as the first jolt rocketed through her breasts.

Taken by surprise, Jessica yelped, her back arching. Pain lanced through her, pulling her nipples into tight knots. Another immediately shock followed before the first had completely receded. This time she screamed behind the gag, writhing above him, trying to pull her hands free and rake away the offending electrodes.

"Easy," he whispered, his gaze never leaving hers. In the back of her sensation-fogged mind, she realized he was watching her for extreme distress. Watching to be sure he pushed her only as far as she could handle. With their eyes locked, he was right in the moment with her, practically feeling what she did.

The next pulse surged into her clit. She moaned, tears pooling on her lower lids. Her hips jerked up and bumped into his groin, drawing a muffled groan from Ryan while the jolts twisted her into a maniacal lap dance. Suddenly, just like when he spanked her, pleasure erupted through her, dragging her toward the dark spiral of release.

Her eyelids drooped.

"Careful," Ryan rasped. His grasp tightened as the shocks continued, moving intermittently between her nipples and clit, the initial pain long gone.

Her eyes snapped wide at his warning. The intensity in his gaze united with the throbbing waves building inside her middle. The continuous jolts shoved her closer and closer to the edge. She sobbed behind the ball trying to hold back her release as it clawed across her womb. This was too intimate. He'd see straight to her soul when she came. He'd see every secret as she was lain open to him. Yet, if she closed her eyes, he'd end the scene.

"Let go," Ryan commanded as a series of quick pulses tormented her. She exploded, her vision dimming, though she fought to keep her eyes open. Her scream crowded out everything else in her head and drove her higher while her cleft gushed around the empty space she needed filled so desperately.

Reaching over, Ryan turned off the remote as her orgasm subsided. He removed the gag. Boneless, she collapsed on him. The muscles in her arms and legs burned and twitched while a sheen of sweat coated her. Carefully, he pulled the metal tabs from her. Without regard for the expensive material, he used his soft coat sleeve to wipe away the gel from her rock-hard nipples. Gently, he kneaded her breasts before trailing his hands to her mound. His fingers slipped through her drenched folds, seeking her aroused bud.

"Well done," he murmured, gently kissing her. She

lifted into him and opening to his probing tongue. She wished he'd give her permission to use her arms and wrap them around his neck but settled for worshiping his mouth. Moaning, she sucked him inside.

She jumped a moment later when someone pounded on her office door.

"Ryan!" a deep voice called. No! Theo. And she was basically naked.

"Just a minute!" Ryan yelled.

"I need to get dressed," she hissed, trying to crawl off his lap.

His arms tightened. "He won't be shocked by this. Before Keera, I caught him in compromising positions a time or two."

Standing, he set her on her feet then shucked off his suit coat. Her eyes widened as he wrapped it around her. The jacket, that smelled distinctly of Ryan and the cologne he wore, enveloped her. It hung past mid-thigh and wrapped around her with plenty of room to spare. He adjusted the top so her breasts didn't peek out of the gaping fabric.

He smoothed the line that must have appeared on her forehead. "Contrary to my idle threat earlier, I don't want anyone else to see you naked. *Ever.* I certainly won't share you. Even with my brother."

"I know." She moved so the open door would hide her when Ryan went to let in his brother.

"Is Jessica with you?" Theo asked, barging past Ryan. *So much for hiding.*

"I'm here," she answered, a blush rushing to her face. Nothing quite like getting caught fucking the boss by *his* boss and brother. Theo didn't seem to even notice her lack of attire.

Worry etched his face. She'd never seen him so agitated. Even during the Clive incident, he'd seemed completely under control.

"What's going on?" Ryan asked.

Theo ignored him and stared at her.

"Where's Keera?" he demanded.

"She's not here," Ryan answered, returning to Jessica's side. His arm locked protectively around her waist, turning her to lean into him. "Look, Theo. I like Keera, but I've got my own woman."

Theo made a strangled, frustrated sound in his throat and waved away Ryan's words. "I know that."

"I haven't seen her since yesterday morning," Jessica cut in.

"She was with me last night." He glanced at Ryan. "I gave her my collar. Today, she's gone with no word or explanation."

"She called in sick."

Theo shook his head. "That's the word I spread. She quit. I found her resignation in my email this morning. I've been trying to track her down with no success."

"What!" Jessica exclaimed. What could have happened between Keera and Theo that had made her run like that? Jess couldn't believe he'd be any less attentive and loving than Ryan was.

Leaving, Ryan's side, she dashed for her cell phone on her desk and dialed her friend. She hoped Keera would answer if she saw a girlfriend rather than her Dom calling.

"Hello," Keera answered hesitantly after several rings. She sounded frightened, but her voice was strong. She wasn't hurt. That didn't mean she was okay…

"Where are you?" Jessica exclaimed. "What's going on? We're all so worried."

A few feet from her, Theo growled. A pissed off mien replaced the anxiousness he'd displayed since storming into her office. Having his girlfriend answer another person's call but dodging his, couldn't help his mood. She could only imagine how Ryan would react—not well. Not well at all. She'd gotten a glimpse of that the day she'd run off.

Keera gasped as the sound of Theo's anger filtered through their connection. "Is Theo with you?" she whispered in dismay.

Jessica glanced over at him. Was she wrong? Had he done something? "Yes. Tell me what's—"

Theo snatched the phone from her hand. "Where are you?" he snarled, stomping across the office. The door slammed shut behind him as he left.

Jessica turned to Ryan. "He took my cell phone."

"You'll get it back or I'll get you a new one with my number programmed into it."

She snorted. "It's already programmed in."

"As number one?"

"Of course, Sir."

He yanked her to him. "Please, don't ever do that to me." He glanced toward the door through which they still heard Theo's demands. "I couldn't handle it. That day you left me because of that misunderstanding... I *don't* handle it well."

"Do you think she's okay?"

"I don't know. Whatever's going on, Theo will fix it. And don't worry. No matter how angry he might get, he won't hurt her. His feelings for her run as deep as mine do for you. I'm sure something just scared or overwhelmed her and she's holed up somewhere in the city coming to terms with it. It'll be okay. Keera will be fine, kitten," he murmured. He locked the door again then slipped off his shirt, shoes and pants.

Jessica swallowed her reaction to his bronzed, well-developed chest and the tribal tattoos on his arm and belly. The sight of them and their meaning would never leave her unaffected. She was his temple, his treasure and he owned her spirit. Over the past couple months, that mantra had cemented inside her. In retrospect, she'd even known on that one day spent away from him, thinking she'd never be with him again. It had ripped her apart. She could only imagine how adrift Keera felt right now. Her friend had been in love with Theo long before Jess and Ryan had gotten together.

Ryan lifted Jess into his arms and carried her to the chair. He sank into it, pulling her to straddle his lap again. He seemed to love this position as much as she did. It left her pussy open to him, and he slid a finger inside her, stroking her engorged tissues.

Her breathing shuddered. If he continued, an orgasm would crash down on her before either of them knew it was coming. How was it possible that she needed him so desperately all the time? He added a second finger, and she braced her arms on the chair behind him, moving her thighs farther apart. She moaned as he jabbed the fingers in and out, finger-fucking her toward oblivion. She could barely think over the sensations rioting through her. The muscles in her belly rippled; her channel spasmed.

She lowered her gaze to where he'd spread her wide. The lips of her pussy glistened with her slippery juices, waiting for him, only ever for him. As if knowing her thought, his eager erection thumped against her mound. Ryan needed inside her as much as she needed him in her. Reaching down, she circled him with her hand and ran her fist over his throbbing cock. Her thumb swept over the glans, taking his pre-cum.

Staring into his dark, gray eyes, she brought her hand up to her mouth and sucked her thumb into her mouth, drawing away his essence. Need and pleasure rumbled in her throat at the taste of his salty flavor.

"Jessica…" he warned, catching her wrist when she

reached for more.

Hastily, he ripped the suit coat down her arms and hurled it to the floor. He cupped her breasts. With long, rough fingers, he kneaded the peaks and pulled at her nipples, dragging fervent groans from her. His wide cock prodded at her cleft. Reaching between them, he guided himself inside her wet pussy, and she sank down him, groaning as the ridges from his piercings, dragged along her clutching walls. Her creamy arousal spread over him, easing her way. She kept moving until her naked flesh rubbed against the crisp hair circling his manhood and he was buried as deep inside her as he could physically go. Spiritually, he was part of every atom of her being.

"I love the feel of you against my bare pussy," she groaned. She grasped his shoulders and rocked on his length, riding the rigid shaft impaling her, spreading her wide.

He grunted as she shoved back down him, eager to please him. "Fuck, you feel good. God, you're so hot! So perfect." His hands clenched on her hips. "Faster, baby. Fuck me with that hot body."

He drew her down harder, angling her wild movements and canting his thrust into her. A moment later, he cupped the back of her neck then tipped them both from the chair and onto the carpet. Pressing her thighs back, he pounded into her.

"Yes!" she cried into his chest, losing any restraint. "Oh! Fuck me. Harder, oh please, harder."

She loved him deep inside her, branding her with his cock. There was no holding back, no control for either of them. Ryan stiffened, shoving into her. His movements jerked as he brought her with him to the edge of the chasm where they'd plummet into their joined climaxes. He rubbed her clit with his thumb until she screamed, arching beneath him and squeezing the erection still lodged deep inside her. His mouth covered hers, capturing the sound before it escaped to the ears outside her office.

They collapsed into a sweaty heap. Ryan rolled to the side, drawing her with him. "I love being inside you," he managed between heavy breaths.

She pressed her face into his neck. "I love having you there."

"How much?"

Jess laughed. "I don't think I can quantify it."

Smiling, he pulled her to her feet then grabbed his pants. "Quantity isn't really what I'm going for—unless it's in years," he said. Her eyes widened at the sight of the black velvet box in his hand. He dropped to his feet. "Today and the day I learn I've filled you with my baby will be the only times your Dom will ever kneel before you and not be feasting on your sweet pussy."

"Romantic," she whispered, barely managing sarcasm as tears filled her eyes.

"I love you, Jessica. I can't imagine a day without you by my side. You've agreed to be my submissive, to be mine forever, but it's not enough. With you I seem to always want more. Nothing will satisfy me by everything. I want everything with you. I want you tied to me in every way—submissively, physically, emotionally, spiritually…legally." He snapped open the box, revealing the platinum band, encrusted with diamonds and surrounding one larger diamond in the center. "Jessica Rush, my kitten, my precious treasure, will you be mine? Will you be my wife?"

"Ryan," she rasped, her voice strangled. She couldn't breathe, and her legs wobbled. She nodded before she could manage the word he wanted to hear, one of the most important words she would ever utter, one that would start their true forever full of confidence and love.

"Yes. I love you. I want you to be mine forever, too. I would be honored to be your wife and have you as my husband."

Happy tears clouded her vision as he slipped the band on her trembling finger, but she wouldn't cry. He stood and wiped the moisture from her eyes with his thumbs before leaning in to brush his lips over her hers. She smiled up at him when they drew apart. Joy flooded her. She belong to him. She belong here, with this company, with his family, and most of all, with him. She'd given him her control, and in return, he'd given her everything she'd ever truly wanted—love, belonging, security and home.

"Feel that?" he said, his warm embrace closing tight around her.

"Feel what?" She felt so many things right now. It was impossible to pinpoint one.

"This," he replied simply. "*This* is what forever feels like."

She closed her eyes, letting this moment sink into her. "Yeah," she agreed. "I feel it, and it's perfect."

It's not over yet! Page ahead for a preview of Theo and Keera's Story, **In My Chains by Brynn Paulin**, the second book in the *Tradition Bound* series.

Plus, a bonus excerpt! Coming soon, a new *Daly Connection* book! **Eye of Her Storm by Brynn Paulin**, coming soon from Resplendence Publishing.

About the Author

When it comes to books and movies, Brynn Paulin has one rule: there must be a happy ending. After that one requirement, anything else goes. And it just might in any of her books.

Brynn lives in Michigan, where she likes to spoil her children and dogs—not necessarily in that order. She also loves to cook, travel and spend far too much time on social media. Brynn conducts workshops at writers' conferences around the country as she enjoys mentoring and meeting new people.

According to Brynn, her writing success can be attributed to an eclectic collection of music, her local road construction crews, a trusty notebook, and of course, the people in her life who've finally accepted that everything is research—or will be.

Brynn loves to talk to her readers and can be found at www.brynnpaulin.com.

You can friend Brynn at
https://www.facebook.com/brynnpaulin

If you'd like to be one of the first to know what Brynn's up to join her group at
https://www.facebook.com/groups/brynnsplace/

Page ahead for previews of Brynn's coming soon books!

COMING SOON: In My Chains by Brynn Paulin

unedited, working blurb

On the run from a stalker, Keera has carefully hidden her attraction to Theo, knowing surrender to her lust isn't an option. She can't put him in danger. Theo, however, is determined to take the choice from her hands.

For months, he's studied her and he has a few secrets of his own. The biggest is his D/s lifestyle. He's a Dom without a submissive, but he's not interested in anyone but Keera.

After a surprise night of passion, she consents to be his. But one minute she's there, the next she's gone and on the run again. Theo is determined to bring her back to his side where he can protect her. Then he'll keep her there forever, wrapped in the chains of his love.

Excerpt for In My Chains

unedited and subject to change

"How are you feeling about this?"

Keera Thornton snuggled into the arms of her lover of five hours and looked up into his gray eyes, captured by her devotion to him. Theo Cress. He owned every part of her and didn't even know it.

He fingered the heavy gold links he'd placed around her neck earlier tonight. It looked like a necklace but in actuality, it was a collar. She wanted to be with him but the thought of agreeing to be his submissive did make her a little panicky.

"I'm okay," she answered. She was sure the few worries she had would disappear soon. She trusted Theo and she knew him well. After all, they'd been friends for six months. She smiled. And she'd been in lust with him since about five minutes after she started working for Cress Construction. Still, she never expected to discover his involvement in the Dominant/submissive community when she came to Pleasure Palace tonight to attend a sex toy party. Heck, she'd never expect to run in to him either.

She grew warm and fuzzy when she remembered how he'd separated her from the others and pulled her to another room where he'd pressed her to the wall and kissed her breathless. She'd been stunned. Since she'd first met him, they'd gotten to know each other, often sharing lunch or dinner. While she'd sometimes caught him regarding her with a strange look on his face, he'd never expressed outright attraction. Last night, right now, it was apparent Theo was out for sex.

His palm slid over her shoulder and down to cup her breast. "You know, the collar is a serious thing in the D/s community," he said, massaging her erect nipple. The sensitive flesh still throbbed from the nipple clamp she'd had on earlier. Still the flesh hardened to his touch while the rest of her body softened to him. Her insides just melted for him.

"How serious?" she asked, realizing she should have asked this before. But this was Theo, the only man she really felt comfortable around, protected. She'd give him everything.

Not everything.

She flinched as the familiar voice of her tormentor entered her thoughts. She would not sink into the fear that man roused. With Theo, she was safe. *He* couldn't touch her while Theo stood watch.

Worry flickered in Theo's eyes. He rolled her beneath him, his body settling between her thighs. His dark curls fell forward around his face while he gazed earnestly at her. "We should have discussed this before."

That hardly seemed feasible while she'd been bent over the end of the bed, calling him master and begging for his cock. A fresh flood of arousal warmed her cleft. Mmm. Yeah. She needed him again. Eagerly, she rubbed against him. "Tell me now. How serious?"

"Wedding ring serious."

Her eyes went wide. "Oh."

"Forever serious."

"Oh," she whispered, barely able to force the air from her lips.

Oh no. What had she done? How long could forever be when a stalker continually sent her running? *He* wouldn't allow Theo to have her. But *he* hadn't caught up with her in six months. If he didn't know... Maybe he'd given up. Maybe she could be with Theo. She had no question in her mind that she wanted to be with him.

"What is it?" Theo asked. "Do you need to think about this? Change your mind?"

He sounded certain that she'd leap from the bed right now. Sure, she hadn't anticipated "forever" but stalker aside, it settled well inside her. Belonging to Theo? Oh yes. And maybe if he fucked her hard enough he'd drive her stalker permanently from her thoughts.

She shook her head, trying to smile. "No. I need you."

"I need you too," he admitted.

She lifted her knees to bracket his hips the way he liked and pressed her wrists beside her head, offering herself to him. She wasn't the only one with demons. She sensed his unspoken pain in his caution. He was a man full of power—in charge of his company, in charge of his world and in charge of her. Yet he needed reassurance.

"Then take me. I'm yours. I accept what you offer," she whispered. "We'll work out the rest later. Just be patient with me. I'm...ah...new to this slave thing."

"You're mine and right now that *is* all that matters." His lips covered hers, devouring her mouth, claiming every part of it. Immediate fire leapt through her. If she ever had any doubt his kiss drove worry away. To think, after years of running, she'd stumbled into the ultimate protective embrace tonight. Theo would never let anyone touch her.

"Yes. Yours. Please don't make me wait." This entire night was foreplay enough.

His cock surged through her drenched folds and stabbed into her sensitive channel. How many times had they done this tonight? Yet every time had been different. How many times had she hovered at the edge of release while he ordered her not to come? Not yet. Not until he was ready and as if he had complete control over her body as well, her orgasm always receded but not far. He'd kept her perched on the precipice of release. Not this time.

Theo drove into her claiming every part of her pussy with the same ferocity as he'd taken her mouth. His wide cock surged through her swollen tissues, branding her as his.

"Yes, Theo," she cried, lifting into him. Already tremors erupted in her sheath as it clutched at him, holding him and claiming him as he claimed her. There was no holding back. Pleasure shot through her and a moment later, Theo stiffened above her on a deep groan, his cock throbbing inside her as he followed her into release. His face dropped to the curve of her neck as they both tried to breathe.

"Quick," he muttered.

"Wonderful." She threaded her fingers through his damp hair. Smoothing her palm over his head. She was so lucky to belong to this man.

"I'm sweating all over you."

"I don't mind."

"Hmm. Well, I'm going to go take a shower and then draw a bath for you."

"You don't have to."

He looked down at her, the intensity in his gaze making it clear that there wasn't just a bath involved and there was no "have to" on his part. This was something he desperately wanted to do to reward her good behavior. "Get some rest. I'll be back in a few minutes."

Rolling on her side, she watched him walk into the bathroom and enjoyed the sight of his muscles dimpling the side of his awesome ass as he went. She turned over hugging the pillow. How did she get so lucky?

She had a hard time squashing the giggle bubbling up her throat. She had to tell Jessica. As soon as she heard the water start, she swung from the bed and pulled her cell phone from her purse. Frowning she realized the display read one in the morning. Oh, that wouldn't matter. Her best friend was a working machine. Chances were good she was still up to her neck in reports.

The phone chirped signaling a missed call. Still smiling, she dialed up voice mail by rote. She had a minute before Theo returned.

"Hello, slut. Have fun fucking? You probably still are since I have to leave a message. You know I don't like that."

No. Oh God no

As soon as she heard the voice through the phone, her blood went cold. Any joy or peace she'd achieved evaporated like water in the desert.

Cary, her stepbrother, had found her again. And apparently, he'd been watching her for a while.

"I want my money, bitch."

She hugged an arm around her middle. "There isn't any," she whispered to the message. If there were some fortune left by her parents, she'd give him every bit just to be free of him.

"I know what you're going to say. Don't bother. If you won't give me what's mine, I'll take my payment in the hot little cunt of yours. And don't think that man you just finished fucking will help you. I'll take care of him if he tries."

No. She had to run. She had to run as fast and as far as she could. Now. Quickly dragging on her clothes, she spared one last look toward the bathroom where Theo whistled cheerfully off-key and took off the collar he'd put around his neck.

He couldn't afford to claim her. And she could never

bear the pain of seeing him hurt.

* * * *

Theo left the shower with his spirit soaring. Keera was finally his and better, she accepted him. Quickly, he ran a towel over his body while he started to run Keera's bath in the garden tub then set about gathering items to assist them in the "bathing". He had a feeling he'd end up in the tub with her.

He grinned. Life would be good with Keera in it.

He turned off the water and silence surrounded him. Too much silence.

"Keera," he called, going to the doorway. She must have fallen asleep. He couldn't blame her. They'd had a strenuous evening so far.

The bedside light seemed to cast a spotlight on the middle of the bed, reflecting off the gleaming gold in the center of the sheets. *Rejected again, you fool.* No…

No.

She couldn't desert him. She'd wanted to be with him and be his. This didn't make any sense. Keera had never lied to him before. Why would she lie now?

COMING SOON: *Eye of Her Storm (Daly Connection Series)*

unedited, working blurb

Two years ago, River Szuzman landed in Daly Wyoming, far, far from the big city. Daly was like no place she'd ever been. There are few women and lots of men—lots and lots and *lots* of rugged men, most cowboys to the core. Two of them, Tai Cauldwell and Seth Daniels, have made it clear she's theirs and they're not taking no for an answer.

River's determined to belong to no man—certainly not to *two* men, even if they've filled her fantasies every night since meeting them. There's still too much she wants to do in life. She doesn't have time for a man—or men, as the case may be. So she's run, but they've chased.

Now, when the unthinkable happens, throwing all her plans into upheaval, she's running right into their arms. She's lost so much time and there's probably no happily ever after for them, but maybe, together, they can find peace in this storm.

Excerpt for Eye of Her Storm by Brynn Paulin

unedited and subject to change

"So…now that your two older sisters are married off, it's your turn, right?"

"Moon and I are twins. She isn't older than me." River Szuzman turned toward the speaker, wishing she weren't decked out in aqua taffeta. Tai Cauldwell. He grinned naughtily at her, his hot whiskey brown eyes scanning unabashedly along her curves. She fought the urge to bite her lip and squirm as his blatant perusal made her wet. God, he made her wet. Between him and his partner, Seth Danielson, who stood behind him, giving her an equally hot look, she could just about orgasm without even being touched.

Feeling warm, head throbbing, she lifted her nearly forgotten drink to her lips and took a sip then grimaced when she realized the melted ice had watered down the contents. But it was cold and she was too hot in this dress. Granted, Moon had picked out kick-ass bridesmaid apparel, and of course, the coloring complemented the bride's complexion and in turn looked good on her nearly identical twin. The sleeveless sheath showed off every curve of her body as it glided against her skin, but something about the silky light-blue dress made her feel…vulnerable. And needy. And susceptible to the charms of the two men standing near her now. They'd pursued her literally since the day she'd arrived in Daly four years ago. And if she didn't get out of here soon, she might finally give in to them.

It was this blasted headache. It seemed to always plague her and never go away with a constant nagging pressure that never seemed to cease. Probably, she needed to stronger pain pills or something. In the meanwhile, the unrelenting ache weakened her resolve against falling into Seth and Tai's bed. She didn't doubt they could distract her enough to block out the pain while giving her mindless pleasure. Even their kisses were a drug. She knew. Because once, just once, she'd caved to their kisses and though it hadn't progressed beyond that, since she'd come to her senses, it had blown a huge hole in her resistance. It had been a bad idea. Such a bad, bad, *horrible* idea.

Seth grinned. "Now, you know that's just not true."

She squinted at him, confused. Had she spoken aloud? It *was* perfectly true that she was minutes from folding to their pursuit and that it wouldn't be very smart.

"Yeah, you are younger. Paisley told us Moon is a good five minutes older than you," Tai clarified.

Oh, that again. Okay. She rolled her eyes, ignoring the pain the slight motion amplified in her head. Paisley, her oldest sister, had married Tai's cousin, Brant, as well as Ace, the third in that relationship. It had been a true Daly wedding, with one bride, multiple grooms and paperwork to authorize shared rights over legal matters, whether societal, health or financially related. And now, apparently, Paisley just loved to talk about her dysfunctional younger sisters, Sun, Moon and Riv.

Today's wedding was more traditional since Riv's twin was marrying just one man, Pete Conlon.

River's stare roamed over Tai before she answered him, briefly contemplating what it would be like to be in a Daly marriage. If she ever caved, she's have a traditional Daly wedding, not an unconventional one like

Moon. How funny that values were so topsy-turvy here—funny and fucking awesome, if marriage and commitment were your thing.

Definitely not hers. No man—or men—would pin her down. She still had so much to do with her life. So, because of that, she did her best to appear dismissive as she surveyed Tai. It didn't stop the craving to have his powerful arms around her tonight—his and Seth's. She knew enough about them to understand they were a package deal. Fine with her libido. She wanted Seth just as much as Tai. She'd never considered a ménage before moving to this town, but now, after witnessing this way of life, the idea just ate at her. She wanted to try two at once, but probably not three…or four like several women around here had.

"Why would it be my turn to marry?" she asked.

"You know…Paisley and Moon are both married; now, you're next in line," Seth answered.

A sharp half-laugh escaped her lips before she could stop it. "Well, you've obviously confused Daly with old-time Russia, guys." She waved a hand to indicate the room. "FYI…this isn't a scene from Fiddler on the Roof."

"Snarky as ever," Tai observed. He stepped closer. "You know that makes us hot, don't you? Your sharp tongue. That's why you do it, right?"

Seth bumped him with his shoulder. "I do have some ideas for that tongue."

Riv fought back a groan as they chuckled, the dark rumbles tingling her clit. She had some ideas, too. Ideas that had her on her knees…their hands tangled in her long hair.

Her brain went fuzzy with them so close—well, fuzzier than her headache was already making it. "Do…what?" she murmured. What had she done?

Seth stepped even nearer, and she felt as if she were suffocating beneath the wave of lust their masculine scents evoked. Dark, woodsy notes of subtle but alluring cologne taunted her, beckoning her to step just a little closer, to close the small space parting them. She steeled herself against the insidious voice urging her on.

Boldly, Tai traced his thumb along her lower lip, pulling at the plump flesh. "What do you do? You lash us with that dangerous little tongue of yours. We can think of something else for it to lash at."

River flattened her hands on their starched white shirts and pushed against their rock-hard chests to set them back a few steps. For good measure, she retreated a couple feet the other direction. She stared at them, wrapping her arms around her waist, her fingers curling into fists beneath her elbows. Her insides shuddered with awareness at the remembered sensation of their firm flesh beneath her palms.

What would they look like naked, their work-hardened bodies moving over her?

"Yeah, okay, boys," she replied, striving to keep the breathless tone from her voice. "Let's back it down a few notches because I'm not going home with you tonight—"

"Not tonight, maybe," Seth cut in. "But some night soon."

"*And…*" She put extra emphasis on the word. "I'm not interested in joining the Daly Way club. I'm perfectly happy as the unattached, single girl I am. Maybe if it was just one of you… Well, maybe, then I'd think about it."

Lies, all of it. Except for the going home with them part. That was true. She wasn't going home with them. As soon as she could sneak away, she'd head to her place and taking some massive drugs. Telling Seth and Tai she wasn't interested in a ménage situation was the easiest way to get them to back off. Several of her female cousins were here tonight, as well as some childhood friends. When they'd gotten to town and seen how things were with Paisley and a few of the other women in Daly, their eyes had gone wide with shock and wonder and definite interest. One of them might surely be interested in what Seth and Tai offered.

Now, why did that set up an ache in her middle?

Be strong, Riv!

The men looked at each other, a silent communication taking place, and she knew she'd screwed up. One of them would offer to back down in favor of the other.

"Don't bother with whatever you're thinking," she put in. She blinked her eyes rapidly and pressed a hand to her chest. "I couldn't possibly go through with anything if I knew I'd broken up the team."

"You're just messing with us," Tai observed. "You don't care that you get both of us in the deal."

"There *is...no...deal*! You're smart for a cowboy. So why don't you get that I want you to back off? Both of you!"

"Because we are smart," Seth replied, unfazed by her outburst. "A lot smarter than you think. You've been running us in circles for four years and we've picked up a few things about you. Cues, if you will."

"Like the way your eyes get dark and you look off into the distance, when you're trying to hide how much you want us."

"And the soft little sighs you don't realize you make, after you take those deep breaths we aren't supposed to notice."

"And the way you bite your lip as you watch us..."

"And how your voice gets all breathy."

"Stop it," she begged. And there it was. All breathy and full of lust. "Fine. Fine, you caught me. Yes, I want you. But here's the thing," she said, grasping for straws,

"I want four guys. Not just you two. The whole thing. Four cowboys—all. Night. Long. Permanently."

Spinning on her heel, she walked away before they replied.

Lies... What she's said was seriously untrue. Dear God, she'd slit her wrists before getting into a permanent relationship with four men. Geez, four sets of muddy boots, four pairs of dirty underwear on the bathroom floor, four smelly, dirty bodies at the end of the workday. No thank you!

But you wouldn't mind two, would you? You like how Seth and Tai smell—all the time and it turns you on, even when they're all muddy.

Her stupid inner voice needed to shut the fuck up.

River had already said spoken with the bride and groom, and they knew she was heading out early, so she made a beeline for the door without detouring to see them. Her bed and the oblivion of migraine meds beckoned.

She liked Seth and Tai, she really did, but she'd sworn off men in a big way four years ago, just before coming to Daly. She was done with the male species, now and forever, which was pretty ironic because when she'd followed her older sister to Daly, she'd unwittingly moved to the one place in the world where she could have her pick of as many men as she wanted—and without the usual female competition too.

River knew the truth about herself though. She wasn't forever material. Even here, the men could find better options than her. She'd been here four years, and the restlessness had set in. Maybe, it was time to move on. Maybe she's think about it later when her head didn't hurt so bad.

The cool fall air hit her hard as she stepped outside the enormous canvas tent erected for the reception. Suddenly dizzy from the rapid change in temperature, she grabbed for the top rail of the fence running beside the path. Her unsteady legs wobbled and she staggered slightly. This damn headache! Breathing heavily, she pressed her palm above her left eye as if the reverse pressure could dull the throbbing. Nothing helped, not really.

"Hey! Are you all right?" A strong arm curled around her waist to steady her, while another went around her shoulders. Seth. Tai. And right now, she had no strength in her to fight them. Weakly, she leaned on their support while they helped her to a bench not far from where they stood.

"I'm not drunk. Promise," she insisted, wishing their arms didn't feel so good as they held her. "I'll be okay in a second."

"Shh…" Tai urged, tugging her onto his lap and pulling her head to his shoulder. Seth sat against him, angling her legs over his thighs. He curled his fingers over her exposed calf, holding her there. With his other arm around Tai, while Tai held her and kissed her temple, she knew they must look like quite the cozy trio. Right then, despite all her protesting not moments ago, she just didn't care. She needed their strength and their warmth. For a few minutes before she went home. Alone. Because truth be told, she was scared. Really, really scared. Not of them or a relationship or being tied to one place.

She terrified her. Her own body.

Being a nurse, she knew this pain wasn't good. The doctor she worked for wouldn't pulled any punches if he noticed her physical distress and gave her a check. He'd insist she saw a specialist in the city.

Not wanting to dampen the mood surrounding Moon's wedding, River had kept it all a secret and probably done the best acting job of her life. Her sister had been through so much over the years—all four of the siblings had, but

Moon had seemed to suffer the most—and River wanted nothing to impede her twin's happiness, now that she'd finally found it.

Still, River had never been so scared. Whatever was going on with her, it wasn't minor and she knew it would be life-changing. She'd suffered migraines her entire life, but this was something else. It presented different from the pain she'd always battled.

Breathing deeply, she fought back the panic that had kept her on edge for weeks now. The men's strong arms, their light touches, helped. And so, despite everything within her that told her just to get up and escape to her car, she sat there with them and let them just hold her and give her their support.

Tai lightly stroked the back of her head and closed her eyes. For the first time, She allowed herself to savor these two cowboys who wanted her so much. Would it be so bad to give in...just this once. She wasn't fooling herself. After tomorrow, her life would change forever. Wouldn't it be better to indulge now before she knew for sure what was going on? But was that fair to Seth and Tai, to give them the opportunity to become more attached? Give them the opportunity to get hurt?

Just for one night. Give them just one time. Take what you need.

She snuggled her face deeper into Tai's chest then grabbed Seth's hand. "One night," she whispered, looking first into Tai's gaze and then into Seth's. Seth's lips parted in surprise, and his eyes seemed to darken with desire. Even in the lamplight outside the tent, she could see the slight differentiation in his irises, one a darker amber than the other. It was just one of the many facets that made him interesting. She looked back to Tai, noticing the scar that bisected the outside of edge of his right eyebrow. He'd told her he'd gotten it in a fight with a cow and a barbed-wire fence.

"One…night…what?" Tai asked, hope lighting his eyes. Seth's hand tightened on her calf.

"Exactly what you think," she said with a small smile, feeling a little shy all of a sudden. It was a weird feeling for her. She was always self-assured and confident, but this was Seth and Tai. God knew they'd been after this for as long as she'd been in Daly.

"Jesus…" Seth breathed. "Thank you, Jesus." He lurched to his feet, knocking River's feet to the ground then, just as quickly, turned and lifted her into his arms so they were chest-to-chest and her toes were a few inches from the ground. Damn, he was strong. She'd known he would be, but she hadn't guessed the half of it. A shiver worked through her as she envisioned him over her. She'd thought about it enough times, but now, flush against the wide breadth his chest, the plates of hard muscle nearly like rock against her sensitive breasts, the reality far-surpassed any imagining.

Then Tai closed in behind her, his equally solid body like a warm marble statue hemming her in. She groaned at the firm press of his strength to her back and his powerful arms circling her.

She wrapped her arms around Seth's shoulders and held on tight while Tai swept aside her hair and kissed the back of her neck. Seth tilted her chin up then his lips pressed to hers with a groan that seemed so much like relief, butterflies erupted in her belly.

"Finally," Tai muttered. His fingertips traced along her abdomen, hampered by the thick layers of silky fabric but seeming to burn her nonetheless. She wondered at the rightness of the sensations filling her, the ease with which they'd all come together. Had this always been a foregone conclusion?

Punished by Brynn Paulin
Taboo Wishes, Book One

Prim Natalia Cooper lives life on the straight and narrow, never veering into naughty territory. But she wants to. One night, years ago, her boyfriend gave her a few swats on the rear as part of their sex play and she loved it. She wants more. But he's long gone and she hasn't been spanked since. When she learns of a club where she can get exactly what she needs—anonymously—she's so turned on and ready she can hardly bear it.

For Ethan Tavish, The Dungeon has served as a place to exert his dominance without making lasting commitments. He can hardly believe his eyes when he enters the play area to find his secretary, Natalia, bent over the spanking bench in a schoolgirl uniform. They're both masked, but he'd recognize her anywhere. In an instant, he has a plan to give them what they both want…and perhaps a whole lot more.

Hottie by Demi Alex and Tia Fanning

Homeless and heartbroken, Phoebe Morris is having a
rough day. The old Cadillac she purchased with the last
of her money, a vehicle meant to get her two states over
to start her new life, is on the fritz and stalling in the
sweltering heat. With no cash to pay for the costly
repairs, Phoebe would sooner take her chances and keep
on driving than become a charity case for the hottie
mechanic trying to keep her safe.

A retired Navy SEAL, Dane West refuses to let the weary
submissive that's putt-putted her way into his life leave
his garage in the deathtrap she calls a car. It's too hot and
too dangerous for the stubborn beauty to be stranded on
the side of a desolate highway, and he'll be damned if
another woman in his care gets hurt by his failure to act.
When a small tug on an engine cable ensures her stay—at
least temporarily, Dane shows the lovely Miss Morris just
how good a little TLC (and BDSM) can feel.

The Pirate Wench by **Melinda Barron**

Can a staid, by-the-book journalist find love with a modern day pirate?

Melani Canton is about to find out. When she travels to Florida to be maid-of-honor at her best friend's wedding, she takes on an extra duty: taking a good look at Ahoy, Matey, the pirate- themed park where the wedding is set to take place, and writing a story that will attract visitors. While there, she meets handsome swashbuckler, Royce McKenna. Royce is a former lawyer who has given up the courtroom for life on the high seas, amusement park style.

McKenna is the co-owner of Ahoy, Matey. When Royce sees Melani he knows that he has to have her. Melani is not, however, the type to sleep with a man she has just met.

So Royce does what any good pirate would do. He "abducts" Melani and gives her a wild night of passion on his pirate ship, where Melani discovers that being Royce's pirate wench isn't such a bad thing. But when the time comes for her to go back to her stoic life, will Royce let her sail off into the sunset? Or will he find a way to keep his Pirate Wench?

Blue Satin by Wendi Zwaduk
Club Desire, Book Seven

Get your rocks off however you want at Club Desire.
We're not easy and we're not free, but we are discreet.
Find your fantasy in the Club.

Two souls can heal with the right amount of heat and kink…in or out of the club.

Can old wounds really be healed? Meghan Stone isn't sure. She's at Club Desire at the urging of her agent. As a writer, she needs to add grit to her stories—grit that can only be acquired at Desire. When Meghan spots the handsome man in the suit, she's smitten. After a conversation with him, she's taken by him. But will the sexy man want more than conversation when he learns about her motivations and past?

James Richards comes to Club Desire to forget his own past. He wants a sub and a lover, but as far as he's concerned, that person doesn't exist—until he meets Meghan. She awakens needs he thought were long buried. Once he sees her, he wants to possess her. But a sub and a life-long love aren't always easy to find, especially in the same person. Will she be the one he's searched for or just another face in the crowd?

Saved by Submission by Laney Rogers

After escaping the clutches of her mother's abusive boyfriend, Megan and her best friend embark on a new life together with little money, but big dreams. Months later, while working as a waitress at a BDSM club, she meets Jacob West, an experienced Dom who introduces a curious Megan to the wonderment and pleasure of Dominance and submission. However, when Megan's past catches up with her, it will be up to her Dom to save her from the danger that threatens to tear them apart.

Pleasuring Anne by Tessie Bradford

Anne hasn't enjoyed the company of a man in three long years and she's over it. Fantasies and fiction are wonderful, but you can't snuggle up with them in bed. Getting back into the dating scene after a lengthy hiatus is nerve racking, and choosing a sleazebag the first time out of the gate is more than a little embarrassing. When two cops show up wanting her to help them nail the wanted felon, she can't stop herself from bursting into peals of laughter. The irony is just too delicious. Standing on her front porch is her vision of male perfection—Detective Garth Slaiter.

Garth is always in control of his emotions, but kissing the gorgeous and quirky Ms. Karmer the moment they're alone together just feels like the right thing to do. When she eagerly returns his attentions, Garth will settle for nothing less than completely pleasuring Anne.